Praise for

Reader

"Captured the whole essence of any amateur group.
… a brilliant read!"

"A book to take your time over"

"Packed with humour and an insight into society that will delight
every reader"

"A hugely enjoyable and compelling read"

"Alice … is such a positive role model for anyone who has
experienced a severe neurological injury, with her ferocity,
lack of self-pity and undaunted creativity"

"The humanity and fun of Liverpudlian life…. A book that will
warm your heart and tickle your funny bone."

"I started out thinking that I knew where the narrative was
going, only to find that I was being led into unexpected and remote
areas, all full of totally believable characters. I loved it!"

"Filled with compassion, humour and unique and valuable insights into a world of amateur musicians, choirs and the complexities and relationships that lie within. If you've loved watching any of the reality shows that form choirs, then this is the book for you."

Amateurs

Gill Oliver

ahBut
Books

Published by Ah But Books 2020
3 Twines Close, Sparkford,
Somerset
www.gilloliverauthor.com

Amateurs is a work of fiction. Whilst the music exists in the real world, the
characters, educational institutions, and many of the places do not.

The quatrain by Emily Dickinson is reproduced by kind permission of Harvard
University press.

THE POEMS OF EMILY DICKINSON, edited by Thomas H. Johnson, Cambridge, Mass.: The Belknap Press
of Harvard University Press, Copyright © 1951, 1955 by the President and Fellows of Harvard College.
Copyright © renewed 1979, 1983 by the President and Fellows of Harvard College. Copyright © 1914, 1918,
1919, 1924, 1929, 1930, 1932, 1935, 1937, 1942, by Martha Dickinson Bianchi. Copyright © 1952, 1957, 1958,
1963, 1965, by Mary L. Hampson. Used by permission. All rights reserved.

Photographic image by ehretkorea from Pixabay

ISBN 978-0-9935976-7-1

For all enthusiasts everywhere, and anyone I've ever sung with, for, or at.

1 Phil

Alice greets me, bobbing up and down in her chair, all smiles.

'My sister, at the Philharmonic Hall!' she chirrups, then reads my face and cuts the gush. 'You were robbed. I mean, they were alright. But you should've won.'

'Cheers, Ally. It doesn't count from family, though.'

'Oh, come on, face-ache, it might never happen.'

'Exactly,' I say. 'Because what does happen next? Big fat nothing.'

It's all disappeared like bathwater, the performance, and the speeches, and my awkward walk across the platform to receive the cream envelope which I'm still holding but haven't opened. *Bethany Collier – Highly Commended.* There were a couple of quick photos, the winners plus the near-misses like me, then just time to zip into the green room to thank the players. And in a few minutes from now, with Alice as my secret weapon in the charm offensive, I'll be heading to the bar to face the noise and the congratulations and my mates Shari and Olly who've already told me, what a shame, to come so close.

At least I didn't have to speak in public.

We're high up in the dress circle, at the wheelchair space from which Alice can survey the whole of the Phil. She prefers not to sit at the front and be forced to look up. I want to ask who's responsible for the crime against hairdressing which is her pudding-basin bob, but at this precise moment the sense of anticlimax is even more in my face, so I add, 'There are no consequences to Highly Commended.'

'Except Mum makes you have a party for all her friends.'

I groan. 'The perfect Friday night.'

'Enjoy,' says Alice.

'I wish you'd come, Al. I need you there.'

'No way. Not if she's invited Snell.'

I sigh. 'It wouldn't be so bad if she'd kept it to the family.'

Side by side, we watch as music stands are cleared from the platform and the grand piano is shifted. The auditorium has emptied, except for our mum, far, far down below, who's collared a stray civic dignitary and whose distant conversation remains distinctly audible, in its tune, its phrasing and its colour at least. Anyone can hear she's after something. Such is the legendary acoustic of this hallowed space: carefully engineered twice over in its lifetime, it's almost too precise. You can't afford to fluff anything in here. No place to hide.

'Jaz didn't come, then,' says Alice.

Now, *that's* opened a chink of satisfaction in a wall of frustration.

'I dumped him. Yesterday.'

Her eyes pop. 'Mum'll be pleased.'

'Mm-hm. I packed his bag and chucked it down the stairs. I ought to have recorded it really, it was quite musical.'

'Oh aye?'

'It was sort of arrhythmical, with these heavy thuds, whoomf, whoomf, ba-whoomf. Be good on a loop? And there was this cheeky little semiquaver ruffle when it hit the front door.'

'Missed a trick, there.' Alice nods, mouth downturned, her lower lip extended: she saw this coming. She's never liked

Jaz, not since their first meeting when he made us late, and her scones were cold.

'Could be the inspiration for my next piece. *Unintended Percussion*, that'd do for a title. Just about sums him up.'

She asks: 'What brought this on?'

'There's too much drama round that man. Too much *static*. He made me realise, I need quiet. That's why I can't work. So, he's had another creative crisis. Only he makes such a big deal about his crisis, that I end up having one too. He goes through this checklist of things he's worried about: maybe this line isn't good enough, maybe that's a cliché, would a reader get on board? I'm meant to look serious and make little cooing noises. And never, ever agree. Well, I told him, if he wants to spend a whole evening gazing into the navel of his novel, fine, but he can do it on someone else's sofa.'

We love messing with words, Alice and me. She's doing our ironic face, so I go on.

'I wouldn't mind, Alice, but we were right back to chapter one. Again.'

She frowns, which only draws attention to the terrible haircut I'm going to ask her about in a minute, once I've told her this ridiculous thing Jaz said.

'Just listen to this. He's realised he's going to have to re-write his opening, quote*: because nobody gets hurt.*'

I pause to let the full import of this sink in. We lock eyes.

'Apparently, right, someone's told him, there has to be conflict. A fight, a kidnap, a murder… A lot has to happen on the first page, he says. You don't start a novel by concentrating on your breathing. And he was really nasty, snapping at me, as if I ought to know. Honestly, Alice, one minute it's *you write music, you're creative, you'll understand*, the next it's *you're a musician, what do you know about writing fiction?*'

Alice nods in sympathy. The fringe doesn't move. It's that short, it could have been painted on. In fact, she looks to have walked off a medieval manuscript.

'Show us the hair, then.'

She twists her neck to give me the full head and shoulders. The only good thing about this hairdo is that it's a delicious magenta. I would never colour my hair, but I love it that she has.

'Like the pink,' I say, after a pause.

'Shame about the fringe,' I add, after another one.

'Yeah,' Alice's exposed brows arch in agreement. 'She got carried away. Shame. The fringe was the whole point. It's our look. For the band.'

'Wow.' It must exist, then, this band. 'Is this with – what are they called – Hands Off…'

'Hands Free. Hands Free Music, yes.'

My sister's putting herself about, these days. Now that she's got her own place in Fairfield, and we no longer live in each other's pockets, there's suddenly loads more stuff about her I don't know. I knew she'd started going to a music workshop, some sort of outreach, part-funded by the City Council. But she's never said what they get up to.

'What's the line-up?'

'Me on vocals. This bloke called John on guitar. Vilma on cushion.'

I've met Vilma. Her housemate.

'Has the band got a name yet?'

'Yeah. Sky Blue Pink.'

'So, what's with the fringe…?'

'It's a tribute.' She sings a high-ish 'Woo-ooh,' and shakes her head, early sixties Beatle-fashion. Nothing much happens, hair-wise.

'Doesn't work, does it? It's too short to do the job.'

'Yeah. No. I wanted all the band to have one. But they won't.'

'I'm not surprised, if they've seen that.'

We laugh and tell each other, 'It'll grow.'

Then we stop and think for a bit.

'That Jaz Ander is a no-mark,' says Alice. 'A mardy no-mark, and a beard-scratcher.'

Our eyes drop down to the stalls, where Mum and the important person seem to be nodding at each other a lot. Mum has so many causes, they could be talking about anything, and I'm almost scared she's going to invite this stranger to the party, but that's paranoia. It's already bad enough. My old music teachers from school will be there, and not just lovely old Joan Pipkin either; Mrs. Ryan from year four who taught me exactly how *not* to breathe; Mr Sprigg who made me go to choir just because I was in the orchestra. Which is where I learnt to lip-sync. And of course, all my mother's friends from the Lyceum Singers. She loves that choir. When Alice realised the guest list included their conductor, Jeremy Snell, she backed out. *Swerve that,* she said. *Not even for me? – Not even for you.* I can't blame her. Can't stand the bloke myself.

I wonder aloud: 'What are they talking about, down there?'

'Lessons. Or bollards. Bollards, I bet.'

'Mm. Probably.'

Mum and the dignitary might just as easily be talking instrumental music lessons as traffic calming, because she's rabid about both. When we were five, Alice, who'd been playing with me in the garden, ran into the road and under a truck. The driver had no chance. It wasn't just her limbs and her fingers got smashed. Her brain got smashed, and her words got smashed, and the only way she got to talk again was by singing. She's got some momentum going with her latest music therapist, who's twigged that, for her, music is much more than a route to speech, or a means to an end.

I can write music, but I can't sing. Alice can sing, but she can't write. In fact, my sister has a great voice, strong and flexible, and she can sing anything Mum sings; although she does flit from part to part, like a bee on speed, because it's all by ear, so you can't be sure whose side she's on.

Some weeks ago now, Alice asked to join the Lyceum Singers, and Jeremy Snell told her the audition would involve a song of her choice (no problem) and sight reading an easy piece of polyphony (big problem). A bit of Palestrina, nothing challenging, he said. That threat of a sight-singing test threw Alice into despair. And it raked up things which the two of us have rehearsed many, many times. How, when I was at school, and they said, *oh, Bethany, do Chemistry with your Physics, you'll always have music for a hobby*, my reaction was – in Alice's words – 'to go seriously mental.' *Only, when you went mental, Mum went mental, and Dad went mental, and now you've got grades, and letters, and a job, and you write music. Which is brilliant. When I asked and asked, to do more music, they said, that's lovely, Alice, but it isn't a priority, is it? How other things were more boring, but more priority.*

Anyway, when Alice told Mum she'd decided to concentrate on her solo career, and pulled out from the audition for the Lyceum Singers, Mum said, 'Good on you, Alice. Go for it,' without really understanding that in Alice's eyes it was already a failure. She's the one with the brave face. I'm the whinger.

Alice mistrusts my silence. 'You OK?'

'It's all catching up with me. Actually being here.'

This is where I heard my first live orchestra, my first Beethoven symphony, my first B Minor Mass, my first Rite of Spring. I've been everything here: amazed, happy, sad, curious, hyper-stimulated; the concert hall is the place I come to find out what I'm feeling. I love every inch of this building, its backstage warren, its folds and clefts and funky carpets, its maddening insistence on squashing a quart into a pint pot, the impossibility, given its layout, of making your way from ice cream to seat to drink to loo without smashing into a crowd of people and being tripped up by someone's stick. Although in her swanky motorised chair, my sister is the equivalent of an HGV, so people shift.

'When we were little, this all seemed so big, didn't it? You know, I always believed that one day, I would hear one of my compositions played in public, in this hall and by professionals. But now that it's actually happened... I don't know what happens next.'

There's a void between me and the art deco muses cut into the walls – so sure, so static, so balanced – as I consider what it means not even to be a runner-up. Nothing, really. This might be it. My career as a composer a flash in the pan.

Alice turns round to face me. 'You ought to join my band... I can fix you an audition.'

She's made me laugh. 'Haven't got the hair for it.'

'I'm getting cold sitting here,' she says. 'Let's take the nishative.'

Off come the brakes and she starts to move.

Once it's all over – smiles smiled, hands shaken – I cadge a lift home from Mum. And yes, it turns out, she and the dignitary *were* talking bollards.

In the chilly privacy of her clapped-out teacher's car, she asks me how I felt it all went. Pretty painless, in the end, I tell her; and I'm thinking, nothing too humiliating was said, Shari raved about my piece, Olly had a good old bitch about the winner. No, says Mum, not the reception after: how did it feel, to hear my piano trio open the whole concert?   I tell her, honestly, that it sounded as if someone else had written it, but it wasn't bad. Was their performance not in line with my intentions, she asks? Oh yes. It's just... outside me now. You can never hear yourself, she says; we never know how we sound; and that's her, talking about singing, again. So I tell her: I heard the other pieces properly and it's obvious why mine had to be the opener. The others were better. Don't be daft, says Mum. Stop feeling sorry for yourself. However good or bad you are, so long as you take it seriously, you're going somewhere. When you start again, you start from where you last arrived, not where you began.

2 Flat

It's quiet in the flat tonight. Well, quiet as it ever gets in the city. Nothing to interrupt the chatter in my head. I do go on. Need to discipline these thoughts. Perhaps now that I've got both Jaz Ander and the showcase concert behind me, I can get down to serious work again, and approach a new blank page appropriately, i.e., with joy, not apprehension. Then, as Mum said, I'll be going somewhere. Already I'm wondering what the next thing will be, and listening out for it. Maybe sidestep the work in progress. Start afresh. But first I need to get over these last few crazy weeks and let them settle.

So much for planning. It only gives you a false sense of progress – anything good that's happened this year has been down to luck. With my post-grad in the bag, no sooner was I back from an amazing trip to Helsinki for the chamber music festival, than I landed a day job here at the uni; the perfect post, nothing too onerous, just enough to pay my way, and with the amazing bonus of working in the same department as Petra Laing. The obvious next stage was to be placed in a national competition; I entered a couple, and come August, there I was in the final of the Arcana, on my way to a performance and a music publisher and the chance of real commissions. I got a bit of luck flat-sitting for Olly's cousin Jo, on a tiny rent, while they're on secondment working on supply chains in Ethiopia; so, privacy and peace and the chance to prove I can exist without my mother checking up on me. And then, mid-vacation, I met Jaz Ander. It was an immediate, potent attraction: we seemed to be so different, yet with so much in common. We both lived double lives: the bread-and-butter life (him a journalist, me an admin assistant-cum-audio technician) and the secret, essential life of the imagination, the pursuit of art and beauty (his debut novel, my compositions). That was what drove us together. We talked next steps, working habits, inspiration, creativity, aesthetics; and it seemed he could talk the birds from the trees. Turned out to be fluent bollocks. And he doesn't know when to shut up.

As for aesthetics... I can't get over that pompous thing Jaz said. How can it even be true? How can it be true, that when you're writing your great novel, you can't possibly start from a place of tranquillity? Because, surely, if you applied that to music, a lot of the really good stuff would never have been written? Now that I'm considering what my next piece will be, this is an urgent question. Do I jump right in, and let the music shout for me? Or seek equilibrium, and listen?

I never got to thrash this out with Alice. I make up a playlist that will prove to us both that music can come from calmness. It takes us back to an age that suits her haircut: sweet female voices in a single, compelling, seemingly endless melody. I listen to it myself in contented silence, running it through noise-cancelling headphones, and wishing I could feel as cool-yet-warm as that. Or write something like that.

Imagine the scene: Hildegard of Bingen, composer-abbess, spinning serenity into the cool air of the vaulted abbey, turns to her fellow-nuns one day and says, stuff this plainchant, what we need here is a bit of action. A loud noise in the first five bars. Hildegard – my heroine – was no stranger to conflict in this world. But the whole point, for her, was that music came from another place.

Not that they even had bar lines in the 12th century. Music then was a seamless and wondrous thing.

3 Friday

Friday morning opens with the squeal of the bin wagon. Croaks, thuds, the slide of wheelie bins on tarmac, the scuffing as they're jolted back onto the pavement. Then the monster glides on.

Beyond the curtainless window, the slates of Arctic Terrace are wet. A gang of seagulls is already swaggering round the tower of the Anglican cathedral, ready for another day crapping on the people. The binnies left the grossest thing behind. Because as much as I'm pleased to have the bed to myself, I've got the same nagging thoughts and the same sick feeling I've had since Wednesday's concert. It's going to wash back at odd moments during the day, like one of Dad's breakfast kippers. It'll be there to meet me when I come to bed tonight. A daily reminder that I am not about to go forth and multiply commissions, or produce a masterpiece, or even get a permanent contract in the half-way job I've got, which is strictly admin anyway, not academic, although it does give me what they call *access to facilities*. The word runner-up pretty well describes my status in the Faculty of Music.

Today's the day. Only my mother would throw a party for a loser.

I told her I didn't have anything to celebrate. I said it was embarrassing. In hindsight, this was the wrong word to use; as far as she's concerned, I got a mention, not only that, I got a performance, so I've achieved something; and she assumes my embarrassment is a pose.

But the more this week drags on, the more it feels as though I've fallen off the edge of a conveyor belt. Shari said it, last Wednesday after the concert: I've never really failed before. It's true. All I've ever had to do, till now, was supply the discipline, put in the hours, and I've come out on top. Not this time. So much for rinse and repeat. I roll forward into my pillow and moan: why did my mother have to invite the whole world? This misery of mine is not something she's aware of. She thinks I'm upset about Jaz. As if he'd dumped me. When in fact splitting up with Jaz is the one good thing in my life. He was a distraction. He was definitely not the Big Tune.

When I groaned at the guest list, she was sharp.

'These people are your supporters, Beth. They've followed you and encouraged you since you were little and you owe them something.'

'Precisely, Mum. My humiliation is complete. *These are the people I've let down.*'

She and Dad are the ones who've made all the sacrifices, but they'd never say that. They don't think that way. To my mind, fair play to her, this thing tonight is her party really, and I don't begrudge it. Also, she's rattling round that house on her own at the moment, which she's not used to, and it must be tough, having both twins move out within a month of each other, when Dad's away to sea.

Makes no difference. I can't help feeling an impostor at my own celebration.

Oh, come on. You need to get a grip, or everything will spiral down. For every bad, say a good; and for every good, find another. That's the trick. I get out of bed and put the kettle on. Leftover pasta, feta cheese and black pepper make an interesting breakfast, which qualifies as good thing number one. Another thing in the fridge is an opened carton of the fancy-pantsy nut milk which Jaz made such a thing about. That's going right down the sink, which can be good thing number two.

On the bright side, life will be easier without Jaz Ander; and I'm better for that mistake; because although we only lived together for a couple of weeks, it was a useful experience. For me that is, not for him. He's never going to understand that there are only two ways of listening to music, properly or not at all. He remains wide open to stupid noises from his laptop and his phone, and can't work without background chatter. But quiet is my favourite perfume. Also, if I don't have to make room for another person, that leaves more space for my kit, so maybe I could take a few things out of boxes to celebrate.

The saltiness of the feta makes up for the blandness of chilled pasta. As I chew, it occurs to me that when bad stuff happens, you feel older.

There was this parents' evening once when my form teacher told my mum that kids who show precocious talent in maths or music or maybe chess are often slow to catch up in terms of emotional maturity. I was sitting there and she just said it, like that, out loud, as if I wasn't in the room, or too immature to notice; and as if it was a given, an unchanging truth, not a clapped-out old cliché. It had the effect of making me want to try every grown-up thing I could, to prove her wrong. Well,

I've waited ages, but now, finally, I can say I've cohabited. And I am so over that.

No hard feelings with Jaz, though. I saw him yesterday, him and his laptop, in the Pen Factory, and we even had a pleasant conversation, in which he didn't ask me to critique his effing novel, just respectfully closed the lid. Result! It sounds as though he's really grafting now, presumably because there are no longer any sexual distractions.

So, our breakup has been a success. Nice work.

When I wake my phone, Dad pops up. He never writes, or at least, not in sentences. So if he's emailed, it's important.

> *Dear Bethany*
>
> *This is just to say congratulations again, and I'm so sorry I can't be with you for the party. Your sister tells me you're down about being pipped to the post, but just remember you wrote a cracking piece there and that's what matters. All you've got to do is write another one, and another.*
>
> *I know you girls don't rate our Jeremy and the Brides of Dracula but if you think they're bad company, try rounding Cape Horn with a shipload of penguin-botherers. Counting the days.*
>
> *All my love, Dad*
>
> *PS Talking of freezing save me some of that pie.*

I love the way he won't call it quiche. I love the way, when he has something to say to you, he says it once so you remember. Then rubs it better by adding something daft.

For a moment I'm a little girl again, my hand in his, and we're walking down a funny, wide corridor with windows down both sides, only it's a corridor where the floor's not flat but crazily steep, so you could almost roll down it, and as you walk your feet run away with you; which is brilliant, because – and this is the really mysterious thing – the angle of the floor is different every time you come; it might have been completely level the last time. And there's that precious scent of nowhere else, a scent of diesel, rope and seawater, that gets stronger and stronger till you emerge at the place where the waiting ferry chafes against the gangplank. To a child, the pier head was a magical place. It was my dad explained to me how the difference in tides here is one of the greatest in the country, and that the city took off when some bright Victorian built a great big landing stage that could float.

Dad reckons you can forget your 'iconic waterfront,' your Three Graces, your statue of the Beatles. That's for the tourists. The real beauty of the pier head is the floating landing stage. The common sense. The vision. Simple.

That's what I need now. My own floating landing stage, so whether it's high tide or low, I can just stride easily onto that ferry that will carry me across… to wherever it is I'm going.

4 Tiger Mother

Menlove Avenue could be a million miles from my flat in Arctic Terrace. Mum and Dad are up the posh end, by Calderstones: close to the park, large detached houses, buffered from the traffic by grass verges, trees, and overfilled front gardens. The crumb-coating of painted pebbledash tells you it dates back before the war, to the days of Empire.

I'm looking forward to telling Mum how easy it was, in the end, to give Jaz Ander the heave-ho. I slip my key in the lock, call 'It's me,' and head straight for the kitchen; on my way, through the open door off the hallway, a flashy expanse of white linen shouts, *special occasion*. We started on the table last night, together. We took out the leaf to extend it, and shook out the biggest tablecloth, Mum and me, then smoothed it down flat. All without saying a word, because we knew what we were doing. I didn't complain about the party – I'm past the whingeing phase with this. Once you've given in, once you've said you'll do something, you should follow through with good grace. Otherwise, you end up bitter and twisted. Also, it's when her hands are busy that my mum is her most tolerable. I didn't mind being asked to take a cloth and shine the cutlery; it was soothing, contemplative, and I got into a nice slow rhythm. I even went the extra mile and set it in a fan shape ready for the buffet. So now I head for the kitchen, safe in the knowledge that the most boring jobs have been done.

But the kitchen is cluttered in a way it really shouldn't be an hour before the guests arrive. Too many unopened packages and paper bags. A few salad leaves have been set to drain in the spinner, but most are floating in the sink. The salmon mousse we prepared a week ago — so as not to be overwhelmed on the day — sits on the counter, unopened, in a frosted plastic box. Weeping at the edges. No chance of thawing now. Eggs have been shelled and dumped in a bowl where they look more like ammunition than food, and eerily, they haven't been covered up. No film, no saucer or tea-towel to keep the flies away. She's particular about that. I check the impulse to cover them myself; I mustn't touch anything, because this might be the scene of a crime.

I call, 'Mum?' and go back to look round the door again. Then to the scullery, the conservatory, and up the stairs. I find her lying on her bed.

Alive!

Thank God. But still wearing her apron over jeans and an old shirt. Her phone sits loosely in one hand and her iPad in the other. She isn't apparently using either, and her hands, turned palms up to the ceiling, make it look like one of her weird yoga poses. The hippy from Marks and Spencer, is my mum. She scowls at me as she lifts her head and grunts.

'Mum,' I say, 'Are you alright?'

'Well, what do *you* think? Of course, I'm not alright.' She hoists herself up on one elbow. 'How could you, Beth? How could you say those things?'

All I can do is stare back at her.

'And as for that Jaz,' she shrieks, 'you're well rid of him!'

Faced with my silence, she jabs, 'Haven't you seen it? Don't pretend you didn't know.'

She passes me the iPad which has gone to sleep. I have to pass it back in order to keep up the pretence of not knowing her passcode.

She has The Guardian open on a feature headed: *Inside the Cage with the Tiger Mother*. With the by-line, *Jaz Ander takes a glimpse at the cost of success.*

It takes me a while to understand. I skim read. The article begins by comparing musically gifted children to tennis stars and identifies the temptation for pushy parents – specifically, mothers – to fixate on achieving success through their offspring. The author homes in on an anecdotal example drawn from his acquaintance, a prodigiously talented young composer whose mother is an amateur musician, and at first, I'm not convinced it's talking about me and Mum, except that it's written by Jaz Ander and as far as I'm aware I'm the only composer he knows. Until I see myself quoted.

'I'm doing what she'd love to do herself, but can't. She wants me to have the life she didn't.'

In a split second my guts are boiling. She wasn't meant to hear that, and he wasn't meant to hear it that way. She doesn't give me time even to scan to the bottom of the piece before she's screaming at me.

'How could you!'

'Mum,' I scream back, 'nobody in the world knows it's about *us*.'

'Well, that's where you're wrong, because earlier this afternoon I took a phone call from Jenny Johns. Who asked if I needed any sausage rolls and kindly drew my attention to an article I would never otherwise have noticed.'

'What?'

'Why couldn't you have picked a boy called Ian? A nice boring name that nobody would recognise.'

My mum impersonates her best pal Jenny Johns, Choir Secretary. Tunefully Welsh. 'I saw the name and I thought, ooh, isn't that Beth's young man? He's doing well for himself!'

I'm gasping for air now. Mum doesn't have that problem.

'And he couldn't just whack it in the freebie. Oh no. *The Guardian,* no less. *Features,* if you please... I'm a *feature* now! And I quote. "Left alone in a room to practise the piano for three hours a day, every day between the ages of five and ten. The line between encouragement and abuse can be a fine one."'

Her glare doesn't waver: she's already got the worst bits off by heart.

'Honestly, Mum, I don't know where he's got it from. He's twisted everything. You've got to believe me.'

'All I can say is, the line between common or garden ingratitude and *complete and utter betrayal* is also, in your case, very fine indeed.'

She flops back on the pillow and screws her eyes up tight. She bashes her head from side to side.

'Jenny Johns! It'll be round the choir by now. Everyone will have seen it. The whole family.' Her eyes open suddenly to horror. 'Mr Sprigg takes *The Guardian*. And *he'll* read between the lines. He's an educated man.'

Typical of her to worry about Mr Sprigg. As if I was still at school. Never mind him, what about Petra Laing? Will Petra have seen it? No, surely not. She inhabits a higher region. She looks down on our petty human squabbles and whispers into the ears of her acolytes, urging us to purge the clatter, to wash it out with pure harmony. That would be the limit of her engagement with Jaz's stupid article. Of course, Mum wouldn't dare invite my Prof into her house and neither would I. We are both in awe of her talent. My mother because she thinks she understands it, I because I know I don't.

'Mum,' I say, 'we ought to get a grip before the guests arrive.'

Her mouth makes a line, her nostrils widen, she gives a little nod.

'Alright,' she says and peels herself neatly up. She sits on the edge of the bed and rolls her shoulders carefully, then turns her head slowly first to one shoulder, then the other, a couple of times. Doing her moves. She stands up straight and says, 'Come on then,' and I follow her downstairs. She stops on the half-landing and turns her whole body to tell me, 'It's libellous, Beth. And God help me, if I had the money, I'd sue. Although that's not the point. What I can't forgive, is you actually saying all this in the first place. Spinning him this yarn. About your *own mother.*'

'I didn't!'

Her body is still but her eyes are searching.

'Is that how you see me?'

'No!' I protest.

Yet I'm the only source Jaz can have had; so, what did I tell him, what can I have said, exactly? About the hours at the piano... that *she might as well have shut the door on me*... I might have said that... Well, for a short time, that was how it felt.

Then, 'No more,' says my mother sharply. 'End of subject.' She turns and walks down the remaining steps.

It's not as though she really locked me in; did Jaz take it literally? I was only dramatising. I shouldn't do that. I must never, ever do that again. It's all my fault. But it was just a thing I said, it wasn't to be written down and repeated! And that quote... *I'm doing what she'd love to do herself, but can't.* It sounds so cruel. It turns my stomach. What else did I tell him? I'll have to read it all again, and the thought fills me with dread. *Obsession*, was a word that came up; *obsession, obsessive*. But it was my obsession too.

We get to the kitchen. Mum points to the half-washed salad and silently takes control.

She knows the short cuts that will get the food to the table. The eggs sliced but unstuffed, the red sprout garnish placed not on the individual canapés but around the plate. I skivvy for her, unwrap, bin, wash up as she goes. As I place food on the serving dishes, I realise she is a brilliant conductor in the kitchen, always anticipating the next entry, communicating her instructions through a raised eyebrow, an outstretched hand. And such a pro. Once she's performing, nothing else is real, her focus is complete. I am mortified and humbled and the best thing I can do is to try and keep up with her. An hour ago, I couldn't conceive of anything worse than failing to be placed in a competition. But now my mother thinks I'm an ungrateful brat. I'm used to her anger, but to see her so hurt… After all this family's been through… I can't bear it. I hate Jaz Ander now, I hate myself for ever trusting him, and I don't know how I'll ever make it up to her.

The catering is dealt with in painful silence. Mum changes into a dress but her hair remains uncombed, snaking out in all directions. The guests start to arrive, and naturally, we divide ourselves between them. She spends a lot of time with Mr Sprigg. I suspect she needs to satisfy herself that he hasn't read the article yet. He's curly-haired but receding, cherub-lipped, and with little wire-rimmed spectacles. A middle-aged Schubert. People like my mother think he walks on water. He taught me a lot, but even he couldn't make me sing.

There's nobody here from my own team, although to be fair I did warn them off myself. Regretting that now. I've known Shari and Olly since youth orchestra. Shari's doing front of house for some Hungarian jazz. Olly's waiting tables, and of course Friday nights are busy, so it's hard to get away.

A good tactic at these events is to attach myself to one of the Greats. Great-uncles and great-aunts. Someone old and deaf who will need a lot of time, and maybe help getting food and drink and a comfy chair and so on. The Greats are not interested in the detail of my work, in fact, not even the outline of it. They just want to feel good that I'm doing it, and reminisce about when they were my age. I can avoid the sorts of conversations that annoy me. And they won't know what's happened. This time I gravitate to Great-Auntie Dot, and get her onto parties after the war, did she remember powdered egg, et cetera, et cetera. She's happy to oblige with the story of her twenty-first at the Mason's Arms in Warrington in 1952 – not long after the Coronation, so did they have the chicken?

– and I'm happy to listen to her authentic recipe as the room fills.

In the doorway diagonally opposite, I catch a glimpse of Jenny Johns-not-Jones. She pronounces the two words exactly the same, only the first time I called her Mrs Jones – just a perfectly friendly *hello Mrs Jones* – she went ape. I was only little. She and Mum have always been great pals. But her phone call about the sausage rolls was quite unnecessary. She doesn't enter the room at the sitting room end. Mum is by the piano talking – no, listening – to Jeremy Snell, Conductor from Hell. I watch the other door, the one that leads from the dining end to the kitchen, and sure enough that's where Jenny Johns reappears, with a huge smile and a cheery, 'Hello Beth! I've put a tray in the oven, just to warm up. Congratulations!'

'Congratulations you! Sausage rolls!'

'Beth,' she says, 'there was something I wanted to ask you.'

'It's all a complete lie and my mother's devastated, if you really want to know,' I say, and her brow knots immediately. Jenny J always wears good foundation, and I have to admire the way it holds up to a high-intensity frown. Then she loosens it and gives a little Welsh *oh*, and says, 'Oh, the thing in the paper? The tiger mother? No, it's not that. Anyway, I told her, she should be proud.' She rolls her r's like she really means it.

I'm perplexed. I remember my manners. 'Auntie Dot, this is mum's friend Jenny. Jenny, Auntie Dot.'

They talk over each other, and it's like a little fizz, an echo repeating before the first sound has died away: 'Oh yes we've met,' – 'Few times, isn't it?' – 'Met here in this room,' - 'You were here Beth,' 'Oh yes, Beth was here.'

Jenny's soft tones bring it to a close. 'We're old friends, Dot and me,' she announces with another big lipsticky smile. It's an exaggeration of the facts but it pleases Auntie Dot.

'I just need to ask Beth a favour,' she explains to Auntie Dot who gives a little twinkle of excitement, moves the teaspoon in her saucer, then looks away, to indicate she's capable of keeping herself amused for a minute.

'You remember Anne, our pianist? Lovely woman. She had that nasty bilious bout after *Israel in Egypt*, and now, can you believe it? She's got a syndrome. Can't play.'

'What sort of a syndrome?'

'Oh, it's got a name,' says Jenny, to stress the seriousness. 'And even if she could play, doctor says no. Strictly no stress for the wrist or hand. Can't even use the remote.' Big eyes, pause for effect. 'And to think it's Jeremy's last concert, too! Poor Jeremy, left in the lurch!' Broken smile. 'You couldn't stand in, could you? Just for this week? Give us time to find someone. Or maybe there's a colleague at the University you could recommend?'

'Oh, I really don't think… I'm not a performer. It's not really my thing.'

Jenny leans forward in a stage whisper to tell me, 'Between you and me, love, *Anne* isn't a performer.' She goes on shaking her head long after the words have died.

With that, up comes my mother, and I can feel my shoulders rise. Whatever this conversation is going to be, I don't want to be a part of it.

Jenny leans across to kiss her on both cheeks, and says 'Hello, lovie, your sausage rolls are in the oven. I've just been telling Beth about Anne and her syndrome.'

Mum smiles broadly. She's taller than both of us and wearing unnecessary heels. Her long neck is a perfect vertical. I did not inherit any of this.

'Poor Anne,' I say, and scrutinise my mother for signs of what's to come. The posture is exemplary, and she's done a good job on her makeup, but that hair is straight from Greek tragedy. The face remains composed.

Jenny leans in. 'And I've asked Beth...' – her voice becomes a low whistle – '... *hyou know hwhat.*'

'Ah, good,' says my mum, and everyone's eyes – even Auntie Dot's – are trained on me. 'It's the least she can do.'

What can I say? This is my punishment. Playing piano for a bunch of amateurs.

They discuss repertoire and I head for the kitchen as if I've got a job to do.

At the sink, I remain standing so as to look busy in case anybody comes in. Which they do. Jenny's daughter Ffion strides in shouting over her shoulder, 'You should knock this kitchen through, you'd have a fabulous space.' She's talking to someone in the other room. 'Oh, hi Beth,' she says, and walks straight in front of me to run water from the tap into her crystal tumbler. 'I'm still getting over last night,' she giggles, and raises the tumbler slightly by way of explanation.

'Cheers,' I say.

She laughs. 'Cheers, Beth. And well done, with the competition and everything.'

She goes back to the party and I push the door to with one foot. *Knock it through?* Dear God. I imagine myself in the tiny box-room recording studio, where you can smell the walls. This grounds me.

A timer pings. The sausage rolls give me a reason to leave the kitchen. Lovely Joan still hasn't appeared. I chat with Mr Sprigg. I don't think he's got wind of anything, but then, I once saw him take a whole registration and not notice that Chloe Clatty had the back of her skirt caught in her knickers. Jeremy Snell is annoyed when I interrupt his story about the time he gave a useful pointer to Jonathan Willcocks, about conducting *Messiah. Of course, it's one of the bits they usually cut.* I've heard this one before and it is sick-making, so I stick the tray of crudities right under his superior roman nose.

After a while, I can stand it no longer. I retreat to my childhood bedroom and close the door before I phone Jaz. I have to find out. How could he do such a terrible thing? What on earth put this idea into his head? And why the rush to print?

'Oh, hi,' he says, as if I were just anyone. 'I thought you might get in touch.'

'What were you thinking of, Jaz?'

'I'm sorry?' His voice is weak. He knows what I mean.

'You might at least have used another name.'

'But… Just a minute… Look… I didn't name anyone. I was careful about that.'

'Not our names, you arse, your name. There's only one Jaz Ander.'

'That's true,' he says.

'My mother's not stupid. She knows you meant us. But you've got us all wrong, Jaz. Completely wrong.'

'Oh, come on,' he whines. 'It doesn't matter. Nobody will ever know it's you. And even if they did…' – his voice is picking up now, ready for a fight – 'It's the truth. Are you telling me that years of musical hothousing had nothing to do with the creation of Beth Collier, wunderkind composer, in the running for the Arcana Prize? Do you really think that if you'd spent your time watching *East Enders* and *Hollyoaks*, like any normal kid, the outcome would have been exactly the same?'

He's doing what Auntie Dot calls getting areated. At least he can't wave his hands at me down the phone. I purse my lips and breathe in slowly, and make him wait for an answer. I'm no wunderkind and I'm not going to justify myself.

'You make it sound as though she locked me up in a room with a piano and wouldn't let me out till I could compose.'

He's tight-lipped now, cold. 'You handed me the material on a plate. What I wrote is what I heard, Beth.'

'It isn't what I said!'

'Oh? Let me quote you. *I'm not used to making room for other people, Jaz. You have to remember, Jaz, I didn't have any friends when I was a kid. It was just me and the keyboard.* Remember? *All eaters are noisy eaters to me. I'm used to eating alone, and I prefer it really.*'

'No, stop there, when I said that, I was trying to be nice to you. You *are* a noisy pig when you eat. Fact.'

That's only made him extra peevy, and now he can't stop. '*I didn't really make friends till I went to college, and I didn't see the point of boys till I discovered sex.* Well, hey, I'm glad to be of service. But let me tell you, Beth, those two weeks we were living together were a revelation. The rules! Every other sentence was 'you can't put that there.' And the whole shelf that has to stay empty, because you need space to think! It was only a notebook, for chrissake. *Do you have to?* about every tiny thing. Do you have to scratch your beard? Do you have to watch that now? Do you have to have the volume up? Well, I'm sorry but yes, I *do* choose to live my life through the speakers. Whereas you don't know how to live a normal life or how to be a normal person.' His voice has distorted as it's risen in pitch, and he's started to sound a bit like a seagull; but now he pauses, and brings it back to land. I can hear his lip curling when he says, 'That article wrote itself.'

'Right, right. You can criticise me all you like. But my *mum*, Jaz. She doesn't deserve it.'

He speaks slowly now.

'When you were five years old – five years old, that's not even big enough for a proper bike – your mother bought a piano. This is what you told me. And by your own admission, she left you alone in that room with the piano for *whole days*. You said. She just walked away and left you to get on with it. Not just whole afternoons, but sometimes *whole days*. That's what you – freely – told me.'

'She never made me. I wanted to.'

I know my voice is feeble. I know it sounds pathetic.

'You can't press mute on me.'

The line goes dead.

5 Sleepless

After the party, it's no wonder I can't sleep. Alice only reads the *Echo*, and lovely Joan takes the *Telegraph*, but by the small hours I'm convinced someone has told them and they're both disgusted with me. I replay in my head all the day's sheared-off conversations, and imagine proper endings for them. Until, cutting even sharper than my own annoyance with myself, something comes to my attention which I've never once considered before: something lurking behind that phrase, *I wanted to*.

Why had a five-, six-, seven-, eighteen-year-old girl wanted to spend her summer evenings in a west-facing room heavy with the scent of baking pelargoniums, playing the piano? To Jaz, and maybe to the rest of the world, it isn't normal. It isn't normal for a child to close the door like that.

At four in the morning, I'm still trying to figure it out. If I was being interviewed on Radio Three, what would I say? How would I explain that degree of musical obsession in one so young?

Well, Petroc (not Jaz, note, it won't ever be Jaz Ander on Radio Three) everyone tells me I'm a control freak. The room with the piano was my territory. I liked being in control. I liked making my own music.

OK… maybe there's a grain of truth in that. And?

It was quiet there. I've always liked quiet. A surprising number of people do, more than you'd think. A lot of people are stressed by the noise at school. But they don't realise, because they've never experienced anything else.

Yes. That needs hammering home. Definitely.

Ah, Petroc will say, you claim to like the silence, but you filled it with music! He has a point. Maybe it's an addiction?

There were things I played that were addictive. Practising wasn't a problem. It's only repetition, after all. I don't know why other people have a problem with that. I started making up my own pieces pretty much as soon as I could play, and I put in things I liked to repeat.

He'd say, so you've always known you were a composer, rather than a performer?

Yes, exactly. Then after a while, Petroc, I needed it to be perfect. In my teens it had to be right… When I was in my teens, it was one thing that could be right.

This would be a good thing to say because the listeners out there know there's so much pressure today on young people to perform. This would link me to my audience.

It's bullshit though. That last bit isn't true. About perfection.

There was nothing holy about it, not then, not now.

It's always been an unholy obsession.

At daybreak, inspiration strikes. I'm going to give up men for a bit. That's my best chance of producing something. There's the *Superscherzo* I started in the summer, which I haven't looked at for, what, four weeks? I'll have it written and performed, while Jaz Ander will still be faffing over chapter one. In fact, I might as well get up now and crack on.

I bound out of bed and head for the spare room, wake the serious PC and open the file. Oh, *Scheisse*. It's not so much half-finished as half-started.

By the time I've made some encouraging toast, Dad texts.

> *Saw the Tiger Mother article.   Don't beat yourself up. Your mother will get over it, she's had worse.*

Immediately followed by:

> *You'd already kicked that lad out.   Trust your instinct and keep kicking love. Xx*

He's right, I suppose. Worse things happen at sea.

At least I can't hear what people are saying about me. This all takes me back to that awful time, just before GCSEs, when I got into an online argument which escalated so horribly I ended up closing all my social media accounts. Not my finest hour, and I'm still ashamed of what I posted about that girl at school; Alice had to talk me out of changing my name by deed poll. *If you change yours, I'll have to change mine. And I don't want to.* I was forgiven, eventually, and I guess I will be again. I won't forget, though.

6 Men, music

When, six days later, my mother finally stops wailing and brushes her hair back into recognisable waves, it's to tell me I really know how to pick them. Men.

I've called round to meet her before the dreaded choir practice. There's just enough time for one of her soliloquies, which she must have been working on ever since the Great Affront, it comes out so pat. She delivers it from the sofa, which she occupies with legs crossed, one hand resting elegantly on her thigh and the other stretched out beside her. I sit back in the velvet armchair and take it on the chin.

'There's no middle way with you, Beth. It's either the blarney brigade, or they're complete *grunters.*'

I frown. She elaborates.

'Blarney. The likes of your man Jaz Ander. All mouth and trousers. As far as he's concerned, discretion is something that occasionally crops up in a crossword.'

She's right about that.

'I'd just like you to introduce me, for once, to a young man with whom I can have an intelligent conversation. Someone whose ears aren't permanently plugged with plastic. Someone who can listen to what a woman says without stealing her words and sticking them, willy-nilly, into his own adolescent scrapbook of fantasy fiction.'

I'm not sure what she's driving at, and ask, 'Do you mean, my words, or your words?'

'Quite frankly, I don't recall ever getting one single incriminating word in edgeways with your last punter.' She cocks her head to one side, to add, 'Which makes me wonder how *you* did. But *something* must have driven Jaz to the conclusion I was a tyrant.'

'You wouldn't let him wear shoes in the house?'

She draws her head back up and blinks theatrically. 'Did *you*? In the flat?'

'Mum, the carpets in that flat came ready-spoilt. Jo's told me, they're getting new when they're back.'

'Hn. Well, yes.' She frowns, eagle-browed, and says darkly, 'I think the last people had a dog.'

'And he wasn't my last *punter*. That was a horrible thing to say.'

'It's the truth. Look at the facts. You're not obese, you're not that choosy, rents are high, and now you've got your own flat. However temporary. They're queuing up to have a go. Every wastrel in town. You might as well be the golden-haired princess in the fairy tale. Worth a try. One of these days the seventh son of a poor woodcutter is bound to strike lucky. He'll catch you on a red wine night and you'll hand him the keys of the bloody palace.'

I'm reduced to stupid noises now. There has to be something I can say. What comes out is, 'You just don't want me to have a proper relationship.' Which is pathetic glossy-mag psychology and not worthy of me.

She is merciful, and simply says, 'I'd like you to be more discriminating. For your own good.'

I check the impulse to remind her that, for the record, she's the one who has the red wine nights.

Time to go, and our way out, like my way in, is blocked. Mum's having another clear-out, and there are cardboard boxes in the hall. When she gets annoyed, she takes it out on the object world. If she needs privacy to rain down curses on the universe, she heads for the garden and some vigorous weeding, pruning, cutting back. This business indoors, though, tells us that if we're not around any longer, why should our stuff be?

Right on top, I recognise some recorder music from when I did Grade 3. I hated that instrument. It wasn't just the fact that you had to play together when the rest of the class were out of time and out of tune with each other and seriously crap at it. It was the way you had to clean the spit out with the hanky on a string, but nobody ever cleaned the hanky. I had to. Took it straight to the toilets, got told off because it came back sopping wet and how was I going to get that home. They tell you off for all the wrong things.

'Don't mix this up,' says Mum. 'They're all sorted for the charity and the recycling.'

'Oh mum, you're not chucking the wind-up metronome, are you?'

'Why? Do *you* want it? You can take that whole box if you like. It's all yours anyway.'

Ooh. I don't want a box of manky old crap from when we were kids. I haven't got room for it. But I don't want her to throw it away, either.

'No, thanks,' I answer.

'Thought not,' she says.

'You *have* still got my bass, haven't you?'

'Of course. Bloody nuisance.'

'It's not getting damp in the garage?'

Mum skewers me with a *what-do-you-take-me-for-after-what-that-cost* sort of a look. 'It's where you left it, in Alice's old room now.'

It took me years to come round to the double bass. In the search for a second, orchestral instrument, wind was out, after the recorder episode. Brass, worse. Few things shocked me more than my first trombone recital. The girl bobbed up and down and made the clown faces that learner trombonists do, but then she took a few bars' rest and revealed to the entire audience that her instrument was full of spit. For the rest of the piece I could not tear my eyes away from the damp patch on parquet which caught the light and took ages to dry up. That ruled the brass section out. Jenny tried to get me onto the harp but I couldn't be doing with the pretty girl image that went with it. I needed an instrument that could bite. The violin would have been OK but I hadn't started young enough, and I couldn't bear the sound that any of us made. In the end, mid-teens, I went for double bass. Lower frequency, wider tolerance. And that way, Mum said with a sigh, they'll always want you. My bass felt like a bodyguard standing usefully between me and the rest of the world. I chose a set of special cloths to wipe her down with and alternated between them.

The bass I never play these days is obviously too big for my flat. But obviously I need access because after all, that's what I'm writing for, isn't it?

OK, so the double bass is a functional instrument; in an orchestra or ensemble, it can be an anchor; but I'm less interested in its earnest contribution to harmony than its virtuosic potential – shared with the bassoon – for silliness and extreme piss-taking. Hence my work in progress, the *Superscherzo*; like Stravinsky's *Ragtime,* but dafter. What I had in mind was a huge joke that even a child could laugh at, with ridiculously high notes as well as the growly low ones, and raspberries and musical pratfalls. Except, that night of the showcase concert at the Phil, my sense of humour wandered down the offy and never came back.

I manage to slither round the boxes and out of the front door without Mum asking how the scherzo's coming on.

On the way to choir practice, Mum drives, I burrow inside my head.

I won't pay too much heed to that bout of rip-roaring indignation which has marked the Great Affront, because that was all about *her,* Melanie Collier, mother of the prodigy, Beth. Events like that were a regular feature of my adolescence. Spontaneous emotional gushers which liberated dark energy at high pressure from the unfathomable wells of my mother's psyche. Each one stopped as mysteriously as it started. I don't attach meaning to them.

But the soliloquies are quite a different matter. There's always something true in them to keep you awake at night. They've been worked on, thought about and polished up over days, months, and sometimes years; old ones are regularly recapitulated, with subtle variations. They have a logic to them. Themes recur. A favourite theme of hers right now is my choice of men.

In the decade or so since puberty, I've notched up quite a few boyfriends; and although she's only met a handful of them, she was spot-on right about them falling into one of two camps. The ones she calls the grunters have been, for example, coders whose prodigious brains might fall out if they took the headsets off for too long, so they never do, except in bed. Then there are the wordmongers, like Jaz; guys who can talk dirty, talk clever, talk foreign, sell themselves, sell you.

I didn't plan this. It's probably an accident of topography. The music faculty is equidistant from the department of Computer Science to the north and Hope Street to the south. The routines and rhythms of each successive term bring a new set of guys you get to know by sight. And there they are on the man-finder app.

Jaz Ander has a real job. Sort of. He's a journalist I met at the dentist's, although I'd already noticed him a few times hanging round the Everyman, with other blokes, or in the cafe, with a Mac, working on his own. Jaz is – was – my type physically; slight, dark, olive-skinned, a bit narrow-chested maybe, but very well-groomed. Right from the get-go, he pretty much bombed me with questions, which I interpreted as taking an interest in me. Thinking about it now, it was maybe just a long run-up to his *In the Cage with the Tiger Mother* article, because the questions were things like how I'd got into composing, where I'd studied, how competitive it was, how I made a living. Generic stuff, really. Nothing particular to me.

The one before Jaz was Nathan. He was a lapsed Quaker with a rather lovely almond-shaped face, whose only question had been, did I mind if he left his own towel in my bathroom. He was a techie. When he dumped me, he said if we took things any further, he'd soon be out of his depth. I never figured out what he meant by taking things further, when we'd tried pretty much everything already.

He must have meant moving in.

Still, whatever she says, that's only two men since I left Menlove Avenue.

Perhaps it was rash to assume that a part-time job was going to pay the rent. I can't teach keyboard without teaching people, and people are challenging. But if it was time for Alice to fly the nest, it was time for me, even if leaving the comfortable house off Calderstones Park was a risk, and premature, financially speaking.

Punters, though. What sort of language is that? When it was my mum who told me that sex between two people was a beautiful thing. She was also the person who said, how do you know you don't like artichokes if you won't try one?

I do listen to my mother, really. Not something to be admitted out loud.

I'm not promiscuous. I'm just trying to find out which men I like.

Maybe there's someone, somewhere, who's already found my competition piece on YouTube, and whose only dream is to meet its composer.

Or maybe it's a trashy piece of nonsensical pseudo-music that nobody will care about and that's destined to lead to other failures. Perhaps the only music I'll ever sell will be functional, for games or advertisements. Media stuff. Tied to someone else's purpose.

7 Rehearsal

Church halls can only be ugly, because they're trying to be all things to all people. This one's typical: laminated notices alongside a frieze done by the Sunday School, the closed doors of a hatch which tell you there's a kitchen, a spiky tower of demountable staging in one corner. Stacking chairs stacked skew-whiff.

The Lyceum Singers' rehearsal is odd, from my point of view. There's almost nothing for me to do. There are no orchestral parts to imitate, it's mostly unaccompanied. To help them learn, I'm required to hammer out odd lines, to give them notes, and occasionally to play all their parts at once which, when there's no piano reduction, means reading open score. OK, so that counts as a skill. In the coffee break, after the notices which don't concern me, I try to prise Jeremy away from his front-row admirers.

'You don't really need an accompanist for this programme,' I venture.

'Oh Beth, of course we need you,' he says in that horribly oily voice. Jenny Johns-not-Jones, always at his elbow, echoes 'Of course we do.' I notice he has dunked his digestive biscuit in a very milky coffee, and one half of it is sitting soggy-edged in the saucer. Ugh. Our collaboration has no future.

'No, what I mean is… you could do this yourself, Jeremy.'

He freezes. There's no other word for it.

It's Mum's pal Jenny who utters 'Conduct from the piano?'

There's a look of horror on her face. When I say, 'It would save the choir a bit of money,' it transitions to a look of embarrassment, and I realise that no fee has been mentioned. I am such a raw beginner at this earning a living thing. And I'm talking myself out of a job.

'But it's all *a cappella*. You don't need a répétiteur.'

Jenny moves closer to him. They stand side by side, like salt and pepper pots, him tall, distinguished, grey-haired, her slightly shorter, dark and rounded; but the body language is identical. Stiff-backed, arms at their sides, they stare in disbelief.

Then he tilts his head downwards and looks hurt.

It's left to Jenny to explain. 'You don't understand. When Jeremy conducts, he gives us his whole attention. His whole attention is on the choir.'

Jeremy's head rises again and he smiles benignly; he fixes a distant, imagined horizon, far beyond the Sunday School frieze with its cotton-wool clouds, its bright birds and irregularly-sized small mammals, its two-dimensional paper people, and the cheerful, rainbow-coloured message, *What a Wonderful World*.

I've just crossed an invisible line. So what? One thing the great Petra Laing taught me is that discord is all about context. Discord implies a context of harmony. But there was never any harmony here. So it doesn't trouble me overmuch. The man's an arse.

The second half of the rehearsal is equally unchallenging, and the vacuum sucks in unwelcome thoughts. Dad, quiet, serious, on the phone: *your mother's taken it very badly*. The unfairness of Mum's humiliation, and the impossibility of ever making this better. The competition, and what's wrong with me, because, objectively, Mum's right, it was a positive achievement even to be placed. And Alice has been having another go at me about my social media, telling me it's professional suicide for an artist not to engage, now I've got something to shout about, why don't I do Insta, video my music? Routine argument: I say, *once bitten, Alice*; she says, *all that business was years ago Beth, move on*. And anyway, why don't I ever share her? Do I even see her posts? My head knows she's right, but my stomach says don't go there, stay away.

I watch my mum's jaw going up and down. She's singing the top line and it isn't the voice I like. I prefer the lullaby register I haven't heard for years. That voice is low and warm and private. If I heard that voice again, I'd cry. I want to cry now, thinking about it. I want to hear it again more than anything.

Daddy's gone to sea. Me and Alice, sharing a bed then. We must have been little. *Just you and me, Daddy's away to sea.* Mummy sang us to sleep. Then later, when we were much older, she started to sing herself to sleep. I don't think I've imagined this. But I haven't heard it for a long, long time. I wonder if she's started to sing herself to sleep again, now that we've moved out, Dad's on tour and she's all alone in the house?

I keep thinking I'm going to be OK, I'll get over Jaz's betrayal and the competition and being at odds with Mum; I'm going to deal with it rationally and power through and write some music. Then I glimpse something that punctures the visible, hard surface of the world, and it taps a memory of things I've felt before, and *oh here I am again* comes gushing out and I'm as bad as her, getting emotional. But where she gets angry, I get sad. Best stop watching Mel Collier, and focus on the rest of choir, and what they're doing right here and now in this room.

That cures it. I've heard this lot many times before, and they're not at all bad for amateurs. They've put in some stylish performances of sophisticated repertoire, but I can see now that it must take a lot of time in rehearsal for them to get on top of the music.

Jeremy Snell looks as though he normally conducts brass bands. It's mostly a steady beat. He might as well be an app.

My mum doesn't trust him, because she claims he can't sing. This might have endeared him to me were it not for the dunking biscuits and everything else I know about him. I've observed his inherent smarminess from a distance. He certainly hasn't sung much tonight, other than to draw attention to the odd problematic interval.

There's a lot of twitching and bobbing about, foot tapping and such like. Look at that woman now: her head is all over the place and the middle finger of her free hand is silently tapping up, down. The pulse isn't inside them; they're still visibly grasping for it, clutching onto it, and when things get difficult, fumbling and dropping it. Bar 42, with its tricky syncopation, is a case in point. The woman's hand stops moving, but it starts again when things are back on an even keel. One of the basses sways from side to side. Several of the men look to be in pain. Conversely, across all the parts there are expressionless types who seem to be made of polystyrene. Pale, rigid, lightweight. Against a cluster of them in the alto section, Ffion Johns stands out. She's substantial. Solid, with enviable curves. A larger version of her mother — taller, wider, more present. She looks comfortable and stands well, feet apart to steady her, as if on deck. I can pick out her voice. It's a *follow me* sort of sound. Maybe by the time the rest of them have learnt the music she won't stand out so much. Mum's pal Jenny, front row of the sopranos, is also note perfect, tic-free, and she blends. Most people look stupid when they sing, though, and my mother's no exception. She stands tall, her shoulders relaxed. But here come some really high notes and — see? — the face-gym starts. She moves the muscles around her nose; her nostrils pinch, as if there's a bad smell. I suspect she's only showing off, because it's a trick not many people can do. She claims it helps her place the note. I have no idea whether that's true.

At the close of the rehearsal, Jeremy Snell says 'I'm sure you'd all like to thank our new accompanist,' and extends his arm in my direction. There's a polite flutter of clapping over the scraping of chairs; a bit feeble as most people are half way into their overcoats and stuffing music into bags, so hands aren't readily available. I smile and stand, tipping my head in acknowledgement. I'm not their new accompanist, though, am I? This is a one-off, surely?

The hall empties. On his way out, a trim middle-aged bloke with oriental cheekbones takes a sidestep towards the piano to say, 'Thanks for helping us out. I'm sure you had better ways of spending a Wednesday night.'

He's got lovely soft chestnut eyes that match the chestnut voice and he's far too old for me.

'Oh… not really.'

Why am I fibbing?

'You can't have found that fun. What do you normally like to do in your free time, then? When you're not working? You must do something to unwind?'

I don't know what to say. I haven't had sex for over a fortnight. I can't say that. Fortunately, he fills the gap.

'I'd be lost without my weekly fix at choir,' he says. 'Heaven knows, I need to let off steam.' Which allows me to ask, 'What do you do the rest of the time?'

'I'm a medic.'

Across the room, my mum, who's also my driver, is deep in discussion with Jenny and Ffion. Most people have gone but these two are hanging on.

'So – what's your thing, then, Beth? Sport? Hang-gliding? Crochet?'

I wince. I shrug.

He tucks his chin to his neck and eyes meet mine in mock disapproval.

'All work and no play?' He shakes his head, then he leans towards me and taps the top of the piano to say, 'Every professional should be an amateur at something.'

Then he turns and glides towards the door, with a backward wave.

In the car, my mother actually speaks to me.

'What did Max Chang want?'

'The doctor?'

'He's not a doctor, he's a brain surgeon. What was all that about, then?'

'He wanted to thank me.'

She passes no comment. But I'd like us to have a normal, unnecessary conversation, like we used to have, so I offer her more.

'Then he asked me about my hobbies. I think he was just making small talk, you know…'

She grunts.

'He said something interesting. He said, every professional should be an amateur at something.'

She perks up. 'He's right about that.'

But she leaves it there.

The heater in her car takes ages to kick in. I'm just beginning to feel something from it as we get back to Arctic Terrace. When the car stops and I thank her for bringing me home, she offers a cheek for me to kiss. It's even colder outside. She waits until I've opened the front door, then drives off.

8 Petra Laing

Having an internationally acclaimed composer in the music faculty was the thing that kept me in the city as an undergraduate. For a fresher, meeting Petra Laing was like approaching the Sibyl in her cave. The first time I showed her a composition – a movement for string quartet – she breathed a lot through her nose and stared at a section of the skirting board with a strange expression, eyebrows raised, mouth arched downwards, nostrils wide; her head wobbled ever so slightly up and down; you couldn't call it nodding, it was more like a palsy, to the extent that I wondered for a moment if she'd been taken ill, what with the tremor and the fact the only thing that came from her tense lips was a straining *mmm*. But by the time I'd graduated, I'd got used to the nasal breathing, and come to realise this was what Petra always did when she was working out what to say; the unnerving motion was like a connoisseur swilling wine round the mouth, prior to spitting it out. That first day, I remember staring at her long grey hair scraped back in a dark blue velvet ribbon, wondering how fast it grew, and how many minutes she must have written while these same hairs were growing. She composes every day, she claims; the sort of large-scale orchestral commissions she commands are years in preparation. That day, she sat back in her throne of a chair and struck a pose with the silver-topped cane planted vertically between the thick carpet and the elegant fingers of her outstretched arm – they're long to the point of cliché – to deliver her verdict.

'Well, Miss Collier, you know your Schubert, your Britten – that treacherous shift to the major, yes?' And she almost smiled at me. 'Looking at this, I can see exactly where you've been. But for the life of me, I can't see where you're going.'

I took this as a rebuke; that I was, naively, tethered to quite a distant musical past; riding a two-wheeler, but still needing the stabilisers. So, as a first-year student, I made it my business to find out what sort of music people were actually writing now.

Five years on, and after my time in London and Berlin, I have a pretty good idea. Some of it is wild. Much of it is melodic, accessible, even naff. There's a new harmonic language out there which listeners find approachable. Opera in particular is hot, vivid, of the moment. Not something I could ever take on, though. Opera means words. Words mean ideas. Ideas are misunderstood, mishandled, mistranslated. In fact, the moment you choose a text, you've had it, because half the world will hate you for your choice. For not writing about their concerns. For writing about their concerns when they should be no concern of yours.

I took this admin job in the department just to stay in Prof Laing's line of sight. Bask in her aura. I get to attend her post-grad seminars, and to see up close the way she reacts to things. But ever since that accursed competition, although ideas trickle in, and although I write them down, and give them drawer time, and review them every now and then, I haven't actually developed anything into a proper piece. The half-started *Superscherzo* is a bitter joke indeed.

At last, today, the sort of moment I used to hope for actually arrived. Prof Laing, back from an uncharacteristically long lunch in town, and in an unusually relaxed mood, offered to cast her eye over whatever it is I've been working on. And I had to tell her, I haven't, really.

It turned into a weird conversation, though. She did the nose breathing thing again, and gazed severely at the skirting board.

'You know what you need, Beth? You need to fall in love.'

She who seldom cracks a smile giggled for a moment. Then checked herself. 'Sorry, Beth, you'll have to excuse me. That was *such* a stupid, trite thing to say. Unforgivable. And personal. Forget I said it. Delete, please, immediately. Blame the mara – marathon... No, not that... what's it called?' Her eyes were wandering round the room as if the word she was looking for was written somewhere on the pale grey walls. She pushed back a wisp of white hair that had fallen from behind her ear, then exclaimed, 'Coffee! Look, I realise this isn't your job, but could you just nip out and get us both a coffee? Be an angel? Double espresso for me.'

Her addiction to caffeine is well-known. We were both so embarrassed, I jumped at the opportunity to calm down, come back with a coffee and take that scene again from the top.

9 B side

The whole world's wagging its finger at me today.

Jaz came round to pick up some book he left in the flat, found me cleaning the splashback, and went for the jugular.

'This is the woman who blamed me for getting in the way of her creative processes. You've got your peace and quiet now, and what are you doing with it? Hunting down the last microbe in case there's some tiny living thing in this flat that might offend your sensibilities?'

'Why would I argue with you? When we're not even in a relationship?'

Nor am I going to protest that sometimes a repetitive and mindless task is what coaxes the shiny ideas out from the gaps between the tiles.

'Displacement activity,' he pronounces, well narked. Then softens. 'Look, Beth... I like you, I really do. It's just...' He raises the flat of his hand to his mouth, as if censoring a thought. Then starts again, calmly, weighing his words, and steadily chopping the air with his right hand.

'Rule number one, right, in The Novel' – in his mouth, I always hear these words with capital letters – 'your protagonist has to *want* something. Same thing goes for you, Beth, in real life. You need to decide: what is it you want?'

'Seriously? *One* thing? How is that enough? I mean, how does that work out, if we can only ever want *one thing*?'

'Where's your *motivation*? If you want to create, create. Sit down and put in the hours. I say this as a friend.' One hand on the door, he exits with his killer line: 'There's only one thing standing in your way as a creative artist, and that's yourself.'

Next up, here's Mum on the phone, making sure I haven't forgotten about choir tomorrow, and encouraging me to wear something a bit more cheerful this time. How can I expect to get noticed in an international jobs market dressed like a scene-shifter?

'International jobs market? What job are we talking about?'

'You know what I mean. What sort of a statement are you making?'

'I dress how I feel. Dark is how I feel.'

'If you dress like a scene-shifter, you're telling the whole world you belong in the wings.' Another one of her instant effing quotes. She pauses in case I didn't notice the speech marks. Then picks up. 'Look at Alice. She always makes the most of herself.'

'Yes, Mum, she does. But we're big girls now and we don't want to dress the same. I love concert black. Anyway, you can talk! Look at the Lyceum Singers. You settle on the platform like a flock of crows. Harbingers of doom. One great big shadow.'

'And that's the whole point, Beth. The chorus has to be the chorus. We're the essential, solid, invisible background to everything you do. You professionals.'

Ah, the chorus. After the *goodbye, love you* refrain which ends the call, I mull over what she's said. Mum's pride in her amateur involvement, when at play, sits squarely alongside her belief in in the inherent dignity of labour, when at work. It's one of her values.

The Chorus dominates Mum's desert island discs, which is all Hebrew slaves and Hallelujahs.

But suppose one week she turns the radio on and it's me?

Lauren or whoever it is asks, 'So, Beth Collier, you were a very unusual little girl, to spend hours each day practising the piano. What was the attraction?'

I'm back in the room with the piano and the green geranium scent in dry air. Why am I there?

I could say it was a way of avoiding my mother.

In a way it was. A place to avoid her heat and temper. A place for escaping the arguments. Arguments about everything, whether I'd brushed my teeth, or been rude to the neighbour; arguments with our dad, things that weren't my business, politics, Iran, the Euro, kleptocracy. The legacy of Thatcherism. And other important, private things, in lower voices. To do with Alice's rehab, and school – not Mum's school, in those days, our schools. Because of course we were split up after the accident. Mum and Dad listened to what we wanted then went off in a huddle and argued in whispers about how to deal with it. I asked Dad once, why's Mum always fighting about something? And he said, your mother doesn't fight *about* things. She fights *for* things.

The thing about my father was, the way he listened. I needed his listening every bit as much as I needed my mother to back off. He'd be watching TV, or in the garden — living his normal life, there'd be other things going on — but all the time his ear took in what I was playing.

Sometimes, if I stopped, he'd pop his head in and say, 'Now that was a tickler,' or 'That was tingler,' or he'd say, 'Why don't you write that one down?'

All the same, I'm not surprised Dad packed in the Belfast ferries and went to work for the cruise line. No wonder he fancied a world tour: he couldn't do right for doing wrong. Was she always so mad, in the days before Alice's accident? I really can't remember. We were only five when it happened. And if I go right back to the time before she threw her energy into the project of my musical education, and made it as much a project as Alice's rehab... If I go right back to those first weeks, I felt then she was avoiding me.

At that time, it could be a very quiet house.

In fact, to be honest, Lauren, the silences were worse.

The music takes you over. It's like driving a car. It's a way of moving yourself through time...

No, no, this is all getting too dark for the listeners, let's move to another disc.

I'd have Thomas Tallis, *The Lamentations of Jeremiah*, and the section called *Beth*. The beautifully ornamented letter B that starts it, as if it were an illuminated manuscript.

The interviewer would pick up on that and say, 'And of course, Beth Collier, your first name is the second letter of the Hebrew alphabet.'

Yes, Lauren, but that's just a coincidence. My twin sister wasn't called Aleph, was she? My twin is Alice.

Oh no: Aleph, Alice. I've never thought of that.

A sister, B sister. A single egg.

A single. And I'm the B side.

10 Dental appointment

More than I blame Jaz Ander, I blame myself for getting him all wrong.

We met at the dentist's. Jaz and I were each sat in the middle of an otherwise empty row of steel-framed chairs, backed against two different walls, at right angles to one another. He was flicking through a copy of that day's *Echo,* looked up and caught my eye.

'Is it true that everybody in this town reads this paper?' Mischief on his face. Never mind the question, he only had to open his mouth for anyone to know he came from down south.

I do remember picking up on it and replying, 'No. And it's a city.'

'Ooh. Sorry,' and he winced comically. That was in the days when I used to think he was a charming apologiser.

He held out the newspaper and said, 'Look at it. The content. I expected the footie,' – the word sounded odd in his mouth – 'but I've never seen so many mug shots. It's either crims, or big-hearted Scousers bleeding pity. Pages of it.'

'You forgot the urban development. And the nostalgia.'

He said something along the lines of, *everything here pulls in two directions, doesn't it?* And that observation was where our – short-lived – mutual respect was formed.

I thought he was bright. Sharp.

He was new to the North West, starting out in journalism, on a placement. He wanted to get to know the North, he said;

London and the home counties were over-familiar. *I went to Leeds for university and that's when I realised it's another country up here.* I'd done my masters at the Royal Academy and come to the same conclusion.

It would have been, *so are you local then?* That classic opener. I probably said, *I can tell you one thing about Liverpool. All the clichés are true.* Whatever it was, he went all post-modern on me and nodded ironically, wanting more. He had a really stylish work jacket on, with a slim black notebook peeping out of the top pocket, and he looked good in dark colours. I was suckered in. We talked and talked.

As one thing led to another, a wonky tooth to a drink to another drink to another day and sex which was not unsatisfactory, not once but twice, and then whole nights, and long, long discourse through the night, I never once suspected that I was simply part of his research. The tried and tested best way to pick up a foreign language.

I can hear him now. Waxing lyrical about how he loved it here, and never wanted to leave the city, people were so warm and open... Yeah. Well. He'd only been here ten minutes. All this talk is great, to start off with. But I told him: a lot of Liverpudlians make better strangers than acquaintances, because they settle into conversational routines which can get boring. Some of them barely get beyond civic pride and their own life histories. You wouldn't want to share a cell.

I find it easy to talk to strangers. Why wouldn't you? But I shouldn't have been suckered in. People in this city wear their hearts on their sleeve, and this is brilliant, or dreadful, depending on how you look at it. *Me Nan's waitin' for a liver transplant. Been on the pop.* Casually shared with the bus queue. It's as if they're missing a layer of skin, and everything bleeds out. Whatever's uppermost on their mind – no, in their heart – is the thing they'll share with you within minutes of first meeting. I've always tried hard not to do this.

I can't forgive myself for giving away too much. I painted Jaz a picture of the obsessive little grafter I was as a child, and let him glimpse my mother through the crack in the door.

11 New Blood

Wednesday lunchtime and Mum phones to say she's coming my way for a meeting, so she'll be able to pick me up from mine tonight. Straight to the point, no natter. She wouldn't talk to the dry cleaners like that; she's got warmth to spare for complete strangers, for a bus conductor or a shop assistant. Not for me, not any more.

Clearly, I'm expected at choir practice. I can't believe it's only a week since the last one. I kept this evening free in case, not that there was anything else on offer; but I'm not sure how long this stand-in role is meant to go on for, and I don't sense this is the moment to ask. Instead, I ask how she is and she snaps, 'What do you mean?'

'Just… you know, how are you? Are you OK?'

'Why wouldn't I be?'

I back off.

I've stopped enquiring what all her meetings are about. Might be an earthquake, might be the scourge of scrambler bikes, or the food bank; one time it was saving the Roscoe Street Rainforest. Some cause or another. She has so many causes, great and small. It's her brand of promiscuity.

Ten minutes to seven. I haven't quite finished tidying my tea things when the doorbell rings, so I invite her in.

'Good meeting?'

'Yes. Interesting.'

She'll tell me more if she wants to. She doesn't. As she stands and waits, her gaze tracks subtly over the surfaces, not disapprovingly either. She believes I get my tidiness from her. She's more dressed up than usual; I recognise one of the good frocks she's using up from work, and she's wearing patent leather shoes with low heels. I wonder who this is all in aid of, which probably makes me a bad person; and I'm not going to ask, either, because I remember the *dress for yourself* discussion. Me, 14, in denim hot pants with the little red heart buttons, off Paddy's market; my dad shifting in his blue Dralon throne, saying, 'Bloody hell Bethany, why don't you just say if you want the window open?' and his eyes appealing to Mum for support. She trained her guns on him, not me. My poor Dad went pink and did that thing where he breathed out and dropped his shoulders, and the colour supplement slid out of his Sunday Times onto the thick cut Chinese rug.

'What's the matter, Keith?' she said.

'Oh eh, come on, Melanie, she's gonna have every feller on the estate running round with his tongue hangin' out.'

'First,' she said, 'this is not an estate.' And she might have been holding the platform at the Women's Group, the way she turned round to me and said, 'Whatever you wear, it's your choice, Bethany. Just promise me you'll never dress to please a man.'

I don't remember what my dad said — probably something like, 'that's me told,' — but I do remember that when he picked up the supplement, the muscle in the side of his jaw was twitching, the same muscle he used to wiggle his ears. Poor Dad.

There I go again. Cupboards closed, I make an effort to bring myself back to the here and now, pick up my coat, smile at my Mum and tell her she looks nice.

'Might as well wear these things out,' she says. Ever the practical one.

This week's choir practice turns out to be as stodgy as last week's was. I've got to make sure I never get roped into this again. I need to able to say, oh sorry, I've got a clash. But I haven't. Wednesday's not a big concert night here, which is probably why they've chosen it for rehearsals. New music and ensemble work – so exactly my territory – get the Wednesday slot, but they are few and far between, and no more this side of Christmas. I can't tell a lie. Who do I ever see on a Wednesday?

About half an hour into the rehearsal, I notice a man sitting on a kid's chair right up against the Wonderful World frieze, well behind the basses, at the very back of the room. He wasn't there when we started. He's too tall for the chair but sits up as straight as he can. He's hanging on the edge of things, listening, his chin raised, and he has lovely curly dark hair that hangs forward over his brow. Slightly built, and in his thirties maybe. He has a Mediterranean look about him; honeyed skin, almond eyes. So, my type. If it wasn't for the fact that a new man in my life is the last thing I need right now, I'd be interested. I'm allowed to be idly curious, though.

At the coffee break, Jeremy Snell goes over to talk to this man. Jenny Jones follows, then my mum, as if there's some sort of pull; they must know who he is and why he's there. They're always looking for men, but if he were here for a try-out, he'd have been singing.

This week I've brought my own peppermint teabag because their instant coffee can only lower my already compromised immune system. The surgeon guy happens to be next to me in the queue for the urn and says, 'I see you've come prepared.'

'So have you.' He's gone a step further and brought his own multi-use rainforest-friendly coffee cup, with a dragon logo on it in gold; the label on the end of the string tells me that his herbal teabag, unlike mine, is top-end pyramid stuff. He flashes a smile.

'Never do caffeine after two pm.'

I don't know whether he means he doesn't, or you shouldn't.

'Very healthy,' I say.

'Max.' He moves the ridged cup to the other hand, to shake.

'Beth.'

I've got one eye on the increasingly large gaggle of people round the mystery man.

'Some of us go to the pub after choir,' says Max.

'Which one?'

'The Irish Bar'

Which hardly narrows it down.

'What, even my mother? Only, last week, she took me straight home. And I was gasping.'

'Ah, your famous tiger mother…'

Oh grrr-eat. He's brought up the Tiger Mother article. I can't decide whether to give him the death stare or to laugh out loud. I can feel my face straining and flickering: it doesn't know which way to crease. Not that Max registers my discomfort. He ploughs on: 'No, she doesn't usually join us. But she will tonight. We've got a guest to entertain,' and he jerks his head over his shoulder, in the direction of the little crowd.

I ask, 'Who is he anyway?'

I don't understand what Max says at first. He starts to spell a name out, but he's drowned by shared stage laughter from the group behind. What I do catch is, 'I'm surprised your mother didn't mention it. She's the contact. He's here to meet the rest of committee. And to hear us, of course. This could be our new conductor. Jeremy's replacement.'

Over his shoulder, the fan club has formed a circle, and now everybody bends backwards and inwards again, like a sea-anemone or a bunch of Morris men.   They must be the committee. Ffion peels away and strides over in my direction. Except it turns out it isn't my direction at all, it's Max Chang she's after. Too late, though, we're starting again. The singers quickly disperse and are seated. The stranger has slipped back to his place under the rainbow. 'Right, bar 56, Herod the King,' says Jeremy with a slitty grin, then raises his elbows and looks both ways.

The rehearsal ends, and now it's Ffion who encourages me to join everyone for a drink. I'm flattered in a way, because she's so different to me; she's properly employed for a start, she does high heels and my goodness, she lets you know if there's something on her mind. I've known her for years, because of our mums being best mates, but we don't hang out.

The pub's only round the corner, so we all walk. I can smell the wetness of the street, diesel and chip fat held in suspension on the city air. I try to tag along with Ffion but she's trying to tag along with Max. Every now and then, I'm barged off the pavement and into the road. Somebody, walking behind me, has a pocket full of keys and loose change, which clank and jingle with each heavy step, never the same twice. Mum in her work frock and patent leather shoes, the interesting guest she didn't tell me about, not to mention the question *what am I doing here*: these thoughts are jangling too, bashing the corners off each other. If I can only focus, perhaps I'll be able to lay them out on the table like the contents of a pocket, and put them in some sort of order before the evening is out. The November mizzle is thick with confusion.

Already from outside I can tell this isn't going to be my kind of pub. Fifties mock Tudor, the lack of customers advertised in flat yellow from the shining windows, and it's all lounge. They didn't build proper cellars post-war. Sure enough, once we're through the heavy wooden doors with their bullseye lights, the first thing I clock is that there are no gravity pumps, just the kind of fizz-gun you might use for coke or lemonade, so a pub without ale. Heartless. Guinness and Irish cider in evidence, a few photos of racehorses, which must be what qualifies this as an Irish bar. There are two kids serving, in emerald green T shirts at war with the garish red-and-gold patterned carpet; they welcome the choir with huge smiles, like long lost mates. They're probably desperate for some action, it's not exactly humming in here. The committee colonises a large bay, giving the man from under the rainbow pride of place at the head of their table. Some of us go up to the bar. I scrutinise the varnished shelves behind the counter; below them, there's a chiller cabinet full of bottled beers most of which are American.

Max wants to buy me and Ffion a drink; when I opt for the Guinness, he thinks at first that I'm being ironic. He's OK with a tonic water which he'll drink from the bottle. A load of us scuffle for places round the remaining largish table and I end up in the middle of the long window-seat, so no chance of hearing what's going on with the VIP. In the squash of damp coats, I'm caught between Ffion and a couple of the flatter altos. Ffi pats the chair to her left and Max obediently sits there. Round the table to his left, at a diagonal to me, a skinny pensioner in a grey suit and stone-coloured mac introduces himself as Ian. I wouldn't have recognised this guy in a line-up, even though technically we've spent two whole evenings together now. But I do know Patrick, the heroic tenor who's sitting next to him, because of the way his voice penetrates;

he's voluble, fair-skinned and blushing, and wearing a tight-fitting pink shirt so cinched at the waist of his jeans that he makes you think of sausage meat in a skin. In spite of the differences in age and dress, from the way they settle in tandem, these two blokes seem to be good mates.

Ffi has a large glass of white wine in her hand; she's forever lifting it up and putting down again without drinking, because, having a mouth on her like the Mersey Tunnel, she keeps thinking of something else to say. There's a lot of babble, with several conversations going on in the room, and soon I'm more watching than listening. Ffion is so incredibly 3-D; so *sculpted*; I don't know if it's down to hours in the gym or the right shape wear, but her clothes are always kind of *explicit*. So different from me. Plus she has these amazingly prehensile lips, and it's fascinating to watch the way they flex and curl, and the distances they cover in conversation. I hope she never changes them. Her attention is fixed on the magnetic north of Max, saver of lives. Looks like he's unattached, then.

He must have made some clever comment, because eventually Ffi turns towards me and taps my arm to say, 'Honestly Beth, what is he like?' And to him, 'Ooh Max, you're so sharp, you'll cut yourself!'

The blokes are grinning into their pints.

'It's the way he tells them,' says Ffi.

I smile as approvingly as I can. I don't want to snarl up the conversation by asking what he said, because I ought to have been listening, instead of staring at Ffion's mouth and wondering how many calories it burns per minute. So I make a contribution.

'Max, you told me the other day, every professional should be an amateur at something.'

He grimaces and makes a couple of movements with his head, as if weighing up an idea he's just heard for the first time.

'Mm. Yes.'

I say, 'Well, that's all very Oscar Wilde, but I don't see why it should be true.'

Ffi says, 'What he means is, being an amateur at something stops you getting too big for your boots.'

Pink Patrick chips in, 'So, like, when the patient says, thank you, Doctor, you saved my life, Max is thinking, ah yes but I screwed up that entry in the fugue last night. Keeps him modest, like?'

Max grins good-naturedly, and when he tilts his head to explain, his rich voice carries.

'Kind of. Seriously, though. Nobody should ever forget how it feels to be only half-competent at something. Not to know stuff.'

'Why?' asks Ffion. Which saves me the trouble of sounding stupid.

'It helps you empathise with people.'

Patrick squeals, 'Yeah, because most people, most of the time, don't know what the Donald Duck they're doing. Incompetence is the default position of the human condition.'

There's a wave of laughter, and as it subsides, grey Ian lifts a hand. He looks pained. His voice is reedy and quiet, and everybody listens.

'Look at our Pamela, though. I can't imagine our Pamela being an amateur at anything. Nothing's too hard. Choux pastry. Standard deviation. She can even explain the offside rule, for godssake.' This is greeted by a murmured rippled of respect. I sense they all know Pamela. His voice wheels plaintively round three notes: 'Everything she touches is perfect, like out of a magazine.'

'Your sister's a pain in the arse,' offers Patrick. 'She needs to loosen up.'

Suddenly, Ian's face opens, the lines smooth out and his eyebrows pop up above the straight metal frame of his glasses; behind the lenses, his eyes are like big shiny glass marbles; he looks almost pleased as he stares at the table and confides, 'Mind you... She can't sing. Can't sing for toffee.'

'Doesn't need to mate, she's got yer great-grandma's toffee-making recipe and the sugar thermometer to go with it.'

Now we're all in bulk. When we stop laughing, Ian is still enjoying his moment.

'No, but seriously... I may be crap, but at least I can sing. It's probably the only thing I can do that she can't.'

'There you are then,' says Ffion.

When Ian adds, 'She can't read music, our Pamela,' everybody cheers. He looks quite impish now. His eyes flit round the company.

Ffion turns to fill me in: 'Ian lives with his sister.' She whispers in my ear, 'Big house in Gateacre. Never left home. Their mum passed and neither of them wants to move out. Can't live together, can't sell up.'

I'm intrigued by this relationship between Ian and Pamela. He must be sixty if he's a day, yet he sounded like some whining teenage lad when he brought up his sister, and now that he's giving her a good knocking with his mates, the whining has morphed into malevolent glee. Maybe I'm sensitive because of being a twin, but I've always rejected the concept of sibling rivalry. It's a fallacy. A social construct. What I'm learning from Ian right now is that once you buy into SR, it only gets worse with age.

So don't buy into it.

I wonder what my twin is doing now. I see her on her own and in pyjamas. I take a sip and wonder if she'd like to be sitting here drinking this creamy, brown gloop. She'd like the noise and the jostling and all these strangers gabbing at once. It's like a big fat chord on a cathedral organ, that takes in every note of the scale, and leaves you to work out for yourself where the harmony lies.

The drinkers round the table all look up. Jeremy Snell is standing right behind grey Ian, who has frozen at the sound of his master's voice; and now everyone's looking at me, because I'm the one he's after. Now, what?

'Would you mind, Beth, for a minute...' Jeremy says, and he's wagging his head and pointing to the big table in the bay window where the members of the committee have fallen silent as if they're waiting for something.

I stand up and nearly take the tangled coats on the bench with me, as the ladies hinge their knees sideways and their shoulders back, so as to let me squeeze myself between them and the table, and follow Jeremy. The visitor looks up and smiles at me as I approach.

'This is Beth Collier,' says Jeremy. 'Melanie's daughter. Beth, this is...' – a name I can't make out – '...he's come to see how we do things. To get a feel for what he might be letting himself into, ha-ha.'

Why would he want to meet me?

I hold out my hand and say, 'Hi, I'm Beth,' in the hope that he'll take the cue to repeat his own first name. But as we shake hands, he just repeats, 'Beth,' with a nod. His fingers are as long and slender as Petra Laing's, but the skin is at once luminous and matt, like golden limestone. It's warm and dry, and this is a proper, honest handshake. Neither limp nor squeezy. He smiles and his eyes flash. His face is a very beautiful shape, almost like a leaf, symmetrical and coming to a soft point at the chin. I can't think of anything to say. My mother actually closes her eyes in embarrassment.

But Jeremy hasn't missed a beat, and the unnatural grin hasn't left him. 'Beth's our accompanist, aren't you Beth?'

There's a great guffaw from my table which grabs everybody's attention. I glance over my shoulder, but it doesn't look as though they're laughing at me. Whatever it is dies down.

'I'm just standing in…'

'And a composer.'

'That's interesting,' says the man. He has a barely perceptible, unplaceable foreign accent. His eyes are dark and bright. 'Do you write for the choir?'

'God, no,' I say, and immediately regret it. That did sound rude.

Mum rolls her eyes, Jeremy flares his nostrils and grimaces. I don't mind offending him. But the man from under the rainbow is a different matter. What I really, really must not do is ask him where he's from, because that would be inept, and I'm concentrating so hard on not saying that, that I end up saying: 'So, how do you rate the talent? I mean, musically?'

His smooth face doesn't flicker. He says, softly, seriously, 'Promising,' and glances round the table, harvesting smiles from the committee. A diplomat, then. 'Promising' is right up there with 'extraordinary' when you want to sound more positive than you feel. I decide to be straight with him.

'I didn't catch your name, sorry.'

He reaches into the inside pocket of his jacket and draws out a business card, which he hands to me. Black type on a glossy yellow ground, with an olive branch logo in one corner.

Stelios Christodoulou
Aphrodite Catering – For All Your Events
1 Faith Place
Liverpool 1A 9ZZ

'Thanks. May I call you Stelios?'

'No. Stelios is my uncle. But it's my address, so this is a useful card. It's the right surname.' He adds, carefully: 'My uncle is my grandfather's brother.' Another pause. 'My name is Theodoros Christodoulou.'

I read the card as I repeat, 'Theodoros… Christodoulou.'

'No. You've put the stress on the wrong beat. The*od*oros. It's not like *Do*reen. It's like the *od*orous. Or the *od*ious. But I'm not. Neither.' The curve of a smile is tickling the corners of his eyes, then he breaks into a huge grin – whiter and wider even than Max's – and giggles like a kid.

'So, I'm guessing I've scored zero on the aural,' I say, and join in the childish sniggering. He's lovely. I'm not sure he understood what I just meant, though. It doesn't matter, he's signalling acceptance. He wants us to get on.

'Everybody here calls me Theo.' Which is at once a mercy, and a disappointment.

They pull up a chair for me and I observe while Theo Christodoulou is pumped for information by the committee. He grins easily, and his eyes open wide, so wide that you can see the white above and below the iris. I learn that he was trained at the Conservatoire in a city I've never heard of, and then in Athens; that he sings, and plays piano, violin, and bouzouki, as well as another traditional Cypriot instrument whose name I don't recognise. It's a stringed instrument. When Marsha asks, 'Plucked or bowed?' I can see him thinking and catch my mum doing hand gestures.

'Ah. Plooked. I plook it.' He's still grappling with northern vowels. Sweet.

Marsha wants to know can we hear him play, and he says, yes, come to the next acoustic night at the Afro D.T. Bar… That must be Aphrodite, Greek-style.

They talk classical repertoire and I watch his face. He's eager to participate, with that look which tells you he's working hard to recognise the foreign names they throw around, and pleased when he catches them. Fair's fair, Bach, Berlioz, Borodin, they're equally chewed up by English, Scouse and Greek, only in different ways. After a while, Jeremy says he's sorry to break up the conversation but his lift home is about to depart, and whisks Mr Christodoulou away. You can tell that this has been stage-managed: the present incumbent tactfully withdrawing so as to allow a clinical post mortem. I bet he'll spend the journey in third gear, warning the poor lad what to expect, i.e., duff tuning and an inability to count four equal beats in a bar.

I'm sorry he's gone. I liked looking at him and I could have looked a bit longer. Now I find myself sitting with the committee. This committee has rumbled in our background for years, prompting the occasional flare-up from Mum, who might come home muttering, *wouldn't pay them in washers, this lot couldn't organise a piss-up in a brewery*, but has never missed a meeting. I'm curious to witness them in action.

Now the candidate's gone, they can get down to business. They're opening the way to all sorts of problems, according to Jenny Johns.

'For a start,' she says, 'he doesn't speak proper English.'

Jenny's voice has just swooped Snowdonia-style up and down a flattened octave. It meets a chorus of tutting and don't-be-daft and what-do-you-mean.

'Well look what happened just before, when you asked where to sign, and he told you to put it *on the backside*? Imagine if you used language like that to a civic dignitary.'

'Everybody knew what he meant.'

'It's pretty good if you ask me.'

'I once told a Frenchman I'd wet myself,' says Mum, steering into one of her top five rants. 'We're all foreigners. Thank goodness some of us are still curious enough to want to learn each other's languages. And if we do, we make mistakes, because you can't learn any skill worth having without messing up on the way. We're so scared in this country of sounding funny, or being offensive by mistake, we don't even try. I mean, anyone here know Greek?'

Before she can get on to the full lecture, she's interrupted.

'*Prima la musica, doppo le parole.*' I think this bloke's called Gavin, or maybe Gareth; he's what Uncle Pat would call a bit of a Fancy Dan. Another tenor, more mature. He's just drawn his Italian like a silk handkerchief from his pocket and flourished it in the increasingly warm air; lingering on the rich, round vowels, rolling his r's, raising an arm, and twirling his hand, which comes to rest elegantly on his sternum. 'The music comes first, doesn't it? Then the words. What's he like as a musician? That's what I want to know. What's his track record?'

'He hasn't got one,' says Jenny.

Mum's warmed up now. 'He's very well-qualified. A post-graduate diploma in conducting.'

'Yes, and the print's still wet. So he's practising on us! And he's only ever worked in Cyprus. Nothing in the UK, so far as I can see.'

'That cuts both ways,' says Marsha. 'We could be missing a gem here.'

I've never really spoken to this Marsha before, but I liked the way she welcomed me by patting the seat next to her just now. She's Scouse as they come, mixed-race; and you don't see that many black or brown faces in classical choirs, so she must be super-motivated.

They fall into comparisons with the other contender, who, I learn, went through the same process three weeks ago. I can't work out whether this person was shy or a sociopath. They might be describing me: fussy, low-key, wiry, suspected vegetarian, maybe of a nervous disposition… Until I learn he's a church organist whose idea of expanding the repertoire is choral arrangements of 'pop songs.' I've no problem with anybody singing anything they like. But if there's one thing I regard as blasphemy, an unequivocal crime against music, it's classical choirs like this one taking great numbers and squashing them into a swing-less straightjacket of strict metre and high Anglican diction. False imprisonment. I keep these thoughts to myself.

People are coming to agreement, and it's not going Jenny's way.

'There was a time when I would have kept my own counsel,' she says.

'Oh aye, yeah. Right,' says Marsha. Gavin-Gareth-Fancy Dan looks sideways and mutters, 'I don't remember that far back.'

'But if we're split on this, I've got as much a right as anyone else to a casting vote, after ten years on the committee, and me being the one who headhunted Jeremy Snell.'

I imagine his shrunken head on a stick, the hair no longer slicked into submission, but hanging scraggily down.

'Funny expression, *headhunted*. Why do people say that?'

'Means they wanted him for his brains,' says Marsha, and leans towards me so that our shoulders touch, and I'm enveloped in a great cloud of vanilla. 'You wouldn't want the rest of him, would yer, though?' she guffaws, and elbows me in the ribs.

My mum's serious, brings us all back to the point. 'Look, the choir is at a crossroads here. We can appoint Mr Limp-

Handshake and get the same old same old, or we can strike out and embrace the new.'

'Time for a woman,' I say.

Mum switches on her best gorgon glare. 'You offering? No. Thought not. Be realistic, Beth. We can only pay basic, we've got no proper arrangement with any orchestra in place, and no real home. Not since the staging collapsed on *Israel*.' Deep groans all round.

Everyone knows this story, and they just love re-telling it for my benefit. The arm-waving tenor shows off his crisp diction: '*Israel in Egypt.* We'd got through all ten plagues, their land had brrought forth frrogs, we'd had b-lotches and b-lains, and we had smitten the first-born of Egypt, when there was an almighty clang. As of a clashing cymbal.'

Sandy explains, 'The back rail fell off and hit the stone flags.'

She sits back for emphasis, and Marsha picks the story up. 'The basses stop first. Then the orchestra packs up. There's, like, complete silence for a second, and some joker on the front row goes, *well that makes it eleven. Quit while yer ahead.'*

Sandy chips in, 'And the headline in the *Echo* was *Amateur Singers bring the house down.'*

Once they've all stopped guffawing, Mum says, 'There *is* such a thing as bad publicity, though. We're a laughing stock round here. People who know say no.'

'That's right,' says Sandy. 'Honest to God, you can't call this headhunting! We've practically been round the bins.' Sandy's the only one of Mum's ex-colleagues she keeps in touch with, and always backs her up.

Mum nods. 'And finally, after all these months, we've got a long list of two. Impose quotas and we take that right up to zero. No, Theo's the man. Person.'

'Young, gifted and kind of olive,' says Marsha, smacking her lips. 'Sign me up.'

She raises her hand and others follow.

'Looks as though we've voted,' says Mum.

'No, we need to do it properly,' says Jenny. 'Beth, you do realise, you're not on the committee, so you don't have a vote.'

'It's absolutely none of my business,' I say, with feeling, to hide the fact that, to my own surprise, I do really care about this decision.

I am quite pleased when Mr Christodoulou is duly selected. Subject to a trial period.

12 Instead of a party

I was feeling quite mellow about this new conductor I met last night, until a voice in my head warned me that he might just be a slightly better-fed, taller version of Jaz Ander. I.e., just my type, and therefore sure to disappoint, given what a rubbish judge of character I turn out to be. By the time I board the bus to Alice's, I've gone right off him, without going so far as to throw away the borrowed business card (I've checked, it's safe in my jeans pocket). Now I'm beating myself up about my errors, not helped by the familiar psycho-chemical effect of diesel fug. It's rank with dismay.

Mum warned me, and it's doubly annoying she was right. 'That lad Jaz… All mouth and trousers. One of these days his karma's going to catch up with him in a dark alley, and give him what for.'

Now a horrible thought has plonked itself down on the seat next to me: it's possible, given the timing, that the Tiger Mother article was an act of revenge. *Doubly* my fault.

Every time I've made this journey, it's rained. Inside the bus, condensation blurs the red brick buildings and the chaos of the shop-fronts; I wipe a little triangular porthole in the window next to me. Edge Lane's so straight, this bus driver can't resist attempting irritating little bursts of speed between stops. Whenever we lurch to a halt, the brakes squeal and I watch the raindrops shiver and collapse onto one another. How easily they coalesce.

Chameleon Close is a cul-de-sac of ordinary pre-war semis, apart from numbers one and three, where a bomb dropped and made room for improvement. The front garden has been bricked over for parking, and parallel ramp and steps lead to a wide front door with a key pad. I press the buzzer.

A stranger opens the door to me and says, 'Oh, I know who you are. You're Beth.'

'Do I know you?'

'Sam.'

'Hey, Sam.'

'She's in the kitchen… Alice!' A shout, like a crease in the throat. Sam shouts again, 'Ali-i-i-ice! Visitor!'

I know the way but Sam steps in front of me, to be first; and tells me that Ginny came today.

They have a huge kitchen-diner here, of the sort that Ffion wishes on my mum's house. It's practical for a wheelchair, and there's almost always someone there, especially since Vilma's Nan gave her a second-hand portable TV which, let's be clear about this, never moves from the corner of the counter.

I look in and see Vilma, slumped at the dining table playing some sort of game on her phone; she's a great pyramid of a woman, narrow shoulders sloping down to massive hips. Her blue jumper has gone all bobbly where it's scuffed by the edge of the table-top. She's got the tiny telly on, with the sound turned down. She glances up and says, ''Lo,' when I walk in, then calls to Alice, 'She's here,' and my sister wheels round from the worktop to greet me, with a flash of red and orange from her folksy jumper. There's a good smell, cheese scones fresh from the oven. 'Hiya! Come in! Welcome to my whirl!' A lot of her speech rehab errors have passed into our private vernacular; they're funny and we don't see any reason to give them up. I hug her and stand back, and we do a silent low-high-five. 'We can have them hot,' she says; her eyes skitter towards Vilma and back to me, and I give a micro-nod: yes, Vilma can have one. I put the kettle on to make a pot of tea.

I load the tray, and Vilma has eaten her buttered scone before we've left the room. Vilma said 'Ta' before and after gobbling it down, otherwise words have not been needed by any of us. Which suits me.

Vilma and my sister got matched by social services, they didn't exactly choose each other for flatmates. Yet they seem to rub along just fine. Same thing with Zoe, whose low mutterings would drive me to distraction, and whose seismic frown seems to flatten out to nothing once my sister's in the room. Alice brings out the best in people. They don't annoy her the way they might annoy me.

On Alice's first day in her new accommodation, a couple of months ago now, she baked a tray of flapjacks and forgot about them. Vilma smelled burning, turned the oven off, cracked open a packet of chocolate digestives, and started a tea party which lasted through till supper time. I'm ashamed to think that, when I left home for the Academy, the first thing

I burned – deliberately – was an old, Novello vocal score of *Messiah,* one of the brown and fawn ones; I tipped the only slightly duller ashes into a jam jar and screwed the lid on tightly. *That's where you're staying.* It sat on the windowsill where it served as a test for potential new friends. Anybody who was affronted by it was never going to understand me. I'm starting to think I was a bit of a prig.

Alice's room is even tidier than my flat — anything visible is in use; so my heart bumps at the little Tascam recorder sitting on the bedside table. This is something new, and I want to ask her about it, but she grabs the conversation first, as she pours the tea. Something's bugging her.

'Mum came. She said shame about not going to the party, and I said, I *told* you.'

'How did she react?'

'Said I should never have worried about the audition, they never reject anybody.'

'Alice, trust me, that's probably true.'

'Yeah, but I don't want to join his poxy choir now, anyway. Not if they'll take anyone.'

'It'll be the new conductor after Christmas. He's nice.'

'Yeah, Mum said.'

'Did she say, don't cut off your nose to spite your face?'

'Yup.'

'And don't burn your bridges?'

Alice frowns under her too-short, too-straight fringe, and nods like a five-year-old, exaggerated, definite.

'Some days I think nobody wants us, Beth.'

There's a crack in her voice, as if she's going to cry. She can be more fed up, more disappointed even than me. Everything she feels is magnified to twice what I feel; she never tries to hide it, and nobody expects her to; and what people forget, or never knew, is that even before the accident, she was the one who specialised in tantrums and delight; she was always vocal, transparent, easy to read. Whereas I'm like a piece of paper on which bad things have been written, so that I have to fold myself in half and half again, and again, and again, pressing down the crease each time to make sure the writing can't be read. When Alice frowns, it's as if I'm watching my frustrations take on physical form. But I know how to stop this.

I jump to my feet. 'Music!' I say. '*Varmints*. Now!' Suddenly I'm brisk, like Mum would be, and I stride across to the laptop. On this feeble set-up you'll never get the volume you want but it will be enough to change our mood. The first track, *Nautilus*, is our favourite. Alice loves the graphics so she'll stare at the screen, which has to be better than watching her own frown reflected on my face. That one-note dotted rhythm on synthesised brass starts up, and instantly we're both distracted from our misery; the music is exciting and urgent; the graphics are block colour, gloriously childish, and they flash in time: tonsils, teeth, tonsils, teeth, tonsils, teeth; the effect is like hearing a fire alarm or a knock on the door, you can't ignore it; and as the rising chromatic scale kicks in – each note repeated, the whole thing still kangaroo-hopping to one rhythm – it all turns into a gurgle of happiness rising from the deep. It's like your dad running upstairs to tickle you. You know your target is the keynote, and that as soon as you reach it, you'll start the whole journey again from the bottom. In no time at all we both have smiles on our faces.

After that one track, I press stop.

'The world needs my voice,' says Alice; she's remembered her mantra, and her face re-sets to a smile. 'I'm not a kid any more, and I do the priorities round here.   If the choir won't have me, I'll just have to be a solo artiste.'

'You'll get a better frock, that's for sure.'

She grins, and asks, 'Any good news?'

'Life is better without Jaz.'

'Good,' she says. 'We don't like him. Mum and me.'

'You hardly knew him.'

'Once was enough. He's a toody, isn't he?'

This is our word for a 2-dimensional character, applied over the years to anybody who only pretends to care, although generally, it's to do with caring for her, not me.

'Yeah, turned out he was.'

'Mum told me what he did.'

'The tiger mother thing? What did she say? She won't believe me, that it was all a big misunderstanding.'

'Good riddance and have his guts for garters.'

'She blames me. Did she say anything about me?'

Alice shrugs, no; but I'm not sure whether to believe her, because she edits out the bits you might not want to hear. All she'll give away is, 'She's still upset about it.'

I look round the room for something to say. Anywhere Alice lives is always tidy enough for visitors. 'So you had a music lesson today? What's this Ginny like? She a toody?'

'No. She's a big round threedy.'

'What d'you do?'

'We did some songs. She showed me how to use this thing, so I can lay it down.'

I've never heard her use that expression before.

'What're you laying down, exactly?'

'My bit. My track,' she says, as if I'm stupid. 'I told you. The band. Sky Blue Pink.'

'Wow,' I say.

'Wanna hear a bit?'

'Pope a catholic?'

She swivels round and reaches for the digital recorder. She might struggle with this, it being so small, and her fingers not as nimble as they ought to be. She passes it to me to play.

'It's Folder A for Alice.'

'You're going to run these batteries down,' I tell her, because it's still switched on from her lesson. There are just two tracks in the folder and the first is only fifteen seconds long, probably a test, so I go straight to the second. My sister has a great voice, unspoilt, strong and with its own distinctive, grainy texture. The song has no words, and it sounds like some sort of dirge. It might be middle eastern, or even Indian.

'What is it?' I say. 'I don't recognise this.'

'You recognise me!' She grins, she thinks I'm teasing.

'Where does it come from?'

'Shh!'

So I listen. It's utterly dismal, but there's a shape to it, with repetitions and a melody. Alice avoids my gaze: she wants to concentrate. Her brow is drawn, critical, and I understand the slight sucking of the lower lip because I do that sometimes.

'*You* wrote it, Alice!'

'I wrote it instead of a party,' she says.

It's at once surprising, and obvious. When we were little, she loved to make things up; she's always been one for humming tunes that nobody recognised, that were special to herself; then, as a teenager, she'd drive us all mad repeating these odd little circular figures, sometimes just three notes, and I was never sure whether it was a confected tic, designed to annoy us, or a genuine, disturbing compulsion. At any rate, I didn't think of it as music; why? Because these one-liners led nowhere. They were never developed. In recent years we've heard less of them but they've never quite run dry. The difference, now, is that she's pushed a basic idea further; not only that, but she's set it down, by recording it.

It occurs to me the recording might have been an improvisation, so I check: 'If you sang it again now, would it be the same?'

'Yeah.' She gives her sharper-than-necessary nod, then asks: 'Will you help me? Will you turn it into real music, in notes?'

'Sure, I'll write it out. But it's real already.'

Once she's pinned it down like that, fixed it, she's writing music. She's doing what I do. Something like an earth tremor runs through me, passes quickly: things aren't quite as I thought; but nothing's broken. It's OK.

And I can help. 'D'you want any backing? You know, harmony?'

'Mmm. Dunno. P'raps. Go on, give it a ticket to heaven.'

She means send it to the Dropbox account. This started when Alice told Father Dominic that God didn't live on a cloud, and he tried to tell us that well actually, in a way, God was like *the* cloud: everywhere, all about us, but invisible, until such a time as we make Him manifest through prayer. Alice laughed in his face and Mum had to pretend to tell her off. I reckon God is dangerously vulnerable to distributed denial-of-service, the amount of praying going on round here on a match day. But obviously I wasn't going to say that to a priest who does the gee-gees.

I grab her laptop and wince at the screen saver which shows a cat playing the piano. Alice watches me as I fiddle around doing the necessary.

I ask, 'Have we got a title for this?'

Our eyes meet, our lips turn down, and in a few seconds, we nod and agree: 'Stead of a Party.'

I re-name the file, drag and drop.

'There. *Instead of a party.* All done.'

'All done,' she sings. 'So long, farewell, ow feeder sane, goodby-ee!' Then she smirks under her fringe and says, wheedling, 'Are you looking for another boyfriend?'

'Why? Have you got someone lined up for me?'

'No, *I* haven't. But maybe Mum has.' Our eyes lock.

'Who's that then?'

'Aah…He's anominous.'

'You mean this new conductor? He's not anominous. I've met him. He's called Theo.'

'Mum likes him.'

This is the opposite of a recommendation; yet, 'I like him,' I say, and I can feel an unwelcome, juvenile smile spreading across my face. I shake my head and look at the floor. She keeps this carpet clean.

'Men are not good for me, is what I've learnt. They only walk mud into your life.'

'You were a bad picker, with Jaz.'

'Hm.'

'I don't trust you with this one, either,' she says. 'That's me judging you, by the way. I'm not judging him. What's he like?'

'How do I know? He's got nice hands.'

'Promise me one thing,' she says, in a Mum voice. 'Before you get involved, make sure he's a threedy.' Then, offhand, 'When's your bus?'

I guess we're done here.

'Cheers, Alice. Thanks for the scones.'

'Maybe cake next time,' she says. 'If we get something to celebrate. Me and the band.'

She raises an eyebrow to say, go on, ask me.

'What sort of something? What are you plotting?'

'Ah,' she says, and narrows her eyes. 'Just something. Wait and see.'

On my way to the bus stop, questions crowd in, and they're questions I could and should have asked. What does she get up to these days? And what about this Ginnie, the music therapist, who gave her the digital recorder? What do their sessions consist of? How long has Alice been serious about writing music?

I ought to have dug deeper, and been nosy about Hands Free music and the band. I should have expressed more of an interest. I'd have asked a stranger. But it was a sister thing. She was so smug, wrapped in her mystery, and that annoyed me, so I walked away like a ten-year-old and left her to it.

Is she thinking of getting the band to play *Instead of a Party?* And if so, what style do they play? Where should I be going with it?

Nowhere. It doesn't belong to me.

13 The Villiers

I'm sitting in the Villiers with a couple of mates I've known since youth orchestra. We usually have a drink after a Thursday concert, chew it over a bit, compare love lives, and so on. Shari wants to tell me about a competition I might be interested in entering. Just lately Olly has had a bit of trouble with one of the trombones who keeps coming on to her, and tonight she reckons she's reached screaming pitch with him, plus the Shostakovich got her so excited she says she needs to expend energy, so we've legged it down the hill and into town where the chances of bumping into any of the orchestra are slim. On the way I've spilled the beans about Jaz and his evil doings. Shari reckons I should have done him over on social media. Tweeted. Denounced and dissed and damned him to tarnation, and got it all off my chest. It wouldn't matter if nobody read it – which they wouldn't – because at least I'd have put it out there for all eternity, just like he did. But in the end, we all agree, I'm better than that. So, now, I'm feeling a lot better about myself.

I love it here. We're in the snug: a tiny room, with cut mirrors, stained glass, polished mahogany, the whole Victorian works on wrought-iron legs. It's quiet tonight, in a noisy sort of way: what the clients lack in number they make up in volume. Olly's a shrill offender, off on a riff about blokes with beards, when does a beard start to look weird (if it points, if it forks, if it contains protein), and trying to get us to play beardy or weirdy as she lists examples. When she flags, Shari gets back to telling me about the competition; it involves choral composition, so I think not; but now, at random and annoying intervals, Olly shouts out another name, scraping the barrel with people we don't know (Troy, who runs the offy at the end of her road). I'm not cooperating with Shari's attempts to interest me in this competition thing, even though I can see she has my interests at heart. Trying to get me back in the saddle. It sounds like another disappointment stacking up, and I already know I've failed. In the end she shrugs and says, 'I'll send you the link,' then throws her phone on the table with a clatter and a sigh. Olly falls silent.

Our attention drifts to the three old blokes in the otherwise empty room, who are arguing about this week's *University Challenge*. They get onto geography versus maths in the hardness stakes. One of them says anyone can do the geography questions, it's just remembering stuff, but if it's maths you've got to think. His friend says that's bollocks because everyone knows that the answer to the maths question is either going to be one, or zero, or a hundred. The third guy says, 'Forty-two, mate. The answer's always forty-two,' and they all laugh, which means their drinking has advanced to that benign stage where even the lamest joke is applauded like a pole-vault. Then he says to the geography sceptic, 'Yer only jealous though, 'cos you know Blondie's a dab hand when it comes to the geography questions. Second to none.' Blondie, I realise, must be the guy with the shock of white hair, the maths cynic.

'Ah, yer got me banged to rights,' says the guy.

'Try me,' says Blondie. 'Ask me anything. Anything Geography.' He pushes his glass away a little and sits up straight, shoulders back, in readiness.

The first guy shakes his whole neck and head, like a wet dog.

'I can't, can I? Cos how will we know if he's got the right answer? I wouldn't know, me.'

'Ask them students,' says the second man, and he turns to us encouragingly. 'Come on ladies, have you got a Geography question for our friend here?'

So I say, 'Capital city of Cyprus?'

And he answers immediately, 'Nicosia.'

Everybody cheers. But of course, me, Olly and Shari haven't the faintest idea whether he's right or wrong.

'OK,' I say, 'That was your starter for ten. Next question: where's the Aphrodite?'

'The Aphrodite? Is tharra ship or a kebab shop?'

'It's a bar. They do Greek music.'

'Ah now, that's not Geography, that's local knowledge.'

'Oh, I've seen an Aphrodite somewhere...' says one, and scratches his cheek. 'Isn't it at the top of Bold Street?'

'Or round the corner from the Crack?'

'Isn't it on Hardman Street? There's a couple there.'

'Is it down the bottom end of Canning Street?'

'Which are you calling the bottom end?'

'Well, I don't mean the brow of the hill, do I?'

'No. Husskisson St.'

'Little Huskisson St.'

'Back Huskisson Street.'

'There isn't a Back Huskisson Street. There's a Back Canning Street.'

'There's a Little Canning Street.'

'Yeah, burritisn't there is it?'

'There's that funny-looking place in Back Egerton St.'

'South or North?'

'Was he a Prime Minister? It's some Prime Minister.'

'Peel Place.'

'Back Sir Howard Street.'

'Now yer 'avin me on.'

'I've got an address,' I say. 'But it's for a catering company. Faith Place. The bar might be somewhere else.'

'Ah!' says one, and raises both arms to the ceiling, 'Hallelujah! Faith Place. That's not far from Hope St.'

'Which end?' I ask.

'Oh, the wrong end, love,' he says, and he's practically crying with laughter. 'You're always at the wrong end of Hope Street. That's life.'

I say, 'Oh, so we're on to Philosophy now?'

'Oh aye,' says Blondie. 'Watch out, he'll be doin' Politics next,' and the other two shout, 'Aar, eh, no,' and shake their heads. Their voices reverberate, bouncing back from the mirrors.

Things flatten out after that, and the conversation separates back into our two groups. So, what's with this Aphrodite, asks Shari, and I explain about this ethnic acoustic night which, it turns out, none of us musos have heard of. Worth a look. Olly wouldn't say no to a cheeky little week in Cyprus, either. Ayia

Napa. The night life is something else. You can fly direct from John Lennon.

The old blokes get up, even though the jowly one's still drinking; he stands to drain his pint, then sets the glass on the bar and turns to us.

'Good luck ladies, with yer night out. And watch out for Greeks bearin' gifts.'

14 All we dread

The laptop pings and I didn't want it to do that, not when I nearly had an idea there, and now, like the Person from Porlock, that email has chased my lovely figure away, because an unwelcome subject has flashed across the screen, *Competition.* The figure had a sort of an E flat minor feel to it, I think. Dark. Really? What business had I hanging around there… bit pretentious, that… only it was perfect and now it's gone, all because Shari has sent me a link about the next competition, or in other words, the next round of the Humiliation Games. Shari is sweet and trying to be helpful, in her sweet world of sweetness. Maybe she's saved me from myself. She wouldn't be doing with E flat minor, and neither would Hildegard – always check in with her – in her plainly-sung world, her world clean of accidentals, too, because there was a time when people didn't need this level of sophistication, of overdoing. *Here's the link.* To click or not to click, what would Hildegard say? And if I do, would it take me somewhere Alice would want to come with me, and what would Alice say? Hildegard says, you need a piece of cheese, and Alice says, go on, open it, find out, and it seems to me Alice and the Abbess would get on just fine.

Cheese first for strength. Wipe fingers, no grease on the keyboard.

Open it. Website bland. Northallen Music Festival. *Download here*. Download. Let's get this over with.

PDF from word, formatting stolid, puts you right off. Skimming to the nub of it, the brief: four minute's worth of choral music, SSATB, and they've even picked the text, so where's the artistic freedom in that?

Although. I don't suppose JSB ever said, *A cantata for the feast of the circumcision? No way, how gross.* And look what he did with that. So I shouldn't be picky. I should be humble.

Can I treat this like an exam question that's too boring to answer, and hijack it? Leave them with the better question they ought to have set? Can you do this with a competition brief?

Not if you want to win. Which I always do.

What's the text? I click on, and find a poem. It's very short. The first line is electric.

Silence is all we dread.

So I read on.

> *Silence is all we dread.*
> *There's Ransom in a Voice —*
> *But Silence is Infinity.*
> *Himself have not a face.*

Well, that's pretty slapdash. You'd think they could manage grammar and spell check. *Himself have not a face.* Maybe it's a translation. By a ten-year-old Albanian. Or a German – every noun but one has been capitalised, which would mean lower-case *face* is only correct by mistake. Should I edit this? Not my remit.

Oh. It's by Emily Dickinson. Wasn't she famous?

I check it out.

Google says it's correct. Can't be. Try another source.

Blimey. It's the same.

Maybe Emily D was going through a phase, like when they tell you not to write consecutive fifths and it only makes you want to do it. Maybe she was just having a go at English grammar, giving it a good shake.

Himself have not a face. Perhaps there's no capital F on *face* because the main thing about the face in this poem is, it's absent.

I'm warming to Emily Dickinson.

Fact remains, I don't do words. They only confuse things.

Music doesn't need any excuse.

Music shouldn't need any pretext.

Another thing about this poem. It doesn't settle into a proper metre. Pa-pa-pa-pa-pa-PAAH, SIX fingers; Pa-pa-pa-pa-pa-PAAH, SIX; Pa-pa-pa-pa-pa-pa-pa-pa, – EIGHT fingers – wrong! – Pa-pa-pa-pa-pa-PAAH, six again.

Unless it's a hymn tune.

Oh my… it fits a hymn tune. The one they used to sing at Saint Stephen's, in the days Mum made us go.

Teach me my God and king, in all things thee to see, and what I do in anything to do it as for thee… Always hated that one. The one about sweeping rooms. That was a poet to blame, and all.

This Emily Dickinson… look at her, with her centre parting, cut with a knife. YouTube offers, *Was she gay?* She was pretty religious.

Do I want to be associated with Emily Dickinson? Being a heterosexual, irreligious word-sceptic? Jaz does subtext, he'd be able to tell me if the whole thing was likely to blow up in my face. But surely nobody could take offence at a part-song about silence?

Another thing about this silence thing is… would this be an ultra-quiet piece, or an incredibly noisy one? Would there need to be long pauses in it? Or could you ask the singers to slap their thighs and stamp their feet and clap off-beat, while they sing at the tops of their voices? And mark it *Frenzied, as if in panic.*

Silence is all we dread. I'm thinking noisy, at least to start with.

Already I'm imagining this piece. I go back to the opening page on the website. I've never heard of the Northallen Festival, or the Northallen Festival Chorus, who'd be performing it. I imagine they're people like the Lyceum Singers. I find their website and view the gallery: a photo of them relaxed in rehearsal, all smiley faces and sensible shoes, dissolves into a more formal concert scene. White tops for the ladies, and black folders held symmetrically, like well-drilled guardsmen. I almost know these people now. I know the pride they take in technical challenges, but I also know the places I wouldn't want to push them.

If I were to write for them, I'd make sure it was a comfortable fit for humans, not something that stretches them to quasi-digital extremes. *Pace* the big Bs, Bach and Beethoven. I'm not in that league. Something interesting and satisfying. This is a discipline. I welcome discipline. It mustn't be too simplistic, too mushy, or too pink. It mustn't be so complex that it falls off the stave. It needs to be… coherent. Centred. Direct. No, the appropriate challenge for little B Beth would be, to get something singable out of this, and write for half-trained voices that are the instruments they are, not the instruments I might wish them to be. I wonder if I can do that?

15 No words

Dad's on the way back from his Antarctic tour. When we phone, I ask whether he's ever been to Cyprus on his travels, and he says no, but cruise liners do stop at Larnaca. He tells me he's sick of this game, wrecking the planet, and he wants to jack it all in. He ought to, definitely. Mum's been drip-drip about this for years now, and he could retire, but I have a horrible feeling that what stops him is the thought of coming home to her for ever. What would they do? If only there was a hobby they could share. Dad claims he was a good boy treble, until the day his voice did the splits and never got up off the floor. He's a choral refusenik, which is daft, because I know for a fact he has a sweet, light tenor voice, the sort any choir would grab.

I did tell him about the Northallen Festival competition, so I must be a bit interested. I don't know whether I write that sort of thing. I wasn't planning to.

It isn't just that I want a break from competitions and the tyranny of other people's whims and diktats.   It's also the whole business of lyrics: I took a stand on that years ago, back in the days when I was sure what I was doing, and I've stayed true to that position without ever really questioning it. It was an easy option, like pleading a food intolerance. I rationalised it, of course; in fact, I seem to remember that I formulated it very precisely. As a teenager, I used to set things down in a padlocked notebook which I kept next to my bed, and I've still got the notebook here, in a shoebox full of old programme notes. I don't keep it locked any more because nobody would be interested.

Time for another look. I thumb through. It's an embarrassing read, sprinkled with bollocks about me and Alice, and the ongoing project of telling ourselves apart whilst tying ourselves together. I'd forgotten about this; most of the personal stuff is in mirror-writing, another thing I'd forgotten. But I do remember all this other, intellectual stuff: my most urgent musical insights and theories, my sacred quest as a composer… And here it is. A classic:

I aspire to Pure Music.
What is Pure Music? Music that reveals the
intimate pathways of the mind, a pure syntax of
thought without content, that describes the
sense of being alive, and therefore needs
reference to nothing beyond itself.
Clean music.
No songs, no hymns, no Shakespeare and the
Bible; in fact, no words.
NO WORDS.

Oh my. What a beaut. But you have to remember, at that age I thought Stravinsky was God. Ah yes, I knew it was here: a few pages earlier, in big block capitals, inside a cock-eyed frame which I've drawn in gold felt-tip, his famous quote about music being essentially powerless to express anything at all. I thought this was so cool. Never mind that the last pages of *The Firebird* sent me into an intense, melting bliss.

Aged seventeen, I made a promise to myself that whatever music I went on to compose, nobody would ever be able to say, 'this piece depicts X,' or 'this is what she meant.'

I told my parents, so as to make it happen. Dad said, 'Sound.'

Mum said I was soft in the head.

I'm still attracted to the NO WORDS promise I made myself in Year 12, and if anything, Jaz and his article have made it more relevant. People talk too much. It isn't just here in Liverpool: it's the age of the motormouth, all over the world. There's an orgy of communication going on; and you can't take part without leaving your privacy outside with the coats. But if I don't get off my backside and go for this competition – bearing in mind that competitions were all part of the plan – I'm going to be the lazy one, the coward, the snowflake. The one who showed promise but couldn't take a knock. And I don't want to be that person.

16 Mocktails

Ridiculously busy handing out pencils at work. Late afternoon, Shari texts.

> *FoH tonight. How about I swing by yours after?*

I reply

> *School night but yes.*

Why not? I've already planned an evening looking through the ideas folder I keep in Sibelius. Shari is bound to ask me what I'm doing about this competition she sent my way, so it gives me a useful deadline. I'm not sure what event she's doing front of house for, but I know it's not an orchestral; it could be a late night, if it turns out to be some comedian. Or a movie. By the time the Phil have chucked out, and she's got herself over here, I should have come up with something.

By 8pm, it's looking like a non-starter. Nothing I've done seems to lend itself to this Dickinson text, which I only half-understand. Or to anything else, for that matter. My stock of unused material is growing, but each file is tiny, just the odd figure, nothing much developed. Sometimes, a fully formed idea will pop into my head while I'm taking out the rubbish or brushing my teeth. I can't seem to grip them, though; as if I have no faith that any one of them is worth spending time on. And such ideas never come to order.

I could turn the letters of a word into notes, using a cipher... A short word... E flat plus B natural would say, *sh!* But that would be taking the piss.

A conventional, modern way to prise song out of nothingness is to sit at the keyboard, or with a guitar, and play about a bit, so I'll try that. After all, it worked for Macca.

I could ask Petra for advice but there's no point, I know already what she'd say: she'd tell me to prime myself by going back to basics and looking at the Lutheran chorale. Her prescription for every musical sickness is J S Bach. But it's not a question of welding epic four-part harmony onto a bog-awful tune. This pseudo-hymn of mine has got to have a decent melody. And unlike JSB, I am somewhere between agnostic and cynical about text.

So with respect I shall ignore her imaginary suggestion and maybe listen to some old-fashioned gospel.

A – Men.

I switch on the keyboard and scoop up a few chords, a few amens, a bit of Queen and Slade, and try to find a new, satisfying cadence of my own, because all the best limericks start from a punch-line.

No luck.

Hands and mind wander in opposite directions.

I'm feeling around for three stresses per line, to start with.

I slump back.

Thinking is getting me nowhere. So I'll be telling Shari, no. In the meantime, I might as well do that transcription for Alice. *Instead of a Party.*

I open the file and listen again. I wonder: how long did it take her to come up with this piece? Did she struggle, the way I've been struggling now? I doubt that very much. If she has something to express, out it comes, one way or another, whether it's a shout or a tune.

It doesn't me take long to get the basics down, so I start playing around with it. I pick instruments. Stretch it, speed it up, add a bass, change the bass; it's so *saturnine*… or do I mean plutonic? Leaden, dark… it needs something like the gleam of a star, to suggest space, depth… Try adding something at a high frequency, something intermittent, percussive, maybe a ride cymbal, for a bit of sheen; yes; no; and I'm deep into experimenting with overlays of my sister's voice against different instrumentation, when there's a thump at the door. *Save.* Shari brings a swoosh of cold air up the stairs, and swings her legendary bottomless tote bag onto the counter; from it she pulls three limes, a bottle of soda water, a huge bag of ice from the offy, and a see-through packet containing fresh mint which looks to have been ironed in transit.

'Mocktails!' she calls.

'Mocktails!' I respond. 'This bag of ice cubes won't ever fit in my little fridge.'

'If a thing's worth doing,' she grins, and sets to work fixing our drinks. She's flushed from running about in the cold air, and full of the cheerful energy you get when glad to escape from recent confinement.

'What was on?'

'Mormon Tabernacle Choir,' she says, and looks me up and down; she takes in the cardigan that's more like a rug, the wrist warmers, the Ugg boots, and says, 'Ah. Should've been mulled cider. Sorry.'

'No, I'm sorry, gone a bit Scroogy there. Jo can afford the heating better than I can.'

Through the open doorway of the spare room, she notices the waveforms stacked on my computer screen, and a look of delight crosses her rosy face. She thinks I'm composing.

'Oh, look, Shari, that... That's just something I was working on for Alice.'

'OK.'

We settle down on the sofa with our drinks and I tell her straight.

'I'm struggling with this competition piece.'

'Really?'

'I've been through the archive, you know, to see if there's anything I can use, but nothing fits. And every time I try to pin the poem down, it's as if my brain is refusing to understand it. Look!' I call up the page with the lyric on my phone. 'Does it make any sense to you?' I thrust the phone, and the responsibility for this whole sorry episode, into her hands.

She's quiet for a minute, reading.

'Well, here's your trouble. *Silence is all we dread.* Says Emily Dickinson. Only, the thing is, in your world, Beth Collier, silence is aspirational.'

I laugh out loud. 'Guilty as charged.'

'I mean, Jaz Ander's number one crime was being too noisy, wasn't it? That was the original dumping offence.'

'Yeah. And when he wasn't mouthing off, he was scratching that bloody stubble. He couldn't do mental arithmetic without making a noise.'

We sigh, throw our heads back into the warm of the chunky old sofa, and stare at the ceiling. Tiredness has claimed me. I'd done a day's work before the real work started.

After a while, Shari gives a low *mmm*, and says, 'There's different kinds of silence, though. There's the silence that helps you withdraw and create. But there's the silence that comes from never being heard, from obscurity… that's not a good silence. Maybe Emily knew something about being ignored.'

'Why d'you think they picked this?'

'Northallen Festival? Because they're musicians. They're all about breaking the silence. They want to perform.' Shari turns towards me. 'Oh, go on,' she says, and touches my arm. 'You can do this. You're always telling me, there's music all around us; so, just grab it!'

I'm touched by Shari's encouragement, but it's not as simple as that.

'It's true that the world throws tunes and rhythms at you all the time, and you can up-cycle all that noise into music. Sound-scavenging. But that drags content in. I don't mind listening to Beethoven's thunderstorm or Mahler's cuckoo, I just don't want to write that sort of stuff myself. And anyway, what do I mostly hear on the air about me round here? People arguing. Drunks. Sirens. Why would I choose to celebrate the 68 bus or the pelican crossing that wakes me up at night? Although the bin wagon *is* a tempting subject. All that scraping, the hydraulic sighs, the banging about, the semi-predictable rhythms…'

'Hm. Maybe not, then.'

We take a sip.

'One thing I am sure about. This demands a tune that ordinary people want to sing. Something that sits as easily on the breath. Like Hildegard. But that sort of choral society won't be interested in monody.'

'Ah, Hildegard. *I am a feather on the breath of God.*' Shari raises her glass to the twelfth-century genius, and we both admire the sparkling greenness of it. 'A lime would have been something the crusaders brought back. I wonder if she ever saw one?'

'She never drank Co-op soda. The scholarship's pretty sound, on that.'

'Just think. She can't have heard as much music in the space of her whole life as we'd been exposed to by the time we left year six.'

Music must have been a more intense thing for her, with a bigger blank margin of silence around it. My thoughts are slowing down. And now I'm daydreaming about the feather on the breath of God... breath being something that causes things to move... Alice's singing... Singing moves the air too. There's something moving about her singing. There's something in this but I'm too tired now to know what it is.

'Alice does tunes.' These words have just popped out of my mouth.

'Really?' says Shari.

'Mm... It started when we were little. She's really getting into it again. That's one of hers on the computer now. I've just transcribed it for her.'

I rouse myself enough to go across to the computer and find the first recording, the solo voice. 'Listen to what she gave me...'

I watch Shari's face as she's drawn in.

'Wow,' says Shari finally. 'That's hypnotic. Her voice sounds like the skin of a peach.'

I nod.

'So, what did you have open there a minute ago, with all those tracks?'

'Just me, messing around with my sister's ideas.'

I come back to the sofa.

'Just messing around with your sister's ideas... About this competition...'

I groan.

'You know what you ought to do?' says Shari. 'You ought to get Alice to help you.'

I don't know whether that's a flip comment or a genius idea. I've been awake for seventeen hours and my brain is turning to mush. I'll put that suggestion under my pillow and in the morning I'll know.

Eventually Shari calls a cab and I go to bed, and I can feel the weight of tiredness drawing me into sleep. I'm almost there, when suddenly, I've bobbed up to the surface and I'm more awake than I've been all day.

We were playing in the garden at the back of the house. Sunny day. What game we were playing? I see the edge of the grass, and the bright red dahlias, but I can't see the game. I can't see Alice. Or the road. Or anything that happened.

It might have been a dare, to knock on the door of the house opposite? Because we were always daring each other. I don't think it was, but I can't swear it wasn't. Alice herself doesn't care, or even ask the question. She seldom looks back, whether out of self-preservation or lack of interest. Her running into the road may just have been for the fun of whipping through space and feeling her body move at speed.

Every now and then, over the years, aunts, uncles, neighbours have voiced their theories as to why she ran out. Was she practising for our first ever sports day? Was she running after something? A dog or a cat? A ball or a balloon? Was she lured by the sound of an ice cream van? Or running away from danger? But that seemed the least likely explanation, in a suburban garden, with a car on the drive and me nearby. I was right there and I don't remember a thing.

After a week or so in hospital, she stopped speaking. People said what a shame it was, because she'd been such a very talkative child. But they weren't listening. Or maybe they couldn't hear the way I could. For a time, melody replaced language; she swapped words for tunes. It was singing, or at the very least, humming, a stream of notes that went up and down. It naturally encompassed growls and squeals, ranging up and down the octaves. I suppose it was a bit gruff, but it was strong and it sat so happily on her breath. To me, she was every bit as chatty as before. I can hear it now in my mind's ear, and it's right there with my mum's lullaby voice, in my secret album of sweet lost sounds, because after a year or two the therapists got Alice talking again properly and the humming thing sort of fell away. She still made up tunes, though, singing to herself. You could always tell the ones she liked, because she repeated them. Sometimes I wrote them down, and added harmonies, and played them on the piano, and Mum would congratulate me; then if I said, no, Alice wrote it, she looked pained. She got our dad to talk to me about it. He sat me down and said, look love, you do understand, don't you? It's very hard on your mum. Your sister's changed inside her head. She isn't like other people any more.

And I said, she's like me.

We'd have been, what, nine or ten when that happened. The serious talk. Looking back on it, they must have thought I was pretending, that it was some sort of twin game where we swapped identities to annoy the grown-ups. You hear of twins who pretend to be each other for a joke. But we'd never done that before, so why would they assume I was playing tricks? That hot, sour, impossible sadness and anger at not being believed… Child that I was, I promised myself never to forget.

My parents believed that everything about this music – not just the chords and the notation – had come from me; everything; when that first impulse, that first spark, was from Alice.

Yet, if they thought I was playing tricks on them, why didn't they laugh it off? Why that awful look on my mum's face?

I've no idea what was going on in their heads, and perhaps it's time I started imagining. My sister's disability – spinal injury, compounded by stroke – was no laughing matter. It meant long months flat on a bed, years in a wheelchair, exercising her smashed wrists, effortfully hauling herself onto the bars and learning to walk a short distance on two sticks. Speech therapy went on right into her teens. She had friends in the special school, all right, but she was lonely too; it wasn't an easy place if you were what they considered *high functioning*. Not that mainstream education was a relief. The promise of more class music collided with reality; she'd been brilliant at this; and now, when it came to clapping a rhythm, the other kids were streets ahead of her. She was the only one in her GCSE class who had ever read music; but now the notes made less sense. And whilst she could sit comfortably at the electronic keyboard, it was like playing in thick gloves, and she was bitterly discouraged. In those days it felt as if I was the only one who could hear her. She's vocal enough now; most of the time, you'd only notice the smudgy fingerprint of aphasia once someone's told you about it.

It's strange to think that all that time my parents were focused on getting what she needed and encouraging every step, and there was always music in the house, yet they didn't hear what I heard.

When we were kids, I only needed one look to know exactly how she was feeling. Not any more. I'm seeing less of her now, and the things that happen in between our meetings are a mystery. But if music is back, and taking over again, that's big. It could change her life; and when her life changes, so does mine.

17 Chameleon Close

Shari's right about the competition. I ought to get Alice onto it. I head back to Chameleon Close. Today, Alice says *hiya* and we scrutinise each other for a minute. She's in acid yellow, which doesn't really suit us. Her gaze dips momentarily to the music case I carry at my side, because she knows I'll have brought a print-out of her composition, for proof. She'll show it to people. They won't be able to read it, but that's not the point.

'Thanks.' She frowns. 'You look like you want something. Biscuit?'

'That would be good. But I need something more important than that… I need a tune, a new one.'

'What sort of a tune?'

'Something that sounds a bit like a hymn, or an anthem.'

'Godssake the queen?'

'Yes, that's right, like Godssake the queen. I've got the words. I've had a go myself, but I'm not getting anywhere.'

'Is this for love or money?'

'Money.'

'Cash, then,' she says, in the same way she'd say, 'Toilet.'

'Mm… maybe not in cash. Also, nothing's definite. It's another competition, so there's no guarantee we'll get anything.' She waggles her head a little and turns her mouth down in a *mm-so-what* sort of expression. 'It might get me noticed.'

'Us.'

'Us. Definitely. It might get us noticed.' Of course, she's right; I'm glad of this correction. Warm honey floods through my veins, at the prospect of going back to our comfortable childhood ways, our twin-signature, ABC. 'Shall we do it together, then?'

Alice nods so vigorously, it seems to me she's trying to shake the terrible haircut right off.

'Yes. Yes.'

'OK,' I say, 'then we're in business.'

I hand over the sheet music I've printed out. *Instead of a Party.* We're both hoping there'll be a better party next time. Then I put the new audio file on her desktop. It's me reading the Emily Dickinson poem in a very deliberate, rhythmical way, so she can make a tune to match the pattern of speech. This Emily was a hundred years dead before Alice and I were ever born, and perfected her use of the English language on another continent. My version might not match the author's. But if there's one thing I hate, it's all those happy-clappy hymns we did at school, where every now and then the words have to scramble to get on board the tune. Too many syllables, or the stress in the wrong place. I'd hate us to be responsible for a mash-up like that.

Alice plays my reading through once, and nods. She'll come back to this. We don't discuss what it means. I trust her instinct.

We listen to some tracks. She offers electronica, then Lili Boulanger; my recent find is a monophonic piece by James MacMillan, in which one instrument takes over the melody seamlessly from another; it excites us both, until the ending, where the forces combine in a final chord; at which point we shake our heads. We theorise: he only copped out because no single player was allowed to have the last word. Although they could all have played the same note? To set things right again, we play the last movement of the Mendelssohn *Octet*, the coda to end all codas, and written by a teenager. Then we sit in silence for a while, trying on each other's smiles. The door opens on a knock and it's Sam who says, 'Ooh, are you still here?'

'There's only one an hour. Buses.'

It is about time I went, though.

The rain has eased off and the pavements of Chameleon Close are drying in patches. At the bus stop, I'm warmed by the thought of having something nice to unwrap in a few days' time. Which is, *work*. Alice says yes to the Dickinson poem. This pleases me, as if something's been put to rights – because how could she be playing with other people, and not be making music with me? I've allowed a chasm to grow between us. I felt destined to make the sort of music my sister couldn't join in with; so that although we might still play together, we'd never really work together; and until a moment ago it looked as though we never would. Already I sense something unblocking, as if working on my own was what has drained me.

The funny thing is, in Alice's room, I don't care about my big issue with setting words, my unholy grail-search for Pure Music. Perhaps it doesn't matter. Perhaps it was always more a fear than a philosophy.

18 Busking

'There she was, bold as brass, you know in that bit round the corner from WH Smiths? With a hat. Seriously, Mel. A hat on the pavement. Singing her head off. Only some bloke reckoned it was his spec, and turns out they didn't have a licence, did they? And the crowd booed him, when he tried to move them on. That's when the police moved in.'

Something like a smile is playing on my mum's lips as she listens to her friend. It *was* faintly comical, the way Jenny took us to one side to deliver her news, during the rehearsal break; something she saw today in town, she said, that we both ought to know about. She insisted we sit down. My sister has been busted for performing without a licence in Liverpool 1.

'I bet she had an audience,' says Mum.

'Oh yes, give them their due, they picked a great spot. Straight to the O2, in busking terms.'

Mum points out, 'She wasn't on her own, then? She's a sensible girl.' This is almost a catchphrase: to her way of looking at it, Alice is the sensible one. I'm the one with no nous and not an ounce of gumption.

I ask, 'Who's they?'

'Her housemate. She's called Vilma. Big girl. But there was a young man too. With a guitar.'

'A young man?' Mum's half way to a frown now; but no more committed to that than she was to the smile. She doesn't fool me: she's trying to hold things in. She'll let Jenny do the what-ifs, then bat them down so as to convince herself that everything's OK.

'He seemed nice enough, but you know…' Jenny shrugs. 'They looked… close, if you know what I mean.'

'She's got a right to a normal life and friends,' says Mum.

'Yes, of course. But at the same time, she's vulnerable to exploitation.'

'Any young woman involved with a young man is vulnerable to exploitation.' Mum gives me a look, as much as to say, *aren't they Beth*, and I'm hoping there was a tiny embryo of forgiveness there. 'What was he like?'

'Nice. Clean. Polite.' That figures, knowing my sister. We don't do scuzzy. 'Very personable. He's called John. They met at the Rocket. He's got her going to some sort of community workshop.'

'Hands free music, yes, we know all about that. He's told you quite a lot then. He's been open.'

'But you hear such things... I mean, if only she'd told you first, Mel, you could have talked her through it all.'

'Talked her out of it, you mean?' says my mum, sucking her lips and nodding her disapproval.

'They didn't have a licence, Mel. You need a buskers' licence for Liverpool 1. They got into trouble.'

'Call that trouble? Not even arrested. It was hardly a night in the cells. And as for John, whether he's a friend or a boyfriend, makes no difference: as far as I can see, there's nothing to worry about. In fact, I'd say, so far, so good.' She slaps her hands down on her thighs, and breathes in through her nose; now she looks like a queen on her throne, having delivered her judgment, straight-backed and sure.

I'm smarting that Alice hasn't mentioned any of this to me. She had the perfect opportunity, when I went round last week. But so did I... I ought to have asked her about the band, instead of barging in with my stuff.

I try my best to sound reasonable, turning to Jenny, to back up my mum. 'Just 'cos she's friends with a bloke doesn't mean it's serious.' But my thoughts are racing... Surely, if it was a serious relationship, I'd have been the first to know about it? I told *her* about Jaz, day one.

Jenny glances between us. She's outnumbered. 'Oh, Mel, honest to God, I love you to bits, I do, but you're too trusting. Always were.'

'She's not a child, Jenny. Alice can stand on her own two feet. It's called autonomy. Things like this will happen. And what if they *are* in a relationship? You can't run a risk assessment on the human heart.'

Wow. She makes up all her own quotes, does Mum. She eyes the clock; then just gets up and walks away from us. Across the hall, she engages the hapless Ian in urgent conversation.

'Anyway…' says Jenny, staring into space.

'Anyway,' I say. 'Were they any good?'

'T'rrific, actually. Specially your sister. Lovely voice. Really carries.'

'What did they do?'

'Standards. Beatles. Gerry and the Pacemakers. Merseybeat, sort of thing.'

I feel sorry for Jenny. She's only trying to help, and Mum can be so scathing.

'Musically speaking, that Vilma's not much use,' she adds. 'All she had to do was shake her little plastic egg, and she couldn't even manage that in time.'

'Maybe she's the chaperone.'

Jenny shrugs again. She's still staring into space and looking hurt, but she needn't be; she and my mum have rehearsed this conversation a thousand times over the years, and it always ends the same way. Mum's too trusting, Jenny's too wary. The next time they meet it will all be forgotten.

'Imagine, Beth, if I'd known and I hadn't said anything? I can't do right for doing wrong.'

The chunky rainbow on the Wonderful World frieze has violet on the outer rim, which means it's inside out.

'Tell me about it. I'm still in the doghouse about the Tiger Mother thing. What I can't get over is, Mum had Jaz Ander down as a waste of space right from day one, and yet now she's taking his word over mine!'

I'm not in complete control of my voice, which has just risen unnecessarily. Tone it down. I'm the rational one here, remember: it's Mum who's off on a wobbly.

Jenny, however, has picked up my intonation, and joins in the complaint: 'And anyway, what's so bad about being a Tiger Mother? It's normal to fight for your children…Are you going for that choral competition by the way?'

'You heard about that?'

Jenny freezes, realises she's let the cat out of the bag. I'll bet my entire vinyl collection that Shari was just acting on a tip-off from Mum.

'I think I read it somewhere,' says Jenny, unconvincingly.

'Let's not talk about me,' I say, and I mean it. 'Back to Alice. If you ask me, my mum's toughing it out. She tries to hide it, but she's been worried sick since the day Alice left home.'

'Oh, lovie, you don't need to tell me,' says Jenny, and she turns to place her hand on mine. 'Your mam's been toughing it out ever since the accident.'

We sit there, silently comparing bruises.

Mum's right, though, it *is* a case of so far, so good. 'It's amazing that Alice is performing,' I tell us both. 'Isn't that the point?'

Jenny smiles, surprised, as if she's found a fiver in her pocket.

'Well, when you look at it like that…'

'She's so talented, and she does it all by ear.'

'Always was,' says Jenny.

'And that's down to Mum. There was always music.'

'Always was.' Jenny's misty-eyed now.

'We need to support her, though.' I cringe at the thought of going back to social media. But I ought to keep an eye out.

She pats my hand. 'Fancy… Little Alice has grown up, and she turns out to be a musician! Who'd have thought it…?'

Which is an odd thing to say. I've never thought about it, because I've always known it.

Once home, I call her. 'Hey!'

'Hey!'

'What about you, then? You never told me!'

'You've seen it, then.'

'Yeah. Great. Well done!'

'You liked me then? You didn't share me,' she says.

I'm wrong-footed by that. 'I… well, it wasn't your post, was it? It was some random bloke uploaded the video… You know I don't really do social media. But yeah, I'll share you, if you're happy… happy with that sort of coverage…'

'Fucksake, Beth…' I hear a heavy, exasperated outbreath. 'I'm happy with *any* sort of coverage. Oh, but eh, there's an entrance exam for your fan club, isn't there?'

'You never told me!'

'I did. I *told you* we might have something to celebrate. Me and the band.'

I stop scrapping. 'You did. And you have. No, seriously, well done!'

She's stopped scrapping too. 'Yeah. Great, isn't it?'

19 A Strong independent heroine

Jaz Ander and I are sitting in the street cafe at the Everyman. In his case, hoping to hoover up the DNA from the lingering sweat of all the talent that's passed through here since the sixties: writers, directors, actors… Bleasdale, Campbell, Russell, Bill Nighy, Julie Walters. In my case, working through some beetroot hummus and flatbread. Nice. He deliberately plonked himself opposite me, when he saw me eating my lunch; it's a clattery place and now I've been forced to take my earbuds out and be engaged in conversation. I've let him bang on about his novel again; he's got both his elbows on the table, hands clasped, and he's dropping each shoulder in turn and swivelling forward, backward, left, right, in a playful fidget.

Jaz is looking for a strong independent heroine. He isn't happy with the one he's got. She's still a bit ill-defined, apparently. She needs a thing, he says. A thing about her that's, you know, individual. Unique. A bit off-centre, a bit wooh.

For a supposed wordsmith, Jaz Ander is pretty crap at defining his terms.

'A bit wooh. What does that mean, exactly? Are we talking magical superpowers here? Or just an annoying habit?'

He smiles like you can only smile when a relationship is comfortably over and acknowledged as an aberration by both parties.

'I really like you,' he says.

'You only wanted me for my backstory,' I tell him.

'Harsh!' He frowns. 'And wrong. Well... Ok, maybe a bit... maybe that was the hook.'

The shoulder-swivels dip lower until he stops suddenly with his chin hovering only a couple of inches from the table top and shoots a conspiratorial look from under his brow.

'I'm hearing things about you,' he says.

I wait. I haven't heard anything about him, but it seems unkind to say so.

'I hear you're playing for the Lyceum Singers.' I shrug.

'Also, your sister's a thing.' And he sits up straight to say, 'Well? What d'you think about *that*?'

'She's a person, Jaz.'

'Obviously, she's a person, yeah. She's also a thing. Don't tell me you haven't seen this?' He takes out his phone and scrolls to a video of Alice singing her head off with her mates, just like Jenny Johns said last night. I've already seen it, now. It's beautiful, and brings a smile to my face.

'People love her. Could be a story in it, once the media get hold of it,' he says, and his voice rises as if he's making some sort of offer. Which is pretty rich, after the last un-favour he did us.

'If there is a story in it, Jaz, it's definitely hers, not yours.'

He offers two open hands.

'Oh, come on. I'm trying to help you here. Trying to get you visibility, you know? Exposure. Twins with talent.'

'Maybe she's surprisingly good at arm wrestling,' I say.

'Alice?'

'Your heroine. Maybe that's her wooh thing.'

He screws up his nose and gives a quick shake of the head.

'S'gotta be believable.'

'Come on then,' I say. I push the plate to one side, get my right elbow on the table and offer him my arm to wrestle. I'm not sure I'm going to win, but he looks like he couldn't kick a hole in a wet *Echo*.

He laughs and clasps my hand, and it turns out to be easier than I'd thought, because I have the advantage of surprise. He's never practised this. He makes it easy for me to work my hand up in an instant, and curl my fingers over his, where I can squeeze like hell. Down he goes. Neither of us has biceps. But he's never played the *Hammerklavier* or worked out with Franz Liszt.

He takes it well, writhing in laughter and pain, opening and closing his hand, grabbing it by the wrist, shaking it in the air. People are looking, and a woman at the table behind him gives me a thumbs up.

I get him a latte.

When it appears in front of him, he stares at it and says, 'Hmm. P'raps I need building up. More meat pies.'

'I swear by lentil bakes.'

'Seriously though, Alice is one to watch.'

Which sobers me up. It's not that long since he used that expression about me; *Oh Beth, something tells me you're one to watch*, drawled as we leant eye-to-eye across a tiny table, not unlike the arm wrestle just now…   What has Alice got that I lack? And why is he even interested?

'You do realise what it's all about?' he says.

He leans forward and stares at me, with the same look my mum used on us when we were kids, to say, you won't be leaving the table till you've finished your dinner. I scoop a bit of beetroot hummus onto a raggedy piece of flatbread and say, 'Go on.' I shouldn't speak with my mouth full, but that's just how the mood takes me.

'They're disabled, aren't they? Human interest. And you know, she's kinda cute, with that fringe and everything.'

There's an almighty crash from the table behind and a cascade of crockery and cutlery hits the wooden floor. A loaded tray has somehow got pushed to the edge and fallen, and the group of diners – all ages, a family out for lunch – start shouting at each other about whose fault it was. There's a toddler, legs dangling from the high-chair, who bursts into tears; a little boy, maybe seven or eight, is laughing, and his nanna is telling his sister off: 'Will you just sit still our Maisie, yer in an' out like a cat at a fair!' The dad's on at the mum: 'See, this is what happens. See worramean!' This is the woman who gave me a thumbs up just a minute ago. She's telling the dad it was *his* bloody elbow on the table, so what sort of an example was that? She shoots a warning glance at the laughing boy: 'An' you can stop starting.' When a waitress appears with a dustpan and brush and begins picking up the bits, the mum's face sheds all trace of anger: she apologises sweetly, 'Oh, I am sorry, love.'

'This is nothing,' says the waitress. 'We had the Mormon Tabernacle Choir in last week.'

'Oh, bloody hell not that lot,' says Nanna, 'I hope you counted the spoons,' and they all start laughing.

Jaz drums his fingers on the table-top. Apart from a quick look over his shoulder when the big smash happened, he's shown no interest at all in the family behind, with its – to me – enviably well-practised exercise in contrary motion: easy conflict, easy resolution. I sigh.

'Jaz. Listen. My mum believes I'm an ungrateful shit. Playing for a bunch of amateurs is my penance. Even as things stand – and unlike these good people on the next table – it's going to take more than a worn-out joke about nicking the silverware to smooth things over; and if you and your publicity machine get anywhere near Alice, it'll all be my fault again, and I'll be blown out of the water without a leg to stand on. And the rug pulled right from under me.'

'R-r-right...' he drawls. 'Cool metaphors, as ever.' He smiles broadly then taps the table twice with the straightened forefingers of both hands.

'Cheers for the coffee. You know where I am.' He jumps to his feet.

'Good luck with your heroine, Jaz.'

He stops, thoughtful. 'Yeah... Maybe she's got beetroot tongue.'

He waves and turns towards the door. I can't be sure that was sarcasm.

I go back to my phone and watch the clip of Alice and her band busking again. Jenny was right, they're terrific, and her voice really does carry. And look at the numbers now! The shares have rocketed since last night. Which is great so long as it all stays positive. How easily it could all turn sour. I don't want her hurt and I don't want her exploited. But if there's a story, it figures that Jaz Ander would be among the first to pounce.

20 Echo

Friday, and Jaz messages me to say, 'See today's *Echo* p 12. Not one of mine btw.' I pop down to the Spar shop and grab one from the counter. There she is, page 12, tucked bottom left, next to *Kind-hearted Scouser does Food Deal with Local Chippy,* and underneath *Sex Pest Threatens Wavertree Mum with Fish Slice.*

It's not a bad photo; she's got her mouth open, which I suppose is OK for a singer. Vilma looks like she's hanging around, holding the shaky egg for a friend. It's a good one of John. He looks quite nice.

> *From Skiffle to Scuffle in Liverpool 1*
> *Shoppers intervened when police asked buskers to show their permit. Alice Collier (23) and her band Sky Blue Pink were well into their sixties medley outside WH Smiths in Liverpool's premier shopping venue, when a rival performer turned up to claim he'd booked the spot. Alice (24) who lives in Fairfield and sings from her wheelchair, was supported by her band, John Melling on guitar and Vilma Wright (percussion). But the crowd who'd gathered just didn't want the music to stop.*

Blimey, she's aged a year in the space of a sentence. That's trauma for you.

According to the Merseyside police Twitter feed

I recognise the house style. What follows is the same story, as sanctified by Twitter, which identifies the disgruntled busker as *Jumping Ted Torrence*. Then comes the official comment:

> *Liverpool City Council recognises the contribution to tourism made by the city's musicians. It has a duty to regulate the issue of busking licences and we the police urge all musicians to make sure they're on the right side of the law by filling in their application online.*

This will only fuel my sister's obsession with what she calls *her social.* I can hear her now: 'Goes to show, things connect, we need to take control. Exploit them before they exploit us.'

Jumping Ted Torrence, though. Bog awful stage name.

21 Faith Place

When I was doing my post-grad, Auntie Dot took me to one side and told me seriously, 'You must never let on to anybody you can type. Or they'll expect you to do all sorts of rubbish jobs for them for nothing.' It was a sweet moment really, a glimpse into a bygone age when keyboarding was typing, and typing was, like pastry-making, a peculiarly female skill. Fast-forward a couple of generations, and I've learnt the hard way that you should never disclose any ability with technology, because the same fate awaits you. My mother is a classic. She calls me a digital native and volunteers my services to the world and her cat. I've tried telling her the digital world is far from monoglot, that there are different countries in that world and they all speak different languages, that I only know the ones I use; but she brushes that off as if it's just an excuse for shirking.

However, I *was* quite chuffed to find Theo Christodoulou on the phone begging a favour. Mum had given him my number, he hoped I didn't mind. He's having trouble with his website. 'I don't know anything about websites,' I said; then mentally smacked my forehead. 'But I don't mind having a look.'

I headed to his place, for three in the afternoon, half-hoping the website was a flimsy excuse. Although the last thing I need in my life right now is another man, so be careful.

From the outside, the house in Faith Place is part of a fine old Georgian terrace with tall windows and steps up to a heavy front door, with white columns on either side. But climb to the top, and look for the bell, and you realise it's shared with an import-export business called Euro Bins, a cosmetic surgeon, and an individual who, decades ago, took a little card and wrote their name on it in blue ink; a name which has now faded to anonymity. Inside, the communal hallway is nobody's territory, clean but bare, decent but unloved. Nothing to see, no pictures, not even any junk mail kicked up against the skirting.

He's led me to the basement, down uncarpeted stairs, then disappeared, and now I'm sitting here with a view of a brick wall through the grimy window; token daylight slips down from the street above. The strip light, on the other hand, is aggressive, illuminating every bump in the cream-emulsioned walls and every fibre of the dark green carpet tiles, which look freshly laid. There's a slight smell which isn't damp; something more chemical, distinctive; maybe vinyl. The room is twenty feet square. There's a radiator, this biggish table and two white plastic chairs, one of which I'm sitting on; all along one wall, there are boxes stacked high, occasionally printed with letters I can't read. In the corner, there's one bulging cardboard box with the parcel tape slashed open, and the lid loosely closed. In short, the kind of place you'd hide a hostage. I haven't told anybody where I am, and I'm beginning to feel uneasy, when I hear footfall on the stairs, light, springy, unhurried.

The door opens and Theo enters the room backwards, because his arms are full. He empties his load awkwardly onto the table: a lever-arch file, a pad of notepaper, a laptop, a mouse, a cable. There's fluff on his dark sweater. The mouse drops onto the floor and lands at my feet, so I pick it up.

He holds out his hand to shake mine and I place the mouse in it. We both stammer and laugh a bit and he says, 'I'm so sorry, I am completely crack-handed, as you say.' We don't, but I might start to now. 'Thank you for coming.'

'Thank you for inviting me.'

He sets about arranging and connecting his objects, and is trying to talk at the same time, with limited success; one minute he's speaking and waving a connector at me, the next he falls silent and I hear the laptop firing up. He made the mains connection last of all. Chaotic, yet methodical. He keeps apologising for taking up my time. At last he sits back and smiles wordlessly across the table. The laptop sits between us. I crane my head round in a pantomime gesture of curiosity, and he says, 'Oh!' and makes room for me to come and sit next to him. I pick up my chair and notice he's left-handed. I sit on his left, in case we end up sharing the mouse.

'I'm so grateful for your help with this.'

Nobody's going to chain me to the radiator. Or anything else, I can tell. He frowns.

'I'm sorry for the room,' he says, glancing around. 'My flat is... not made.' I can't read his expression; he's frowning still, but his head is waggling in a slightly exaggerated way which suggests he might not be serious.

'What do you use this room for? I mean, what usually happens here?'

'Nothing. My uncle keeps things here. You know he has a business? Tins, bottles.'

'Stock.'

'Yes, for the bar, only. The Aphrodite Bar. He has a catering business, too, in Speke. My uncle bought this place in the days when he was King Krisos, then when he stopped the import business, he kept it for an investment. It's OK, it's not great, but it's right in the middle of town, and that's perfect for me. I have my freedom. I can go to a different bar every night if I want. It's my party.'

'So, does he live here too?'

'No, he lives over the river.'

'Over the water.' Oh no, I sound like my mother, correcting his vocabulary, improving his grasp of local idiom.

He turns to the screen, says something about a 'catagraph E,' and logs in to what looks to be the back end of his website. My usual approach, faced with any new dashboard, is to take a quick look round, get a sense of the geography, open a few menus and see what's inside the box. I like to tell myself I've as good a chance as the next woman of making sense of any new software. But not today.

'It's Greek.'

'No,' he says, 'It's English. See.'

He clicks and we've navigated straight onto the site, which is almost as featureless as the hallway was. There's a header, yes, in English, *Theodoros Christodoulou,* a ridiculously tiny thumbnail of him in concert dress, head and shoulders, and a short bio. Nothing balances. It looks terrible.

'I need to change this,' he says.

You're telling me. I want to see a *much* bigger photo for a start. I'm nosy to read the bio; but he's already clicked away and back to the dashboard. Greek. A few more clicks, a few more screens, and the page I saw before is back again, but this time with an additional bank of editing icons. At least that bit works in English.

'How?' he says.

How indeed.

'Can we see how it renders on a phone?' I point at the tiny icon. He clicks, and yes, it looks even worse, the proverbial white cat on a snowy day. I ask him: 'Have you got a structure for this?' I've noticed what must be a nav bar, with nothing in it but the word Home.

He shrugs and smiles and his eyes shine like a child's. 'I want it to look good.'

'I have to be honest, I'm not familiar with this. Even if it was in English. I've never built a site on this platform.'

My own website started with a flourish, only to die in my arms as I lost all belief that anyone would ever care to visit. Theodoros looks surprised.

'Your mother says you like to do this. I think computers are your *meraki?* It means, a thing you do for love. She said technology makes you happy.'

What is she on? Where did she get this idea? And what must he think of me? I have to put him right on this one.

'No. *Music* is my… whatever you said.'

'*Meraki.*'

Although there are times when music is a royal pain in the arse.

'Theo… I know my limitations. You need to find someone else to help you here.'

He shifts his chair diagonally so that we're no longer side by side, pushes it back to make space between us, and arranges his long legs so that the left ankle is balanced on the right knee. He grins.

'Forget the website. We just speak.'

'We'll just talk.'

'Yes,' he says, 'we speak. So, Miss Collier, tell me please your musical journey.'

His expression is one of mock seriousness. He clasps his hands loosely in his lap, like a real interviewer, and takes a generous breath. I'm slow to respond, so he opens his arms to invite whatever crazy confession is going to pitch up.

My throat tightens. I can't remember what I prepared for Petroc on Radio 3, or the woman on Desert Island Discs. I want to be truthful, which means I must like him. But he might be taking the rip, and I have a feeling that somehow I'm going to say the wrong thing, or the right thing in the wrong way.

'Ask me a question, then.'

'Very well. Of course, I know about the piano trio. I'm sorry I missed the performance. Is there a recording?'

'I'll send you the link.'

'So, what are you writing now?

Tricky. In a month's time he'll be asking me how I'm getting on, and I might not be. I tell him, 'I'm between projects.'

'So, who are your musical influences? You are a pupil of Petra Laing...'

I squirm. I can't put my work in the same category as the music I listen to.

'You'd have to ask other people what influences they hear.'

'Your heroes and heroines, then. Personally, I have a great admiration for the music of Petra Laing.'

'Same.'

I'm ashamed of myself. What on earth made me use such a childish expression? When I was at school, the girls were obsessed with comparing tastes. *I like this one – Same; That's awful – Same. Same* was the password to acceptance and I often said it, although I seldom really cared.

The almond-eyed man deserves something more than teenage shorthand. A proper sentence, with a verb in it.

'Well, I have a special relationship with Hildegard of Bingen. But my greatest hero is JS Bach.'

He quickens: 'And I.'

'But not just for the technical brilliance. I love him for the emotion.'

'And I.'

'Because it's no use having a musical brain the size of a planet if it isn't attached to a beating heart.' I've never said these words before, or even thought them, but they sound right.

He touches his chest. 'For Bach, I have no words.'

I hear myself say, 'And I.'

He has nicely proportioned lips and a gentle, balanced smile. He pauses for a moment before looking me in the eye and asking, 'What led you to composing?'

'I don't have a performer's temperament.'

He leans forward confidentially, and gives a shake of the head; a narrow, rapid movement.

'That's not an answer.'

I'm tempted to say, there's nothing else I know how to do; but that's obviously untrue. I can wait on tables, I'm a passable admin assistant and good enough in tech support. When I try to remember how the music started, though, it feels like an addiction.

'When I was a kid, I liked playing the piano, but I never wanted other people in the room.' As I say this, I can smell the sour green of my mum's crazy, knock-kneed geraniums on the window sill. I feel the high round door knob turning on its loose spindle and hear the click of the latch, because I always closed that door.

He chuckles. 'When I was a child, I used to practise the *bouzouki* in the attic. Nobody could stand the noise I made.'

'Where do you practise now?'

'Over the shop.' His English is quite idiomatic, apart from the times when it isn't.

'Is yours the flat without the name, then?'

'That's me. Room at the top. A room with a view. It's all thanks to my Uncle Stelios. He came here in '74, after the invasion. First thing he's washing plates at a Chinese on Lime Street, then he started his own Kebab shop, then he went into import-export, small scale for the Brits back in Cyprus. Halloumi in, brown sauce out.

'Right.'

He gathers pace. 'I tried to find work as a musician back home, and that's OK, but it's hard; it's not a big place, the tourists can only take so much bouzouki, and they don't want classical, just hotel lobby piano, which makes you weep and dies in the winter.'

I know nothing of this world he's come from. I'm fascinated by the way his eyebrows dance. I love it. He wasn't like this when we met with the committee. Perhaps because they're older than him. Us. Is he more at ease because of me? Or being on home ground? I remind myself: the last thing I need... be careful...

'So, I end up twenty-six years old and still living at home and my mum sees me get depressed, and my dad says you need a proper job, and my mum says it must be a clean job; and they end up screaming at each other. Then one day granny cooks stifàdo and says if you could do anything, Doros, if I gave you a thousand euros right now, what would you do? And my mum looks sick and worried because *yia-yia*'s eighty-two and maybe she's planning something. 'Oh *Mamà*, she says, you're not going to leave us!' 'I'm not going anywhere,' says my granny, 'I asked a serious question, I want a serious answer please. If I give you a thousand euros, what do you do?' I say, 'I'd travel.' So my mum smiles, and my dad bangs the table and curses at the ceiling, and my grandma says, 'You go and stay with your Uncle Stelios.' And my dad sits up and says, 'That's a good idea. You can go to England.' Like all his friends' kids have done, of course, which makes him proud. (Trust me, we are everywhere.) And that day... oh, it was... like the clouds breaking and a golden sun in the sky.'

He slows down for a moment, and lifts grateful hands.

'I thought, of course, this is beautiful, why didn't I think of it before? In those days I only know three places in UK: London, and Birmingham because of the orchestra, and Liverpool, because of the Beatles. This is the capital of music, and my uncle lives here, so of course, it's the place for me. So, I say, 'Yes, sure, when can I leave?' Granny says, 'I call your Uncle Stelios.' 'My dad says, 'Great. And you know the best thing? You won't even need a thousand euros,' and he takes out his wallet, and starts counting notes onto the table. 'Easyjet. I give you two hundred myself, for starting.'

He ends with deep-throated laughter, tossing his head back. I've been watching him with growing amazement: I didn't realise he could be so animated, doing all the different voices, frowning like his mother, slapping the table like his dad, re-enacting before my eyes the annoying, tender spectacle of a family who argues for love. There's so much to know about him.

'So, you have a day job. Like me.'

'Oh yes. I work for Uncle Stelios... But it's not what I thought. The export-import is over, he sold it years ago and he's back in catering. He has a unit in Speke. He makes me wear a – hairnet?' – he raises his hands to his head, checking the word, so I try to look encouraging – 'and blue gloves, and there's a lot of machinery, big mixers and things like that; I have to measure ingredients and chop it up, so they can say the food is made by hand' – he's doing the gestures, his long fingers chopping and kneading – 'but it's like a factory. The smells don't make me hungry. So maybe this is just my empty year, then I go home. I do an extra shift when people let him down. That's all the time.' He laughs, rolls his eyes, shakes his head. 'I work with strange people. Scousers. Every shape and colour of Scousers. Some of you never stop talking, some of you never talk at all.'

He sits back, takes a breath in through flaring nostrils, and suddenly snaps his laptop shut with a smile and a shrug. 'I'm just talking about myself. No. Don't apologise, it's my fault. He stares at me with one eyebrow raised.

'You...' he says, and pauses, thinking. 'I think perhaps you still don't want other people in the room?'

This sounds like criticism. He doesn't like me. I defend myself.

'I'm happy with my own company.'

'You're not like your mum, then.'

'No, I'm not.' That sounded way too emphatic: but what's she doing in this conversation? It's all slipping away from me. He's right, though, I'm not like her. She's nicer, or at least, the sort of person people like. Although I suspect she needs to have other people around her to prove she exists.

'Oh, my mum... She can't just *be*; she has to *be things for* people. She's what we call a do-gooder. She's a compulsive joiner, you know? She joins everything. Specially since she left school.'

'She taught languages, yes? She retired?'

'Sort of. There was a big drama and she told them where to stick their job.'

'Oh?'

He wants to know more. He's more interested in her than me.

'I think she regrets that now. She tutors a bit. Dad's at sea most of the time – I mean literally, he's on the cruise ships, what they call an Environmental Officer. Means he takes the bins out. Me and Alice left home, so now she's on her own.'

'She is lonely.'

We nod at each other, silently.

'My Uncle Stelios is lonely. He lost my aunt Maria, a long time ago now. But we think maybe he has a new lady. A mystery lady.'

Family. That's what he's talking about, what he's curious about. There are lovely creases by his eyes as he moves from seriousness to mischief. They disappear as he goes back to business.

'So, you're sure you can't help with the website? I'm sorry I wasted your time. I owe you lunch.'

'That would be great,' I say. We sit in awkward silence for a few moments; but no arrangement is made. However fluent he is, you never really know, with people from another language, whether what they say is what they mean to say, or just what was drilled in the textbook; or some random phrase they find attractive, like my over-generous use of *der Teufel liegt im Detail,* which I'd never say in English. The next thing I know, he's on his feet, and showing me out.

22 Greek

I've decided to learn Modern Greek.

I'm teaching myself online. I can already count up to ten. I'm not telling anybody I'm doing it in case it turns out I can't. Also, it sounds pretentious. Like telling people you're writing a symphony – the time to talk about it is after you've done it.

Or a novel. Jaz Ander, take note.

Besides, I don't want the nudge-nudge brigade (choir) to speculate on my reasons.

It would be satisfying, though, to speak a language my mum has never even tried.

She's a tough egg, my mum. As well as the big drama at the end of her career, there were plenty of horrific ends-of-term along the way. One time, she got picked up for using a long word in some kid's report, and she flipped. She still does the rant that led to her resignation: how you're patronising working-class kids by telling them that foreign languages are too hard for the likes of them, when you've just watched little Ibrahim acting as interpreter at his own parents' meeting, for chrissake. It was a collision between the national politics of league tables, and the school politics of the jobsworth v the loose cannon. Knowing her, she went over the top, dug herself in, then couldn't back down.

As a volunteer tutor, she's barely been called upon as a linguist at all, and has ended up teaching English as an additional language. Which she'd never have countenanced in the context of actual employment.

She fought for me to do German A level, alongside Music and Physics, practically stalked the poor timetabler who said it couldn't be done; came up with a solution which involved supplying two hours' tuition a week herself at home, to make up the hours. She seldom has an idea without trying to make it happen.   She never taught at my school. *Gott sei Dank.* I hope this Greek experiment works. I hope she's going to be impressed.

23 Mincemeat

'Petra said go for it.'

'Oh, well, if Petra Laing said go for it, that makes all the difference.'

Mum sniffs and turns her head slowly to the right, then to the left, then back again, three times. She's releasing tension. I don't know why she's making such a big thing about this lately, but she's always doing shoulder-rolls and inappropriate stretches. Even now, when she's in the middle of bottling mincemeat for the underground WI (standard-labelling-averse, black-market ops). Maybe this display is a way of reminding me that I'm the main cause of stress in her life.

'Alice said the same.'

She takes in a deep breath through her nostrils and exhales slowly through barely parted lips. She seems to be trying to see how long she can make it last, which just makes me impatient to get the disagreement over with.

'Alice says, an audience wants something they can sing along to. Even if it's in a concert hall, and they can't.'

She tips into sarcasm: 'So, you've got an agent now?'

'Better than that, I've got a collaborator.'

She puts the sticky spoon down on a saucer and drops her chin to look at me. Her tone softens when she says, slowly, 'Oh, Beth…'

'She's doing one of her tunes, Mum. They're great.'

She bites her cheek and when she shakes her head this time, it's not therapeutic.

'Just don't get her hopes up.'

'What about my hopes?' I mutter. It bugs me though. We project this image of Alice as independent and strong and entitled; then we pussyfoot around making sure she doesn't get hurt. Instantly I'm taken back to a time when Mum couldn't make sense of Alice at all, whilst I, who could, was accused of making things up, putting all manner of communications into my sister's mouth. But I'm going to *make* Mum take us seriously this time. 'Anyway, she's not a baby. Look, Mum, Alice is the one who wants to put herself out there, isn't she?'

She makes the opposite of a frown, a sort of *if-you-say-so* face.

'What did Petra have to say?'

'I haven't told Petra about Alice.'

'Beth, you're being wilfully obtuse. Nobody expects you to "tell Petra about Alice." What did Petra Laing have to say about the brief? Did *she* think it would be so hard to handle? Because you thought it wasn't right for you.'

'She said it's an opportunity to shed a skin, take it.'

At that, Mum smiles and raises an eyebrow.

I'm not going to tell her what Petra actually said: *Attempt it in all humility.* When I asked, *But is it the right thing for me to be doing?* she looked at the skirting board and went all mystical on me. *That becomes a valid question once you've worked out who you are, Beth. How are you going to find that out in the absence of action? The way to being is through doing.*

Mum's eyebrow settles back in a frown: 'What about your word-setting thing? I hope she told you to stick your scruples where the monkey stuck his nuts.'

'Kind of.'

'Good. You shouldn't ever limit yourself as an artist.' She picks up the spoon again and finishes packing the jar. My job is to wipe off any last traces of sticky with a damp cloth and add the disc of waxed paper. I push it down gently with the tip of my finger to expel any air. The scent of brandy is pleasingly warm.

'Well anyway, I'm over that.'

'Are you? Handsome is as handsome does. What time do you finish on Tuesday, then?'

'One.'

She tuts ironically: 'Call that a job?' She knows quite well I'm only there part-time, in fact she knows my hours.

'Great,' she says, 'You can be at the Grafton by three, no problem. Don't look at me like that, it's not a pub, it's a care home. It's about time you did something for someone else. In fact, better still, if I pick you up, we can take your keyboards. They've got a piano but it hasn't been tuned since the Blitz. Sounds like ten cats dodging bullets down the bottom of a well.'

I groan. We're barely into December and Christmas has started.

'In fact, we'll get you some music, you could start with a keyboard medley.'

'Do I *have* to? It's bad enough playing for Jeremy Snell… And anyway, isn't Anne better yet? How long is this all going to go on, Mum?'

'Anne?'

'The regular accompanist?'

'Oh, she'll not be back. You won't let us down with the concert coming up.'

I've seen the posters without reading a word: the usual flat-pack madonna and child, their annual ugly baby competition.

My name might be on it, which would be treachery. My name might not be on it, likewise. Neither payment nor recognition.

'Mum – were you expecting me for the actual gig? Only you didn't ask me and I haven't got it in the diary.'

'Oh no, we don't need *you*, there's an organist. He's playing a couple of chorale preludes as well.'

My scalp tingles because, whilst Christmas music generally fills me with apprehension, there are some things that transcend even religion.

'Chorale preludes? Bach? Which ones?'

'Oh, ones people know. *Sleepers wake* in the first half. *In Dulci* at the end.'

The organ may be a fusty old instrument, but Bach's chorale prelude on *In Dulci Jubilo* is a shower of pure joy that blows every bit of dust off it. I almost feel left out.

'You can put the lid on that,' she says.

So, my sentence runs right through to mid-December, with no hope of parole.

24 Routine

Nobody under forty likes to admit they're a creature of habit. But the regularity of rehearsal schedules provides something useful to complain about: it gives an urgency to precious, so-called 'free' time, a sense that if I don't use it today, I will have robbed myself of something, because the rest of the week is made up of obligations to other people, the boring stuff that pays the bills and so on. Wednesday nights with the Lyceum Singers are dire, but at least the rehearsal adds its own phrasing to the week, a steady build-up of resentment which starts quietly about Tuesday lunchtime and grows steadily louder, then drops away again at bedtime, Wednesday night. Something to work against. Which seems to suit me.

It's Jeremy's last rehearsal in the hall, and they're all carolled out; they know those pieces back to front; and he's promised, as a special treat and a last goodbye, to revisit two old favourites from their wider repertoire, one nominated by the choir, and one by Jeremy.

The choir's choice is the *Cantique de Jean Racine*. It turns out to have a busier accompaniment than I'd remembered and this edition has far too many page turns; the singers drone along while I work up a sweat. I send the whole thing flying off the piano at one point, and have to keep the ostinato going with the left hand whilst the right grabs the music back from the floor. It's a tidy piece though. They're predictably flat in the descending phrases; the more often they return to a particular note, the lower it has to be. As if they're knocking a tent-peg into the ground.

Next up, a Bruckner motet. Ooh, they say. *Os justi.* Someone asks what the words mean, and Patrick the sausage-skin tenor – who went to St Francis Xavier's and therefore counts as the resident classicist – helpfully gives his gloss on the whole anthem: 'You gorra tell it like it is, and then walk the talk.' *The mouth of the righteous speaks wisdom*, it says on my copy. I'm back with nothing to do, and I'm only half-listening to start off with because all I can think about is that Theo still hasn't got back to me about lunch. But the piece seduces.

Jeremy's reading is meticulous and I'm beginning to think he really cares about this music. Harmonically, it's inventive, thoughtful, generous. The loud sections are wonderful cascades of sound, and when the singers complete the calm plainsong coda with poise and tenderness, I see my heroine

Hildegard in her abbey church, winking at me, and decide maybe Jeremy isn't a complete arse after all.

Then it's back to carols, and the jury's out again.

25 Ransom

Alice phones, about her idea for the competition. She says to come round to hers so, next chance I get, I take the bus to Chameleon Close.

Sam isn't there today. A different stranger answers the door, a woman in her thirties with a lisp. I can smell baking.

'She'th exthpectin you. Dunno what she's purriner cornflaketh. Like a dog with two tailsh, she is. Off er ed. Buzzin.'

'She's been working on a special project.'

'Workin, you thay? Ah, tharr'd be the band.'

The woman's mouth gapes. I notice she's got a piercing in her tongue, a steel ball. Perhaps it's new, and that's why she's talking like this. Or perhaps the piercing is meant to fix the lisp, the way pirates thought an earring helped long-distance vision. I'm dying to know but you can't possibly ask a thing like that, it's too rude.

'I'll leave you to it.' She heads upstairs with a clipboard.

Alice's door is open and she's sitting at the desk, ready for me, with the little black recorder standing to attention, next to a plate of biscuits. We hug and she tells me, 'Business first!'

She's cued the track already and all I have to do is press play.

Alice's voice is strong, C major confident. It starts brilliantly, like one of those songs you've never heard before yet feel you already know. Next comes something close to an

inversion of the original tune, rising and therefore rousing –
this works; then it takes an unexpected sidestep – which is
interesting – but it closes pretty lamely. Well, adequately. Just
not as spectacularly as it began.

'Bad end,' she says, and we nod at each other.

'But the rest is brilliant, Alice.'

'I know.' She's all smiles. 'I gotta leave something for you
to do.'

'The words fit really well. So, what we need to do now, is
develop this. Stretch it out in time. It's a fine judgement, how
much to repeat, and how long to hang around each idea.'

Her expression changes; she's serious now.

'I like these words. It's what I want to say! This is my
chance to tell the world. This is urgent, Beth.'

> *Silence is all we dread.*
> *There's Ransom in a Voice —*
> *But Silence is Infinity.*
> *Himself have not a face.*

My sister knows what it is to live in a place without speech.
And how it feels to be, in many parts of your daily life,
ignored.

Her eyes are round: '*Dread* is the most important word.'

I nod. I hadn't seen it that way.

'Like what I did with the ransom bit? Ransom in a voice:
it's the upside-down. The upside-down of the dread. I don't
get the end of that poem, though.'

'Most things you don't get aren't worth knowing.'

'You know what Mum always says. When you don't
understand something…'

'Yeah, yeah. *Stand on the thing you do understand, and
you'll be tall enough to see over the top*.' I've heard her say

this to Alice a thousand times, in the same sing-song. Another one of her inspirational quotes. Not one she used on me.

'Didn't work, though,' says Alice.

'I claim my biscuit. I'll get the tea.'

We eat and drink. Alice wets her fingertip and picks up every last crumb. Then she announces, 'I did a bass.'

Really? She hasn't done that before so I'm not sure what to expect. 'Did you lay it down?'

She looks confident enough. 'Yeah, but I can't stick them together. It's noying, that thing.'

'Noying, yes. Noyingly small and fiddly.'

She giggles. 'Niddly.'

'Yeah, niddly. That's the word. Let's hear it first, then maybe I can join them.'

'There's rubbish next. I'll find it,' she says and stretches her hand out for the device. Her hands look smaller than mine but logically they can't be. Vilma makes a thing about doing her nails, so they're always manicured, peppermint green today. Her slender index finger alternately extends and bends, slowly and deliberately, to do all the real work, while the remaining fingers of both hands hold themselves up in a cup shape, like that gesture you see in old masters, where it's some saint admiring a miracle.

The recording of the bass track goes off in her hand, which makes her giggle for a second, after which she becomes serious, studying my face, and sucking in her bottom lip.

My pulse quickens, because in so far as I can tell, from just one listening, this bass line sounds strong. Which means that Alice has got her head well and truly into harmony; she might have a view on how it should be figured; she's handing her idea over to me, yes, but who's to say she'll be happy this time with the way that I develop it? I sense that soon, our collaboration will be much more equal, much more real. Our names will be together at the top of this music. I'm hot with excitement and with fear at the direction in which she's driving: one day, she may not need my help at all. Although I suppose I'll still be her technician.

This time, I remember to ask how the band's getting on. She's non-committal. *Yeah, good.* I push for details: any comeback from the Echo article? *Yeah, good. Got a bit of attention. Vilma was worried about her Nan seeing it. But it was the crowd did the bad behaviour. I said, get in first. Ring her up and say eh Nan I'm in the Echo.* What are they working on? Any new pieces, or just, you know, rehearsing? *Rehearsing, yeah.* How's John? *Good. He's good.* We both dry up. Right. I'm not going to tell her about my trip to Faith Place. I don't know what to think of it, success or disaster, significant or insignificant; and if I start telling her about it, I might find out.

I say, 'You ought to write something for the band. I mean, covers are just a start...'

This raises an eyebrow: 'Oh aye?' There's a mean look when she asks, 'So what about you? How's your *work in progress*?' I can hear she's put inverted commas round that expression, because she knows full well that, in the kitchen of my creativity, it's consigned to the back of the fridge.

My visit ends with a share of the file; a hug; and a *love you.*

26 So here it is

Mid-afternoon, and it's already growing dark outside, but the overhead lighting in the Grafton Care Home is powerful enough to keep even the moribund unnaturally awake. My mother leaves me to set up whilst she and the manageress or matron or whoever it is go off to talk about something. The lounge is full of high-backed armchairs, the sort you don't so much sit down on as back into, and against the basic wishy-washy colour scheme of the soft furnishings, the crimbo decs stand out like wild, loud, colourful graffiti. Several of these chairs have occupants, who watch my every move. I've got a designated spot for the keyboards in front of the infamous piano. Setting them up is a two-minute job, after which I suddenly have nothing to do, and realise I've been racing all day.

I don't want to stare back at the watchers so I just smile and drop my gaze to the keyboard, where I set the volume to zero and retreat into JSB; there are pieces my hands just know. Inventions, some of the forty-eight. Playing without hearing is the nearest thing to meditation I can manage. I'm drawn today to the busiest pieces. I've had a pig of a day so far, not a minute to myself. My morning kicked off with two first-years acting like a pair of prima donnas over the set-up for their assessed recording, arguing first with each other and then with me over microphone choice, as if either of them could hear the difference, or indeed as I pointed out, as if it was going to affect their marks. Only a few years ago, that could have been me, and surely, I wasn't ever as bad as that? They treated me like a minion. All I could think was, *you don't realise who I am*. I repaid them though by saying at the end, 'Gosh, did you write that all by yourselves? It's ever so good. Reminds me of *Lez Mizzerables*.' Then I had to deal with some old bloke with a sharp suit and an accent I couldn't place who insisted on seeing Professor Laing, without an appointment, and on a day she wasn't there. He refused to believe me and plonked himself down in the faculty office. He was a personal friend, he said, but wouldn't leave a message or give a name. Wanted her telephone number, her personal email, got ratty with me when I wrote down the public numbers on a compliments slip on which they were already printed. He was still there when I left. I didn't like his manner or his moustache (halfway between Saddam Hussein and that guy from the Marx brothers) and I have a bad feeling for Petra. Ought I to have texted her? To say what? If he's a former lover, or a debt-collector, or a lunatic, her day would not be better for knowing he was there.

I'm starting to loosen up when one of the tiny lady residents calls across in a faltering voice, 'You've got to switch it on, love. Is it on at the mains?'

I bristle. 'Yes, thanks, it is switched on.'

She thinks for a moment and says, 'But I can't hear you.' Her hand goes up to her ear, and twiddles a bit. 'I can hear you talk, though. Well, that's funny.'

It occurs to me that maybe she actually wants to hear what I'm playing. Astonishing. If she does, I ought to play something a bit less manic than the D major prelude, so I switch the volume up and go for the famous C major; and as soon as the arpeggios start to ripple out, a blissful smile comes over her face. 'Oh, I love classical,' she says. The smile lasts right through to the final bar.

'D'you know any Show Pan, love?'

'Mm, not by heart. I'd need the music.'

'My Anthony could play by ear,' she says. 'We went to all the Industrials, when he was with Leyland.'

'My mum's told me about them. But that all finished a long time ago.'

'Well, they went down the same chute as Leyland and the rest of them. How about Fairy Lise?'

I busk it. The room is filling with residents and carers and there's a comfortable murmur as they work out who's sitting where. Mum comes back, looking surprised.

'I haven't heard you play that since you were a little girl. I thought you hated it.'

'It was a request.' I nod to my fan, and look at her properly for the first time: her hair is thin and white over a pink scalp, and she has a crocheted rug over her lap, all pastels and grey, papery colours, so that when she eases herself up on her elbows, she looks like a little butterfly about to emerge from a chrysalis.

Mum smiles at her, 'Hello, love.' Then turns back to me: 'Where's the *Sounds Like Christmas*?' I plonk the thick volume on the stand. It's been about a bit, and the fissured spine tells me the pages will stay open. 'I've done a list, but you can choose, any of this lot will be OK. You've got twenty minutes' worth. You start at half past three. Us lot are going to make an entrance so we'll be waiting outside. Tell me what your last number'll be and we'll know when to come in.' She places the list flat on the ledge of the keyboard for me to consider. *White Christmas, It's beginning to look a lot like Christmas, Jingle Bells, The Little Drummer Boy*, and the rock standards: *Slade, Wizard*.

'I'll finish with Slade.'

'Right you are. Now, this is your carol book. Jenny's put little stickies on the ones we do, see? And this is the order we're doing them in. With the page numbers in case.' Down goes the second list.

The clock on the wall opposite tells me I have ten minutes to go before showtime. I'm not going to sit here like one of Lewis's, waiting for things to start formally at half past three. I don't want any introduction. I'll start with one of the gentler numbers while they get themselves sorted. *When a child is born*. It's usually played lounge-style, *molto con schmalzo*, but it stands up well to my chaste rendition, and the chrysalis lady looks pleased. I like the way it's stepped, the phrases in the first half reaching up, and in the second, reaching down until the perfect landing. Easy listening.

I play on. From time to time, through the open doorway to my right which leads to the entrance hall, I catch glimpses of people I recognise from choir, walking straight past as if they know where they're going. The armchairs fill and the carers in their funny short-sleeved tunics occupy the spaces by the wall. Every single one of them has broken the uniform rules one way or another, by wearing reindeer antlers, elf ears, or a fake white beard; not to mention the jewellery, brooches and earrings that flash coloured lights. In fact, there's one bloke who has a set of tree lights pinned all over his top. Perhaps I ought to have made a gesture? I'm wearing exactly what I wore to work this morning, dark blue baggy jumper and black jeans. Mum says I dress like my own shadow. I don't like people looking at me, that's all. Except that here, I'm the one who sticks out.

Once the room is full, I shift gear into Jingle Bells and we're off. They sing along to everything, crashing the rests and shortening the long notes to create their own cheerfully random canon. Before I know it, the clock says 3.45, so time to bring on the ultimate rock anthem of Christmas which is Slade. From my place at the keyboard I can see upturned faces, smiles, hands waving in time to the music, exchanged glances. This might be the most useful thing I've done all day, certainly the most appreciated, and almost fun… I've always claimed to hate this sort of event, so it's a shock when one of the carers sticks her phone under my nose to show me the video she's just taken, and I see myself, bony as usual, but with a huge smile across my face. I carry on pounding away, wondering, what's going on here then? *Oh, I wish it could be Christmas every day…* They all go wild in the choruses, which is most of it.

It ends in applause. Then there's a flap of greetings cards against the wall and the door nudges open, threatening to pull down the decorations with it. In comes Jenny Johns wearing a red and green bobble hat and matching scarf over her silver lamé. It's time for the carols, then. The others sidle in – Max Chang is there, and my Mum, maybe eight or nine in total — they must all be sweltering under the terrible knitwear – and there are song sheets being passed around.

A red-faced, bald resident who's been singing his head off turns to his neighbours and shouts, 'Any requests, ladies?' Someone bellows, 'Silent night!' and that sets them all off, 'Silent night!' 'Oh aye, silent night!' 'Silent night. Gorra be.' Jeremy Snell, who's hardly through the door himself, gives me a startled nod from the back of the room, raises terrified shoulders and mouths *Silent Night.* It wasn't the first thing on the list, and I doubt his timing, but I give them two bars in and just hope the singers can edge their way to the front before the carol starts without them. Jeremy looks embarrassed by the crush, picking his way past the old folks as if they were lepers.

His obvious fear makes me all the more determined to have a good time. The room was already full, so the singers have to squash right up against the keyboard, and I wonder how Jeremy is feeling, with no podium to cling to, only people. He's teetering on the end of the row and I can see him leaning in to keep the beat with his left hand. I didn't know he could do that. And yes, he's singing.

There's an energy in the room, and maybe it's the energy you get from rubbing coloured balloons until they stick to the walls, but something is making this lot stick together. The great-grandmas and the great-granddads sing *Silent Night* as I've never heard it before. Everything from raucous to tender. Some of them study the song sheet in scholarly reverence, as if the words are new to them. Others just weep. It's hot and airless, the place stinks of carpet freshener and berry candles, and it's a complete visual nightmare, but I'm maybe beginning to see the point in this… in this and all my mum's crazy do-gooding… all her causes…

This could be my Scrooge moment coming up. The day when Christmas, and specifically all that awful Christmas music, starts to make sense to me. Maybe I'll be able to write sentimental carols, to be marketed by small boys in frocks, with ding-dongs and no-wells on every page, and dog-whistle-high descants, and fa-la-la's swinging around like skipping ropes. Because I don't need to believe it: I just need to understand it. This isn't an act of faith. It's harmless fun. I could be minted.

As *Silent Night* ends, I turn to give my mother a huge smile, to say thank you, Mum, thank you for bringing me here. Then I choke, because immediately behind her, with a carol book in his hand and an orange ski hat pulled down over his lovely chestnut locks, is our new conductor. Who thinks I'm smiling at him and looks suddenly embarrassed. Something in my tummy flips, and I think my face must have mirrored his embarrassment, because when he throws the smile back, I'm not quite ready to receive it. We both drop our eyes and pretend to look at the music.

27 Toothache in my brain

I look out onto a concrete sky and walls without shadows. The flat of the metal-framed window is flecked with rain, and little streamlets elbow their way from drop to drop, at once purposeful and awkward, without rhythm; condensation collects on the aluminium inside, inviting black mould into an otherwise smart environment. Petra is so fortunate to have trees outside her room, even if they do look skanky right now, naked, broken. The faculty is almost empty during the holidays, but at least it's heated. I ought to be able to get loads done, now that we've finished our competition entry. I thought I'd be so in the groove, and getting on with my own stuff whilst Prof was away. So why is nothing working?

Something's out of whack.

Perhaps I ought to find another day job, one that uncouples me from the seasonal stop-start of academia. For the last couple of years I've looked forward to the summer holidays, and they've turned into a nose-dive, because the summer schools are too short, then in the empty weeks I get low and bad-tempered, wondering why I haven't written more and hating what I do write. September comes and I wind myself up again. I've just about found my focus, I've just about got things to cohere, when Christmas comes like a great big karate chop and sends the whole lot flying out in bits. Dad came home in time for the not-celebrations. He never stays long enough.   This year he and Mum spent more time together. There were no arguments, and he even took her out for a meal, not once, but twice, as if in search of privacy. Something's brewing. I bet it's one of those amicable divorces. It's selfish of me to hate the idea, when they both look so much happier. But I do.

Alice stayed with them for the duration and we all groaned at Mum's *Messiah*, predictable as turkey and stodgy as stuffing, in her northern choral cast-of-thousands recordings. Me and Alice retaliated with our own playlist. It started with an original German *Mack the Knife* and finished with Black Sabbath. I got accused of egging my sister on, and she sang *I like it, I like it* – Gerry and the Pacemakers – at the top of her voice and shook her fringe like the Beatles in '63. That was the best bit of the entire Christmas festivities.

It was the same argument we were all having ten years ago. I'm a bad influence.

Then Alice went back to Fairfield and I've been feeling royally bad-tempered ever since. As Alice would say, *there's toothache in my brain*.

2020. Yet again the New Year isn't nearly new enough. I'm waiting for the rest of the world to move forward the way I want it to, i.e., with me in it. I can only just afford to heat Jo's flat, but those two weeks with Jaz have made me wary about taking a lodger, and now I've set up my serious kit, with the big monitor and the recording gear, in the spare room. So I'm posing as a vegetarian to conceal the fact I'm skint. Theo must have got someone else to do the website. I looked yesterday, had some trouble finding it, and it's still shite, but nowhere near as bad as it was. Our lunch date never happened: Theo went back to Cyprus to spend Christmas with his family. Without telling me. Though why should he? It's later there, Mum says. Orthodox. He must be back by now.

Why am I so gloomy? Is it his fault? Or the weather? Another slow-moving depression.

Olly and Sarnie have families to go home to. The campus is dead and I actually miss the people who get on my nerves. The Lyceum choir goes back next week.

They're having a second attempt at *Israel in Egypt* this term, a year after the staging debacle, hoping this time to make it across the Red Sea and into the promised land before the vicar halts proceedings on health and safety grounds. Don't know what they're doing about an accompanist. I bet my mum expects me to carry on. I'm saying nothing. Nobody's asked me.

Unpaid.

Amateurs.

Never did monetise my Scrooge moment, did I? The mood has left me. *The thrill is gone.*

There are half a dozen starlings in that tree. They're all facing the same way, into the wind. Stock still.

Oh my God, an email from Theo.

> *Dear Beth,*
>
> *Thank you for the link to your composition. I give it first prize. It's cracking fab and when I played it to my family my mother cried. This is just what the doctor ordered.*
>
> *I take over the choir and I am nervous. I'm back in the pool now, can we meet?*

Ooh – now I've got his mobile number.

> *PS I owe you lunch*

Right. I'll give it a couple of days. Keep it low-key.

28 Can't

The morning started so well. Petra's in town again, and called me in to run through a few things ready for the start of term. She's come back with a funny little smile on her lips. I'm dying to know what she got for Christmas and have a feeling my childish question would get an adult answer. It must be something big. A nomination? Maybe some high-profile coverage for this first performance she's got, coming up in March, with the Phil. That's not far away now. She's always calm, poised as ever, but there's something soft about her.

And she's showing a positive interest in me. What have I been up to over the vacation, she asked?

Petra smiled when I told her I was ready to send off the competition entry, and wanted to know more. When I recited *Silence is all we dread*, an odd thing happened. Her mouth drew into the shape of a pink banana; the top lip, with its pearly lipstick, became suddenly smooth and silky, the bottom lip found an exact symmetry; first I saw her teeth – large and even, almost American – and then I saw the whole of the inside of her mouth as she threw her head back and laughed at the ceiling. She has some big fillings, at the back.

I've never seen her laugh as heartily as that before. It isn't what she does, not with other people. She only seems to laugh at me.

'I'm sorry,' she said at last, and waved one elegant hand as if to say, take those chocolates away, you know I don't do sugar. 'I'm really pleased for you, Beth.' And she swapped the madwoman look for her previous enigmatic smile.

I don't know whether it was that rare laughter which encouraged me, or her congratulations that I'd *shed a skin,* but I started to tell her all about it. First, about the metre and the hymn/anthem idea, and how I knew it had to have something of the sound of an anthem, but an anthem unmade; and my musings about whether *Silence is all we dread* ought to be loud or soft, the decision to avoid long pauses, because – didn't she agree? – mimesis should be more than just the surface noise of things – more than cuckoo-calls and cannon fire – but should describe the heart of an emotion, the way it feels to live, to be alive; how I'd gone to my sister who had a basic knack for melody, and did she know about Alice; then I started to fill out the detail on the little she already knew; and I told her about our twin signature, ABC, and how exciting it would be to see that printed at the top of the piece; when her brow became rippled and uneasy.

'You can't do that, Beth.'

I apologised for getting carried away. I don't normally get this excited... do I? But it wasn't that.

'You can't enter a competition as two people.'

'Why not?'

'Check the rules.'

So back at my desk, I'm doing just that.

It doesn't say. That means it's OK, surely?

Absence of proof is not proof. A sick urgency overtakes me as I type my query. Impersonal, strictly factual, it betrays nothing of the somersault in my gut. I rationalise: OK, so I put my weight behind this project, and that proves I can, which is a good thing to remember; but I wasn't sure about this in the first place, was I? And I'll only need to tell Alice if it's bad news.

On Wednesday morning, confirmation comes. Petra Laing was right.

I've emptied all the contents of the kitchen cupboards onto the draining board and I'm scrubbing the insides clean, careful to get right into the corners, where the dust sticks. Where does it come from? I've thrown several packets out (there were tiny weevils in the flour); and I'm trying to find a better way of re-stacking the shelves, only I can't. There's a terrible racket from gulls screaming on the roof, it sounds as though they're laughing at me. How do I tell Alice? I need to get this over with.

29 Rules

Alice has switched her mobile off, I think. I ring the house in the end, and get Sam, who reckons something must have happened, because she's shut herself away, playing some terrible dirge on a loop, and it's doing all their heads in. Something she calls *Instead of a Party.*

They get her to the communal landline, after a bit of thumping on a distant door.

'Is your mobile dead?'

'Oh. You. Good. So, you've heard?' she says, and she sounds to be in a right paddy. Then, distractedly, 'My mobile? Yeah, prob'ly. I've hammered it. Look, give me time to go back and plug it in.'

I give her five minutes, call back, and the moment she picks up, she blurts out, 'How could they turn us down! Oh, Beth, I *hate* them.'

I'm gobsmacked because while the two of us do intuit many things about each other, we're not psychic.

'How did you find out?'

'Normal way. Blue letter, came yesterday.'

'No!' This makes no sense.

She slows down to read: '*We are sorry to inform that your request for a performer's licence has been unsuccessful at this time...* Blah blah...'

'This is about your buskers' licence?'

'What did you think it was about?' She stops, heaves a heavy sigh, and her voice drops. 'You haven't seen it, have you? My social? Course you haven't.'

This is about as bad as it can be. Double trouble. I listen as she rails against the City Council, who don't realise that busking is all part of her career plan. They don't say why they've refused her and the band; maybe they don't look right!

Typical! Maybe, I venture, it's because of the police moving her on, and that piece in the *Echo*. Well, she's *not having it, no way, ho-zay*; of course, she's going to appeal, because *people are up in arms*! At any given moment, half the city's up in arms; it's our birthright; but it's impossible to persuade her that an appeal has to be based on something more tangible than that. Apparently, the Council will be forced to back down; she knows that from her social media; and I would too if I wasn't such a chicken. 'Honest, Beth, you never look at me. You don't know what I'm doing. Then you post *one thing,* and expect us all to like it. Then you delete it, to be on the safe side. Cos you might communicate something, by mistake.' She tells me my trouble: I'm just running scared in case the whole world unfriends me. Yeah well, they've got to friend me first. It must be a full ten minutes before the old aphasia kicks in, she ties herself in knots, and I get a word in edgeways.

'There's more bad news, Al. I'm really sorry to lay this on you. Specially today.'

''Kay,' she says, 'go on.'

'We can't do a joint entry for the competition. It's against the rules.'

There's a pause, then she asks, 'How do you know?'

'I checked. I asked them.'

'You *what*? You *idiot*. Why did you do *that*?' The words are released at high pressure and high pitch, like a kid who's just learnt how to squawk through a double reed.

'Petra said be careful…'

'Oh, well, if teacher says… That's that, eh? Fucksake, Beth, you are *such* a wet.'

'But Alice… It's an online registration, there'll only be room for one name.'

'So? Just put one name down, then!'

That pulls me up short. This would be cheating.

'Whose name?'

She doesn't miss a beat. 'Mine, of course.' Then pauses. 'Or yours. Doesn't matter.'

'How can it not matter?'

'Either it's worth it, as music, or it isn't. It's an important message and I want it out there.'

'What is?'

'Silence. Silence is all we dread. People like me, and Sky Blue Pink. Silence is what we dread. Being ignored. Like the Council, trying to shut us up.'

I'm trying to work out what I think; she falls silent too, then cools down: 'But of course, looking at it from your point of view... This competition was part of *Bethany Collier's* career plan, wasn't it? To get noticed? Because silence is what you dread, too. So look...' She speeds up again, snaps, bad-tempered: 'Enter it. Put your name on it. I don't mind. You can have it.'

Which is rich. 'Just a minute... I'm sure you think you're being incredibly generous... But actually, Alice, you've got a nerve.'

'What?'

'This whole thing was down to me!'

'My tune.'

'My reputation!'

'Beth, you haven't *got* a reputation. Nobody's heard of you and that's what this whole thing is about.'

'I won't be a cheat.'

'All that work for nothing,' she growls. 'Wouldn't mind, but it's good.'

I tell her, 'The way I see it, it doesn't belong to either of us, it belongs to both of us. It's a collaboration. And that's the single most important thing about it, for me.' I've only just fully taken that in; but here are times when it seems my sister, my second self, really doesn't read me at all. 'Look Al, look what we're doing. We're kids again, fighting over the two halves of a recorder, when you need them both to play.'

'So, we take turns,' she says, triumphant. 'You have no common sense.' She's channelling Mum, to signal that this argument is officially over. There's a long sigh, then she adds 'Honestly though. Haven't they heard of Lemon and McCartney?'

I sigh too. 'I'm sorry, Al.'

'Don't you worry, little sister. We can work it out. Well, I can.' She hasn't called me *little sister* since before the accident, and I'd forgotten she ever did; it was how she teased me, for a season. 'Leave it with me.' Next, she's breezy: 'Wanna join the band?'

She's joking, of course.

30 Rehearsal

I decide to clean the bathroom and find something else to think about. Choir tonight, Theo's first rehearsal, and perhaps he's expecting to fix our lunch when he sees me. Last term was my penance, and now, according to Mum, they want me to continue on a formal basis, i.e., for a fee. But nobody's been in touch to confirm. I've got to hang in there with this choir, at least for the time being. Or how will I know whether to be bothered with Theodoros Christodoulou? After more than a month, I might have gone right off him anyway.

When the doorbell rings, it's Ffion, in a deep red coat, one of those down-filled things that cost a bomb, tailored, and with a huge fake-fox trim round the hood which makes her face look like a pink ball inside a big hairy donut. Her gaze drops to the rubber gloves I'm holding in one hand. 'Come on Beth! Aren't you ready?' She's my lift tonight, she says, because Mum isn't well. Nothing serious and I'm not to worry. Mum's never ill, so it's odd she didn't let me know. Although I was on the phone to Al for ages.

'I'm ready. All I need is a big empty bag for the music I haven't been given.'

In some ways it would suit me to make us late, just to make a point. But turning up late is too horrible.

'I mean, for chrissakes, what do they take me for? What happened to communication? They think they've got me on a string. This is real zero-hours stuff.'

'But then again, Beth... whose job was it to tell you?'

'*Tell* me?' I twist round and aim the rubber gloves right across to the other side of the room, with as much force as I can muster, aiming for the sink of the kitchenette. One falls in with a good clear thwack. The other lies awkwardly over the edge, fingers akimbo. I'm pleased enough with that. 'What do you mean, *tell* me? *Ask* me, maybe.'

Then I remember, Ffi's mum is the Choir Secretary. 'Sorry... I'm not having a go at your mum...'

Ffi shrugs it off. 'Can if you like, she drives me round the bend... Oh, come on Beth. You never said you wouldn't, you know. Alright, so our mothers are still trying to run our lives...'

'Which is only one vowel away from ruin our lives...'

'Whatever. Beth, you do realise, don't you, you're an adult in charge of your own destiny? Seriously, though, asking or telling, surely you ought to hear it directly from the conductor? It's a mark of respect. One professional to another. So, the way I see it, it's his fault. It was his responsibility.'

The second glove slithers and drops to the floor, rubbery and pathetic. Theo's fault.

'Is it? Oh. Well.' I tell myself it must have been a misunderstanding, he can't have known the protocol, it must be different in Cyprus.

I glance across to the deflated glove. 'Sorry about the tantrum. It's been a crap day. Sometimes you need to let it out, you know?'

'Time for a good sing, then,' she says.

When we enter the hall, Jenny Johns is stationed at a little table with her attendance sheet, handing out music, and there's an awkward look on her face as she greets me, which only feeds my suspicion that our choir secretary has been a bit shifty here. What's more, her daughter knows it and is decently ashamed on her behalf. Ashamed, not annoyed, though. There's the difference between me and Ffion. You wouldn't catch me being ashamed of my mother. That would be tantamount to accepting responsibility for her.

Jenny says, 'Ooh, I've got your music for you, Beth, sorry for the mix-up, Mel told me you didn't get it. I hope it's all OK.' She hands me a score of *Israel in Egypt* and a fat anthology with angels on the front.

Theo's there, across the hall, with Marsha, whose amply cut cascade cardi is swinging about, while she's doing a sort of shaky dance, laughing, waving her arms around and generally looking supportive. He smiles and nods back. Alongside her, he looks tall. And calm. Or maybe tense. He's noticed me, darts a quick smile and raises a hand, nodding all the time. Then focuses back on Marsha and whatever helpful hints she's passing on.

I like that people recognise me, wish me happy new year. Max even leans on the piano to tell me, 'I thought for a minute we'd lost you.'

'Why would you think that?' Not that he's wrong, but I genuinely wonder how he reads me.

'You missed the concert.'

'I wasn't booked.'

'Oh, you missed something there. It was amazing. It's always better in the performance. Part of it's the building, of course.'

A Catholic church? I'm thinking, cold and creepy with pictures of lacerated bodies and weeping women on all sides. He says, 'It's so warm.'

'Warm?'

'The acoustic. The stones. The high roof. The building is always part of the music.'

'Oh, yes. True.' Hildegard has just kicked me in the shins.

He looks up at the ceiling of the parish hall, whose wooden joists have been painted a sea-sick green, and says, 'This isn't bad, as these places go. You couldn't record here, though.'

'You can record in a cupboard,' I tell him with a smile. 'In fact, I have.'

He looks sceptical.

'You add whatever space you want. Dry, echoing, big, small, near, distant. It's just sound waves. That's all it is.' I would have thought he'd appreciate that. Surgeons do technical, don't they? Technicians is what they are.

'Ah, but what about feedback?'

I wince. I want to tell him you only get feedback if you're a complete amateur, but that would be rude, in this context. 'You only get feedback if you slip up on the basics.'

'No, not that sort of feedback. What I mean is… you sing into the building, don't you, you sing into that enclosed space, and all the time you're singing – or playing, same thing – it's sending the sound back to you. And in the right building, the sound comes back better than it left you. Which encourages you. It's all happening on a scale of milliseconds, but the brain can process it.'

I'll defer to him on the human brain. That's amazing. And it's true, in terms of performance, that the instrument has to match the hall; or else the player has to find a way of making it work. *A nine-foot Steinway in a cage, throws all of heaven in a rage.*

We're interrupted by the start of the rehearsal. It's Marsha, not Jenny, who calls the chattering singers to order and welcomes our new conductor. He thanks her and says how much he's looking forward to working with the Lyceum Singers, then turns in my direction to say he knows how happy everybody will be to learn that Beth has agreed to play another term, so thank you, Beth. All I can do is smile an idiotic smile and shake my head.

Theo wants to start with a warm-up, which sends a ripple through the ranks; it isn't what they're used to; the smiles and frowns are pretty equally balanced. Max is a smiler, so is Patrick, our *Heldentenor*. Ffion looks bored, her mother positively irritated, Marsha in her element.

Then Theo walks up to me with a generous smile, nods to the piano, and says, 'Um... It might be easier if I... Do you mind?'

'Be my guest.' I get up and he wheels the instrument round to a better angle, leaving the stool behind. He stands at the keyboard to face the choir, and starts on arpeggios to *ma*. Up he takes them in semitone shifts. Changes vowels. And into a sequence of exercises.

Back on my stool, legs crossed and arms folded, with no instrument to hide behind, I watch the way he takes them through the warm-up. (I could easily have picked that up, why wouldn't he have trusted me?) His hand gestures are minimal and clear. Good. His facial expressions, though, are even more animated than when he was talking to Marsha just now, and sometimes they're so silly that I have to look away. I flex my foot, stare at the scuffed tip of my left boot, and consider. Who, here, am I most annoyed with? Jenny Johns is first in the dock for looking shifty. And definitely one of the accused is my own dear Mum, who isn't able to be here tonight (well fancy that), and probably told everyone that *of course* her daughter would *love* to play for them. She keeps telling me I need taking out of myself. What sort of an expression is that?

Theo, I decide, is either naive, or ill-mannered, or just as manipulative as the rest of them. He still hasn't even said a proper hello to me. And he ignored me for long enough when it suited him.

Warm-up over, he pushes the piano back to me, with a beautiful smile; then addresses the singers.

'As you know, in March, we will perform the Handel which was interrupted last year. But I don't want you to get stale.' There's a murmur of approval. 'So we'll be able to make a start on some music for our summer concert.' Nods and smiles. 'Anyway, you've all had the email with the dates, and I hope you're as excited as I am.'

I catch Ffion's eye, shake my head and shrug.

'I haven't,' I say. 'I don't think I'm on the distribution list.'

'Oh,' says Jenny. 'Didn't your mum pass it on?'

'My *mum*?' I'm narked and I don't care who knows it.

'We can fix that,' says Theo, 'can't we?' and he smiles at Jenny, who nods.

We start on their first big chorus, a sort of establishing shot in which the Israelites are having a hard time, which the choir lumbers through convincingly. Then God gives them hailstones for rain, and I realise I ought to have used the warm-up time to have a look at the music, instead of getting myself worked up about the treachery.

In the break, there's such a thick scrum of middle-aged-to-elderly women round our conductor that I haven't got a chance. Weirdly, it calls to mind a video they showed us once at school, of what happens when a sperm penetrates an egg: instantly, a protective wall is formed. Other, unlucky sperm just can't get through. The men of the choir are similarly rebuffed, and talk amongst themselves. I'm going to tackle Jenny Johns, who hasn't joined the fan club and is busy with her lists. Which means I can pick her off. I stride up to her little table but when she looks up at me, she bites her lip, shakes her head, and says, 'Oh. You didn't know about your mam.' A little tut. Another shake of the head. 'That's it, isn't it? Thought as much. Thought you looked a bit – you know, out of sorts. When you came in. '

'It's not just that. Nobody's even contacted me officially about playing, Jenny. I mean, taken for granted or what?'

She's affronted. 'I don't think it was *my* place, was it?'

'Besides, we haven't agreed a fee.'

'Oh. No. Well, um… I suppose it's standard rate? You'd better invoice the choir. Ian deals with all that. I'll send you his email.'

Ah. Ian, the old bloke in the mac who lives with his sister. Pamela.

'Seriously though, Jenny, what's the matter with Mum?'

'You haven't seen her this week.' The level intonation means it isn't a question, and it might be a cold accusation.

'Have *you*?'

'She's poorly. Her old problem. Like she gets sometimes.'

I don't understand. My mother's as strong as an ox.

Jenny reads my disbelief, and corrects herself: 'Like she used to get. When you were little.'

That's not something I remember. There's a kindly lilt in Jenny's voice as she explains, 'I don't think she's finding it easy, now you've both left home. With your father at sea half the time. Empty nest, they call it. And this is the worst time, after Christmas, when it's been so busy, and suddenly it's dead.'

This pulls me up short. Anyone can see Mum's over-filled her diary since she left teaching. Over-compensating. She might just be burnt out. Although... I wonder what she's doing now, all alone in her empty nest. Maybe she's sitting on the sofa, in the dark, listening to Schubert sonatas, because she did this a lot after that last horrific end-of-term when she finally got written out of the timetable. Schiff, Brendel. I joined her once. She was quite low. We got to the end of the last, great B flat major, and she said, 'Well, that's just about it, isn't it? It wasn't all bad. You've just got to deal with whatever comes next.'

'I ought to call her.'

'Wait till the morning, lovie. She's alright. If you call her now, she won't sleep.'

It occurs to me that Jenny and I are holding different bits of the same puzzle. She tells me:

'Your mam misses Alice.'

Another shock. But fair's fair: after all the ructions and the arguments that contributed to my departure, why would she miss *me?*

'I think it's brought it all back, now that Alice isn't at home any more. Like after the accident.'

'You're saying *Mum* was poorly?'

Jenny looks uneasy again, as we both realise how little I know of all this. Also, that I'm old enough now to be told.

'It was cruel, Beth, the timing. A little girl, just started school... So musically gifted.'

'I know.' She's often said that; in fact, it's one of Jenny's refrains, whenever she gets sentimental about my sister.

I offer, 'I remember us playing chopsticks together...'

She shakes her head. 'Chopsticks? Oh, but she was a prodigy, your Alice.'

I don't remember that. I thought the prodigy was me.

At the end of the rehearsal, Theo seeks me out. I get in first.

'You're lucky I've shown up. I wasn't invited.'

'But I spoke to Mel...'

There's a deep V-shape etched into his brow.

'Nothing on paper. No email. No contract. And I ought to be paid, if this is to go on.'

'You are so formal here. Excuse me, I forget. I apologise.' The V-shape flattens. 'I still owe you lunch,' he says.

I smile, but after all I've heard this evening – on the back of the debacle with Alice and the competition – I'm losing belief that any bit of my life can go right.

'Strike with a hot iron... how about Friday?'

'Yes, sure. Have you got my number? Look, I'll message you.' I send *Hi, Beth x*. Which was foolish, because now he knows I'd already added him to my contacts.

Ffi is waiting at the door, keeping an eye on me from distance and with a smile puckering her face. No drinks tonight, she says; she's promised to get me home. Unless I wanted to? I don't. I have a gathering sense of *allegro*, of things moving forward, things that must be, things I'm about to find out, for good or ill.

31 Snake

When I phone Mum from work the next morning, it rings fifteen times, before she picks up in her usual way. She denies there's anything medically wrong. Just tired.

She's never tired. What if she's got some awful underlying condition? Something she's been suffering from all these years, perhaps, since we were five? Heroically silent? Perhaps she wants me involved with the choir precisely so that we can share her last season? That would be awful.

'Dad's back soon,' I say. 'You OK on your own?'

The question surprises her. 'Yes. No change here, you don't have to worry about me.' She turns the subject to my news; do I have any? I start to tell her about the competition, and how we can't enter after all. I'm trying not to dramatise, but my words are met by heavy sighs that mean, I knew it, you've disappointed her, I knew you would.

'How did Alice feel about all that, then?' she wants to know, when a first-year wanders into the faculty office with a short lead dangling from her hand. She's holding it aloft by the jack, like a snake rendered powerless.

'I have to go, I've got a customer. Sorry.' I nod to acknowledge the girl.

'How did she take it?' says the voice on the line, louder now.

I swallow. 'She understands. She was more upset about the performing licence being refused.'

'Now, *that* was a wrong decision,' says Mum, roused to anger. 'Very wrong. But we can't just roll over and accept it, can we?'

'No.' She can't, but I might.

'Did you tell her in person, about the competition?' There's impatience on her breath.

In the anonymity of the faculty office, I'm trying to pretend this isn't a personal call. 'We've discussed it over the phone.' I'd like to point out that I couldn't trek over to Fairfield last night, could I, because of choir; but the pleading eyes of the drippy girl with the faulty connector help me not to. Faced with the first-year's haplessness, I'm the capable one here.

'I can't forgive you, Beth. I saw this coming. You've built her up, and now you've let her down.'

'I've got to go. Talk soon.'

'It was a good piece and it deserves a performance,' she says.

I deal with the student, find a replacement lead for her, spend an unnecessary half hour being as helpful as I can, checking the set-up, listening, even offering encouraging comments on her performance. Then back to my desk in the faculty office to contemplate my mother's sign-off: *Leave it with me*. That's exactly what Alice said about the competition, although in her case, it was probably just a form of words; she was modelling our parent, trying to sound assertive. But when Mum says *leave it with me*, it's anybody's guess what might come next.

32 Lunch

My lunch with Theo is happening. I speed towards my destiny, at the top end of Hope Street; off the pavement, through the door, down the steps into a world of up-cycled anti-décor, and industrial aluminium ducts hanging overhead; so glad to be here; and there, at a table near the bar, staring at me as I walk in, is Jaz Ander. Damn. I've made an effort with my smartest jumper: will he notice? And make-up. Hope he doesn't. I want to look naturally beautiful. Except he's seen enough of me to know the difference between everyday me and the enhanced version. A glance round the bar tells me Theo isn't here yet. As usual I'm the embarrassing side of early. I can't ignore Jaz but there's no way I'm sitting down at his table.

'Hi,' I say. 'I'm meeting someone.'

I peer down at the sleek laptop open in front of him.

'Good,' he says. 'Good. You OK?'

I nod. 'You?'

'Me, yes, I'm OK, but this…' he frowns at the keyboard. 'I've hit a wall with the book. You're creative, you'll understand…' He pauses, looks into my eyes, and attempts a winning smile with a losing ticket. 'You know, Beth, that's one thing I've always liked about you.' I'm not going to respond. 'So,' he continues, undeterred. 'Thing is, about the book, I know where I need to go with the plot and what needs to happen when I get there; and I'm thinking, great, I'm powering along, and then out of nowhere, wham, someone takes the wind right out of my sails.'

I try to compose my face in such a way that he can tell I'm not rude but not interested either. If I edge around the table a bit towards him, I'll be able to keep an eye on the door. He's off on his favourite subject.

'So, it's my contact, right, I told you about her? Katie in publishing? The house share way back in Camden? So, she's said yeah, she'd love to see anything I'm doing, just send it, so I did, and, oh man…' He hangs his head and shakes it from side to side. Then looks at me to say, 'You must have got this sort of thing from Petra Laing all the time? Like, an insight that makes you think, I'm doing this all wrong, why did I ever start?'

I've never needed Petra Laing to do that. I can manage that all by myself. I can see he wants to tell me what Katie in publishing had to say, and to prove I'm not a total shit, I feed him a morsel of interest: 'She didn't go for beetroot woman, then?'

Another theatrical swipe of the head, 'No, no,' and he laughs as his shoulders sway from side to side. Then he becomes serious. Grave, even. 'No. It's, like, more *fundamental*?' His shoulders hunch, he slouches back, and he looks mightily sorry for himself.

He's going to prose on now and I will skim-listen.

I position myself so as to keep an eye on the entrance. I can make out shapes passing along the pavement.

What I glean is that Jaz's novel lacks grit. It's mostly middle-class people living in their heads because they are privileged enough to afford to do that. Katie says. Katie says X, Katie says Y, Katie says write about what you know but only if what you know is interesting. Katie says if we keep on writing books for the sort of people who read books then the sort of people who never read books won't ever read them. He interrupts his monologue to take aim at me.

'It's ten times worse for you, though. Because say what you like, the concert hall is elitist, and chamber music is the most elitist manifestation of all. Pure music – who's interested in that? At least I can move the setting of my story to a night shelter, or a prison. And make my villain a prison governor. In fact, that's what I ought to do.' He brightens. Then darkens. 'Although I'd have to research that.'

'Why not make him-stroke-her a gang master-stroke-mistress, say, on the windswept beet farms of Lincolnshire?' I can't be bothered to argue and besides, we've slugged this one out before. I shrug, 'You have to write the stuff you need to write.'

His eyes narrow.

'So, what's your output right now?'

'Yeah. Good,' I lie.

'Do you ever actually finish anything?'

That's rich. He's only checking I haven't because he hasn't.

'I did a piece with Alice. Only we can't submit because it's a competition and you can't be two people. So.' I shrug.

'What is it?'

'Have you ever heard of Emily Dickinson?'

He screws up his face, hunches his shoulders and stretches out his arms, insulted. Then drops the arms and leans forward, on the attack.

'Words, then? I thought that was against your beliefs. But it sounds like Alice has got more sense.'

I'm mustn't let my voice go too squeaky. 'Look, this is just one small piece of work. There's other music I can write. I'm all ears. If something else walks into my head I'll welcome it with all my heart.'

'Jesus,' he sniggers, 'I'm just trying to visualise that. Anatomically challenging.'

All this *you're creative, you'll understand* bollocks is a one-way street, with Jaz. He sees no need to reciprocate because to his mind I'm just pathetic and wrong. He's trying to wind me up. Don't react.

He dips his head to look up at me, somewhere between questioning and sympathetic: 'Still playing for the amateurs?'

'So long as they pay me as a professional, yes.'

'When you could go back to Mummy and live rent-free. You're crazy.' His index fingers chop at the rough table-top.

Now I've had enough, and besides, through the glass I can see a tallish thinnish man approaching. I feel a sort of bubble under my ribs. 'Anyway… didn't Katie in publishing give you any advice?'

'Yeah. She said, find your minority.'

The door opens and in walks Theo. He plays an instrument I've never heard of, and muddles up *talk, speak* and *tell.* The things I know about him are few but growing in an exciting way. I feel sure his hair must smell really nice, and I already know his hands are warm and dry.

At first Jaz doesn't register the impending shift from monologue to soliloquy. He's staring right through the man in the doorway. 'Find your minority... I mean, which one?'

'Well, that's me,' I say by way of closure. 'See you later.' Then a look of recognition comes over his face and he shoots a glance between us. I hope he registers that this man is seriously hot.

I guide Theo round the corner of the bar to a place where neither of us has to look at Jaz. We both want the haddock and Theo lets me advise him on the ale. I learn that he usually drinks bottled beer. They don't have the beer herb in Cyprus, because it doesn't suit their climate. They have fine red wines. Maratheftiko, Mavrodaphne. I confess I've never drunk Cypriot wine, and the only Greek wine I've ever tried is Retsina. I screw up my nose, and so does he.

'Top notes of garden shed. You have to be drunk to drink it.'

'It's like Gwinness and Marmite,' he says. 'No, not together... What I mean is, nobody is born to drink this wine.'

'It's an acquired taste.'

'Exactly. It's an acquired taste.'

I'm approaching this lunch date like a big interview, hoping he'll ask again about my own music, and that I'll do rather better than the complete cock-up I made of it last time. I've been going over it in my head all day, likely questions, and possible answers, always hoping I'll get a second crack at the big one. Tell me please your musical journey. I think I've nailed it. I'm not just telling Radio 4 and the world, though,

I'm actually telling him. I must have got myself over-excited about this, because some time past midnight Alice rang to check up on me; the vibes had reached her all the way out in Fairfield. It always steadies me to hear her voice. She told me to be myself. I said, can I tell him how we wrote this thing together, and she said, great.

I'm ready for him. I set off at a rattling pace. 'I've been thinking about what you asked, about my musical journey, and I reckon it started with my mum singing to us. Well, me, because I was born insomniac! She was so desperate to get me to sleep that once, she nearly threw me out of the window. Anyway, she used to sing hymns and Beatles' songs and stuff. She gave us our first piano lessons. Then we had percussion instruments at primary school, and we made rain sticks which were like cardboard tubes with rice inside, and eventually I started piano lessons with Joan Pipkin, who was just the best…'

'That was after Alice had her accident.'

How did he know? Also, although chronologically, that was probably true, he seemed to imply a connection I've never made myself.

'You know about the accident? Has Jenny Johns been talking about us?'

'Your mother told me, first.'

'Oh, holy shit!'

That sounded bad.

I'm in the centre of this story, but everybody else is telling it. Everybody has a perspective on it except me. Perhaps I was too little and too close to it to see. Perhaps that's normal.

'I'm sorry.' He lays his hand on his chest. 'This is painful for you. I apologise.'

I fall back on the anger I've rehearsed. At least I know this speech by heart. 'What I meant was, it's exasperating, the way my mother always has to give her account of me. I feel like I've never once been allowed to start writing on a truly blank page with anyone. She's always got there first. She's ruled the margin, written in the date... Underlined the title even. My Musical Life by Beth Collier. I'm the clever, annoying one. Alice is the nice one. Although, actually, she is. Nice.'

'I'm the youngest of four children,' he says. 'So, by the time I arrived, all the good jobs had gone.' I'm puzzling to work out what he means, but there's a soft look in his eyes and I think this is intended as sympathy. He's read my confusion. 'We already had a clever one and a pretty one and a brave one. The only vacancy was for an entertainer...' He gives an ironic shrug. His teeth are even and very white. 'Look, Beth, our parents have to find a way of telling us apart, they're writing a story where the characters have to be as different from each other as possible; otherwise the authors themselves will lose the plot.'

'Maybe.' The canines are particularly nice.

'I don't mean to investigate.'

'I don't mind talking about Alice. Not with you, anyway.'

'It's interesting, that you're twins.'

'Identical twins,' I tell him.

'I know.'

'She likes every sort of music. We both do. Classical, old-fashioned rock, R+B, electronica, garage, house, even jazz. Except folk. You have to draw a line somewhere.'

Then I remember he's a real ethnic musician and I feel a bit sick. He looks faintly amused.

'And your sister was musically very gifted,' he tells me.

'She was. She is.'

'A prodigy, in fact.'

'A prodigy?' This is the second time in a week I've heard this.

'Yes. Jenny told me all about her. I think this is painful, for your mother. It must have affected you deeply, Beth.'

'So… what did Jenny tell you?'

'She told me Alice taught herself to play by ear. And she was so talented, your parents bought a good piano and they'd just started lessons with the best teacher they could afford, when came the tragedy of her accident.'

Did it? It must have. But we were only five. I don't remember it that way. Or that the piano was bought for Alice.

'I remember the piano. Mum's still got it. I do remember it being delivered.' A great dark but fragile thing that entered the house on a mobile see-saw.

I'm trying to take this in. I'm trying to remember Alice before the accident, and I can't. Or Mum and Dad, before the accident. Or myself. It all turns into a horrible mangled chord inside my head, jarring, jamming every thought. Then into a hammering, as if I'm beating my fists against the heavy closed door of memory.

There's a hand on mine. 'Beth,' he's saying, 'Beth… I'm sorry. Are you OK?' It's a warm dry hand. There's no pressure, only warmth.

Our meals have arrived and I stare down at my plate. The fish has curled up in the cooking, with the batter bubbled into boils, pock marks and ridges, all crisped just one shade too brown.

He reads my distaste. 'I never eat the coat,' he says. 'Its only purpose is to protect the fish.' He takes his knife and fork and makes a careful cut, turning a blubbery flap of batter over to point with the knife tip at the milky white flesh. 'See, it's good inside.'

I don't feel like eating. And I don't feel like talking about my musical life either because maybe I've been living someone else's.

And now Jaz bloody Ander walks past, on his way to the gents.

Theo eats and I decide he's right about leaving the batter. We've stopped talking, which suits me because suddenly there isn't anything I want to say.

Jaz reappears and he's actually stopped at our table.

'Sorry to interrupt,' he says, smiling to acknowledge me then turning to address Theo. 'but am I right in thinking you're Theo Christodoulou?'

Theo looks immediately delighted. Maybe this has never happened before.

Jaz hands him a business card, which Theo examines carefully. 'I hear you're working with the Lyceum Singers? The choir that literally brought the house down?' He grins at us both. 'So, at the Echo, we're doing a series on the Rushworth heritage, cultural life, amateur groups, that sort of thing. Are you by any chance related to the guy who runs the Greek nights at the Aphrodite Bar?'

'My Uncle Stelios!' He's delighted. 'Sometimes I play there too.'

'Really? Two generations, two traditions... Maybe we could talk some time?'

'Yes, yes of course!' Theo beams and stands up so as to release his wallet from the back pocket of his jeans, opens it, takes out a card and hands it to Jaz. I hope it's got his own name on it this time.

'Great,' says Jaz, grins at us both, and takes his leave.

Theo waits until he's out of sight. 'You know each other?'

'Oh, yes. Look, if you and I are going to work together, I'd be grateful if you'd give him a wide berth. And so would Alice.'

His eyes have narrowed gradually and he looks puzzled. I don't think he can have seen the Tiger Mother article, at least. This much is a relief.

We eat. I tell him about Alice. Her huge musicality and total lack of training, her busking, and the incident in Liverpool 1. I show him the clip, and he's impressed, moved, even. I tell him she helped me write something for a competition, but we couldn't enter because there's two of us.

'You're a team, then.'

He's exactly right. 'Yes… Yes, we are.'

Yes. We really could be. This is how it looks to him, from the outside, from the little he knows. He makes our collaboration sound a perfectly reasonable state of affairs. I tell him: 'You know, what gets me about all this is the sheer unfairness of it. So here am I, trying to carve out a career as a composer, and it may be stunted and inadequate, but at least I can see a way to do it. But for Alice, there's no clear pathway.'

And out it all spills.

'Alice can't read music properly, but she's the sort of person who'd have been able to play an instrument by ear, if she hadn't lost so much manual dexterity. Her singing voice is great, she stays in tune, in fact she's got a good sense of relative pitch, so with the right training, who knows what she might have done? If she hadn't spent so long in hospital, if walking hadn't been the big deal everybody focused on, if her speech had recovered sooner and she'd started mainstream earlier, if everybody's expectations hadn't been so low, she might have taken theory exams and more… I always knew her life was unfairly harder than mine. I got the piano, the teachers, the applause. What did she get? Painkillers, physio, a better wheelchair…'

These are thoughts I've often tormented myself with. But to learn that the piano was bought for my sister casts a filter which threatens to change every colour.

The more I talk, the worse I feel. Yet the more inspired he looks.

'You are going to carry on working together, aren't you?'

'I'd like to. Especially if I can help her in some way.'

He tilts his head to one side. 'From what you said about the competition, I think she's the one who helped you.'

Another jolt. And of course, he's right: I sought her out when I was stuck. I think he can see that I've wobbled, because he gives a generous, re-balancing smile, and says, 'Anyway, I'm so glad I found your family.'

'Wasn't it my mother who found you?'

'Mm… perhaps.' He glowers ironically. 'Your mother is a face to be reckoned with.'

That's another one for the album. I don't feel like laughing, though.

'Yup,' I say. 'And I'm in her bad books right now. For leading Alice up the garden path, about this competition.'

'I don't understand.'

'It means… Well, she thinks I was wrong to involve my sister. Because Alice gets excited, then she gets disappointed.' I think, but won't say, *and so do I*; only, whatever Alice feels – disappointment, boredom, elation – she does it out loud. 'She's had so many knocks. School. Everything.'

'She's not a child, is she?"

'No. Just because she's vulnerable – that's the label they give her, the word they use – just because she's vulnerable doesn't mean she's fragile.' This is probably confusing to what Mum would call a non-native speaker. 'She's strong.'

He understands. 'She's strong. Then you must persuade your mother of your combined talents. *Show* her.' He smiles broadly as if this is going to be the easiest and most natural thing in the world.

But I'm not sure any of the talent is mine. My stomach is one huge stone. A sore, heavy, rounded piece of granite.

Flimsy, disconnected thoughts walk past my head. He really likes me. They haven't cleared our plates.

The main thing now, though, is the stone.

33 Piano stool

It's hard to write a really funny scherzo when you're not in the mood for a joke. There's nowhere I can settle down to work; Jo's flat's too cold, the faculty's too full of distracting people who might want things from me, and public places are full of the public. I know where I want to go. I want to go back to the piano in the big house on Menlove Avenue, only as it used to be, before they made a big through room; the way it was when you could close the door. That was the original door. It must have dated from the thirties – the round knob that rattled on its spindle was set high, so aged five I would have had to raise my arm to close it. I'm racked by all the things that I've forgotten. If I could only sit there, and smell those smells again – not just the geraniums, but the polish, and fragrant woody scent when you lifted the lid of the piano stool to get the music, and that funny loopy fabric on the old armchair that used to release a smell like ironing when the weather was hot – if I could just sit there and breath it in, I'm sure I'd waken all the memories from that terrible time, when my twin, my second self, just disappeared. I don't remember ever trying to forget. And yet I did.

Alder Hey. Which I thought was Hay, like on a farm. She was in Alder Hey for ages. It was full of clanky, rattly noises. I dimly remember a long, white ward and being frightened by her silence: she was bandaged like a mummy, which I think I can see, except that those words, *bandaged like a mummy*, are the ones the family use to tell the saga, so maybe I'm imagining. Did I really know then what a mummy was? At five, did I understand that a mummy was a dead person? And how many times did I visit her there? I have no idea at all.

When we got the piano, it was for her. All those hours I spent, practising, on the wide piano stool... You buy a bench like that if you're expecting duets to be played. I've never given it a moment's thought before. Was it meant for me and Alice? Or Alice and Mum?

All those hours... Who was in the house? Other people were looking after me. Dad. My nan, my aunties. Where was Mum? Because I'm sure, I'm absolutely sure, a lot of the time, she wasn't there. I could ask Auntie Dot. Wouldn't she just give me the official version all over again, though? I'll ask Dad, he'll be back in port soon.

I used to be so much in love with going forwards that looking backwards never crossed my mind. Now that I've glimpsed what might have been stacking up behind me all these years, I've frozen. The muse, in which I don't believe, has departed, and when I replay the past, it's never going to sound the same again.

34 Sorted

Alice messages me.

FYI – competition sorted. Entered in my name.

Then there's a 'fingers crossed' emoji and a couple of kisses.

I shout aloud, 'I can't believe you've done this to me!'

I'm on the point of phoning her immediately, when I remember that in effect I've already written the whole thing off, so it would be pretty hypocritical now to say, I don't want this song and you can't have it either. Nevertheless, I'm wrong-footed.

It means she found the files – OK, on our shared space – but she also found the competition web page, filled in the entry form, paid the fee, and uploaded it without any help from me. I've always done the admin, the fiddling round. She's always let me. Was that habit? Convenience? Or have I underestimated her all this time? Perhaps she got somebody else to help her, maybe Ginnie, the music therapist I've never met. Or John? This hurts; she might have asked me, I'd have let her have it her way, I'd rather hand the piece over to her than have a stranger's grubby fingers going through our shared documents.

In a way, *Silence* does belong to her. It's her tune. And Theo was right: she was the one who helped me, not the other way round. Vocal music was never my territory. The piece has meaning for us both, yes, but a more intense meaning for Alice; and I know how badly she's been knocked back, not just over the busking licence, but not being able to join the Lyceum Singers. I ought to concede.

I start to type:

OK but you cheated

Then delete. Then type:

Good luck

Then delete that, because it sounds as though I'm condoning it, as if it's all absolutely fine and I've nothing to say.

Next, I scroll through available emojis, but I can't find anything with the right blend of shock and ambivalence. A question mark will have to do.

35 Rocky Lane

Great Uncle Pat is a minor celebrity on Merseyside. While you freeze on the doorstep in Tuebrook, with the traffic thundering past and the buses squealing to a halt, waiting for him or Dot to shuffle down the hall and open up, you can't help thinking about all the people who've brushed against the privet and knocked on that door, on one kind of Union business or another. Come for advice, for strategy meetings, for a drink and a gossip. Rumour has it he once lent their holiday money to Derek Hatton. One thing we do know, because there's archive proof – and I'm staring at it right now, in floor-to-ceiling shelves full of old-fashioned videotape, audio cassettes and DVDs – is that back in the eighties he swore to visit every European capital behind the Iron Curtain, and managed to bag the lot before the Berlin Wall came down. He had a little video camera, in the days before phones. Dad says he made a big deal about being allowed to take it to these places, but that the family dreaded having to watch any of the tapes, because they were, in my dad's words, 'all meetings, handshakes, and paint drying in Bulgaria.' The tapes sit on the long shelf above me, neatly labelled and in chronological order. *USSR: Russia; German Democratic Republic; Poland; USSR: Belarus; USSR: Ukraine*, and so on.   At eye-level, his personal chronicle of the Miners' Strike includes *Flying Pickets* (numbered I – VII), *Police Brutality – Highlights*, as well as *TV coverage I – XII;* there's a couple of shelves on the Liverpool Dockers' Strike, and he reckons he's got every available TV interview and documentary about Hillsborough, switching formats to DVD to bring the story right up to the present day. It was a struggle for him to walk upstairs and let me into his den, the old box room, but nobody else can show me how to work the antwacky technology. He's in touch with an archivist from the TUC who's slowly copying them over to digital, so at the moment a lot of 1983 is missing, he warns me. He was made up last week when I asked to look through his historic VT collection. And now he's hugely disappointed in me because I've told him what I'm actually after is footage of the family.

Every Christmas, Uncle Pat was there with his video camera. I hated it at the time. But the tapes might be able to take me back to that front room with the geraniums and the piano. That's my destination.

'Oh, Christmases? That's all off the camcorder,' he says, and points to the lowest shelf. There's a layer of fluff on the old brown carpet. 'They're all down there. I'll leave that to you, makes me dizzy, bending down. We can use this one for demo purposes. You might learn something.'

He picks up from the window sill a cassette marked *1997: Women of the Waterfront* and we sit down at the table where various dusty great video recorders are stacked. There are wires everywhere.

'We're switched on. You put it in here. You wait. See that light? You're good. There's play. There you go. Just don't press record.'

The monitor shows a crowd of people holding a long banner at waist height, *Victory to the Dockers.*

'Do you have bookmarks on this thing?'

'Oh eh, love, does it look like a book? You're in luck, though, this one has a real-time counter. State of the art, this. In its day, like. You can fast forward, only just remember, it's mechanical, you have to give it time to react. None of your back-and-forth, stop-start malarky. Or it'll jam.'

'Thanks, Uncle Pat. I'll be careful.'

'And that's the eject button.'

He looks deflated by my narrow horizons and isn't going to hang around. I can hear him puffing, taking the stairs one at a time. Perhaps he hears the clicks as I press stop and eject, because he calls up to me, 'She was there, you know. On the picket line. Yer mam.'

He's near the bottom when he adds, 'If you ask me, the women were more organised than the men.'

I've found Christmas from the year 2000. There's a dramatic bit, a dark screen, then what I think must be my Uncle Pat's voice saying 'Oh, here she comes, the crimbo queen,' – way too loud, but he'd be the one holding the camera – and you can see a tiny flickering light, then there's applause and a child's voice saying 'Yak, what can *I* have?' And in the gloom, edging through the door, you can just make out a smiling woman – my young mum – carrying a barely flaming object into a darkened room; holding it aloft above the table to applause; then the lights are switched on, the room is sort of browny-pink, and the shaky camera tries to focus on the pudding, and a woman's voice says, 'Oh your holly's lovely,

Melanie, is it real?' The camera walks, juddering, round the table. That must be Auntie Dot, but she looked so different then, so plump, you were hardly aware of her having bones at all; I recognise our cousin Jason, who was really skinny as a lad; there's Mum's brother, Uncle Trevor who died of malaria; and that's us, twins, looking chubby with eyes wide open; and I think I'm the one on the left because it has to be Alice who looks out and smiles for the camera. We're wearing the same blue dress and we both have hair in a pony-tail, with a little fringe. My Dad looks like he's had a couple of drinks.

I remember that dress. We liked the idea of wearing different colours. But when it came down to it, we always preferred the same one. *Oh, come on girls, take turns. Whoever gets first pick for the dress, the other gets first pick for shoes.* One of us said, alright then, you can have the blue one; and the other said, no, it's alright, you have it. And we both ended up having the same. That feeling comes rushing back: being sort of pleased, but a bit fed up at the same time.

Everybody's in the minty-green front room now, for the turns. Auntie Dot goes first, with a medley from the shows, and everyone sings along. The piano jangles, with some duff notes. It's Nan's old piano, the one that even Rushworth and Dreaper couldn't fix. I'd forgotten Auntie Dot ever played. When did she stop?

Then the two little girls who were us come up and face the audience and giggle a bit, and Mum scrambles into shot, to accompany them on the piano; they sing *Jingle Bells*, quite nicely, and strong. I'm not sure which is me. We both stand still, arms by our sides. Applause. Dad says 'Thank you ladies, that was very good, but come on, let's hear your Snowy Song. They wrote this themselves.'

The girls grin and give a heavy nod, that exaggerated way that children do and Alice still does. They squash side by side on the little piano stool with their backs to the camera, and begin a duet. The bass part is very simple, just four notes that walk up and down, up and down, growling between G and C, and the girl on the left is playing this with her right hand, steady and confident. The girl on the right uses both hands; her left hand has the same walk an octave higher and in contrary motion to the bass, while her right hand makes funny little splashes – snow flurries, I suppose – at descending intervals, in the high register. These tinkly notes are random but they start from higher and higher, and the gaps between them get bigger. Sweet, very sweet. She's just having fun, making it up as she goes, playing quietly then loudly, then quiet again. Anyone can see, she's the musician. That must be Alice. The piece ends with her slapping her whole hand noisily at the very top of the keyboard, at which the other girl, me, obediently and instantly stops playing. We must have practised that.

That final slapped non-chord was like a snowball in the face. Brilliant. I'm laughing and crying all at once. Oh Alice, Alice. It's not fair.

Now it's Mum's turn. She starts to sing, and it hits my heart because this isn't her choir voice, it's the lullaby voice I've so longed to hear again. I was right about it. It's much lower and warmer, a fine, straight, honest voice full of love.

'Oh, you are a mucky kid, Dirty as a dustbin lid, When he hears the things that you did, You'll gerra belt from yer da.'

But the song itself… that's another thing I'd forgotten all about. The words get worse and soon they're sobering me up. It's basically about child abuse; well, domestic violence.

'If you're norrasleep when the boozers close, you'll gerra belt from yer da.'

My dad's just in shot, listening seriously, misty-eyed; and at the end there are sighs and 'That was lovely, Melanie,'

'Aye, lovely, Mel. Nice one.' Weird, the way they accept it. Nobody in that room would lift a finger against a child, but instead of being outraged, they've gone all sentimental.

Nobody should sing that song. It's wrong to normalise violence. What bugs me is, my mother Melanie Collier didn't become politicised last week, she was already a dyed-in-the-wool feminist *then*. Why did she choose it? Surely the woman in the song ought to have kicked her husband out, changed the locks, protected her child?

In those days, there were lots of things you didn't talk about, so maybe that was the point. Just proves, though. Words can have a terribly ageing effect on music.

I play back the bits with Alice. The longer I watch, the more I'm certain who's who. I study her movements. She moves exactly like me, quickly, easily, turning from one adult to another, grabbing a sleeve for attention.

Christmas 2001, when at last I find it, is a very different affair. It's not at our house, but here with Auntie Dot and Uncle Pat. Alice isn't there, and neither is Mum. I see myself but can't read my own expression. Calm, tense, spaced-out, thoughtful: don't know. I don't remember how I felt. I smile when I open my present: a wooden recorder. I do remember that, the woody taste of it. My Dad looks worn out. Jiggered, he'd say.

That's enough. I can't do any more. Maybe, like the clunky playback mechanism, I've jammed with the strain of going back and forth. I head downstairs where Uncle Pat's watching his telly in the back room, while Auntie Dot's in the front, watching hers. She brightens to see me: did I find what I wanted? No, not exactly. I make us a cup of tea. I tell her I've been looking at Christmas 2001, when we came here for Christmas dinner.

Auntie Dot's voice is thin, rising, questioning; she's pulling at a thread of memory: 'Oh, you did, that's right.'

'Did Mum go to live in hospital?'

The question panics her. 'No,' she protests. 'No. She was poorly, she had a bad do alright, she wasn't herself, but she wasn't ever...'

'I meant with Alice?'

Her mouth puckers. She knows she's given something away. She revises.

'Well, yes, she might as well have lived there, she was in that hospital every day.'

'Where was I?'

Her voice calms: 'You were at home, love. And you went to school.'

'Who looked after me, Auntie Dot?'

'Well, your dad, of course. Don't you remember? And me. And all your mum's friends, they helped a lot, her friend Jenny in particular, she was a brick... There was a rota, oh, for ages. Because you know, your mum's always taken care of other people, so a lot of people owed her. Everybody pitched in. Don't you remember them?'

'I remember people. I just don't remember a person.'

How long did our dark ages last? That period between Alice falling silent and Alice talking again is the period I don't remember, although I'm beginning to see why. I do remember the relief, as she got better, and starting to think that maybe *I'd* be alright after all.

What was going on in the house, what the story was with Mum and Dad, I have no idea. But I do know how the time passed for me. I was in the front room with the door closed, playing the new piano, where everyone would leave me alone because they could hear what I was doing, so they knew I was alright; and if Alice was going to tell me something, this would be where she'd come to find me. It was my way of listening out for her.

36 Olive branch

There's a chilliness about my thoughts these days, now that I've seen the Christmas videos; my mind's eye replays an image of myself, a silent, wooden child, playing duets *secondo*, faithfully helping realise my sister's musical fantasies, because she, playing *primo,* was clearly the one who had all the ideas and all the personality. I used to think I had a vocation. Now I'm not so sure.

I can't be cross about Theo's observations on Alice and me, because he was right.   Imagine, if there was another person who helped you make sense of yourself and the world, and stopped you screwing up…   I wouldn't have to explain anything, because my true intentions would be obvious. Nothing would be misconstrued. Every hasty judgement – because we all make a thousand micro judgements every minute we're in company – every hasty judgement would be accurate; haste would be a sign of ease, not carelessness. This is what I imagine it would be like to be truly loved: your heart becomes an open book in the hands of a skilful reader.

I don't know whether this is something that could happen in real life, far less whether Theo might be that person. Up to now, the book of my heart has been skim-read by idiots looking for a story. That story comprises *things that happened to her*, and *things she did*. Early trauma, got this, won that.

These events lie exposed, white and naked, in the sun. Nine-tenths of the iceberg that is me are under water. My hurts are solid, cold and crystalline, and I long for them to fall apart and melt into the less frozen ocean.

Find an interest. Greek lessons. I've got this Blue Book with olives on the front now, and I'm going to do half an hour a day, to supplement the diet. It's much harder than I expected. I found this group online, where you can share resources and experiences and chat to other learners for *support*. (I can hear my Uncle Pat: 'Your generation. You can't pick your nose today without *support*.') The Go Greek Group encourages you to share your motivation. *What are your aims? What is your dream? Post them here and check in with them from time to time as you make progress over the next few weeks!*

People write stuff like 'To get by on holiday,' 'To help me in the villages off the beaten tourist track,' and more intriguingly, 'To make my in-laws like me.'

My aim is to understand at least some of what Theo's friends are talking about, at the regular Cypriot acoustic nights in the Aphrodite bar. Starting tomorrow. My dream? Ah, my dream, after weeks, maybe months of secret study, is to astonish him by saying exactly the right thing at exactly the right time, just... casually.

This is about as realistic as making your début as a flautist with Act One of *The Firebird*. As my mum never tires of telling people, languages are a performance subject, and it's not enough to practise on your own: sooner or later, you have to perform in front of other people. She'd tell me to regard the Aphrodite crowd as a resource.

I'm not sharing any of this with the GGG. I post that my aim is *cultural understanding,* and my dream is *global harmony.*

37 The Aphrodite Bar

Me and Shari often meet up at the photo-op crossroads. It's handy for the bus stops on Myrtle Street, and if you stand behind the vintage, brick-built advertising panel that came free with the Philharmonic Hall, there's a chance of shelter from whatever the sky is throwing at you. Although tonight a wind is whipping straight up from the river, so no escape. The crossroads at the top of Hardman Street is one of my favourite places and definitely my favourite impossible photograph, one that only human eyes can take and only the human brain can process. Sure, the view to the new cathedral is one for the postcards, with the other, bigger, rectangular job – floodlit now – staring it out from a safe distance at the far end of Hope Street, along the brow of the hill. This noisy, diesel-infused spot is where tourists attempt selfies with the Philharmonic pub behind them, flowery and colourful by day, cut-glass and sparkly as it is now, by night; curse the passing double-deckers as they launch themselves through the traffic-lights. But it's the whole patchwork 3-D puzzle of the city that I love; things I can't literally see but that I know are there; the flat lines of the Everyman, the drop of the hill and the towers of the Liver Building, which is a long walk away and yet will loom close enough to spook me if I walk a few steps along the front of the Phil; the flat, grey Portland stone of what used to be an art deco blind school, and is now a coffee shop, bar, pizzeria; the cobbles on the southern end of Hope Street, and all the places that you know are tucked aside round corners, the Cracke, the Roscoe Head; and further than you can comfortably see, the bombed-out church at the foot of the hill. Somewhere near that top end of Bold Street is Theo's Uncle Stelios's Aphrodite Bar. Where we are heading for the monthly Greek Acoustic Night.

Shari pitches up, we hug, agree it's Baltic, and set off down the hill.   She's excited about some top-notch choir from Finland, and moaning about having to trek all the way over to the other side of town to hear them.

'Honest to God. Two cathedrals, and neither of them fit to perform in.'

It's true, they both mash music to a pulp. Gilbert Scott's sarcophagus has an 8-second echo, while the concrete wigwam funnels the sound up and whizzes it round like a great spin dryer.

Personally, I wouldn't bother with the choir from Finland. But, she claims, you only get to hear this piece – whose name got swallowed by a gust of wind – once every Preston Guild. And it's some liturgy or other, and a liturgy belongs in a church.

Shari has tonight's destination on her phone. Soon we're back on the flat, past the garishly lit filigree of the bombed-out church – whether that's to attract the tourists or deter the smackheads I'm not sure – and threading our way into the cobbled backstreets whose uneven pavements are a threat to my smart-heeled boots. I smell kebabs.

You can't miss it. The Aphrodite Bar has big picture windows which send colours across the narrow street, slamming into every reflecting surface from door frames to puddles. There's condensation on one side of the window, and Cypriot music is sweating out into the damp air, happy, plinky-plonky, rhythmically intriguing, to my western ears.

The room is two-thirds full of people sitting drinking, some eating, some in front of rolled-up, oily serviettes on plates that ought to have been cleared away. We're not the youngest people here, but we're not the oldest either. There's a sort of disco lighting effect going on which adds to the confusion. Three guys are playing, crouched over their instruments in a tiny performance area; bouzouki, mandolin, I guess; and guitar. Near the bar, an arm is raised; that's Theo, who stands and beckons us to his table.

'So,' he says, 'This is my band.' And he introduces us to a couple of blokes, sounds like Georgios and Paul, I think, and a woman with the most extraordinary eyes. Heavily made up, a sort of Amy Winehouse look, but even without the lashes and the eyeliner they would be the most beautiful eyes, huge, dark. She is so lucky with these eyes. She has a slightly chubby neck, which makes a little crease where it meets her torso. I had a doll like that. Her hair is dark, long and piled artlessly on top of her head, stray wisps snaking out. She's all in black, like me; but the difference between her black, which is stylish and suits her, and my black, which is routine and, by my family's account, doesn't, is huge. Suddenly, I feel so pale. It's time I thought about another colour. Her name is Eleni.

Theo makes room for me to sit on the bench seat alongside him, and Paul moves a chair to place Shari between himself and George, doing that boy-girl-boy-girl thing that old people get so hung up about. Theo, me, Paul, Shari, George, Eleni, and back to Theo.

Wine gives me a headache on its own. I opt for Cypriot lager, like pop with slightly less sugar. They're talking about people I don't know, with Theo mostly asking questions, and it sounds as though he doesn't know them either; and whilst George is as Scouse as they come, Paul, who's closest to me and easiest to hear, has an accent I'm not sufficiently familiar with. I can't hear Eleni, and in any case, I've tuned in to the music. Each successive piece is seemingly in a different compound time which my western ears are working to identify; sometimes I feel I've got it, only for an extra, unexpected measure to be thrown in, that makes the whole thing sway to a stop, before starting off again.

Flashing lights shower us all with colours, the men laugh in waves, the music thrums and rattles, and eventually Paul gets up and takes the floor: a young man dancing on his own. We're squashed together behind the table, and I can feel a gentle, happy sway run through Theo's body too, as he watches his friend.

The dancer has become a kind of human corkscrew, twisting lower and lower, rising again, arms tilted, head aslant, tipping in different directions, so that you might think he was simply drunk, but for the persistence of the dance, the repetitions, which mark it a performance. Everyone's eyes are on him, and they smile and nod. I lean in to Theo, and I'm wondering whether we feel this music the same way, or whether we're hearing different things, when an old guy with black hair and huge, bramble-patch eyebrows rolls up, and pinches Theo on the chin. The way a pantomime dame might do to Buttons. Then slaps him on both cheeks and laughs, revealing big, even teeth, like piano keys. Then he shoots a look at me, and Theo says something I don't understand, before introducing us in English. This is Uncle Stelios.

The cuffs of his crisp white shirt – which glows under the muted lights and re-interprets the disco ball pinks and blues – are folded back, his forearms strong. I check his hands for rings; yup; and yes, a fat watch with a gold bracelet. I am ashamed of myself for seeming to recognise him; my imaginings of Uncle Stelios were stereotypical, although they were not all wrong. He smiles at me – the full octave – and his dark eyebrows rise as if he thinks I'm somebody.

'You are the sister!' he exclaims, then walks round to grasp my hand and pat me on the shoulder. 'Welcome, welcome! You know,' he says, 'I've shared your sister with the whole family. Soon, in Cyprus, she's gonna be famous! Ha, ha!' Then he shoots a theatrical look at the table and says, 'You need food. Do you like Cypriot food?' Now he's looking at me. 'Of course you do, everyone likes Greek food. D'you like souvlaki?' One minute his brow is knotted, interrogating, and the next it clears as he answers his own question; 'Or the dips? Everybody likes the dips. Vegetarian, very healthy.'

'I'm good with souvlaki,' says Shari. 'Just whack it in a pitta, that'd be great.'

He tells me and Shari that we want chips with that.

'On the house,' he says, hand on heart.

'No, I can't...'

Theo is laughing broadly. 'It's my uncle.' He puts his hand on mine and says in my ear, 'Let him. This is his ...' and a word I don't recognise, which must be Greek and sounds like a disease.

Shari is giving me a behave-yourself look. 'When in Rome! Go on Beth, don't be an ice-maiden all your life.'

Is that how I come across to strangers?

'Alright,' I say, giving my permission, before I do remember to say thank you.

Stelios goes off and I ask Theo what was that word he used. He goes public, glances round the table with a look of glee: 'Here comes Beth's first Greek lesson!'

Everybody's listening now, and when he says, 'Repeat after me: *philoxenia*,' they all join in.

'*Philoxenia!*'

The mandolin player looks across to our noisy table, smiles and waggles his head.

Nobody, though, will tell me what it means. George insists you can't translate it. This is an argument I've rehearsed many times with my mother, who holds that some concepts really do defy translation, which strikes me as a load of mystic nonsense and implies that a foreigner has no right of access to other people's notions. So, I deduce, *philoxenia* is either some sort of tradition, or a nice way of saying a close relative is in your face.

They simply can't be bothered to tell me, and in any case, it's time for our table to play their set. Theo stands first; he motions for me to hand him the instrument case which is leaning against the wall beside me. George gets up, and Eleni; Paul shakes his finger from side to side, no, he tells me, he's no musician. It takes maybe ten minutes for the three of them to sort themselves out with seats and microphones. In the meantime, as from nowhere, little dishes are placed on the table, olives, bread, some hummus, tzatziki. On the other side of the room, Uncle Stelios beams across at us, nods and raises a hand to say, enjoy. He's standing next to a tiny round table tucked under the spiral staircase. This table is at odds with the rest of the décor, just big enough for one, and unlike the other tables, it has not only a white damask cloth but also a pot of cyclamen, in a little basket. Our table, in contrast, fills up, as other arms deposit a huge oval platter loaded with souvlaki in halves of pitta, with shredded cabbage, grated carrots, tomatoes all spilling out. And chips, 'for the ladies.'

Shari's eyes pop out of her head. 'That's my five a day sorted. What're you lot having?' Paul chuckles, and like a mate, I reach out for a chip.

The music starts, nothing I recognise, pleasant enough, the sort of rhythm that reminds you of being bounced on your dad's knee as a baby, in two, a simple dotted rhythm with exaggerated downbeats, and at the end of the sixteen bars, a sort of heavy sit-down – plonk! – and a pause for it to sink in. The way this game works, first time round, you startle the baby: but with each iteration, the baby moves from smiling to the gurgle of anticipation and, you have to hope, wild laughter. It occurs to me that this kind of music invites you to play that same game, subliminally. For the next number, they all sing along. Theo's instrument is called the laouta. It has a slender neck and a body of dark, glossy wood, with a blonde, decorated soundboard; he wears it well. His long fingers manage it easily. Eleni's a passable guitarist, but as they get to a faster, trickier song, it's clear that George on the bouzouki is in another league. The notes are little points of light, scintillating, soon gone.

It bugs me that Theo never did explain that word to me. I want to understand. I want it to matter to him that I do.

With Paul mainly talking to Shari, I pick at the food, watch Theo play, and let my mind wander. I'm uneasy about my mum's state of health, past as well as present. I want to ask her straight about the piano, too, but I want to do that face to face, or she'll just fob me off.

I'm listening again. The music's changed. It isn't background any more. Eleni has stopped playing and sings alone. Her eyes are closed, the brows rise to an arch, and the sound comes from a different world. Rich, deep, sustained, warm. Slow stretches to slower, as if the voice is reluctant to leave each note. The whole room stops to listen; and at the end, when Eleni's extraordinary eyes open, everybody claps and hoots in approval.

I have a very bad feeling. I can't name it, and it passes as quickly as it came. Like pricking your finger on a needle.

The musicians go back to the folksy stuff; people start dancing, Paul gets up and coaxes Shari to her feet, and the already modest floor space is jammed with a skein of dancers, women, but men too, side by side, holding hands up in the air, all smiling; they step back and forth and forward, and the stumblers like Shari are carried along by the two-thirds who are footsure. I wonder if this is normal. I don't want to join in, and nobody tries to make me; there's pleasure in watching other people happy, dancing, and I press my back against the wall, allow my foot to tap, and feel melancholic.

As the evening wears on, I seem to watch Uncle Stelios age. After all, he is a great-uncle, with a lot of history, so not a young man. A manager runs this place, he only comes for music nights. Eventually he allows himself to sit at the table for one, which has remained unoccupied.

It's late before the whole thing breaks up, and I'm desperate to have spent a whole evening with Theo without us sharing anything worth taking home to think about. Cake has been brought, and little glasses of some sort of clear liqueur that might be oven cleaner. There's a cab outside. Hugs all round, instruments away, coats on, tables clearing. Shari is glowing, tells me that was the best night for ages, and that we must come back next month. Eleni and George are arguing in Greek. Theo turns his back on them and flashes a broad smile at me: so glad we liked it, yes, we must surely come again. Uncle Stelios, sparked back to life by everyone's departure, steps in, all smiles. 'Yes,' he says, 'you'll have an ouzo with me. Beth, please!'

'Really, no more. Thank you.'

'No? Let me tell you my idea!'

His idea is this. Thursdays he has live music. Open mic. Some Thursday, I must bring my sister, the famous one, and we'll hear her sing.

38 Visit

That was the third bad night in a row. I've definitely overslept: the sun won't get much higher at this time of year. I don't know whether it's my dream, or the noise, which has woken me; a series of gentle thumps with regular pauses in between. Or maybe it was the noise that generated the dream. Because that's my sister, hauling herself up the stairs one step at a time, with her sticks, which she'll be carrying in one hand, knocking against every riser. Then a clatter. I open the door and there she is, wedged in the narrow staircase, only a couple of steps down from the landing, where she's already thrown them. She's a rascal. Looking very pleased with herself.

We both know what to do. She heaves herself up the last two steps, and waits for a moment while I fetch a chair and place it on the landing where she needs it. She grips the back of the seat and uses it to steady herself. I hold the sticks in one hand and with the other arm help her in.

Once on her feet, she grins. She's in turquoise today. She knows I like that colour.

Inside, she looks around the flat, just as Mum would do, checking for mess, and pronounces, 'Nice.' My bed tee shirt draws a frown, though.

'Bad night.'

'I tested you.'

'You texted me? Oh, sorry, I was awake all night, and then I've been asleep all morning, and I never…'

I've darted into the bedroom for my phone, but it's dead.

'It was out of charge anyway. But I've been thinking about you… We do need to talk.'

The last time we spoke was on the phone, about Uncle Stelios's invitation. She bit my hand off: *yes, when?* I had to persuade her to give it a couple of weeks. When I raised the competition entry, she made a lame excuse and said she couldn't talk now, bye, love you.

I ask, 'Are you getting a set list together, then?'

She grins and the stupid fringe almost bounces off her face when she nods: 'Oh yes.'

'How did you get here, anyway?'

There's mischief in her eyes. 'John brought me. He's parking the car. We've got something to ask you. Two things.'

'John's coming? I better get dressed.' I zip into the bedroom and grab yesterday's clothes. Alice sits on the sofa and we talk across the room. She's very perky today.

'And you came all this way to see me, when you could have just Face Timed?'

'I wanted to see what you'd done with the flat.'

'I haven't done anything. I'm keeping it nice for Jo.'

At speed, I brush my teeth, comb my hair, and join her. It's good to be side by side again. She gently pushes her shoulder against mine, I push gently back, and we slide back and forth a couple of times.

'About the competition, Al…'

'Oh, that.' She sounds casual, even bored; it's not what she came to talk about.

'Have you thought about what could happen?'

'What, you mean, it might win? That'd be a blow, wouldn't it,' she growls. Here we are again. I'm trying to be serious, and she just meets it with sarcasm.

'I hope it doesn't!'

'What?'

'I hope it doesn't win, Alice, for your sake! I mean imagine. Imagine the shame if it all came out that you'd cheated.'

'The shame? *Cheated?*'

'It'd be terrible. People would say horrid things about you. You bent the rules. Because you didn't do the whole thing, did you? You didn't score it, or harmonise it, or… anything.'

I can feel her stiffening into anger. I shift on the couch so as to make her look at me. She's not impressed.

'You and rules, honestly,' she sighs. The family cliché raises my temperature in an instant.

'And what about *me*? You've just pushed me aside.'

She bites her lip, and tells me straight: 'This isn't about us, it's about the music. It's a good piece and it deserves a life. Wouldn't you like to know what people think of it?'

'No. No. I don't care about it! As far as I'm concerned, you can have it, it's yours…You needn't worry, I'm not going to tell anybody, nobody's going to find out the truth from me…'

'And that's the point,' she says. She's sharpening every word to stab me: 'If you don't believe in it, you don't deserve to own it. *I'm* the one who believes in it, and that's why it belongs to *me*.'

I flop back and think, why do we keep doing this? All our arguments seem to end like this, with one killer blow which leaves me winded, incoherent, dazed.

Alice lets her head fall back into the comfy sofa and gazes at the ceiling, then round the room.

'These colours are very you.'

'Really? Blue?'

'Mm.' We fall silent, and I've started to wonder what's going on with her and John when she announces: 'This is a good location. I don't like my new house.'

'What, seriously? You don't like the house in Chameleon Close? But it's lovely. You've got everything you need.'

I'm shocked. After all the preparation, the ringing round and checking out and chasing funding and everything… Not to mention leaving Mum all alone when Dad was at sea.

'You left Mum all alone,' she tells me.

'D'you want to go back to Mum and Dad's, then?'

Alice peers at my bedroom door.

'I could move in here.'

'But Alice, what about your chair? There's hardly room in the hall. And even this room's not big enough for you to move around, everything's too tight… and where would you sleep?'

'Show me round,' she says, grabs one stick and with a huge swinging motion, gets to her feet.

'What's wrong with Chameleon Close?'

'Vilma. Zoe.'

'But you get on so well. They love you.'

'Zoe's tone-deaf.'

'That's a horrible thing to say, Alice, nobody's tone-deaf. There's no such thing.'

'Zoe can't sing. Vilma sings like a cat. I can sing with you. You can play.' The logic pleases her.

It only demands a few paces to show her the rest of the flat – the bathroom with the frosted window, the spare room which is half-filled by my desk and a load of kit piled on the bed, the main bedroom so cramped that she frowns. We step back into the living room and she tells me, 'You can have the sofa.'

I play along and say, 'We could always get a bunk bed. Not great for the love life, though.'

We slept on a bunk bed once when we were very little, on holiday near Caernarfon, and we both thought it was brilliant. We took turns, we didn't fight. I remember the weight and the lovely free feeling of my arm hanging down, her fingers meeting mine in the dark.

She frowns. 'Why d'you move up here? You're so high up. On top of everyone. Why d'you put yourself so far away?'

'Independence,' I say.

'Ivory tower,' she bats back.

'It seemed like a good deal at time, didn't it, with no deposit.'

'OK. Where's the studio?'

'Recording studio? You've seen it. I haven't even got a proper piano. I'm 100% digital here.'

'I'm not. I'm real. Me and my band. We could practise here.'

Holy cow, she's serious.

'Alice, it's not practical, with the stairs.'

She breathes out noisily and the frown deepens.

Now I'm wondering where John has got to, parking his car. I put some music on and we just hang out on the couch together, side by side. Me, Alice, and Hildegard of Bingen. Soothing, seamless, sweet and easy. Until she tells me, 'You need a lodger. You could use the money. Since you kicked Jaz out.'

'Jaz? That wasn't ever about money.' I've let her rile me again. 'Anyway, what about *your* boyfriend?'

'I haven't got a boyfriend.' Her denial is dead-pan, and she doesn't move a muscle.

'Yes, you have, I know you have. What about this John, then?'

I turn slightly to face her, and watch her embryonic frown: just the small, curved print of an upturned thumbnail at the place Mum calls the third eye. But her cheeks are rising to a fury.

'He's my guitar.'

'Course he is.'

I ought to be ashamed for teasing her.

I lean my head and my shoulder against hers to ask: 'Is he a toody, or a threedy?'

'He's a threedy.' I can hear that her answer is filtered through a smile.

The space that's grown between us in these last few months is more than geography, more even than the adolescent years of *I've got, you've got,* which has lowered over everything like a big dark wardrobe full of stuff you know is there and never want to take out and examine. Now that we're older, that space between us is packed with other intimacies. Things which trouble us, and which neither of us want to share.

I've seen and heard this John on my phone, but we haven't met and I'm looking forward to seeing him pop out of the video to reveal the superhero within. I can't help feeling protective of my sister, even though I like to think she's sufficiently savvy not to be led up any garden paths here. But as Mum and that French bloke said, reason is a stranger to the reasons of the heart.

At last we hear the street door, then a knock on the bottom door, *'Allo?'* and a steady, even tread on the stairs; the top door opens. John is one of those tidy blokes, quite small but athletic-looking, clean-shaven, drainpipes and fitted puffa jacket, with short hair that's gone sort of bubbly on top, as if there's a little bit of personality trying to get out. That Beatle cut which Alice wanted for the band was never going to work on him.

He looks at Alice, then me, then Alice again, then back to me as he says, 'All right then? Great. Here we are. So. Beth? Pleased to meet you. Oh God, parking round here, eh? It's a mare. I've got Alice's badge, like, but even so, it's mad down there. Honest to God, it's unreal. Anyway, we're all sorted now. Great!'

He's got one of those round faces that creases everywhere when he speaks, and his mouth probably looks wider than it is because it works so hard, especially with *great, mare, unreal.* It reminds me of the fortune-telling things we used to make with folded paper when we were kids: open, shut, open, shut, never still. When he says *great*, he rolls his r's in a way Mum only tolerates from outside the family; if we spoke like that, she'd have a fit.

'Hi John,' I say. 'Tea? Coffee?'

'Tea, great, cheers. I'm gasping for a brew. One sugar, please.'

'No sugar in the house, sorry.'

'Oh, go on then, I'll have it al denty.'

'Have a seat,' I say, as I get up and head across the room to make our drinks.

He ignores the low armchair and takes my place on the sofa next to Alice. 'Ooh, you've warmed it for me, lovely! It's parky out there, though.'

One arm rests along the top of the sofa; he doesn't wrap it round her shoulders.

She takes a huge breath and says, 'So, my big ask number one.'

The two things they wanted to ask me, the reason they're here.

John's voice is reedy, squeaky. 'You haven't asked her yet? Worr've you two been talking about all this time?'

'You. So, Beth. About this open mic at the Aphrodite Bar.'

'Mm hm.'

'You know we mostly do covers?'

'Mm hm.'

'You need keyboards and we haven't got keyboards in the band.'

'Right.'

'So we need you, really. In the band.'

I'm wrong-footed, and protest, 'You've already got Vilma and John.'

Alice shakes her head. 'We need a keyboard player. For a real gig. Also, I want drums, not the shaky egg.'

'You got a drummer lined up?'

'It was that shaky egg lost us the licence. If you ask me.'

'Vilma's a bit weedy on the old shaky egg, but at least you can hardly hear it, so it shouldn't put the rest of you off. It'll be serious damage if you let her loose on drums.'

'We need keyboards. That way we get drums, two for one. And we need the best.' She tilts her head upward and grins.

John's face is making horizontal pleats again. 'She's right, you know.'

'What will Vilma think, if I come barging into the band?'

'Never mind her. It's about you and me. You and me should work together.'

I can't argue with that. I change tack.

'I've got so much on, Alice…'

'Oh right. Like playing for the choir. You've got time for them, but you haven't got time for me.'

That's a low punch. I need us to make up, though.

'Look, I'll help out this once. I'll give you two rehearsals max, and the gig. That's my best offer.'

Alice turns to ask John, 'Will that be enough?'

'Why not?' he says. 'Beth's a professional. It's like doing a session, isn't it? But it's up to you, Alice. You're the boss.'

She beams and her eyes pop open. 'Yeah,' she says with a little jut of the chin, 'I'm the boss. Sister, you're hired.'

The kettle has boiled and I make the tea. I'm in two minds about this band. Alice, yes. But Vilma and the nice lad who isn't her boyfriend, *per-lease.* I stare at the soggy teabag I've extracted from John's drink and foresee artistic differences ahead. It's not lost on me, either, that this is the second time I've taken on a job I didn't want because somebody made me feel guilty.

'So,' says my sister once we've all got our mugs of tea to warm our hands on, 'Second big ask. You know our anthem thing?'

'*Silence?*'

'*Dread,* yeah. D'you mind if we do it with the band?'

'How will that work?'

'Mm…me and John've got some ideas. We might change the ending though. D'you mind?'

I give an encouraging glare. 'Well, it's your music. Do it. Do whatever you want with it.'

'Whatever I want?'

'Whatever you want. It's all yours.'

Utter delight suffuses my sister's face, and makes her eyes sparkle. She pronounces herself *made up,* starts telling jokes, and I can see she's going to be in high spirits for the rest of the day. I might as well shake off my bad night and join in. We *are* a team, Alice and I. The three of us burble along, chatting about this and that, and John lets slip that they're looking for somewhere to rehearse now that Zoe – the supposedly tone-deaf Chameleon Close flatmate who can't sing and isn't in the band – has made an official complaint about the noise. I can see where this is leading. There's only the Spar shop downstairs to annoy, and I'm feeling generous. Sure, I say, you can practise here. Some of the time.

39 Sunk

The day after my dad's back home, I phone him. We've already exchanged texts, so I know he's alright. We always make that assumption about each other anyway: it's a kind of pact. At the start of every tour, there's a look that passes between us that says everything, that reminds me how to behave while he's gone and what are the things that matter. Then he's off.

'Dad… can I ask you about something?'

'Ask away.'

When he gets back from a tour, he's zonked out for the best part of a week. At 2 pm, he's probably still in his pyjamas, catching up on the rugby. I rush without a breath from question one to question two.

'Are you busy this afternoon? Can I buy you a pint?'

There's a pause, and I can guess the expression on his face as he pretends to himself he's mulling it over.

'Aye, go on, I've got time for a swift one. Your mum's down the centre, balancing her chakras. Each to his own.'

We meet by the Phil and I steer Dad to the Cally. He loves the kind of city boozers he can't take my mum to; an old building with a proper cellar, where the seats make you sit up straight, and there's no danger of a sticky carpet, because there's no carpet. For him, it's pure nostalgia: he can pretend he's a young seaman again, and that his old bones don't mind the lack of upholstery. He'll turn a blind eye to the vegan burgers. And of course, any pub with shipping connections has an extra pull for him. Even if the real *Caledonia* sank.

It's quiet, in the late afternoon. It'll be heaving later, and full of music, because they're having a Cajun night. We sit by the window; it's overcast but bright, every wrinkle on my father's face is equally visible, and there's a puffiness about the eyes. He's pale underneath the tan. When we've both said 'Cheers,' and drawn that first pensive, testing mouthful, Dad licks the froth off his top lip and says, 'Alright. Out with it. What d'ya wanna know?'

'It's about when we were little. I remember some things about when it happened. Like that special nurse at the hospital, and the cards I made, and some of what they did at school, but that's mostly because of what you've all told me...'

'Oh, that school... They didn't have a clue, did they?'
'No.'

'She was mustard, your mother. Stormed in, all guns blazing, because without so much as a by your leave, they'd given Alice's desk to some kid… without any thought to *your* feelings, Beth… Like she'd died. And even if she had… Your mother gave 'em down the banks that day.'

'Yes… Only I don't really remember that. It's just a family legend. I don't even remember hitting that kid. Or the kid. At all.' The cuckoo child in Alice's seat. 'I don't remember any of that.'

'You were in shock, love. We all were.'

'Where did Mum go?'

'She didn't go anywhere, love.'

'The way I remember it, Dad, she wasn't always there.'

'She had a lot on her plate.'

He stretches his hand across the table to hold mine, and turns his head ostensibly to stare across the street, raising his chin. He doesn't want anyone in the bar to see. Cars go past.

'Dad… someone told me something… Remember when you bought the piano? That the piano was meant to be for Alice.'

He hesitates. 'Well… It was for both of you, wasn't it? And for your mother, too. That old one of your nan's was shot. Past mending, they said at Rushworth's. It would've needed a whole new action.'

'But Alice could already play, couldn't she? She taught herself, didn't she? Dad, I don't remember! I don't remember what she did! I do remember both of us messing around on the old piano, playing chopsticks and stuff. But she was the one with the real talent, wasn't she? She was the one who wanted lessons. I didn't realise. All these years.'

I can feel a crease in my throat. My dad frowns, which doesn't happen much. His broad forehead seems to press down and squash the whole of his face. He's stopped looking out at the street. He's thinking what to say. Seeking a channel.

'You both had talent. Course you did.' His voice rises in pitch, and drops in volume: 'And anyway, who says we bought the piano for Alice? Who's told you this, Beth?'

'Jenny Johns.'

'Oh aye, the voice of the valleys…Why've you let that get to you? What's the matter? What is it?'

He must have realised before I did that I was going to cry my eyes out, and that once I start, I won't stop.

'It should've been her, Dad! It should've been Alice! Studying and playing and writing music and winning prizes and going on foreign trips. Only if it'd been her, she wouldn't be a runner-up! She'd win every time! She's the one with the instinct.'

'Oh, Beth, love! But look at all that's happened since. You love music, and you've stuck at it. Everything you've done is real. And nobody's more proud of you than Alice.'

My tears are rolling down his cheeks. And anybody who can see us through the window or from across the bar is welcome, welcome, welcome to stare.

That's it. I've said it out loud: it should have been her. These last months have been a series of modulations, groping towards a once-distant, now compelling key. We part company on the pavement below my flat in Arctic Terrace, with a big long hug and patting hands to say goodbye. Upstairs, it's even colder than the street, so I swap my coat for another jumper, tip a carton of soup into a mug, heat it up and take it to bed, to get warm. I switch the radio on to a brief silence which turns out to be the pause before the piece starts, and find I've stumbled on exactly the sort of slushy music that facilitates a good long cry. This is healthy: I've got a lot to weep out. It's slow, a violin solo against muted strings and broken chords on the harp. High romantic, sugary, wallowy. I don't know what this music is, and I'm surprised when a voice comes in. Also, the soprano's first line has the shape of an ending, not a beginning. She comments on the violin melody rather than joining it, as if she's settling but not quite settled yet, like those little pats on the back and arms that my dad and I exchanged just now.

There's a modulation, the violin stops, and now the voice has taken the lead, and works through a series of harmonic shifts that feel like thoughts which gather and re-form, once the crying's done.

It says to me, life is crap, but it may not always be.

The soprano line is left hanging, unresolved, and it's the violin that reaches up high to turn off the light.

Applause. The announcer identifies it as Richard Strauss: *Morgen*. I probably ought not to like Richard Strauss. I once told my mother it was emotionally incontinent. I'm not at all certain this piece is in good taste. I want to hear it again, immediately.

I open my laptop, track down the song, then listen to it over and over in different performances: Jessye Norman, Renée Fleming. That first soprano phrase is nearly, but tantalisingly not quite, the cadence that belongs to the preceding violin melody. Which is searching and beautiful, but also confident, underpinning the whole piece as if it were the distillation of a sort of wisdom.

Eventually I look at the words. *Und morgen wird die Sonne wieder scheinen.* And the sun shall rise again tomorrow.

He got me. Snared me with his word-setting.

40 Crossroads

Perhaps identity is less who you are, than where you think you are and how you think you got here. How you notate your past, at any given time; the changing ways you constantly re-write it.

Wednesday lunch break, and I go to sit in the round cathedral, Paddy's wigwam. It's the best place I know for stepping outside myself; you can't really think, because it's such a hot bath for the senses. Incense greets you, more or less subtle depending on the timing of your visit. By day, the light show never disappoints; shafts of intense blue from the side windows warm the building, and you're soothed, even by the single blood-red stream that spreads across the circular pews. The lantern both conceals and reveals the play of clouds and weather outside; you're in a bubble, which a sunbeam can transform. On a dull day, you might be under water. A rain shower can be the perfect slow crescendo whose beginning was unheard. I love the way sound curls round on itself, in any circular building. Small things carry, the scuffle of a shoe lingers and softens. But anything hard – say, a walking stick clattering to the floor, dropped by a doddery nun – will shock and multiply; the squeak of a trainer can be unbearable. You recognise the tunes of speech, more than the words; and blessedly, a cathedral is pretty much an argument-free zone.

My guess is, half the visitors are good Catholics, the rest are opportunists, thrill-seekers and impostors like me. The air is thick with the sense of other purposes than mine. I sit down, settle, and abandon myself to whatever the tide washes into the cathedral today.

Rich blue light. These are short wavelengths – high energy; and yet somehow the brain flips this over, and translates it all to calm.

Time looses its moorings. My breathing slows.

Gradually, one ill-defined, strong feeling tugs at me, like shallow waves lapping against an idea. *Unison.*

When it feels right, I get up and step out onto the flat of the concrete ziggurat, where I'm met by weak February sunshine and a painless breeze. At the top of the steps, I stare for a moment down Hope Street thinking, maybe unison is what I seek. In music, in life.

Not to be alone, but to be at one with something... or someone... else.

I don't interrogate this feeling, just carry it with me, down the concrete staircase, and across the road. As I walk past the Everyman, an idiot steps out of the Street Cafe, right in front of me. Jaz bloody Ander.

'Beth! Hi!'

'Hi.' He falls in step with me, uninvited.

'Wi-fi's down. I'm going to try the Old Blind School.'

'Right.'

'So, I've re-drafted the novel.'

'Oh yeah?'

'I fixed the context. Because, like I said, it was all wrong. The setting.'

'Good.'

I'm rude. I shouldn't be rude. I'm not going to lift my eyes from the pavement ahead, but I ask, 'Did you fix your heroine? The one who needed a wooh thing?'

His tone implies a problem dismissed, oh, weeks ago.

'Yes, yes. Done all that.' The bag carrying his laptop whacks me in the side, once, twice, as he adjusts it on his shoulder. How does this man manage to fidget even when he's walking? And he talks. 'What I'm struggling with...'

I knew it. Here we go.

'It's like, character and how it drives plot?'

The traffic lights force a stop at the crossroads. He must be thrilled, he's got me now. 'Thing is, I've got a great plot twist, only it's completely out of character for my protagonist; so, I'm thinking, can you get away with it, so long as you've explained it, or foreshadowed it, or something?' His tone changes: 'So, I'm reading this book. Turns out, personality isn't fixed. People change all the time.' I can tell his hands are dancing around. 'So, introversion, extroversion, classic example. Depends where you are, and who you're with.'

'You mean, that's why people don't shout in a library? Who knew?'

He makes a teacherish sort of noise, half-sigh, half-tut. 'No, that's social norms. The world has conditioned you to be introverted in a library.' I've annoyed him. Hah. 'But look, the point is, this. Plot-wise, I'm thinking, at this point in the story, it would be great if my character stole a car and drove to Harwich.'

'Harwich. Exotic. Local colour.' Although actually the east coast *is* exotic, because the sun sets in the wrong place, over the land.

The beep beeps, the lights have changed, we cross Myrtle Street in the company of a couple of Chinese scousers who are cheerfully mid-barney, and an old lady muttering to herself.

'Harwich for the Dutch drugs ring and the sand flats, actually.' We reach the other side, and he just stops stock still, so as to prose on a bit, and turns to face me. 'Only… my character wouldn't steal a car, my reader won't believe it… Except maybe they ought to, because maybe my character has decided to be someone else, and she can if she wants, right?' He readjusts his bag, and his brow clears. 'And in a way, on a deep level, shifting identity is what this novel is about.'

Holy shit. What mighty bollocks.

'You can afford to be experimental, then.'

When he says 'Yes,' he says it in a surprisingly middle-aged, sensible sort of way. 'Yes. Within limits.'

There's something shifty in all this.

'Are you aiming to sell this book?'

He's indignant. 'It's a serious project. I can't afford to stray too far outside the tropes of the genre, if you know what I mean.'

I don't.

'Seems to me, so long as your readers have read the same books as you have, you're home and dry.' I smile straight at him. 'You need to cross. I'm going this way. Bye.'

'Wait…' he says. 'I haven't told you…'

I look up and notice he looks a bit older. In the flat light, I can see little lines running from the side of his nose down to the edges of his mouth.

'First up, Beth, I want to say how brilliant it is, what you're doing with Alice… What you and Alice are doing together.'

I don't know what I was expecting him to say, but it certainly wasn't that.

'Thank you.'

'Yeah.' He makes a sound like a piston, or the air brakes of a bus, expelling a breath rapidly and with exaggerated force through his nose; he's uncomfortable about something.

I hate silences, so I ask, 'Just checking I've got you right… What is it you think we're doing exactly? Me and Alice?'

'The music, of course. Creating music together.'

'It's what we do.' It brings an easy smile to my face. I just loved saying that. 'But how did you know?'

'Oh, I follow her. Look, I was wondering… because I've got this contact, right, it's a guy who runs a video production company – I mean they're small, but they're on the up, and small means it's quite personal, not one of these faceless corporations – I've got connections, and there's a little pot of money going at the moment for the arts, and I was wondering if there might be something we could do... together? To bring Alice to a wider public, you know? You and Alice. Your initiative.'

'I don't understand. What do you mean?'

'So, there's the City Council doling out funding for access initiatives, because obviously access is the big thing, and these guys have got a small budget for a YouTube channel – just short videos – which is a win-win to promote what they do and also to showcase people's work – so that's a platform, right? And say they were to give a grant to you, which isn't impossible, I'd be proposing we expand that and think big because I truly believe there's scope for a really interesting documentary there, you and Alice, twins separated by a terrible accident but here you are years later united in... Art.'

'Jaz,' I say, 'This platform costs nothing. You can do it on a phone.'

'Yes, but it could be so much more professional...'

'And as for the music. We don't need funding for an access initiative. Alice is my sister. We just do it.'

'Yes but, you know, long term... you could maybe scale it up... Reach people. People like Alice.'

'Other people are doing that already. Hands Free Music, for a start.'

My next gambit is a dangerous one but I need to make a point.

'Look, Jaz. Remember rule one in the sodding novel?'

I judge a pause: short enough to stop the flow but not long enough for him to interrupt. 'Motivation. Your protagonist has to want something. Well, I've worked out what my motivation is, Jaz. And I have to tell you, it isn't love of humanity. It's not general, it's specific. It's about my sister. I don't want to do things for other people. I don't even want to do things for her. I want to do *my* things *with* her. I want us to do things together.' I'm thinking, like we used to.

He makes a whimpering noise which might be the start of speech so I cut him off.

'And as for *your* motivation... You may read the right papers. But you're no do-gooder. Oh, but I'm guessing we'd need someone to guide us through the media minefield, wouldn't we? To articulate our message?'

He shakes his head. 'I'm only trying to help, Beth. To make amends, because I know how much I upset you all with that article. Although I still don't see why that was such a big deal. But...' He shrugs at my loss. We smile at each other and go our separate ways.

His revelation of the obvious, and the shifting nature of personality, though, is almost psychically in tune with my mood.

I quite like the idea that you might be half way through your life and decide to change it. Take a sudden turn. Surprise everybody.

41 Artists

Today there's a window-cleaner outside the faculty building. He's got a snake of yellow hosepipe leading to a long pole with a sort of brush thing on the end. It's dripping water and he doesn't want me to trip up, so he steps aside and tells me he only cleans windows part time, because his big thing is writing poetry. He's got a new collection out, called *What's in a Name*. The proceeds go to charity. His name's Jaz

MacMahon and he does customised birthday poems, printed up in a nice card, to order.

'I know a bloke called Jaz. He's a writer, too. What's your Jaz short for?'

'James. Like 007, only I'm licensed to chill.'

'This one's Jaleel.'

'Jaleel, eh? *Jaleel, Jaleel, what's the deal? Is he fake or is he real?*' He laughs at himself. 'Haven't gorran off switch, have I? What's he write, this Jaz?'

'Pretentious crap. Very niche.' We laugh. 'But, fair's fair, at least he's doing his thing, eh?'

'What's your name anyway? I'll do one for you.'

'Beth.'

He grimaces. 'Oh eh, you haven't gorra lot going for you there. I mean, breath and death, that's about the long and short of it, isn't it?'

'Crystal meth? Maybe not. It's Bethany.'

'Aw, no, you got me there.'

'Anyway, nice to meet you. Good luck with the poems.'

I head for the door and he heads for the hosepipe, but the sudsy, soapy water is now irradiated by his bliss, the bliss of being recognised as a maker of art; and any lurking dampness when he changes out of his clothes tonight will be a reminder of the conversation he had with a young woman at the University who recognised the artist beneath the disguise.

They're all at it, round here, making stuff, making art.

To all intents and purposes, I too am an undercover artist. My cover involves, this morning, a double booking for a mixer desk and a boss in meltdown because she's lost something, and it must be something important because she won't tell me what it is. Something's bothering her about this first performance she's got coming up. Worse, since I deleted Jaz Ander from contacts and blocked him from my already withered social media, I find he's used his journalistic skills to worm his way into my work account. He's started by contacting the Prof about this access initiative, and of course she's pinged the email to me, with a note saying 'Open the doors, yes in principle to using our facilities, find out what they need, I've given him your contact.' So I can't ignore it.

He's written to ask are we already involved in any access initiatives, in which case, would we like to showcase our work, blah-di blah; or if not, would we consider supporting musicians with disabilities in another way by sharing our facilities?

He knows quite well that nobody accesses our facilities without swinging by me, in my minion capacity of pencil monitress and key holder.

It's a great idea, though. How could any decent person block it? There are lots of people like Alice, who want to make music. In fact, that was what she asked me, didn't she, when she visited my flat: *Where's the studio?*

Why wasn't I the one making overtures to Prof Laing? I'm stupid not to have thought of this.

Is there anything worse than ending up in the debt of someone you despise? Someone you'd choke to thank? I'm choking now.

42 Small world

Later, at my desk, I'm trying to imagine myself in Alice's band when Petra Laing turns up and announces that she's going to be in a meeting all afternoon. 'It's not in the diary,' she says, in a tone which implicitly swears me to secrecy. I should only text if it's urgent, which it won't be. And she's gone. Quick as she can, which is not very. The light stick, the heavy foot. Tha daa, tha daa, tha daa.

I slope behind her desk. Well, she said I could. She's got twin monitors and she knows how useful that is to me. And I *am* on faculty business, with the studio bookings going bananas and the end of semester looming. I log in and while I wait for the system to load, I enjoy swinging around in her chair. It's more solid than mine, mesh so as to keep you cool in summer, with all the extras – lumbar support, arm rests that go up, down, back, forward, swivel to the diagonal. It was me who sold her on the idea, when I realised she was needing the silver-topped cane for more than just the image. It's a real gamer's chair. I don't dare adjust it because I'd never get it back to the way it ought to be. And Petra Laing would know.

The swings get stronger until the side of my foot thumps against something. She's left her handbag, and I've just spread its contents all over the floor. On my hands and knees, I scrabble to pick everything up and return it to the bag; beautiful, in blue leather, and worn over years to softness, it gapes generously. No phone; she must have that with her. A fountain pen, pencils, notebook; a locker key on a leather fob; two lipsticks, unexpectedly heavy in my hand, in a brand I don't recognise; and a wrapped sweet that's got squashed and sticky, leaking sugar. It's the sort you get given in restaurants; in fact, I've seen this before: *Aphrodite Bar.* Uncle Stelios's place. Small world.

43 Pulling strings

Mum and I ended up arguing again tonight. She said I was over-reacting and told me to sleep on it, but of course, now, it's keeping me awake. To her way of thinking, the facts are simple: the twins wrote an anthem, for four-part choir, but they were barred from entering it in a competition jointly; therefore she's asked Theo if the Lyceum Singers can perform it, and he said yes, without even seeing the music. Very generous of him, and so supportive. What's the matter with me, asks Mum, who thought I'd be pleased, and why am I being so mean in blocking my sister?

Alice can't have told her she's uploaded the files and entered the competition, passing it off as all her own work. I'm not going to snitch. But Theo knows we wrote it together, and Mum does, and given her legendary discretion the whole choir will too; so there could be consequences.

How awful, if it won, and the Northallen Choir found out that some other outfit got to give the first performance? We could be sued.

No. Alice could be sued.

I warned her: she could end up seriously exposed on social media.

Or I could, if *my* name ended up on the top of *her* music, which is how some people would read it, wouldn't they, and they'd all pile in on *me.* That would be the end of me.

But I couldn't say any of this to Mum, so I had to fall back on a different line of reasoning – a variation well-rehearsed in the set piece argument on my ingratitude. I go over and over our conversation in the car.

'This is embarrassing. You pulled strings. You put Theo in an impossible position. How could he refuse?' 'You ought to be grateful.' 'How can I be grateful? You embarrassed him into it. It doesn't count.' 'I helped you. I just, sort of, nudged him. What if it had been Petra Laing who'd pulled strings? That would be a completely different matter, wouldn't it? That'd be fine, a leg-up from Petra Laing.' 'She's an eminent professional.' 'Oh right, because we're only an amateur choir. We're not good enough for you. But look here, Beth. If you two had been able to win that competition, or say you'd even got an agent and a music publisher, who do you think would be performing your work? Amateurs, that's who.'

I stare at the dark ceiling because screwing up your eyes as you try to get to sleep is what makes them hurt the next day. My dad taught me that.

Was she right, though? Objectively: ought I to be grateful?

Objectively... the best thing that has come out of all her machinations is Theo, but I don't dare acknowledge that. She might weigh in, and try engineering things to get the two of us together, which she is well capable of doing, because she has this motherly way of seeing what I want and trying to give it to me. If she knew how often I think about him, she'd be in there, setting us up, because let's face it, Theo has every attribute she'd approve of in a boyfriend. Musically educated. Polite. Non-boring, non-British, and a polyglot.

A pale lozenge sweeps across the room, the ceiling, with the note of a taxi engine and swoosh of wheels on tarmac. Come and gone.

Back to the point. Another thing that wound me up was way she went about it; she didn't consult us first, just asked Theo straight out; so now we've got no choice, have we?

Who's she doing it for anyway? Did she do it for Alice's sake, or mine? Because we can't have Alice disappointed, can we. *I let Alice down,* remember.

She's only showing off to her mates in the choir. Me and Alice are currency in a game of parental one-upmanship. Now that Ffi Johns has got her promotion with the Estate Agents.

When we drew up outside the flat, she said, 'Well, it's up to you. Sleep on it. If you don't want us to perform your music, pull out. This won't be the first time you've embarrassed me, and I'm certain it won't be the last.' Emotional blackmail. Plus, she tells me, I'm the one who's going to have to explain it to my sister. *Just make sure you do it face to face this time.* Well, here I am, sleeping on it.

The choir's going to hate it, anyway. And what must Theo think of me?

Fat lot Alice would care. She's unembarrassable, that's her secret weapon.

Did he really agree, just like that, without even seeing the score? Is he squirming in his bed tonight, wondering how to get out of an awkward obligation?

I can only think how much he's going to hate it. Although he did like the trio I wrote for the Arcana Prize. *Cracking fab.* OK Beth, admit it, you've prised a smile out of that tight-lipped gob. Now go to sleep.

But it wasn't meant to happen like this. I wanted to turn up casually to a rehearsal and have somebody say, 'Hey, Beth, what's this about the Emily Dickinson piece? I caught it on the radio…' I need them to *want* to perform it. Mum's just… forced it on them.

I'd love to do a Mozartian Wunderbrat: turn up at Faith Place unannounced, and say, 'Yes I'll make music for you, but first tell me you like me.'

He might not get the joke, though. You shouldn't foist humour onto strangers. Or foreigners with whose culture you are unfamiliar.

He might take me seriously. He might take me in his arms and carry me off to his private apartment. It's delicious not knowing how that would feel.

I'll have to go back to Fairfield tomorrow, talk to Alice, find out what she thinks. Although I can guess. She'll say, go for it, who cares about the rules?

No need to switch the light on, it only hurts your eyes. I grab my fleece and scrabble around for the two thick socks which lie somewhere on the floor near the bed. That'll do. Once my already chilly feet are further protected from the cold, I head for the bathroom. The air is different, sharp and faintly medical. I fundamentally resent the street light outside this window, but tonight it's useful; the distorted blob of white behind the frosted glass, which looks a bit like a spaceship, throws an icy pallor over the walls, and makes it light enough to get the gist.

I stare at myself in the oblong mirror. My neck, wrists and hands are skeletal and pale. It only takes a little while, then there's my twin, as narrow-shouldered as me, with her big familiar eyes under the terrible, alien fringe; she's smiling, and singing a gentle tune to la, in C major, four bars' worth.

It's going to be a yes, isn't it? She says yes to everything.

Back to bed.

Oh no, the buses have started. I'll never get to sleep now.

My nightmare-filled insomnia must have given way to a dreamless sleep. First light brings clarity: I don't want us to pressure Theo, and it would help sort out the muddle if he declined. There are loads of possible excuses he could make – wrong forces, bad timing – to avoid having to say, no thanks, your music's crap. I send him a pdf of our score with a note saying, *caveat emptor,* let the buyer beware, if you want to change your mind we completely understand.

He pings back an hour later, *that's all Latin to me,* smiley face. And half an hour after that: *why would I change my mind? It's great. I love it. I believe in yous.*

The sore-thumb cathedral tower which I can see across the roofs is slammed by a sudden surge of light. It glows pink, and I'm ecstatic. It was obvious. Why *wouldn't* he love it? Why wouldn't the choir love it? Why wouldn't I be *pleased*? Although it still leaves us with the problem of attribution.

The more I think about it, the clearer it is that I'm going to have to ask for my name to be removed. I can say, it was Alice's tune and she deserves to take the credit. Mum won't like it, though. She'll think I'm posturing. I can imagine what she'd say: *you don't have confidence in your own work so you're passing it off as your sister's mistake, just in case. Getting your apology in early.*

I can withstand that barrage. But it's a ridiculous situation, wanting *Silence* to be good enough for successful performance, and not good enough to win a competition.

I walk to the window. The clearing sky means the play of light on the world beyond this flat is positively magical.

I Face Time my sister. We'll work something out.

Squashed by the phone, she looks drained as well as distorted.

'Mum told me about the choir doing *Silence.*'

'Is she still calling it that? *Silence?* S'pose she would be. I officially re-named it. *Dread.* Yeah, she says they're going to do it in the summer.'

The Lyceum Singers tend to save the lighter stuff for summertime. There is nothing more nauseating than a classical choir 'letting its hair down.' Popping the consonants back in place, as if the Beatles dropped them by accident. Not that I'd dare programme our piece next to that Bruckner motet they rehearsed the other week; maybe the summer concert is where me and Alice belong, after all. From the corner of my eye, I'm distracted by a flurry of pigeons; they descend on the ridge of the terrace opposite. The sun hits the iridescence on their beautifully ugly necks, all those colours that don't go and shouldn't be there.

'Look, Alice, I've been thinking. It's great to get a performance and everything. But we've got to get my name off this. I'm going to say, it's your tune, so it's your music, I just took it down from your dictation. Only, if it is a finalist with the Northallen Festival, well, it's like I said…'

'You'd do that for me?'

'Us. Yes. Mum'll think I'm just being horrible, or neurotic.'

'And Theo? *He* knows. You told him all about us.'

I'm going to be embarrassed. But I can't let a bad thing happen.

'Look, Alice, remember, when you said, you're the one who believes in this music, so it belongs to you? You're right. It's like… the judgement of Solomon, you know? Two women are fighting over whose baby it is, and King Solomon says, OK then, cut the baby in half; then the real mum backs down and says, no, no, she can have the baby. So, King Solomon only said it, because he knows the real mum is the one who cares about it, and wants the baby to live. You're the one who believes in our work. It isn't enough to create something you think is beautiful; you have to believe it has a right to life outside your own head. I'm useless at that.'

She frowns, and snorts. 'This is weird. I've been awake all night worrying. About the rules. About what you said, about how people might have a go at me – although actually, Beth, they might hate both of us.' It's sweet she thinks she's telling me something I hadn't realised. 'And I know I always skit you about following the rules, but they're only to make sure it's fair for everybody. So… this cut-the-baby-in-half story of yours is a bit weird. Because first thing this morning I emailed them. I've withdrawn from the competition.'

'Oh, Allie…'

'I did the right thing,' she says. 'I thought, this is a dilemma, what would Beth do?'

We're silent for a while, staring into each other's faces. Then I realise: 'Mum doesn't need to know anything about any of this, does she? We won't have to explain.'

My sister's eyes are suddenly awake. 'Nobody needs to know,' she says with a wicked grin.

'We've got our first performance, then. Open goal! Strike the viol! Halle bloody lujah!'

'Can we still do our version with the band?'

'Course.'

'Good. John and me have done a special ending. *Dread dread dread* and out on a high.'

'You ought to come to one of their rehearsals. See what they're doing. In fact, you ought to sing it with them.' It's as plain to me now as the muck on this window.

'No!' she snaps. Then drawls, sullen: '*They* don't want me.'

'What do you mean?'

'They won't have me!'

Oh dear, we're back to the audition and Jeremy's threat of a sight-reading test.

'But Alice, you *wrote* the music. It's your tune!'

She's in a bad groove. She growls. 'I won't be able to keep up.'

I hate this distance. 'Oh, come on, Alice. That's rubbish and you know it. Besides, Jeremy Snell has finally gone to hell, it's Theo now, and he likes you. *I* want you there. I need you to be there with me. It's your place.'

'I'm not coming. I'll be sick, like Italy. It's too far, it's on a plane. And it won't be good when I get there.'

I slow down, lower my voice. 'It isn't on a plane.'

The only answer is a frown. She's enough to make a cat weep at times. I look away and scan the sky. Another flock of birds swoops from west to east, driven on the wind; starlings, sleek, too high and swift for me to see them, but I know their sharp beaks are skewering the air.

'Alright. Alright. Forget I suggested it.'

Across the street, something has set the row of pigeons fidgeting.   Here we are, winding each other up without really trying. All at once, the fat birds take to the sky, wheel around, up, up, and down again, lost in the next street.

'You ought to bake a cake today, anyway, to celebrate. It's a good day, Alice. We're winning.'

'We're winning.'

'Don't worry about the singers. It'll be great. And Mum's made up.'

'Made up. Dog with two tails.' The smile is coming back.

'Happy as Larry,' I keep up the riff.

'OK, I know the score,' she says through a big grin. 'We are her sunshine, her only sunshine.'

She's right, of course.

I don't accept the view that I'm an incurable neurotic, while everybody else in this family is sensible. But I have to admit, that last sleepless night was a complete waste of time. This morning, all my laborious workings-out have big fat underlinings and crosses next to them in red pen.

Next up, Mum. I owe her an apology. It isn't going to wait until after choir: besides, we have all our arguments in that car, they cling to the upholstery like sour spilt milk. I'll ambush her after yoga. She's been banging on about the Palm House for ages, trying to lure me over for a nice pot of tea, as if I'm interested in tea and bought cakes. Well, time to meet her half way. At least we'll both behave, and it won't blow up, if there's someone else's china on the table.

44 The Palm House

The parks in February are a cold, damp world whose mingy attempts at spring are worm casts on the grass, and a few slits of colour that are meant to be crocuses; so the minute I step into the Palm House I understand Mum's affection for the place. Warm, delicious air to breathe, a round lacework of wrought iron, softened by foliage and curtains of cream, pink and red flowers I can't name. The Palm House smells of nothing I recognise, and its scent changes as I walk around. The glass roof is a shallow cone, which captures the chirp of a sparrow and funnels it straight down to my ears; he's hopping round the vines, high overhead, near a dainty staircase which spirals up to heaven behind palms and creepers. I could inhabit this glass house every bit as happily as my round cathedral; in fact, it's more human, with a bloom rather than an echo, and without that blood-red streak from the window, that stains the pews and is designed to trouble your conscience. Around the circumference, here, plants swirl and trail and spray, conferring decency on the unremarkable statues that pop up every few feet along the wall. A sort of performance area, with a low platform in the centre of the building, takes up almost a semicircle; this must be where the yoga happened. Against it there are huge leafy plants, and to one side, tables hidden behind a screen: the caff where Mum will be waiting for me, after her class.

She looks well in this natural light which comes at her from all sides. Her face is nicely plump, peachy-pink from exercise.

She gets up. We hug briefly, and sit down.

'So. What do you think?' Her gaze skims the hanging greenery.

'You're right. It's beautiful.'

She nods, and the corner of her mouth describes a very quiet *told you so*.

She's drinking mint tea. I get one for myself, and break into my apology while I wait for it to cool.

'Look, Mum, I just wanted to say… I'm sorry I lost it yesterday. I'm sorry if I sounded ungrateful.'

'You *were* ungrateful.'

'Well, I'm grateful now.'

One brow arches: 'Will you take up Theo's offer, then?'

'Yes. Of course. And I've talked to Alice about it, we're fine. Thank you. I don't know what got into me yesterday.'

She sighs. 'For practical purposes…Why don't you try to forget I'm your mother? Try to think of me as a useful contact. Like any other.' She reads from my expression that this isn't going to work for me, because she adds: 'You know, Beth, generally speaking, you could make a little more room for gratitude in your life.'

She's fresh from the yoga mat, so I let this pass. 'OK. Fair point.' She tilts her head.

'You always have to resist, Beth. Right from a baby. You used to push your little feet against me and stretch your little legs and dig in, while you stared at me with these big grey eyes, as much as to say, see? See what I can do? See how strong I am? And you'd send your arms out and beat the air, and squirm, and cross one arm over the other, all tensed up. And then you'd kick.'

In family legend, I was always the awkward one.

'I hear you've been round to Uncle Pat's. Visiting the archive.'

I didn't see that coming. But there's no emotion on her face.

'I wanted to see our old videos. I wanted to see what we were like, before the accident.'

A tension creeps around her eyes. 'You were the quiet one.' I've been told this so many times, this, and my legendary awkwardness, it's as if that's all there is to know.

'It wasn't – it *isn't* – just about me and Alice. I'm curious about all of us. What about you, and Dad?' I lean forward across the flimsy little table. 'I've got this version of what happened, the version I tell people when they ask about Alice. But I'm older now, and I'm thinking, maybe that's only the version we've rehearsed. Just lately, I've started to realise how many gaps there are. Things I don't remember, because I didn't try to; maybe I didn't realise they mattered at the time. Things nobody explained.'

'Such as?'

'What happened to *you,* Mum?' It occurs to me that teasing might work. 'For example, I know for a fact, you didn't always stand to attention. You used to be normal.' The woman on the VT was definitely her, cheerful but bending, slightly round shouldered, none of that poker back stuff we get these days. An ordinary woman who hadn't taken her pinny off and didn't sit up particularly straight, looking to other people, ready to bend so as to pass the plates and feed them.

'Well, it was pre-yoga.' She takes that with a smile; I have the sense of getting close to something. I have to push on.

'Where did you go, Mum? Even just… physically? Where were you? When Alice was in Alder Hey?'

Her eyes dart to the wall. 'There was a lot to do. It was a terrible time.'

The less sure she looks, the easier this gets, and the more I sense the child in me is growing distant now. I need to be specific. The interrogator always tries a different question.

'Where did you sleep? Were you always there, at home? Only, I seem to remember a time the goodnights stopped.'

She breathes in slowly, frowns, and her shoulders adjust ever so slightly, as she checks they're horizontal.

'Mostly, yes… I wanted to be there with you,' she says. Her eyes search mine. She wants me to say it. She wants me to be the one who understands.

This means she thinks I can.

I reach out to take her hand.

'You had to be with Alice. And that meant you couldn't be with me.'

She nods, sighs, and for a split second her shoulders dip as if she's going to slump like the ordinary woman in the video; then pulls herself up again, and grips my hand.

'I thought… We all thought we were going to lose her. I'm so sorry, pet.'

'Yes.'

'I've never been so frightened in my life. And it just went on. On and on.' The voice is muted. 'At the time, I told everybody I was living in hope. But looking back… I lived in terror, Beth.'

'We both did, Mum.'

'And once or twice… Maybe more, it only happened a few times… The worst days… I came home from the ward and I didn't come to you straight away, or even tuck you into bed, because I couldn't risk you seeing me like that. I was in such a state.'

The brightness of this palm house is overwhelming. The warmth, on a winter's day. How strange, that those few times are the times that I remember. How unfair.

My mother's voice is steady. 'We were all dealing with the physical reality – all those broken bones – and we'd just about come to terms with that, and the physical disabilities she'd have to live with, when it all turned into something else; something popped in her head – the bleed – and she couldn't communicate any more. She'd been getting better. Suddenly it was back to… well, not even square one. There were times I looked, and it wasn't even her in that bed. God forgive me, I didn't know my own child.'

She's never used those words to me before. Or said anything about how she felt, beyond the *terrible time* which is a shorthand. The medical facts are facts I've known for ages; I've heard them, and expressed them myself, in iterations whose language subtly changed as I got older, the vocabulary sharpening as I became an articulate teenager, then blunting again as it all receded into the past.

'She was such a chatterbox before, you know? And clever. Reading, writing; you were both way ahead of the other kids.'

How can I tell her? How it felt to hear the front door open, and her footfall in the hall, and up the stair without *hello, I'm back*. That behind that front room door, with its high knob that rattled on the spindle, and clicked when it shut, and without the thought ever forming words in my head, I was sitting at the keyboard waiting to find out whether Mum was home and whether I was… viable. Whether I would live another day. How can I tell her this? What would be the point, now? After all these years?

'Did *you* end up on meds, mum?'

She nods. 'Mm. Yes, in the end. You can put only on a brave face for so long. I was off sick, for the best part of a year. I couldn't be doing with other people's children.'

This would be my chance to ask her straight: could you be doing with me? But why hurt her now?

'Horrible,' is all that I can say; thinking, I sound like Alice.

'It was. Without work, there was too much time to fill, waiting for you to come home from school. I couldn't concentrate. I started playing the piano again, in the afternoons. It was almost automatic, you know? The notes were there, written for me, I didn't have to decide what came next. It helped, to practise something long and complicated. Well, complicated for me.'

'What did you play?'

'Schubert. The slow movement from the A minor, I could just about manage that. The last, B flat, particularly… don't laugh… I couldn't play it really, not beyond the first page. Not like you. But I became addicted to things that were difficult for me, things that would force me to repeat, repeat…'

'The legitimate pursuit of mindlessness.' My favourite addiction.

'And the Schubert is special because… The thing about him… This probably sounds pretentious,' she warns me.

'Right up my street then, Mum.' I squeeze her hand.

'His music had the shape of my fear. And it talks about comfort. A lot.'

For a split-second I think, here we go; we'll never agree; music, for her, always has a purpose beyond itself, and it's never pure, because it always has to bend to the imperfectly human listener's requirements. It's not even about beauty. For people like my mum, music doesn't take on the shape of thought: it takes on the shape of feeling. And yet: when did I last think a thought that had no feeling in it?

We drink our tea, and it isn't long before we've talked ourselves back round to banality and what we've each got on for the rest of the week. She takes me home, because it's raining, but also because she wants to. She pats my hand after we kiss goodbye. For a long time afterwards, in the grey and then the twilight, and through into the evening and the night, I carry this capsule of white warmth which was our conversation in the Palm House, when I said sorry, and discovered that I really, really meant it.

45 Email

Wooh – email from Theo.   Subject: Yoton Yo Saturday.
Sounds like a club but it isn't one I've heard of.

> *Hi Beth*
> *I saw Shari today in the Old Blind School. This
> is great. Did you know there is a great concert
> two weeks Saturday? Yötön Yö choir from
> Finland. They do Rachmaninov St John Liturgy
> with incense and everything, at St Faiths Crosby.
> This is rare and beautiful in UK. They have no
> audience!!!!! I thought, strike with a hot iron! A
> bunch of us are going, will you join us?*
> *Also Emily Dickinson.*
> *Can we read through next week? Can you
> make copies in the faculty, in time for
> Wednesday?*
> *Kind regards*
> *Theo*

Well, obviously, I want to go out with him. But, honestly,
is it worth trekking to the North side of town, and sitting
through an evening of choral music and holy smoke?

> *Hi Theo,*
> *Sounds great. Yes, I'll get the copies.*

I type *x*, then delete it and just sign, Beth.

46 Silence

Thou sentest forth thy wrath. Theo Christodoulou, tall, brown eyed, so smiling and in control, has spent the first twenty minutes with the choir on Handel's *Israel in Egypt*, which they all know, trying to persuade them that no, they don't. I understand his frustration. It's a viciously energetic piece, with an un-Christian emphasis on meting out violence and devastation to your enemies; and they *are* being awfully nice about it. He stops, brings – very beautiful – praying hands up to his nose, stares at the dusty floor as if it confers some sort of inner strength; then looks up again to ask, 'You remember the last time you sang this?' Smiles, nods, *yes, yes, oh aye.* 'Well, I need you to forget.' Then he makes them sing the last four bars of the movement at double time, and we repeat it over and over, ridiculously fast, with just a bar for breath between each reprise, until we're all dizzy. At last he raises his hands for us to stop. Nods approval. 'There,' he tells them quietly, 'I knew you could do it.' Then practically shouts, '*No rit!*'

A lot of them are chuckling so I think he's charmed them, although you can feel the static off some of the altos.

'Let's try something new. We have a part song by Beth and her sister, Alice.' He holds up the music, exhibit A.

I've gone all quivery inside. I adjust the piano stool up, down, up, push it back, push it forward. The sick I'm feeling is a different sort of sick to the other times people have played my stuff, though. Because it's *our* stuff. If they don't like Alice's tune… If they don't like Alice's tune… I won't like them. I won't play for them next week.

I mustn't cry and I mustn't swear.

While they all rummage to find the piece that Jenny Johns dispensed from her little table at the entrance, he tells the choir they'll be doing this in the summer concert, alongside some part-songs from all over Europe. *Part-songs from all over Europe,* he said. A nausea hits me: Jaz Ander, telling me, most authoritatively, a propos his bloody novel, how much it matters to be familiar with your genre; and me saying, well that's all fine and dandy, so long as you know what your genre is, so long as you *have* one; and thinking, ha, sucker, who wants to be defined by categories? But now I see as plain as day that Part-songs is a whole Genre, capital G. A *European* one. Before we even started this, I ought to have been studying loads of these Part-songs, instead of playing around with rock anthems and half-remembered hymns. A fatal error. It's too late to undo it.

Theo asks me to play though the piece for them first, and they make the sort of noises you get when you pass round a plate of eclairs. *Mm. Very nice.*

Jenny raises a hand: 'I think there's a typo in the underlay. It says *have* instead of *has.*' She looks around; they mutter, *oh yes, so there is, well spotted, I saw that.*

I don't have to say anything, because my dear old mum raises her teacher voice: 'That *is* what Dickinson wrote.'

More mutterings, shrugs, frowns.

Theo looks across in my direction. 'It really is,' I say.

Why? They chunner. *What was she on? Gorra be a mistake.*

Patrick's OK with it; he folds his arms and looks to our conductor for agreement: 'That's poetry for you, isn't it?'

They begin. It's well within their sight-reading ability and it sounds OK. In fact, it sounds the way I meant it to, apart from the section where they merge into unison, because they've each got their own version of what unison should be. Theo takes the piece apart, tells them where not to breathe, works on a few of the trickier moments for the inner parts, clarifies the duplet rhythms. Tries the whole thing again from the top. And looks pleased. When we get to the end, there's applause, which you *don't* get for a plate of eclairs. So maybe we got away with it. 'Thank you, Beth,' says Theo. 'Great piece. Are you happy with that?' His slender eyebrows rise to a beautiful arch and the whites of his eyes shine.

I have a choice here, to speak up about the unison problem, or not. Petra might. Alice wouldn't.

'Fine.' That was just a first shot, after all. I remember to thank everyone.

We break there. Jenny gives the notices. Some Christmas music not yet returned, and you know who you are. Then this flu business. People are getting worried about large gatherings, and choir practice is a large gathering, so just to let you know it's under review and we're taking advice.

'Oh, we have this every year,' says pink Patrick.

'It's all right for you,' says grey Ian, sharply. 'Some of us have got conditions.'

Jenny looks perturbed and turns to Theo for support. All he can do is stare back at her, smile, and stare heavenward, open handed like Our Lord. She says maybe we should have a quick show of hands, who's got a condition; a couple go up and drop down again, as Ffi protests, 'You can't ask that in public! That's personal!'

The discussion fizzles out.

In the ten minutes of socialising before we start again people seek me out to make their comments on *Silence*.

'I thought it would be, you know, more modern, less tuneful,' says Jenny Johns. I'm not sure how to take that – modern has been tuneful for a long time now. Ffion was expecting it to be harder, and almost sounds disappointed. But basically, the choir liked it. Very singable. 'That's down to Alice,' I say. Smiles all round, thumbs-up from some of the altos who've already taken their seats again. The singers around my mum make the sort of friendly fuss that women do, congratulating her. Then it's back to Handel. *The horse and his rider He hath thrown into the sea.*

After the rehearsal, which has seen Handel's enemies well and truly eating dirt, Ffi ambushes my mother. Yes, go on, she'll come for a drink.

'Let's go down the *Bessie*. Check out the makeover. Loads of different gins, apparently.'

'I'm driving,' she says; but that smile means she's ready to spend an hour basking in her twin daughters' glory. I really don't mind any more. Not since the Palm House.

Patrick piles in: 'Oh go on. Be sociable.' He turns and calls, 'Eh! Maestro! Come for a bevvy?'

Theo flashes a smile.

'We're having a little celebration for the girls,' says Ffi and gives me a big squeeze.

He beams, with that open-handed gesture I like so much. 'Sure.'

We bowl down the street in a big, noisy gang. All the fun people. Except my sister.

It takes Max the brain surgeon two minutes to shift the furniture in the Bessie and we're all seated round three small tables. That's nearly half the pub. On the other side of the lounge bar there are two old blokes on the Guinness, and a couple who can kiss goodbye to any chance of a romantic drink tonight. There's a swift, well-practised drill when it comes to rounds: pink Patrick, grey Ian, Max; Marsha and her admirers, male and female; Ffi and Jenny with Mum and me, although of course, we're not paying tonight; Theo, who's not in anybody's round, gets them in for us. I stand by his side at the bar, ready to help carry the glasses, and while we watch

the barman pour, I say, 'Shame Alice wasn't there to hear it.'
He turns to me and asks, 'Why doesn't she sing with choir?'

'She got spooked when Jeremy described the audition.'

He laughs. 'Tell her, I heard her audition outside WH
Smiths. She's in.'

'It would have to come straight from you. I've already been
on at her about this, she was adamant. She'll just think I'm
being manipulative.'

He takes a pencil from his pocket and hands it to me, with
a beer mat. 'I need her address, then.'

Once we're all seated, he proposes a toast. 'To Beth and
Alice. Cheers. *Yia mas*!' Lots of noise.

'Absent composers!' I say; and, feeling cocky about
reaching chapter ten in the blue book with the olives on the
front, I throw in my own, '*Yia mas!*' with gusto.

Ffi asks one of her intelligent questions: 'Where did the
idea for it come from, Beth?'

I don't really want to answer this so I'm quite relieved when
Marsha jumps in to say 'That poem's just written for us lot.
For this city. *Silence is all we dread.* I mean, we do. Don't we?
Dread silence.'

Nods all round.

'Quite honestly,' says Patrick, sitting back and resting his
pint on the cummerbund cushion, 'silence isn't something I've
got any personal experience of.'

Marsha says: 'You should spend a day with me.' She works
in the Royal, like Max, but I imagine background music is
forbidden in the mortuary. She's quiet for only a second; then
explodes, 'I loved the loud bit. The *dread, dread, dread.* It's
just the sort of thing I feel like singing after a shift!'

'I liked the quiet bits,' says Ian, and his grey eyes find mine,
as if he thinks I might not otherwise believe him. 'Lyrical.'

'What does it mean, though, that poem?' Jenny searches round the table for an answer, or a supporter. 'Doesn't make sense to me.'

Patrick is eager to explain. 'You take two things that belong together. You put them side by side, and what've you got?'

'Harmony,' says Ian.

'Well, yeah, maybe. But that wasn't what I was trying to say; I mean, basically, all you've got is, two things that belong together. But if you take two things that *don't* belong together, and put them side by side... Bang! Wham! Shazzam! You've made *art*.' Patrick is glowing. 'And how do you know?' Pause. 'You know you've made art, because you've got people saying, what the fuck's that? You've got people thinking, haven't you? You've got them making connections. Answering a question. You've got them *involved*.'

Max and Theo chuckle, Marsha laughs out loud, and Mum joins in.

'It's like the lambanana, then,' says Ian. 'Lamb plus banana equals art.'

Jenny contemplates the white wine spritzer in front of her, unconvinced; then appeals to us all: 'I liked them when they actually looked like bananas. Yellow, you know?'

Ffi coaxes her mother: 'Well, at the end of the day, it's the music that matters, isn't it? And it's a nice piece.'

A micro-wince crosses my mum's face. She's the one who taught me not to trust that word.

'We need it though, don't we?' says Marsha.

'Art, oh aye.'

'No, not just art. And not just music, either. Singing. Look at me. I'm living proof.'

From their sudden solemnity, most of them already know her story. I ask her with my eyes, and she addresses herself directly to me, although she's got everyone's attention now.

'I hated choir at school.' Her speaking voice is deep, full and steady. I'd love to sound like her.

'I lost everyone, Beth. All at once. Mum, Dad, Dwayne – my big brother.' People's heads have dropped. They know what's coming. 'It was an accident. Big smash-up on the M6. The details don't matter, do they? Point is, *they* died, *I* walked away. It wasn't fair. And it screwed me up, for years. I avoided people. I got panic attacks. Some do-gooder somewhere along the way told me to breathe. Which I thought was ridiculous, because as far as I could see, I was breathing. Only, not much else. Then I read something in the paper about this community choir; and in the end, what got through to me, was this scientist on a podcast talking about what happens to your brain when you breathe in sync with someone else. And it broke my heart, because the very thing I couldn't do was breathe in sync with someone else. There wasn't anybody there, was there? And for the first time in ages, I just *wailed.*' She throws her head back and I see the dark pink roof of her mouth and the white teeth as she repeats, 'I *wailed.*'

Jenny murmurs. Ffi shakes her head.

Marsha is still fixing her gaze on me, her smooth eyebrows raised: 'And that's what got me singing.' She nods through a pause to make sure I take this in. Then carries on.

'And I found something out,' she says, majestically. 'People who're s'posed to know – nurses, doctors, personal trainers, experts, like – they're always going on about how important it is to take deep breaths. You know what they say. Any shock, any panic, before an exam, before a race, before you go on stage – take good deep breaths, that's what they tell you, don't they?' Marsha's gaze sweeps around us all; she's sure that everyone agrees with her. 'Well, what *I* say is, the breath you take in is *nothing,* nothing, next to the breath you let out.' Slowing down, she speaks almost in a whisper:

'Singing is all about the breath you let out. And everything that comes out with it.'

'That's true,' says my mum.

'All the glad, and all the bad.'

There's a solemnity in the air for a moment. It's almost atavistic, as if the tribe is gathered round the campfire to recite the time-honoured legends that bind them together; we might be Anglo-Saxons, Ancient Greeks, Māori people… and it's all directed at me, the uninitiated. The outsider.

I don't know what to say.

The others begin to cover the silence. *Natural. A basic human instinct. You always feel better for a good sing.*

'I read this article,' says Sandy. 'They think humans could sing before they could talk. Which is amazing. Because, singing is closer to what animals do than talking is. I mean, just listen to animal noises. Some animal noises are very close to singing.'

'You speak for yourself,' says Patrick, lifting his pint and elbowing Ian.

Sandy joins in the laughter, but she hasn't finished, in fact she's getting more excited. 'As a matter of fact, they think the most ancient languages are what they call tonal languages, like Chinese. Which is dead hard for us to learn because it's basically musical. Goes up and down. Am I right, Mel?'

'Right,' says Mum.

Stuff everybody already knows, and stuff nobody knows; it's all equally exciting to Sandy.

Soon, there are two conversations going on: the Patrick / Ian/ Sandy crowd are swapping viola jokes, *what's the difference between a pizza and a viola player*; while down our end, Jenny Johns announces, 'Apparently, I could sing before I could talk.'

Ffi rolls her eyes. 'My mam's a racial stereotype.' I can't suppress a giggle, because she did sound a bit Welsh herself when she said that. Jenny's completely defrosted, all smiles again.

'Welsh and proud!'

'And bloody loud!' comes from the raucous end.

Jenny takes the floor. 'No, really though! Your grandma Morris stopped telling people in the end, because they didn't believe her. There was I in the pram, and she'd say, *Our Jennifer's singing now, not bad at six months, is it?* And the other mothers would give her a look, as much as to say, *Oh, yes, pull the other one it's got bells on, we're not as green as we're cabbage-looking.* But my mam knew what she heard. *That's just a baby gurgling*, they said. *They all do that. But of course, it's your first.* But it was a tune. Real tunes; I was already singing *Myfanwy* in my pram. And you know what I think? I think they were jealous. Too jealous to hear it.' She grins from ear to ear.

Ffi grins too, and rubs shoulders with her mum.

'Did *I* sing in my pram, Mam?'

'No,' says her mother crisply; then snorts and laughs at herself, because that did come out rather more harshly than she'd intended. 'Oh, sorry love, listen to me! I've only closed the piano lid on the poor child's fingers!' The pair of them are swaying about and practically crying with mirth. Jenny raises a finger. 'But I will say, you had a good pair of lungs on you, mind, even when you were tiny. Hear you in the next street.'

A good pair of lungs is an asset in a singer. It's something I signally lack. Etiolated: that's my body type. So how come Alice can belt it out?

All this time, Theo has sat opposite me with a beer on the table and a smile on his face. I'm not sure he's followed that last foray into Welsh culture. He notices my glass is empty, gets me another beer.

In the next forty minutes, as the alcohol and the talk polish all the evening's previous anxieties clean away, Theo and I just smile and listen, while the heroes round the camp fire talk of triumphs past. Hardest sings. Best final pages. Which are the bits that make you cry. Whose Requiem would you choose for your desert island. Because seriously, that's the most likely outcome, if you're dumped on a desert island.

I'm catching something of their warmth; it's like watching other people dance – quite enough to give me pleasure. From time to time, I catch Theo's eye and our smiles broaden. He was so kind, about Alice. I'm tuned to his presence; I always know where he is in the room, and he's stayed close to me, even if we're not officially together. Against the hubbub, I'm basking in our shared silence, the sure sign of a deep connection. But most of the time, my eyes are settled on Marsha, so present, so sure of the space she occupies and of her right to claim it; her hands move steadily, as if the air were solid and she were smoothing it around her. Her speaking voice has a focus that makes it carry; only Max comes anywhere near, in terms of projection. But it's also the words themselves that claim attention. *All the glad, and all the bad.* She wasn't always magnetised like this, as surely as my mother didn't always sit up straight. I sense that the three of us might have an understanding.

She's right. The details don't matter, do they.

When my sister nearly died, and all our lives had to be re-made, my mother would have been, what? Thirty? So, six years older than I am today. She'd already been teaching I don't know how long when she got married, had us twins, and we'd started school; so it's as if I were pregnant with twins today… Which is unthinkable. I'm not ready and perhaps I never will be.

But in terms of years, when she gave life to me and Alice, she hadn't much more experience on this earth than I do now. She had stuff she didn't know. She wanted things, worked for things, avoided things. She had off days and holidays, work crises at the ends of term. She was probably ploughing through life with a sense, like mine, of how she wanted her future to be, this sense that's as robust as it's vague. It occurs to me now that, before the accident, she was still a learner, and she would never have been completely in control. And when Alice nearly died, Mum wasn't ready. Can't possibly have been.

47 Meeting

I take Theo's solicitude over my sister as a sign that he's interested in me; and even if our only touch has been a handshake, he's invited me out with his friends, so the direction of travel is promising. And now Alice has invited us both round for tea, ostensibly to say thanks about the choir and everything, but actually, I'd say, in the hope of nudging us towards coupledom.

At Chameleon Close, we get off to a good start. Alice has plumped for a Traditional Victoria Sponge, with Mum's Continuity WI strawberry jam. No additives, no labelling, no surrender to Trading Standards. Theo doesn't do any of that *ooh you do look like your sister* stuff which we both hate; there's no pretence of *how do people tell you apart*, which is a game a surprising number of people play even though it's obvious that one of us can't walk properly and has a nightmare haircut.

While they talk cake for a bit, I examine the letter, which she has stuck on her bookcase as befits a trophy. It's in black ink with a fountain pen on proper cream writing paper. Never before has she received such a letter, and I've told her, she's one up on me because I'm still waiting for mine. Theo invites Alice to give the Lyceum Singers a trial; the word audition isn't mentioned. It contains no mistakes or misjudged colloquialisms. Mind you, I'm more interested in his handwriting than his grammar: he started life in a different alphabet from us; and a person's hand is as revealing as a handshake, so it's a shame you never see it once you've left school. Theo's writing isn't joined up, but it *is* elegant, and leans very slightly forward, which is my preference. My own jumps about all over the place. Perhaps this would change if I ever stopped fidgeting inside.

All the time I'm watching: does she like him? It's obvious he likes her, but everybody likes Alice, she's fun. He thanks her for agreeing to join the singers; that ploy seems to have worked.

'D'you rate them, then?' she asks.

'The choir?'

That V-shape reappears on his forehead.

'They're very… safe,' he says. 'Honestly? I think they need a kick in the pants.'

They both laugh briefly. He moves fluently on to the Aphrodite Bar, and the open mic night.

'The band mostly do covers,' she warns him.

'Uncle Stelios won't mind. Covers are what people expect to hear, in a bar.'

'You know me and Beth have written loads of songs?'

I feel myself redden as she turns around to reach for the remote. 'They're not exactly songs, though, are they? I mean, it's just music. There aren't any words.' I don't want him thinking we're going to shoe-horn our teenage experiments alongside Gerry and the Pacemakers, and alienate his uncle's clientèle.

'D'you want to hear some?' She doesn't wait for an answer. He looks at me and smiles. I'm not imagining it. We *do* have a real connection. Give us time alone, it will just… develop.

I'd thought she was diffident about our music, but Alice has cued up all our original compositions ready for Theo to hear, going right back. The titles are crazy things that made sense to us when we were teenagers. *Cloth Ears, Die Quietly, Four Hands Good.* It seems to me now that some of the simplest things we did when we were kids are better than anything I've laboured at in these last few years. It's as if I know too much about it now, and it's all become difficult.

Cloth Ears, electronic version, is first up.

A few moments in, he smiles. It *is* quite good.

He accepts a second slice of cake.

'By the way, Beth, you did me a big favour with Jaz Ander. Thanks for the introduction.'

Christ on a bike, what's brought *him* up? Alice's eyes are big as saucers.

'Really?'

He settles back in his seat, a sign I'm about to hear something he's been looking forward to telling me.

'Yes. He got back to me about the feature they're running in the *Echo*. All roads lead to Rome, and all musical roads lead to Liverpool, sorta thing.' His slight Cypriot accent, with its strangely bent vowel sounds, disappeared with that *sorta thing*. Fleetingly, he sounds like a man who's spent his whole life in the Dingle. 'Each week, a different piece of the music scene. The Rushworth heritage. You know, one time, they used to have the biggest music shop in Europe here? I learned this from Jaz Ander. Amateur music-making is in your blood. So, they're gonna come to choir practice, take photos, interview the singers. It's great publicity for the choir. And the Aphrodite Bar will get a mention. Of course.'

He sees my face and his smile drops.

'Beth? I thought you'd be pleased. It was your hot tip. You said, take this man seriously.'

If he's mirroring what my face is doing now – pantomime panic – I must look quite stupid. Then I remember.

'No, Theo. What I said was, *give him a wide berth.*'

'It means, give him a big space, no?'

'No. It means, put a big space between you and him. It's a saying.'

He sighs. 'This is your Liverpool way. Everything you say, you mean something else.'

'It's a metaphor, yeah.'

He waggles his head and purses his lips. 'Your metaphors are very… confusing… I don't know my blindness.' He raises his eyebrows and those brown eyes are so shiny, so innocent.

'You have no idea what you're doing here, Theo. Whatever happens, that man and my mother must never be in the same room. Understand? *Never.*'

'Why?'

'He… *used* us. He wrote something incredibly offensive. About her.'

'About your mother? About Mel?'

'Mm-hm.' Alice is staring at him. I let the silence hang. No way am I going to talk about it.

He frowns, nods. 'A messed up, then,' he says, all Scouse. Then extends open hands, like Jesus at the Last Supper. 'It's too late now. I've done the damage.'

'The damage is done.'

'Yes, and I did it.'

He hasn't twigged that I was polishing the idiom for him there. He's thinking. His eyes are busy, as if he's looking for a jammy dodger in a box of broken biscuits. 'But Jaz Ander *is* a real journalist, isn't he? He looks like a typical journalist. He has that jacket, like an intellectual, y'know worramean?'

Alice pipes up, 'They had a relationship. She kicked him out.'

'Cheers, Alice. Never mind me, this is about Mum. This could all turn out like… oh, I don't know, what's that woman who kills everybody? Electra? Medea? She's gonna go apeshit.'

'Medea killed her children,' he says, knowledgeably Greek.

'That'll be the one, then.'

He sighs.

'You've got to put them off. I'm serious! I mean, if he turns up at a rehearsal… Well, he *can't*. You *have* to keep them apart. Seriously. You hear what I'm saying?'

'But I've already told Jenny the *Echo* are coming. She was *made up*. I didn't say who. Maybe they send someone else?'

He takes me back to Arctic Terrace but doesn't come in because he has to make a phone call, business. He says. I Face Time Alice straight away for her verdict, and also because I'd like to know what the hell she was playing at.

'So, Theo. What d'you reckon?'

'Mm.'

'What d'you mean, mm? He's not like Jaz. He's not a toody, is he?'

'He's a threedy.'

'Exactly.'

'He's not sure about you, though,' she says.

'Alice!'

She's like this with people. She's like a dog that can walk into a room of strangers and sense who's good for a stroke, or a titbit, or neither. So many people have handled her, from when she was small. I put it down to that.

'He likes *you*, Alice. I could tell.'

'He likes cake,' she says, with a sly smile. 'And he likes Jaz. Your ex.'

'No, he doesn't! Look, Theo messed up there, but it's for a good reason. He didn't know Jaz from Adam. And I really don't think he knew anything about the Tiger Mother thing.' Even as I say this, I realise what I've done, and feel sick: because he'll want to know now, won't he? He'll go straight to Ffion, or to Jenny, and say, what's all this about Mel and Jaz Ander, and they'll lead him right back to the *Urtext*.

'Y'know Jaz...' drawls Alice. 'D'you think he's got... useful contacts?'

Where on earth is this coming from?

'You mean like a black book? Oh, yes, for sure, and it'll be full of self-important sconeheads like him. What *are* you on about?'

Slowly, quietly, she makes her pronouncement. 'Beth. You worry too much.' I snort. She's repeating Mum's line, which makes me mad, it's such a terrible short-circuit of reasoning. And she's doing the silly face that goes with it. I'm getting frustrated to think how little Alice really understands, when she throws in the one bit of family wisdom she knows we can agree on: 'Mum likes a fight.'

I agree: 'She's very touchy.'

'Yeah. Very touchy.'

We allow a few seconds of silence to seal our truce.

Then Alice says, 'He's nice.'

I'm glad she approves. 'I saw him first, remember.'

'Oh, you can have him. Only I bet you won't get him. You'll put him off with your scaredy-cat what-iffing.'

48 People like us

Mum wants help bagging stuff up for deliveries at the food bank. I ask her about this Rachmaninov gig. The Liturgy of St John something-or-other. I don't know much about his choral work, except that back in my teenage, neo-Stravinsky, pure music phase we heard the Philharmonic Choir do *The Bells* once, and had a big argument about it afterwards because it represented everything I didn't want to do in composition. Lots of imitative stuff, which really bugged me in those days. When I used to be opinionated.

I tell her they haven't sold many tickets and wonder aloud if this Liturgy thing might be a bit like *The Bells*. Big choir, big sound. In your face, you know? She arcs into excitement. 'You really must hear it.' She wants to come along too. Next thing, she's on the internet, trying to find the listings in *Culture Liverpool*, she's reading out the cost of a ticket; she wants to book but maybe Jenny would like this, in fact lots of the choir, we ought to give out a notice in the break, if they haven't got an audience. Me and my big mouth. I was looking forward to an evening with the beautiful, almond-faced, warm-eyed Theo, sure this would be the night we become unprofessional, and now my mum's hiring a minibus so all her friends can be there too.

Then she breaks off. Oh, no. *That* Saturday? The eighth? She's already committed to a fund-raiser for the Open Door. And of course, she's roped all her pals into that already. This is one of those moments when I almost believe there is a God and He does love me. She's crestfallen. 'You never get to hear this piece live,' she says. In a rush of benevolence, I try to soothe her disappointment, and ask what's so special about it.

'It's beautiful.' Her gaze is no longer in the room. 'And the heart of it, for me, is an actual job description for the choir. Bang in the middle.'

My experience of job descriptions is slight, and not positive. 'OK. What's that then?'

'The Cherubic hymn. The words say, here's the deal, we're not really cherubim, we're ordinary people pretending to be cherubim, with jobs and families, and we have to set all that to one side in order to do this job properly.'

Typical Mum – she's dumbed it down for a class of year tens. I'll elevate our discussion to post-grad seminar with a knowing cultural observation: 'Ah. You mean, it breaks the fourth wall.'

She raises an eyebrow, then takes a breath. 'At the beginning of the piece, it's about achieving calm and focus. That's the *how*. Then comes the *what*. Ecstatic praise. Radiance. That's the task. As you sing it, you do it. Well, that's how I hear it, anyway.' She pauses, then tells me: 'It all starts with one note.' She knows a single perfect note will get my full attention.

Then, out of nowhere, she says, 'You know, I think you're either born a praiser or not. Your sister's a praiser. Always was.'

I must have frowned because she says, 'Beth, love, the wind'll change and you'll look like that for ever.'

'Alice isn't religious.'

Mum tuts. 'She has a way of homing in on what's good, and amplifying it.'

'Whereas I was born to criticise?'

'People like you and me, Beth, are never satisfied. The world needs us too. Or everything would just stagnate.'

That's why we're here in a cold church hall putting little boxes into bigger boxes. But I'm warmed by the casual way she put us in the same category. *People like you and me, Beth.* She sees a likeness where I never had.

49 Band practice

Band practice, at my place. On their way up the stairs, I can hear John telling Vilma it'll be OK, and not to worry, no, go on, just push that door… Vilma, monolithic in black, drags a frown into the room which vanishes as soon as she sees me and we say hello. Then her eyes wander round the flat, taking it all in. John gives a cheery 'Y'alright, eh?' dumps his guitar and goes back to help Alice, who's soon made her noisy ascent and is wearing rose today. She has that adolescent smile that says, aha, I'm carrying a secret – the smile which makes it no secret at all.

She sent the set list in advance:

> *We are allowed 3, there are 6 in case*
> *1 Ferry cross the Mersey*
> *2 How do you do it*
> *3 I like it finish?*
> *4 This boy in case*
> *5 Or don't let the sun in case*
> *6 Bonus track – Dread*

Apart from the last one, this is their busking repertoire, and they have it well under their belt. We chug our way happily through the first three numbers, sticking to the usual sort of rendition; I supply a strong bass, since that's what they lack, plus drums. Nothing fancy, people don't like the classics messed about with and, I observe, we're not trying to make a statement here.

At that point they glance at each other and Alice says, 'Well… We are, actually. Show her, John.' There's a look of mischief and excitement about her which John doesn't share. Quite the opposite. He's been burbling away happily for the last hour, but now his elastic mouth has stopped twanging around and slackened into doubt.

'Bonus track,' she grins, and shouts, 'Dread!'

Serious-faced, he passes me a crisp white copy, headed *All We Dread. ABC.* I laugh out loud. I was warned, after all.

'It's Alice's arrangement, like. For the band. I just wrote it down. I hope you don't mind.'

'He's too modest,' says Alice.

'Let's have a look at it, then.'

Alice takes control. 'There are four lines in this poem, and there are four lines in the basic melody. The first line is catchy – Silence is all we dread – everyone'll get that. The rest is complicated.' So, you make the first line the main song, you use up your best bit of melody by singing that first line of words four times; and you make the rest the bridge. Then you go back to the first idea, only stronger, and wow them with your reprise. Then when they've played it a few times they'll start thinking about the rest of the words. That's how they sink in.'

The copy he's given me covers voice and the keyboard. It's strange to see this so reduced. He hasn't transcribed my meticulous dynamic markings, and they've moved the whole thing down a major third. That figures, now that Alice is the only voice. The harmony has been simplified and some of my proudest details have been erased.

Vilma confesses: 'I still don't know all the words.'

John says, 'No worries. Just do the *dread* and join in the shouty bits, Vilma. Your main job is the egg, remember?'

He counts us in, faster than I'd anticipated; and when we start to play, I realise his rhythm guitar is adding a strong offbeat. I fall straight into the swing of it, amused by the transformation. When Alice's voice comes in it's clear that my dynamics have been not so much omitted, as trashed. From the way she belts out the word *silence*, I can see she aspires to deafen; and when the music pauses, it's electric. They've added some pauses of their own, too, so that it seems to stall repeatedly; with each one, John damps the strings with a smack of the hand; Alice snaps the word *dread* shut with a grotesquely clear consonant, and the musical gap that follows makes the hair on the back of my head stand up, so much that I want to hear that effect again. This is genius. When they get to *silence is infinity*, things smooth out and quieten down. There's a whole page of what I felt were rather thoughtful choral modulations which has been lost in favour of repeating the words and tune. But this is Sky Blue Pink, not the Lyceum Singers. When Alice sings, *himself have not a face*, there's a sudden tenderness in her voice. Then it wraps up by going straight back to the beginning, ending with more volume and two last electric silences punched in between the final *dread, dread, dread.*

'What do you think?' asks Alice.

'We didn't quite agree on the timing there. Bit scrappy. First time, though.'

John says, 'We could do with a good strong beatbox under that lot.'

'I'll play around with it.'

'No, but what do you think?' says Alice. 'Do you like it?'

'Yeah. Great. I really think Mum might hate it. Nice work, Alice'

'John did it too.'

'Nice work, John.'

Hours of my toil have gone straight in the bin. I like it so much better. It's turned into a song that anybody would remember.

I tell her, 'It suits your voice, Alice,' and she nods.

'Gonna be my signature dish.'

But Vilma's dark eyebrows are heading for her nose. 'Do the words matter?'

My sister goes up like a rocket. 'Yes! It's not *be-bop-a-do-wah-diddy*. It *means* something. And the music has to mean the same thing. Or what was the point?'

Vilma looks suspicious. 'What's this *ransom in a voice* about, then?'

John checks: 'You know what ransom is? When you take someone hostage, and you have to pay to get them back?'

She nods solemnly, and he asks, 'What does it mean to you, Alice?'

'Everything.'

Alice and I both look at the paper, and read it over.

> *Silence is all we dread.*
> *There's Ransom in a Voice —*
> *But Silence is Infinity.*
> *Himself have not a face*

We can all see that Alice is thinking, and they give her time to get her explanation out, which proves they're really good mates.

'When someone hears your voice, it's as if they pay your ransom. They set you free. If they refuse to hear your voice, you're just in solitary for ever.'

'So, silence is like infinity.' John lifts his eyes to look into hers and says, 'God's honest truth, Alice, you are one amazing woman.' My sister flushes crimson.

'That's clever, Alice,' says Vilma. 'I just come in with dread dread dread, right? That's all I have to remember.' She's as serious about this responsibility as a child cradling a newly-hatched chick in her hands.

We're all busy nodding, when she comes back with: 'So what's this *himself have not a face* about?'

This is the line that we just couldn't handle, and possibly why we were never really satisfied with the ending of our first version. But Vilma's eyes trust Alice to explain. In rehab, they used to do this game where they hid little objects in a bowl of rice, and she had to put her hand in, grab an object, and work out what it was, without looking. She has the same expression on her face now, the opposite of concentration; excitement: what random thing will it be? What will I pull out next? Only this time, it's not an object out of a bowl, it's an understanding, something hidden in the back of her head; and she grabs, quickly, impulsively, for the first idea.

'It's a boyfriend, that she knows she can't have.'

'OK,' says Vilma, satisfied.

Then we start to practise properly.

As I play, I watch my sister, and John. They're close, but not that close. Their eyes meet, often, but their hands don't ever touch. The longer we rehearse, the more she digs in to the music; she can deliver any trashy lyric with utter conviction and therefore persuasion; but *Dread* brings out something more again. Her eyes close on tenderness, soreness in the middle section, and the expression on her face is one I know from the inside; one of sadness and of longing, of disappointment and dismay; and after what she said to Vilma just now, I'm thinking John is on her mind. A couple of hours and a packet of biscuits later, we come to a halt. That expression is gone. John puts his guitar back in its case. Vilma smiles at the shaky egg, and polishes it lovingly with a hanky before slipping it into the pocket of her cardigan. Alice is back on song, her moment of intense sadness, like a necessary piece of kit, packed away. It seems to me that without that pain – and also, without that easy access to joy, which my sister has always had – her singing would be unremarkable.

Alice and I have played around with music over the years, but this has been different. I've never seen my sister *at work* before. She's the boss here. She knows things, decides things, tries things out, rejects, approves, all at the rapid pace of intuition. Why can't I do this? Why do I scratch my head and worry? I'm ashamed to think how apprehensive I was about John and Vilma, too. You'd think, from his conversational style, that John would be full of notes, a wannabe Clapton or Knopfler, a Hendrix even, all show; but he's a regular, rock-solid rhythm guy, thoughtful and generous, sensitive about playing down against the voice when the music demands it. You'd think Vilma's lack of rhythm would drive him wild; but he's the one who's christened her *Vilma the Rhythmic Randomiser*, and pronounced her the band's secret weapon, persuading Alice that this shaky-egg layer might have its place in the texture, so long as Vilma observes the silences; because how hard is it to keep up a truly random cross-rhythm? He's kinder to Vilma than Alice is; he's the one who keeps eye contact, and gives her the signal that it's time to stop, with wild eyes and a vigorous nod.   The looks that pass between myself and Alice are of a different nature. We're more like dancers holding hands; it's physical, this coming together and stepping apart; we each know where we're going, and we read the other's steps and trust our hands will join again. It all feels right. It all feels to be leading somewhere.

As they leave, I give my sister a tight hug and tell her, in her ear, how this is the best thing I've done, and the best I've felt for ages. Then, as we break apart, I tell her how brilliant she is, and especially, how well she explained the poem. 'Ah, well,' she says, 'You always notice, when a poem concerns your life.'

'Your life? My life?'

'Our life.'

50 The Stonebreaker

Alice and I like to meet up at the Walker from time to time, to check out the special exhibitions; she's big on colourists, so the green and orange splodge they're posting to advertise this one was bound to draw her in. They could do with a bit of colour here, in the entrance hall, where I'm waiting among the marble statuary. You'd think an art gallery would get that. It's freezing outside; I nearly got blown away getting up the steps, and every time someone walks in through the tall doors, it sends a little shudder across the hall and right through the café area. It doesn't help that they're all virtually naked in here, especially the bloke in the middle, who holds his short sword in the air and has a woman draped over his other arm like a coat. I suppose he's meant to be a hero, not a sex pest; the man they put in the middle usually is.

It's busier in here than I'd expected. The conversations make a sort of acoustic soup that bubbles away. Above us, I can hear little kids running around the circular balcony; every now and then they stop to peer through the balustrade and send their voices down to us punters below in joyful whoops and squeals. Alice and I have done all that. Probably got told off like them, too. *Don't run,* echoing off the marble.

At last, here comes my sister; she glides through on her magnificent chair; and the big grin on her face, together with her ridiculous hat – the sort of thing Rembrandt would wear to Glastonbury – mean you could almost forgive her for the slice of cold air she's brought in her wake. Rosy-cheeked and gleeful, she sails straight to my table. A smooth transfer from chair to seat, and I head off to the counter. Once I've got her behind a hot chocolate, I challenge her.

'You're looking mighty smug today. Something's up, isn't it? Go on, spill.'

Her eyes narrow and she leans forward.

'Jaz wants to help. He made us an offer.'

'How? When?'

'Last session he came to Hands Free, at the centre. He just turned up.'

I screw up my face. 'Really?' Then unscrew it, because that annoyed her. 'What's the deal?'

She sits back and snaps, 'Interrogator voice! Stop it! I'm meant to be the one who talks like that.' She means, in shorthand.

'Sorry.'

'He wants us to do a video, on this platform thing. He says we can use the studio at your uni.'

I shouldn't have closed my eyes in response. A minute ago, she was chuffed to bits about this; but now she's hit the miserable great iceberg which is my dislike of Jaz, she's been knocked off course.

'What did you say?'

'I said, have you told Beth, what does she think? So, he said, yes you were in the know! *You* didn't tell me he's got the Uni onside, though, did you?'

'Well… there was a general enquiry about an access initiative, just in principle. No mention of anyone, by name. Not you or anyone. Nothing on the calendar.'

She gives me a straight look. 'Blah blah. You just won't deal with him, will you? You can't get over yourself about that article. Not even for me.'

I'm suitably ashamed; but I'm not at ease with this plan yet.

'I don't trust him, Al.'

'Yes, well. That's your problem, it shouldn't be mine. Another thing he reminded me. I have *agency*, and I don't need anyone's permission.'

'Agency. Yes. He's right. Even if he is a toe-rag.' I shrug. 'And it's not just about me, anyway, it's about Mum. It's about *family.*'

'He never mentioned me, though, in his article, did he? He never said, this composer had a twin who used to make up music too.'

I stare across at her. 'Why do you say that?'

'Because it would've been a good story… Look, Beth, what do you want from him? Isn't he allowed to make it up to us? Isn't that what ought to happen?'

'He hasn't ever apologised. Not in words.'

'Fucksake Beth, you don't judge people on their words.'

We're both quiet for a moment. Slightly peevy, or maybe just ashamed, I point out that she's the one who spends hours each day scrolling through other people's disagreements. She pushes back: that isn't what it's about, and anyway, I ought to look at Jaz's posts some time instead of criticising. Then she realises her chocolate's going cold.

I'm pondering what she just said – *it would've been a good story* – and she changes tack, as if to rouse me from something, and cheer me up.

'Anyway. It turned into a boy-fight.'

'Tell me more.'

'So, after I said about Beth, John says, *no, but really, have you talked to Beth properly*. Then Jaz gets all excited and swears and waves his hands in the air.   Then John does his calm-down voice. And he says, all casual, like, *Beth's in the band now anyway.* Bombshell, or what?'

'We should do it,' I concede. 'It's all performing experience. You've got a little frothy moustache there.'

My sister's warming me up again; she opens wide eyes to tell me, 'Jaz said, we ought to change our name!'

'Sky Blue Pink? But it's a brilliant name!'

'I know. He said we had to get the right message across. Something less flimsy. Something that says *we-are-boss.* He thinks I'm five and he's reading me a story.'

'He's an idiot.'

'But he *was* trying be helpful, Beth… Anyway. John said, Sky Blue Pink, it's a triad. Three short words, equals strong.'

'Like it.'

Alice's bright eyes tell me, John was brilliant. They were fighting over her, and John won.

I beam back at her: 'He's a threedy, John.'

'Mm-hm.' Her eyes twinkle, and she licks the chocolate moustache.

'You were great, the other day, with the band practice, and everything. And us working together… It feels right. Did you think that?'

'Yes… Yeah.' She looks as if ambushed by that thought, surprised, but not unpleasantly; and gives me a little punch on the arm.

I'm mellow enough to ask: 'D'you remember the piano? When it was new?'

'Yeah.'

'I've been thinking about it. Who was it for?'

'Us.'

I nod a 'thought so.'

Alice shakes her head. 'Beth. It's never good, when you go back to that time. Never mind that. What happens next? That's the only question that needs an answer.'

I groan. 'I wish I knew. Sometimes it seems that everything's going to come together, and all those near misses before – with Jaz, and the Arcana Prize – went wrong for a purpose. Only I don't trust myself not to screw up the next time.'

She puts her mug down, clasps her hands to rest them on the table, and leans forward slightly: 'Look. Smiley eyes, serious mouth.'

This is our counselling face and means she's going to psychologise me. I nod permission.

'OK, pretend I'm your fairy godmother and I can grant you one wish.'

'One wish? If you're only allowed *one thing*, it would have to be save the planet, obviously; and where would that leave me? In real life?' Then I remember… 'Just a minute. Jaz asked me the same thing after I kicked him out. What did I want? And *he* said I was only allowed to want one thing.'

'Did he? Maybe the universe is trying to tell you something.'

'This is Mum-talk.'

'You're always worried about what happened last time.' Fair comment. I'm listening.

'OK,' she says, 'three. Three wishes. Only they all have to be for yourself.'

'Three wishes is always two good ones and one bad one that ruins everything.'

'Three things. Go on.'

'I want Theo to ask me out. Properly. On my own.'

'Granted. Easy. You ask him first.'

I close my eyes. Unthinkable. But maybe she's done this with John, so I ask, 'Would you do that?'

'Course. If I was sure he'd say yes. Theo might say no. But if you're desperate, best get it over with. Move on. OK. One down, two to go.'

'I want you and me to be together more.'

'Granted. How d'you think you got into the band? With no audition?' She cocks her head. 'Wish number three?'

'Number three… I need to be sure I'm not wasting my time, trying to write music. I want a sign.'

Alice picks up a teaspoon by way of a magic wand, when suddenly everybody's attention, including mine, is grabbed by a wonderful sound coming from upstairs. Two little girls, maybe three or four years old, have stationed themselves at opposite sides of the circular balcony – for us, the hole in the ceiling – and are sending owl calls one to the other, *te-woo, te-woo*… They grip the bannisters in both hands, and push their shoulders back to summon all their strength. After a couple of repetitions, one of them stretches the call a bit longer; her sister imitates; and in their impatience to see who can make the note last longest, their voices overlap, and rise in pitch and volume. It echoes round the gallery, upstairs, downstairs.

The mum stops them, in the end, and we both get the giggles.

'There's your answer.'

'Come on, soft lass,' I tell my sister. 'Sup up, and we'll do the art.'

We can't leave the exhibition without saying hello to all our friends in the permanent collection: Queen Elizabeth, the babies with the bubbles, the cavalier kid and the Cézanne murder, Dante and Beatrice, Murillo's yummy mummy. I execrate the wallpaper, as I always do; and Alice gets too close to the paintings, as she always does, hoping for a telling off, thereby luring the guards into a pleasant conversation. We skit, and admire, and are grateful to have something else to talk about. We've stopped in front of *The Stonebreaker*, mesmerised by the searching sunlight and the heat and dust that come off it. A poor country boy sits high on a hill, between a way stone and a dead tree, smashing rocks with a hammer, eyes on the ground, and his back to the beauty of the landscape that rolls to the horizon behind him. All his focus is on the particularity of this stone, and that.

The little kids who were doing the bird-calls earlier are still a presence, and every now and then we're aware of them practising stage whispers, or making their trainers squeak, or heaving big sighs, to see how far their pretend boredom will carry.

Alice says, 'If you're going to behave badly, there's nothing like a public place. It's so limiting at home.' She's right. Smooth floors, glass doors, gratifying echoes bouncing off everything. Such a great space, a place to play, to be tutted at and shushed. 'God, Beth, were we like that? Poor Mum.'

'You know, Uncle Pat's got video of us when we were little.'

'You mean, before?'

'Yes. Last time I visited him and Dot, he let me have a look.'

'Oh, I'd like to see that!' Her eyes light up. 'What were we like? Were we the same? Can you tell who's who?'

'Same dress. Same hair. It was Christmas, on the video, and we played a duet. Snowy Song. We wrote it.'

'Oh! Did we?' She grins and shakes her head. 'Was it any good?'

'You were good. I was rubbish.'

The grin broadens. 'Ha!'

'I think you were always the one with the talent.'

'Correct.'

'No, really, I'm not joking…' It's going to come out in a rush. '*You* were the one who wanted to play, the old piano was shot and you were already so good, they knew you needed something better… In the video, *you* were the one with the ideas, and I was pretty lame really. It was only after the accident that I started to practise seriously. Because of it, even. It was something I could lose myself in, and they didn't need to worry because they could hear where I was and what I was up to. They knew I was safe. On my own, nobody could look at me with that look. And I was left holding something; I was taking care of it, for you… But you never came back to it, and I just carried on with the piano lessons, and one thing led to another, and… Alice… seriously… Lately, I've started to wonder if I'm on the wrong path, and it's been the wrong path all these years.'

'What are you trying to say?' Alice turns from the painting to me, and her eyes narrow.

'Allie… I've started to wonder… Have I been living your life for you?'

Hotly, she answers, 'I bloody well hope so.' Then cools: 'No, you haven't. You've just been making the best of a bad job. We both have. Or… is there some other big thing you want to do, instead of music?'

'No.' I feel forlorn and a little stupid, realising this.

'We're stuck with it, then.'

We turn back for one last look at the boy at his labour. His cheeks are pink, and he doesn't seem unhappy.

51 Fuel

I woke in the night with ideas coming out like stars, so I've scribbled them down in this white notebook I got for Christmas. Figures, riffs, possible projects.

Yesterday, I heard some third-years give the sort of chamber music performance that Jaz despises on the grounds of elitism. It only confirmed me in the belief that music is truer to life than any words can ever be. One instrument states a musical idea, and hands it to another; they hand it back. They pass it round. They might argue what to do with it. They might chop it into bits. But by the end of the movement, they've each listened to what the other said; something's happened, and that original idea has morphed into a more powerful, more persuasive, more beautiful thing. I think back to what I wrote in my teenage diary, about music revealing the intimate pathways of the mind, the syntax of thought without content. That was insufficient. So much chamber music is more than a depiction of how it feels to be alive: it's a moral demonstration of how we ought to behave. How human discourse ought to be, that is, marked by listening.

Perhaps, in ten years' time, this thought will appear as overblown as my teenage manifesto, in the old padlocked notebook, seems to me now. That doesn't matter. If this is the fuel that's going to drive me forward, nobody needs to know.

52 Dark

Everything seemed to be zipping along. I flew down those stairs at such a speed, with my coat half-buttoned, careless of the February dark and the drizzle. An hour ago, I came back alone to the bare light on the steep staircase, and nobody's, everybody's, anybody's mail under my feet.

I imagined there would be time, on the journey over to Crosby and back, to talk. I thought we'd discuss ways of giving the choir a kick in the pants. I'd ask Theo what he really thought about *Silence*; and I couldn't wait to tell him what Alice and her band have done with it. I imagined he'd laugh and we'd laugh together; and I might tell him about Alice's John and my relief that he turns out to be so solid; I imagined telling him why I'd been just a little bit worried that Alice was getting too involved, and setting herself up for a fall. And how I couldn't tell my mum because she'd tell me not to over-react, then worry herself sick on the quiet. He might take my hand. I could even imagine myself telling him, some day, how Alice and Mum and I were getting on each other's nerves so much we couldn't carry on living together, and how incredibly hard it is proving to live apart. As if each one of us is homesick for a place that hasn't existed for many years. Or maybe ever. I was ready to tell him anything, all the very things I'd never think of telling Jaz. I was nearly that woman at the bus stop: *Me Nan's waitin' for a liver transplant. Been on the pop.*

But the doorbell rang, and I flew downstairs, and behind the rain-spattered window of Shari's mum's Renault, there was Eleni, sitting in the back with Theo, deep in a conversation which barely faltered when Paul gave up the front passenger seat for me, and joined them. I got a friendly hello from Theo, but it placed me firmly in the background. As we drove, I struggled to follow the conversation behind me, which was in

English, but mostly about people I don't know. Eleni was doubtful about something, and Theo tried to reassure her. Paul kept out of it.

The church felt like a mausoleum. By daylight, in summer, it's an ugly, hulking box; the red of the brick and sandstone beats back at you, dominating the main road. Tonight, dismal inside as out, it seemed waiting to receive the disappointment I carried inside me. So drear. A liturgical performance, with no interval. Now, hours later, my throat's still dry from the incense, which accounts for the first beer but not the second. This second bottle is to help me swallow it all.

The programme explained that Yötön Yö – literally, nightless night – is what the Finns call the midnight sun. Astronomically speaking we're miles away from that. Dim electric lights in the nave were switched off at seven thirty exactly, leaving only the singers in the chancel able to see and be seen.

I sat on Theo's left, Eleni on his right. I gave them space and faced the front. I made sure to be still.

The first notes of the first deep intonation electrified me. Listen up, it said. Don't move until you've understood.

That huge sound came from a little stick man standing far ahead. He looked so flimsy, narrow-chested, in his funny robes, yet held such power. Theo, and Eleni. Theo and Eleni. I should have realised. Why wouldn't they go out together? Why wouldn't they be in love? Why wouldn't they have things to say to each other that they wouldn't say to me? Things which, simply, don't translate?

I gave myself up to it. It was the most extraordinary singing I've ever heard. Then it ended, and we all would have to speak.

This music, with its extraordinary spaciousness, its solemnity, its excitement, its radiance, and its consolation – the consolation of knowing whatever pain and grief and disappointment there may be in the world, there is beauty too; this music is still resonating, running through my very bones right now. And yet, at that moment when Theo turned and asked me what I'd thought, all I could grope for were platitudes. How the Finns, like the Russians, are famous for producing super-deep basses, how accomplished the whole choir was, how worth the journey, how worthy of a bigger audience.

I said something like, 'I wonder if the span of this music comes from the composer's hand. Deep chords. The low notes are so very low, aren't they? The wavelengths are so wide, you can hardly identify the note. You're just guessing. It's more a rumble than a tune.'

I was thinking aloud, and I am genuinely intrigued by this: the way we as listeners guess, and fill in the shape of a musical line that stretches our actual perception. Theo's frown made me feel so stupid.

'It's a dialogue between heaven and earth. Part of us can fly, and part of us needs to feel the earth beneath our feet.' Then he shrugged and smiled, and said, 'You're a pianist, you come to Rachmaninov from a different route,' as if that were some sort of excuse.

He thinks I'm shallow. He does.

Eleni was nice to me. She said I had a point, that there was a lot of illusion here. The low notes are very low, yes, because he had deep basses to write for, and that makes the high seem higher than it really is.

Of course, she would know. She has the most extraordinary voice. She is all warmth and vigour, and there are no hard edges about her person. Her eyes are huge and bright and when she wears black, it seems to make her shine.

Afterwards, as we walked back to the car, he put his arm around her.

Mum was right about the music, too. I didn't follow the programme, I was just letting myself be carried, *a feather on the breath of God*, when a number started so exquisitely, from one high note that opened downwards to a chord, and I remembered: this must be the Cherubic Hymn, the bit my Mum was talking about.

I'm playing it over and over now, at home, and yes, it is as she said. Voices descend quietly to earth. They gather. They deliver a loud and thrilling message. Then they float back upwards, moving close yet not quite together, but helping each other up, up to the top of a scale, and – implied – silence and calm; and the place they end up in is a different place from where they all began.

I get the world so wrong because I live in my head. Because even as I explain this to myself, it sounds like dry analysis when what I long for is that sense of transformation, for my life to transition, through surprising yet convincing modulations, into a different key. Not to be alone. And to be at one with... I don't know... someone. Something.

53 Feedback

When people say they're *reaching out,* does that mean they think you need their help in some way, or that they're fumbling to make contact with someone who might be as messed up as they are? I'm sitting at work, looking at that official email which the Prof pinged over to me some weeks ago, and which set this whole thing going with Alice and the band. It's got me thinking it would be worth spending a chunk of the afternoon checking out those aspects of Jaz Ander that didn't concern me when we were sleeping together.

Of course, his social feed might be a bluff. He obviously spends lots of time liking, and replying, sharing and generally joining things together; it's as if he has to pass on every rumour, from the sinister meaning of blue stripes in toothpaste to the abdication of the monarch, just to prove he's right on point. Few threads start with him. He's always agreeing with people, so he probably changes his mind a lot. But Alice is right, there is a huge amount of disability stuff, and brain injury stuff. There's loads of it. He shares everything, not just posts from charities which anyone might see, but specialised things about research projects, and medical matters, in language I don't understand. He follows boffins and warriors and therapists, all over the world. Social-wise, he's a bulimic, but these things are a constant in his diet.

It goes back a long way, too. But there's nothing personal to tell me why.

The other thing that's interesting is the push-back he got on the Tiger Mother piece. Old hat. The pushy mother is just as unhelpful and outdated a trope as the authoritarian father-figure, says some wordy person called Erin. Can't we get beyond this? Can't we imagine better?

Then it occurs to me that there's something odd about Jaz Ander's behaviour in the months since I kicked him out. He's been pestering me, yes. But only about Art with a capital A, notably his novel, and Alice. Perhaps he really has been trying to make amends. Through all our recent irritating exchanges, and in spite of the sense he's always in my path, he's never made any sort of move, far less come near to suggesting that we get together again. He's so platonic it's almost offensive. Add this to my humiliation over Eleni, and the evidence suggests I'm not very good at reading men. I need to nail this, to figure out how I've got it so wrong not once but twice.

Although I promised myself I wouldn't ever initiate communication again, I have to message him.

Hi Jaz. Srs Q. How come I didn't break yr heart?

Two hours later, there's a reply.

How come I didn't break yrs? Same reason, prly.

Then after a few minutes:

It was never going to work and we both knew it.

I enter his number and he picks up.

'Look,' I say, 'I'm not trying to get at you here, Jaz. No hard feelings. But you did say you loved me. I might have expected you to be a *bit* sad.'

'Did I? Yes, I suppose I did. But you said it first, and… Well…'

'Well?'

'It's a thing girls say, isn't it? A girl says, *I love you*, so you say it back. Be fair. What was I meant to say?'

At least he's being honest, so I might as well be, too. 'Well, Jaz, I thought I did, but I was wrong. I suppose we were both a bit daft.'

'OK. I get that.' He takes time to swallow; then moves on. 'All the things I liked about you, Beth… I do still like them. And the things I didn't like so much… well, they're not my problem, are they?'

I'm more curious about Jaz Ander now than ever I was in the fortnight we lived together.

'Can I just ask… all this stuff about helping Alice… Do you have some special interest in disability?'

'I'm interested in a lot of things. But I'd rather leave disability journalism to disabled journalists.'

'And brain injury? Only… I'm looking at what you share.'

When he sighs, it's more weary than sad. 'I had a friend… Look, we all know someone who's experienced that. It's not easy.' His voice shifts from downbeat to upbeat in a moment: 'You have to fight for resources! I made a promise that I would, and I do. I try.'

'You never said. We never talked about it.'

'No.' He's not going to talk about it now. If we'd been closer, I'd have known that.

'Where are you living, Jaz? I never asked you because it wasn't any of my business and I truly didn't want to know. But it isn't a state secret, is it? Did things work out OK?'

'I got a flat share, pretty easy as it turned out. Off Newsham Park.'

'Cool. Well done. That's a relief. It's such a pain, combing through the ads.'

'Oh, I didn't have to. I ran into an old friend from Uni. Just, random, you know…So that worked out well. Similar tastes in music.'

I laugh. 'So you can play your goddamn awful cheesy pop twenty-four seven, full volume, no problem.'

'Yeah, pretty much.' I can hear the grin in his voice and imagine the way he's nodding; I'm feeling almost affectionate towards him now. 'Downside, though, she doesn't read much, so with my writing she's a bit, like, *whatever*. I just crack on. It's not personal.'

Oh. I get it. Friends with benefits. A random encounter, maybe with the help of an app. What was it my mum got so mad about, during the Great Affront? If a woman's got her own flat, they're queuing up to have a go. *Every wastrel in town.*

Jaz waits for me to say something, and when I don't, asks, 'How's the choir?'

'I think I'm going to have to knock it on the head.'

'Amateurs, eh?'

'Yeah. Amateurs.'

'Nice talking.'

'Yeah. Bye.'

There, I've set my intention, Mum. I'll have to find a way of telling the singers it's all over, because it's going to be a terrible thing, week after week, to have to sit opposite Theo, the man with the beautiful face who has shaken my hand and touched it once or twice but never put his arm around me or kissed me and probably never will, who thinks I'm shallow and an idiot, on which points I'm inclined to agree. What a raw beginner I am.

54 Adhio

Brilliant. Here's another thing to give up.

The Go Greek Group have been on my back, reminding me with their silly cartoon notifications that *Learning a language needs daily practice!* They've missed me, they say. Missed the chance to earn a few bucks by waving a load of irrelevant ads in my face; a sonic device for pest control was the latest. Well, there's more chance of meeting a mouse or a cockroach in my flat than a Greek speaker, now. So it's *adhio* from me.

A week on, though, they want my feedback on their online offer. I will take the survey, if only to tell them how pissed off I am.

Most of it is radio buttons. I don't read the text, just select 0 for everything.

Aha, this is what I want. There's an open text box to vent my spleen. Here goes.

Please note

Nobody goes into a bank, this is a waste of vocabulary.

No British person haggles, they use supermarkets when abroad. If a thing's too expensive they leave it on the shelf. Again, language-free transaction.

I don't wish to talk about pets, I'm an adult. Also, hamster is like Google, it's the same in any language.

Family vocabulary. Mother, father, sister, brother, well, maybe. Niece, nephew, cousin – now you're being intrusive. Godmother, godfather, godson, goddaughter? WHO WANTS TO KNOW?

Right. That's me signing out.

I can't get out of this appearance at the Aphrodite, though. I can't let my sister down. She's already gutted that Dad's going to miss our performance by a matter of days. Meanwhile, they've quarantined a cruise ship in Japan because of some lurgy, so Mum says she'll settle on him getting back at all. That'll do me.

55 Open Mic

The guy on Liverpool Live made it rhyme with hermaphrodite; so here I am ready for the open mic at the Afro-dite bar. Seats are disappearing; I'm sitting with Shari and Paul, at the far end, waiting for Alice and the band, keeping an eye on the road outside, and hoping that Theo won't be here tonight. I dread seeing him again. This will be my last visit. A shame, because I liked this place; the plinky music on the CD, the elegant chalk script chalked on the specials board which I now can read in parts, although I wouldn't understand without the translation that accompanies it. Across the room from us, and tucked under the stair, the single table with the pot of cyclamen is reserved and unoccupied. Uncle Stelios hovers over it, simultaneously greeting the public and preventing anyone from sitting there. I can say *Yia sou* to Uncle Stelios and tell him the setup is *polì kalà*. I've got one eye on the street, through the plate glass window which is already licked by steamy patches here and there.

A white people carrier draws up outside; the driver walks round to open the door. This will be Alice. Yes. Two sticks emerge first, which he takes into his hands, and those are Alice's feet swinging round onto the pavement. Tall, wide, slope-shouldered, and in black, here comes Vilma, the random factor, ready to shake her egg. There's John; regular guy; he stands by as the driver opens the boot for him and brings out his guitar. But who's this? Someone else is getting out of the back of the cab and walks round now. They must have picked Mum up on the way. Sweet of them. And a peacock blue headwrap pops up, which can only be Marsha from choir. Marsha who knows stuff, *all the bad, and all the glad,* as well as being the queen of fun. And she's not the last to pop out of the taxi, because here's Jenny Johns in her mac.

Uncle Stelios steps forward to greet them all as they bunch in the doorway, open armed: '*Yia sas, yia sas*! Welcome! Let me shake you by the hand.' Alice, in her technicolour dreamcoat, delighted; John, broadly grinning; Vilma, surprised into giggles; then Mum explaining, 'I'm Alice's mum. Mel. We're the groupies.' He leads them through the tables, and they bump their way towards us.

I manage to engineer it so that Marsha sits near me. She's the one person I can talk to right now. She reminds me of the great Jessye Norman, as seen on YouTube, for the bicentenary of the revolution, draped in a monumentally billowing tricolore, and belting out the Marseillaise whilst apparently gliding on castors around the monument in the Place de la Bastille.   Because for all her wisecracks and her off-duty pursuit of fun, Marsha has a poise about her which is unattainable by skinny types like me. There's a certain gravitas that comes from spending her days amongst the dead; and she has a beautiful profile which she often holds, like the diva, tilted slightly upwards as if seeking the light.

No sooner are they all settled, and introductions have been made, than a big bloke with a dark curly mop of hair gets up from the other side of the bar and walks across, carrying a pint of lager close against his chest. The glass alone puts him closer to Mum's age than mine. He looks Greek and sounds very Liverpudlian when he tells them, 'So this is Alice and her band! I'm a big fan,' and barely pauses before steering into 'Can I ask you something? How did a lovely girl like you end up on crutches, eh?' 'Big accident,' she says. 'Aw, love, that's terrible, how're you doing now?' 'Good,' she answers with a big grin. 'A lorra people can't be bothered, they just give up,' he says. 'Good on you, Alice, well done, it's lovely to see you here, have a great night,' and he puts his free hand gently on her shoulder and gives a little squeeze. She smiles. He repeats his good wishes to all of us, and moves off, still cradling his drink.

We exchange glances.

'Fans!' Shari beams at Alice.

'You're public property now,' says Jenny with a cockeyed look.

Mum says, 'He meant well. He's harmless enough.'

I'm watching the easy smile on my sister's pink face and thinking: there's a fine line between intrusive and interested. It reminds me of another great humdinger barney that we had when I was maybe sixteen, when Mum dragged me to church one time, which ended up with her screaming something like, *for pity's sake, Bethany, you might not take communion, OK, but why in God's name would you refuse a blessing? If there was one on offer?*

Alice has always been open to blessing, in any guise, even the ham-fisted, red-heart emoji-care of a stranger.

Baskets of pitta bread and plates of hummus, tzatziki and taramasalata appear, without anybody having ordered them. From the other side of the room, Stelios nods and smiles, *enjoy.*

Several conversations set off at once, and my mum is holding forth.

Marsha leans towards me and says, 'That last rehearsal was a shocker, eh?'

'I got a telling-off from Mum for my bad behaviour.' I'd let out an audible groan when the tenors missed their entry for the nth time.

'I tell you, our Theo's got the patience of a saint.'

She tilts her head away from me now and gives me a good hard look; then brings her lower lip over the top one and nods. 'What's going on, Beth? You look like you've lost a quid and found a button.'

'Nothing's going on. I'm just... stuck, really. In the doldrums.'

'But surely things are going well? With *Silence*, and everything?'

'Oh. That. Well, yes. Although in fact Alice's band have come up with a much better version.' At least this thought makes me smile, even as I acknowledge my underdog status with a shrug. 'The thing is... You put your heart and soul into something, and hours of work; then once you've done it, it's... dead to you, really. Anything you've actually achieved in life looks so small. *Dead pants,* as the Germans say. *Tote Hose.*'

'So young, and so bleak,' says Marsha. 'Bloody hell, kid, you've got your whole life in front of you. The world's your lobster.'

I stare at the table top and all its tiny dents and scratches, thinking: is that a good thing?

'I've not finished anything of my own, nothing I wanted to, for ages. *Silence* was thrust upon me.'

'Scared you've lost it, eh?'

'Maybe I never had it in the first place. Oh, I get ideas.' Little does Marsha know, I'm being taunted by them nightly. 'It's just that they seem to crumble once I try to grip them, I don't know how to turn them into anything. I don't know what they are.'

Marsha rests one elbow on the table, cups her chin in her hand, and takes a different sort of look at me.

'How old are you? You've spent, what, most of the last twenty years on a treadmill from one exam to another, you've got all the grades and the letters after your name, collected all the stickers, and now you expect to produce something? Where's it going to come from? If you haven't lived?' She leans back and plonks her hands back together. It's that obvious to her.

'What do you suggest? A gap year? You have to *fill* a gap. What would I do?'

'Take a break. Travel. Go abroad. Fall in love.'

'Hm.'

'Well, that's what other people do.'

And he's here. Him and Eleni. I'm sick to my stomach. He grins and waves to us all, catches my eye for a split second; Eleni waves too; conversations stop, greetings are shouted across the room, above the tinned R and B. At least there's no chance of him coming over to sit with us, with space so tight. They head towards the cyclamen table, but Stelios steps forward with open arms, embraces the pair of them, and guides them to a couple of seats on the end of the long table where a big family group, who are tucking into *mezedes,* greet them like old friends and budge up. I look away.

Alice, Vilma and John are squashed around a table for two, which has been drawn close to ours, and close to Mum and Jenny. Jenny seems to be interviewing them; against the music, I can't hear her questions, or their answers, only John's fulsome 'Oh, yes,' 'Oh no,' and an intriguing 'Oh aye, we do, we always do.' She's got her eye trained on John, more than Alice. Checking him out. Alice looks so happy.

We're well into our second round before the live music starts. A pair of old blokes with guitars shamble up to the platform, which is barely a platform, more a trip hazard; one of them is the man who greeted Alice, earlier. As they set up, his partner drawls words of welcome into the microphone whilst looking at the wires around his feet, and checking the amp; only when he's happy does he lift his head to face the crowd with the confident grin of somebody at home. They lead off with *Take me Home, Country Roads.* A few people join in.

There's going to be a twenty-minute break in an hour's time, after which the shaggy MC and his pal will signal the start of second half with another classic, and then we're on.

I'm not nervous about playing – although I am a bit concerned to know just what Alice is drinking. It's some sort of cocktail which may or may not be alcoholic. I don't think she's as used to drink as I am, not combined with performing. I dread Theo's eyes upon me. In a few hours, this will all be over and I can put it all behind me. Tomorrow, first thing, I'm going to get up and write my formal resignation from the role of choir accompanist. And think about what Marsha said. Get off the treadmill. Maybe I should pack in my job at the

University; hanging round Petra Laing only makes me feel inadequate, after all. I'll not be able to afford the flat. I'd have to go back to Menlove Avenue. Or find a job abroad.

One lot of performers takes over from another, on and on, until the room joins in a boozy chorus of *Hallelujah,* which signals the break. The table gets talking again. Mum's holding forth.

'Trouble with Liverpudlians, we *are* awful. We do talk too much, and we do skit too much, and we shout and we cry too much, and we're no respecters of status. Why would you be?'

'You forgot modest,' says Jenny. Everybody laughs.

'Jesus, Mum, you'd go ballistic if I tried to say the French were self-important or the Germans ate too much red meat. You're the one who's rude about professional Scousers, and now you're turning into one.'

'We-e-ell…' I can see she's having fun. 'Anyway, if you take the clichés out, what have you got left but a whacking great mush that could be anywhere? That's how people end up talking about the weather.' She raises an eyebrow and sniggers like a teenager. 'That's what they do, down south.'

'That's all they're allowed,' says Shari.

I groan. 'Oh, right, that's all we need. Bring on the north-south divide. Any other unhelpful notions we'd like to put out there? Honestly, this is the sort of stuff you read in the sort of newspapers you don't read.'

'Number one Scouse skill: you've got to laugh at yourself.'

'Oh, Jesus, there goes another cliché in the bucket.'

Shari turns to Paul: 'Anyway, what's wrong with Cypriots, then?'

'Too hospitable. Too hospitable by half.'

He gestures to the table-top, which is covered in glasses and bottles, full, empty, half empty, and the little plates smeared with the last mouthfuls of the dips that we're all too polite to claim, grins from ear to ear and shakes his head.

'We're here on a mission to entertain you.'

'To entertain, to nourish and to educate,' says my mum. 'Don't forget the stuff the Greeks did for the Romans before they did anything for us.'

Something catches Paul's attention, and he points to the far side of the room. 'Also, we're too passionate. See, Theo's Uncle Stelios, seventy-five years old, and he keeps a table free every night for his lady, and she never comes; and he pines... But look! Tonight...'

Sure enough, Uncle Stelios is helping a smartly dressed woman to her place at that very table. She's standing with her back to us while he moves it out into the gangway, so that she can get round the tight space and into her seat, which is wedged against the staircase.

'Aw,' says Shari, 'Sweet!'

'Aw,' says Jenny, wrinkling her nose in appreciation.

The woman wears her hair in an old-fashioned chignon. It's grey. And familiar.

He's taken the woman's stick, and placed it carefully against the wall. Once she's seated, she looks up at him: a fine, handsome face, hair scraped back. I let out an expletive as my mum hisses, 'Isn't that Petra Laing?'

'What? Your boss?' says Jenny.

'Your guru? Your role model, eh?' says Marsha and digs me in the ribs. 'Ah well, all work and no play...'

Now the old bloke who kicked the session off comes over to Alice's table, and says, 'Eh, come on, ladies, shake a leg, yer on next, after me and Norrie. You need to get yourselves set up. We're just doing the one. Warm them up for yer, like.'

John helps shift things so that Alice can get out. Table, chair or human, no leg is safe from her two sticks in this crush. It's sensible for me to lead the way, because I'll be standing behind them when we perform, but I don't want to draw attention, so I carry the upright keyboard like a shield in front of me; Vilma brings up the rear. I copy the veteran MC, and busy myself with the kit, eyes down. I ignore the argy-bargy over which mic to use; John tells them, Alice will stay seated. The MC and Norrie, guitar and now banjo slung round their respective shoulders, have to place themselves in front of her, and the stand they're using is almost in the audience, close enough to nick a chip. I'm safely tucked away on the back row. John, breathy, asks: Which two? Because we've prepped five songs thinking it was three, but in fact it's only two. Alice is in no doubt: '*Like it.* Then *Dread.*' I can't protest, it's her call, and anyway, there's no time for discussion, the guys have finished tuning, and look poised to start, when Vilma gasps, 'Oh! I forgot my egg,' and for a moment looks ready to push her way back through the scrum. Jenny, realising what's going on, grabs the shaky egg off the table, and waves it aloft, shouting 'Here you are, love!' and it looks like she's going to hurl it through the air.

The guitarist with the mic protests: 'Arr eh, we're not *that* bad!'

Jenny rocks with laughter. A couple of people cheer as the egg is safely passed forward. We settle down.

The room is silenced by three chords on the guitar. A decent pause, and the other imitates. Ironic groans and knowing chuckles: *Duelling Banjos.* They're well amped. They milk the pauses in the slow call-and-response intro; but before long, the gaps are infiltrated by the scratchy sound of a very human argument going on.

I can't help tuning in to this. That's Uncle Stelios' voice, deep, pleading; and a woman, dry, indignant, whispering, but cutting. A voice familiar to me but never before heard in this register. The venerable Prof Laing, whose utterances, *ex cathedra,* are scant, and precise; who always leaves space for an echo round her words; bun or no bun, Prof Laing is frankly, unleashed, and off on one. It's a relief when the main section starts and the two players race away noisily into the blue grass. This musical ride is a real bone-shaker; they're well in control; and I hope John isn't losing his nerve as I hear him mumble 'Holy shit,' because he's the guitarist who's got to follow that. Meanwhile the argument by the stairs rattles on, but it seems to have ended before the music does. There's applause, for some time.

Then the mic rings out. 'You've seen them down Liverpool 1, you've seen them on YouTube and now we've got them here. Give a big Aphrodite welcome for Alice Collier and Sky Blue Pink.'

At these words the two blokes step aside. Right in my line of sight, Stelios is bent over the cyclamen table, apparently pleading, gesturing with both arms towards the band. So now she's seen me. Petra Laing's eyes pop wide open and we stare at one another.

I blink first. I'm not meant to know things like this about Petra Laing. She's not meant to have a personal life, or at least, I'm not meant to witness it. I need her to be a modern-day, secular Hildegard, the embodiment of dedication, scholarly detachment and wisdom. She can only be embarrassed by my presence and the fact that I've caught her arguing with some old geezer in a bar. And what's even worse, it's no longer watertight, this seal between my hapless private life and my life of music. All these thoughts are compressed into an instant, and instantly dismissed, because I have to turn my focus to our set. As much as I want the ground to open up and swallow me, this is my sister's big night.

John counts us in, and off we go. The way Alice sings *I like it* makes everybody want to join in. Except Petra Laing. We get to the end, and I don't believe she's moved a muscle. I daren't catch her eye again, I can only look at the table next to her, with unfocused, performer's eyes. I'm not even sure she's joined in the applause. Which suddenly makes me really cross. I feel like shouting, 'Don't diss my sister. Listen to her. Treat her with respect!' Although perhaps she's as mortified as I am.

Now, it looks as though Alice is going to introduce *Dread* herself, and something flips inside my chest. This could all go wrong; she might stumble, speaking in public; and although this crowd are a good-natured lot, anything which dents her confidence could make her – or the others – more likely to flake when it comes to the music. The less experience you have, the more peripherals distract. I have no idea what she's going to say.

Alice takes her time. 'We wrote this with my sister.' She looks over her shoulder, to identify me. 'Not the words.' She grins; and says, slowly, darkly, 'That's someone else's fault.'

As we all chuckle, a liberating thought streaks through my head. I RESIGN. I resign from everything apart from this one moment now. I resign from the Faculty of Music and the booking system and Petra Laing's perfectly disciplined tutelage; I resign from the Lyceum Singers. I'll never need to see Theo Christodoulou again; I'll never set foot in the Aphrodite bar again; I'll never need to watch Theo and Eleni sharing the dips. And I've already stopped learning useless things in an impossible language. IN THIS MOMENT I am going to give this song everything I can throw at it. I have nothing to lose.

The change in style from sixties' Mersey beat to *Dread* is brutal. I can feel the audience wince, but soon they're just so many sheep and cattle in a landscape that flashes by as we cut through the air on a motorbike. The engine thrums. The gear changes sing. Alice gives it large, we all do. *Silence is all we dread, dread, dread* – so we're not going to leave room for any. Until the volume drops for *ransom in a voice*, and Alice's voice, now tender, rich and warm, becomes the focus. Even Vilma has the musical sense to cut the shaky egg for this section. This piece has a shape, and far more definition than my first scoring offered; and yes, I want that final reprise to sound even shinier and more important than the first statements, so I modify the chord by adding a genius, minor sixth, which I also sing, *molto con belto*: *Dread, dread, dread.* I can do this.

I wasn't miked up, so my vocal contribution probably got lost. I don't care. It felt good. There's applause, some people nod approval, jut their chins, waggle their heads, well it was different, wasn't it? We know that was better than any of our rehearsals. Alice is like a dog with two tails. And from her table cramped under the stairs, an internationally acclaimed composer dips her head and raises her hands in applause. Then seeks my eye, beaming.

We trek back in single file to our camp, at one end of the room. It feels a quarter of the journey it was last time, although the physical obstacles haven't changed. Everyone looks pleased. My responsibility is discharged, and a bottle of Keo is waiting. I allow myself to float. I'm gliding on the notion that everything about my life, now, is going to change, because I'll make it change; I don't need to know how, but simply that I've *set my intention*, as my yogini mum would say. Look at her. Chuffed to bits with the pair of us. Alice raises her lurid glass to me and we congratulate each other with a look. I'm pretty sure it's full of sugar.

There are so many congratulations, exclamations, observations flying round that it's a while before we realise that the next act hasn't materialised. In fact, the shaggy MC is watching, apparently waiting, while Uncle Stelios is no longer pleading with my Prof, but with Eleni; he clearly wants something from her. Now Theo and Eleni have stood up. Theo works his way across the room to our table, nods to each of us and congratulates Vilma, John, Alice, then me, generously. I ought to be thrilled but it's just making me miserable. I'm happy to let my sister speak for us both, which she does: 'Not bad for beginners, eh?' He laughs beautifully, straight from the gut. Nods for a while, his eyes darting between us both. Then the broad smile drops and it's clear he wants a private word with Paul.

He stands behind his friend, and the melody tells me this is Greek. The only word I can make out – because it's repeated several times – is *Eleni*. Probably the easiest Greek name for a beginner to recognise. Or else I'm paranoid. Paul reaches for his bouzouki case and looks across in her direction. Perhaps they're about to perform? It looks as though something's wrong; Theo's voice has dropped; he's whispering into his friend's ear, and I was already straining to hear. Couldn't help myself. I'm trying to liberate myself from an attachment here, and he's never looked more desirable; so now I just want Theo to go away and walk out of my life. Then the dial on this whisper opens up to the start of a proper conversation, or maybe a dispute; and Paul, who's been shaking his head, says quite distinctly one thing which I don't understand at all, followed by another, which I think I do. *'Eleni, Eleni... Eleni ènai i zàderfi sou, kai òxhi dikì mou.'* He stresses the *sou* – yours. *Eleni's your cousin, not mine*. I know the word for cousin because it was over-represented in the Genesis-rivalling family section on the Go Greek website. I know the sentence structure, because my irritatingly capitalist online course was obsessed with ownership, what's yours, what's mine, dogs, godparents, carrots, and drilled it endlessly. Theo frowns, shrugs, works his way back across the room.

It's not easy for Paul to extricate himself and his bouzouki from behind the table, ready to perform, so I jump in: 'Is Eleni Theo's cousin?'

He's astonished. '*Milai ellinikà*?'

No way is he getting a Greek answer, because I keep confusing yes and no, so I just say: 'Not really, no.'

He appeals to my mother, across the table. 'She is her mother's daughter! She learns Greek! Nobody learns Greek.'

I feel awkward; but Mum's reaction is classic. She's not interested in why I took it up or how long I've been learning; she just wants to know, 'Which method are you using?'

'Um… Osmosis?' I lie.

Paul guffaws, *òsmosi,* and he's on his feet.

'No, but *is* she?'

'Of course.'

It does seem Mum was right about one thing: no knowledge is ever wasted.

I start flicking backwards through every meeting I've ever had with Theo, like one of those silly cartoons you'd do in the corners of an exercise book, to watch them jump into awkward life. Where the end is the beginning.

Eventually, the squeal of feedback wrenches me from my racing thoughts. I look up to see that Paul, Theo and Eleni are about to perform. It's a Greek song, intense, passionate; a complete mystery; and when her singing is utterly perfect again, it doesn't trouble me one *iota.* Even her eyes, when she finally opens them to acknowledge the applause, don't have quite the same effect on me as before. Might it be worth upping my game? Do I have it in me to capture his affection?

The after-scrum, as people leave, is equally momentous. Petra has just made her way across to our table, congratulated everybody, expressed delight at our chance meeting, shaken Alice by the hand, asked – with the smile of an assassin – why didn't I tell her that this was the band involved in the access initiative, and told my mum she must be very proud. Now she's gone back to pick up her coat from the cyclamen table, and has engaged Eleni in conversation. Stelios is waving what looks like a big ice-cream box at them both. Jenny's sharing a joke with John, Mum looks to be having a heart to heart with Alice about something but Paul and his mates are shouting their farewells across the room at each other, so I can't work out what it is. Then Theo's at my elbow.

'*Milai ellinikà?*'

'No! Not really. I understand a bit. That's all. Strictly passive skills only.'

'You never told me.'

'It's… recent.'

'You never said.'

'It was going to be a surprise.'

'Well, it was.' He waggles his head slightly, and takes a comical in-breath which makes his nostrils flare and lifts his whole chest up and forward, as he leans towards me: 'Congratulations on your success.'

I squeeze my eyes tight shut, which doesn't make me invisible.

'Why?' he asks, 'Why would you do this?'

All I can do is shake my head: 'Dunno.' I open my eyes again, and he's scrutinising me with a serious expression. 'I just wanted to… understand you.'

'But you're not interested in me.' His tone is completely neutral, as if he were telling me *the plate is on the table,* and his face betrays no expression.

'Yes, I am.'

'Are you sure?'

'How interested?'

'Very!' I'm looking at him and something strange is happening with time, because even as I'm gripping this moment for dear life, it's overlaid with the recent memory of my sister dispensing advice in the draughty caff at the Walker. *Ask him. Go on. Ask him out.*

'You're always polite, Beth. But I'd say, you don't like me. Sometimes you look so cross, sitting at that piano.'

'No! In fact, I've been wanting to ask you out,' I blurt, as if another, different me has taken over the microphone.

'Oh.' An eyebrow moves. 'Where do you invite me?'

I have no idea. 'Wherever. Wherever you'd like to go.'

He looks downward, apparently dejected.

'But Beth,' he says, lifting serious eyes in my direction, 'you haven't seen me in my hairnet.'

We hold that seriousness for a moment; then, with magical synchronicity, snort into giggles. It's the best measure in the whole piece. I've never been so glad to be so wrong.

56 Grammar

That was a first, Mum calling me at breakfast time. Something she didn't get a chance to tell me last night, because their taxi came and that was it. I didn't like to say, I was too busy re-writing the book of Theo, you wouldn't have got much sense out of me anyway. The urgency of this early morning conversation, which turned into a sort of benign rant, deserves examination. It was very Mum, and there were bits I'm going to want to remember.

The thing she needed me to know, i.e., how proud she is of what we did yesterday at the open mic, was just the opener, the excuse for calling. Then she rabbited on about us twins being good together, always had been; and emphasised, *she's* good for *you*; and then came this – grammar lesson? As I grew up, she says, I was trained to help my sister; well, I said, I wanted to; *No, but listen to what I'm saying... that form of words... She was always the object of that verb. We were the ones who had to help her. But who was helping you?*

Maybe Mum feels some guilt about that. She mentioned guilt herself.

We've both been guilty of infantilising her, Beth, at times...But look at Alice now, there's plenty she can do for other people. Entertain. Inspire. And she doesn't want to be helped. It all came out in a torrent, like one of her soliloquies only less polished. She sees, now, the ways in which Alice is helping me. Things she wants for both her daughters. Things she wanted us both to know. We all need help sometimes. But you've got to grip life. Don't just be trained – learn. Don't be told – find out. Don't wait to be chosen – choose. And then she came out with her stand-out quote of the day: *I don't want any daughter of mine to live her life as the subject of a passive verb.*

Bonkers. But I did agree with what she said, especially about having the wrong perspective about who's helping who. Whom.

And then – my phone confirms, that was a long call, over forty minutes – then, she started reminiscing. Did I remember, when Alice came home from rehab, she couldn't tap a rhythm? She couldn't balance on the piano stool; if she tried to play from the wheelchair, the arm was in the way; how bewildered she was that all the things she'd learned to do – playing scales, reading music, reading words, all the things she'd absorbed so easily – had just run away from her. Did I remember trying to give her theory lessons?

I'd forgotten that. But it brought back a vivid memory of how it ended, in a huge paddy, tears, and a slam of the lid.

I didn't say much in this call, only to remind Mum what a big deal it was that she and Dad got Alice back into mainstream education at all. Over the phone, we raked it all over. I can feel it now, the aching inevitability of it: my secondary school couldn't or wouldn't have her. She was out of sync with the whole curriculum. She had to have her own assistant because of the *complex needs*. Mum said, *Complex needs my arse. The main thing she needed by then was a good shout.*

And that's how our phone call ended, with me saying, well she's having a good shout now, and us both laughing, and *love you lots, love you, love you, by*e.

57 The hind leg off a donkey

I catch myself daydreaming a lot. Various rhythmic patterns visit my head; they twist and turn and hammer themselves out in the background, while my conscious mind obsessively re-capitulates all those things about Theo which I didn't know a week ago, and do know now, touches, scents and words fused from the night we talked the stars down from the skies. This awareness has such protective power that things which were embarrassing yesterday barely register at all today. Now life has a sinuous, rhythmic strength, because behind the twists and turns and stop-start syncopations, there's a steady beat that's pushing me forward.

Theodoros Christodoulou is Doros to his family, and grew up in a world different from mine. He practised the laouto in an attic where, when the Turks had invaded back in '74, his grandfather cut a notch in the window-ledge for a rifle-rest, just in case. Great-uncle Stelios had been a young man then, in a village further north, and ended up dispossessed by the conflict. They grew up close to mountains scented with pine and cedar, where copper was mined in ancient times, on an island lapped by the sea from which the goddess Aphrodite sprang.

Is it wrong to be drawn to a person because they're different, if different means exotic, bathed in myth? When exoticism is close to being patronising?

But then, what sort of voice is it who instructs you to stick to your own? I can't help liking people who are different to me. And anyway, attraction is only the start. I'm accumulating things to love.

Big things. Theo told me how, as a child, some big lads pushed him off the harbour wall, which was how he learned to swim. Little things. Like, he's afraid of spiders.

We talked and talked that night. It turns out Eleni is Stelios' granddaughter, born in Liverpool like me. He told me all about Eleni and her standards. How she's always riding the reed, which means, I think, being a bit of a diva. We compared the colours of our favourite sayings, Greek and Scouse. Doing the duck, being in dock, slowly the cabbage, being in bulk. We laughed again about giving Jaz a wide berth. I warned him, though, that if Jaz came anywhere near a choir practice, my mum'd give him down the banks, and he said, ah, you mean, he'll eat wood! On that point, though, I wasn't joking.

My myth of Theo is a powerful one, in which he's kind, wise and idealistic. Bathed in light. And funny. That he's a looker is factual, and came before the myth. Probably invited it. I'm thinking, though, that if you harbour a myth about a person, it means you really are in love. This is new to me and it feels like a sort of fuel. So, what's the mileage in this relationship? Will it be a forever thing? Or will I end up slinging it in that rusty old skip with all my other big mistakes?

Because right up there at number two in the top ten seduction techniques, after *make a woman laugh*, is *let a woman talk about herself.* And oh, he let me talk.

All I know is that before the night was out, I'd unfolded the crumpled ball of paper on which were written all my recent workings-out: from confusing childhood memories, to Uncle Pat's recordings, and finally everything that Mum confided to me in the Palm House. Worst of all, the terrible jolt which forced me and Alice into different lives. I cried, as I smoothed that crinkled paper out. It's a tremendous thing to cry and not to be alone. Theo held me and listened. We lay still for ages. Until he said, 'You are so serious, Beth. I will make you smile.' And he tickled the sole of my foot, so I kicked him and we rolled about laughing.

58 Seminar

For somewhere to park my eyes, I'm staring out of the window at the soft, flat, slow-moving clouds which hang over the dull building opposite the faculty. It's almost demure, the way silver daylight sits behind these windows. Brown bricks meet the sun without warmth, let alone combustion; we've not yet reached that point where you can believe spring's on its way.

I'm sure Prof Laing has claimed this meeting room because, like her office, it's purged of all distraction: clean walls, and a fine, flat wooden table, around which the post-grads sit expectantly. Today she's back to her priestly self, elegant in camel cashmere. She stands, the long fingers and pearl-varnished nails of her left hand opening and closing every now and then around the silver pommel of her cane. Slow and measured in her speech. Cryptic, too: five minutes in, and we still haven't a clue what the theme of the seminar is going to be.

'Imagine, for a moment, you're a sculptor.'

We're easing ourselves into that thought, when suddenly, it gets personal.

'Is your method additive, or subtractive?'

Silence.

'By which I mean, as your work takes shape, are you assembling it, finding bits to stick together?' A slight sniff. 'Additive.'

She's explained that because she suspects there's a divvy in the room. I hope it's not me.

'Or is your work subtractive? Are you chiselling and shaving something away? Perhaps scrutinising the material itself, and reaching for that idea inside the marble?'

Oh, holy smoke, which am I? Is there a right way? Am I doing this all wrong? What do I say? If I've done nothing with these new figures bubbling in my head, perhaps this is the problem: I don't know what I'm doing.

I snatch a glance around the table: quiet smiles, some puzzlement, but none of us wants to be first to reply; and although this is strictly a post-grad seminar, and none of these people are fools, they all look as stupid as I feel. In this light, those who are white-skinned seem to have wintered to an extra pallor, and this must include me.

Like any class caught off-guard, we sense that if we keep our mouths shut, and look embarrassed enough, the Prof will oblige us with her own answer. Which she does.

'Surely, it's both. Surely, it always has been.'

You can almost feel the room exhale.

At the end of the seminar, she stops me at the door with the light tap of one finger, cranes her neck, and fixes me with exaggeratedly wide-open eyes until she's shamed me into returning her gaze.

'Did you find that useful?'

'Yes, of course. Always. Thank you.'

'And yet you seem to be elsewhere.'

'No… I'm just, you know, reflecting.'

There's a downturn of the lips and a slight shake of the head as if to say, plausible, but I'm not convinced.

'You don't share your work, Beth.'

'I haven't got anything new to share.'

'*Dread*?'

I wasn't expecting her to bring that performance up.

'Oh… *Silence,* you mean?'

'It was very strong. Alice has confidence in it. Why don't you? You could learn from your sister.'

Mum has been using that form of words for almost as long as I can remember, and I haven't been inclined to take it literally. What always I heard was, *you annoy me and she doesn't.*

'Alice made some major changes, for the band. I've only got our first version, the choral one. But that's not so good.'

'You were happy enough with it a month ago, when you were ready to enter it in a competition.'

January. A lot has changed since then.

'Show me.'

'OK. I'll send it later.'

'No – show me now. You can access the pdf, can't you?'

I'm filled with panic. I want to read it over again; I might want to make some changes.

'Can I just look it over first?'

'No, Beth. I may not be interested tomorrow. Ping it across, and come to my office.'

This is like going to the dentist for a check-up and being told you need three extractions *now*.

I fumble at the login. This is all happening too fast.

Once in her room, I make sure to close the door behind me.

She gestures and I sit. Her eyes neglect me now in favour of my work. I watch as she clicks, stops clicking, stares, reads, begins to scroll. Nothing is said. Nothing moves, on this usually mobile face. She scrolls back, then forward again. The very fact of her scanning it over means I already hear it with new ears.

At length she sits back with her hands in her lap, and asks: 'So why did Alice make the changes she did?'

'Instinct.'

'Don't give me that guff. What were the changes that she made?'

'The ending's stronger.'

A nod.

'More of it is louder.'

A frown. 'Irrelevant.'

'It takes on a different shape.'

'Go on.'

'Some of the material comes to the front, so that by the close, when it's re-capitulated and re-worked, there's a sense of recognition, but also escalation.'

'Which adds?'

'Direction, I suppose. Energy.'

'Yes. Energy. Energy!' Her open hand is slanted towards the screen. 'This piece here loses energy. It flags.'

I want to say, wake up, Grandma, it's the beginnings that count, look at what's happening outside the classical world… It's statistically proven, long intros are out, you have to make your best statement first, and jump straight in. Yet it's true that in much of the music I admire, it's the way you make landfall that counts, because there ought to be a journey in between. Pop is different. In a three-minute track, your main task is to create a distinctive place, and make sure you stay there.

'You're too careful. Too afraid.' She stretches her arm across the desk and says, 'Give me your hand.' She grips me by the wrist, but not as a doctor would; roughly; she shakes my hand in the air, which makes my open fingers look absurd.

'What are the tools in this sculptor's hand of yours? You're happy enough with fine sandpaper. But that should be where the process ends. It begins with a bolster and chisel. Stand back, look at what you've got. Then strike!' She shakes my hand. 'Do anything, write anything, but let it produce energy. You're seeking the wrong perfection. And listen to your pulse, Beth. You need to *run* to meet your music. Not creep up on it.'

Suddenly gentle, she drops my hand, and her dark eyes flash wide open in a way that reminds me of Eleni. She nods, and beams at me. 'There.'

I suppose, technically, that constitutes assault. She doesn't think she did anything wrong, just as she doesn't realise these lapidary statements, quoted back, sound like so much meaningless bollocks. Art, art, arty-farty Art. She's done a big interview for Radio 3 in advance of this first performance coming up, and it's gone to her head. I can't imagine Hildegard coming out with anything like that. Or JSB.

59 Salad

Tuesday, and Theo has a day off from the food factory in Speke, so we can meet for lunch.

The Aphrodite Bar is altered. The mean daylight which has nudged its way between the spotlights betrays fading upholstery, and with so few punters, it's obvious the marble floor tiles are made of vinyl. There's no Uncle Stelios, and no white damask on the little round table under the stair, although the cyclamen is still there and looking perky. No live music, either, but a thin skein of bouzouki through ancient speakers – I've thrown better ones away; no background hum of chatter, no friends and relations; no excitement, apprehension, jealousy or joy. And yet these are the things that echo around in our heads. We're still full of the open mic night, so we start by paying our conversational dues to that. Then Theo asks me how the post-grad seminar went.

'Ah… It started out very vague and ended up very personal.'

I tell him about the sculpture analogy, and show him how Petra gripped my wrist and held it in the air while she banged on about the tools in the sculptor's hand. He laughs. I gather speed.

'Who would have thought it? She always looks so… Like a statue herself. Well, she did, until the other night. Apparently, I ought to swap the sandpaper for a chisel, or something. Or maybe I'll take a sledgehammer to all my music and have done.'

Grinning broadly, he suddenly seems to notice I'm more rueful than mirthful, and checks himself.

'What d'you mean by that, Beth?'

'I showed her *Silence*. She made me! She says it lacks energy and I ought to take a lesson from my sister.'

His eyebrows rise and he's searching into my eyes, as if looking for a clue how to respond. I can see he's not going to speak until I say more. I put him on the spot.

'What do *you* think?'

He'll either *say, she has a point* – which I don't want to hear but would believe; or *no, no, no, stuffed aubergines, your Prof is talking rubbish* – which I do want to hear but won't believe. The question that's uppermost in my mind, though, is, will he be honest? Because if he isn't, we might as well split up before the bill arrives. His eyes leave mine, and now he's staring right through the table.

'It works best when you and Alice are in the same room.'

This is a jolt. How does *he* know? Is he another of those self-important people who like to tell you things about yourself? Jaz was always doing that. Maybe Theo's no better, and he just hit lucky there? We mirror each other's movements as we both reach for more bread, push it round our plates, scoop, chew, mop, reflect. I'm struggling to capture a black olive, chasing it round the dish.

'What makes you say that? Is this a theory, or an intuition, or what?'

'An observation,' he says. 'Your sister lights a fire in you.' Then he looks at my second-class eviscerated tube of an olive and suggests, 'Fingers?' with a shrug.

Why not. I pop it in my mouth, and it's such a chemically tainted specimen that I wonder why I ate it anyway.

'I bet, when you eat peas, you squash them on the back of the fork.'

'Yup. But I don't do the soup thing.'

'I bet your mum does.'

'Yes. Except when she's abroad. She's a when-in-Rome sort of person. But I'm sure Petra Laing never scoops any of *her* vegetables.'

'Oh, you can't be sure of anything with her. She's a deep horse.'

For harmonious but slightly different reasons, we send smiles around the empty bar, shaking our heads. We can agree on that.

'Seriously, though,' I say, and leave it there to see what happens. Nothing, at first.

Then, 'I had an idea, this morning,' says Theo.

After Jaz, I can't help being impressed by any man who can have an idea without waving his arms about.

He leans forward. 'The choir is competent. But it's safe and boring. My idea is a collaboration. What if we get you and Alice to work with the Lyceum Singers? Give you a... what do they call it – residency. A partnership. We make you our partner composers. For maybe six months? A year? We create a new piece, and we perform it, and everybody learns something from everybody else.'

I swallow. It's painful enough working in the privacy of my own room... but screwing up in public?

'The singers'll run a mile,' I tell him. 'They like what they know.'

He doesn't disagree. But he frowns and tells the table, 'I have already thought about this.' From the way his brow is dipped as he addresses the salt and pepper, I guess he's practised whatever it is he's about to say and needs not to be distracted.

'We won't stop doing those pieces, the Bach and Handel, Mozart, whatever; they're great pieces and besides, that's what their audience expects. But we can add some workshops. Only – and this is the great thing – you and Alice, as composers, won't just be names on another piece of sheet music. You'll look the performers in the eye. You bring them your musical ideas. You learn from them what works, what feels good for a voice, for *their* voices, and you find out where everybody's edge is so that you can push them over it.'

Underneath the creative use of English, that's my mum's yoga-talk. 'It's a fine idea, Theo. But once you get down to specifics... how would it get off the ground?'

He brings out his phone, his long fingers fly, and seconds later he passes it to me, opened on a web page. *Making Music – Adopt a Composer.*

'It's already a thing. People have done this. They do it. See.'

I scroll down a list headed *Pairings.*

These groups are all amateurs. The composers, though, seem mostly to be people like me. It's been going on under my nose for years. And it occurs to me that in all my lavish training, the matter of how to go about finding an audience for my music has been left untouched. No wonder I'm stumbling around. I've always regarded my attention, my ability to focus, as my most precious creative asset, I've set it at a premium; so that the very voices which might have helped me, have formed the background I've deliberately tuned out: distractions, so much spam, unread posters my shoulder might have brushed against on faculty notice boards. In short, I've been so busy looking down a microscope at art, art, arty-farty Art, that I haven't seen the giant at my elbow.

All the same... 'Would that be ethical? I mean, you already know me and Alice. And our Mum's in the choir. We all know each other. Is it even fair?'

He looks profoundly confused.

'No, it's normal.' He sits back and his eyes skim round the room. 'I'm only here in Liverpool because I have an uncle who runs a catering business.'

'Hm.'

'Beth. You're in that room again. In fact, you've never left it. Just you and the piano.' He shakes his head. 'Let people help you, Beth.'

'I wish Alice were here right now. I can hear her asking, 'Love or money? I mean, is this a paid gig? How do we fund it?'

'I don't know.' He frowns.

'What if the singers don't want to?'

'The first thing is to decide what you want yourselves.'

Even as I'm stacking up the reasons not to do this thing – too complicated, in practical terms, not to mention the artistic ones, because how on earth can you make music by committee? – I know I'm being a coward, and that I'm going to rely on Alice to talk me round. She's the positive one. She's the open one. She'll sweep all my flaky *ah-buts* out of the door and off the step.

I clock a special Theo gesture: he lifts open hands, arms loosely bent like Our Lord blessing loaves and fishes; and says 'We call Alice, yes?'

I'm onto it. There she is. The phone makes our nose look big, and I don't like the Collier nose at the best of times.

'Hi Alice. How's things?'

'I'm trying to buy a talking drum.'

'Good. Look, I've got Theo here. He's just had a big idea. For us. He'll tell you.'

I pass him the phone.

'Hi Alice! So, the idea is, we get the Lyceum Singers to adopt you.'

'Swerve that,' she says. 'I'm not going to be anybody's effing mascot.'

I call, 'Oh, Allie!'

'Or maybe a tabla,' she says. Her eyes track away from us to the laptop we can't see. 'Only I can't sit cross-legged.'

Theo's unperturbed. 'No, you and Beth. It's a scheme called adopt a composer. We make a partnership, for a few months. You and Beth write another piece, but this time it's especially for the Lyceum Singers... To start off with, for example, you'd discuss with them what it's going to be about.'

I'm pricked by the idea that this music is going to be *about* something.

'It's Beth's kind of music they want.'

'They liked the last piece we wrote.'

'Being polite.'

Theo protests: 'No, they appreciated it.'

'What about it, did they appreciate?'

I tell her, 'They liked your tune.'

She snorts.

'They'll take all the *Dread* out of it.'

I'm only too aware that it wasn't *Silence*, but *Dread*, as performed by Sky Blue Pink, that got Petra Laing's vote. I'm grabbing a lifebuoy when I say, 'But Alice. You and I have to find a way of making music together.'

This shuts her up. I'm not going to let go. 'We need each other.'

She nods, so I pursue. 'My music needs your music. Your music needs mine.'

There's a short pause, then she says, 'Mm... dunno. It's not my culture though, talking drums. Come on Beth, you're the worry department: do I need to develop a Scouse version of this instrument?'

Why is it only when someone tells you, no, you can't have that, that you work out it was the thing you wanted most of all? All I can think is, oh come on, Allie, I need you to persuade me, I need your courage, because I so want to do this but I'm not a strong enough swimmer to make it ashore on my own.

Now she's actually turned her head round to scroll through drums. Theo and I exchange glances. I'm frustrated; he seems to be waiting.

She sucks in air: 'Seventeen quid, has to be crap. Hundred and fifty, what if I can't play it?' She comes back to us. 'Your music needs my music. My music needs yours, right?' she says.

'Yes!'

Theo jumps in, 'Performers need creators. Creators need performers.'

'And the idea is we all work together?'

'Yes! You'd get to exchange ideas, work with them...' He's barely started gathering momentum when she cuts in.

'OK. If the band can come too.'

'Sky Blue Pink?'

'I'm not changing the name for anybody.'

Now I despair. She'd just made a hard thing harder.

'You mean we'll have everything from Jenny Johns' wannabe coloratura to Vilma's rambling rhythm section, all written into the same score? Seriously? How's that going to work?' I'm aghast, and look across to Theo for sympathy. But he's just doing that thing with his hands again.

'I hadn't thought of that. The band. Now, *that* could be fun,' he says. 'That really would be a kick up the pants. Loosen them up.'

Fun? *Fun?* We're talking about Art here... And with that thought I catch myself out. Because in the end, what *is* the matter with me?

'Think of it as a scherzo,' he tells me with a definite look of mischief.

Alice frowns. 'Beth! For, fuck, sake.'

'What?'

'The gob on you!'

My protest is a strangled, silly noise. 'It's not an easy fit for me, is all I'm saying.'

'Be grateful. Honest to God, Beth. You literally are the princess with the pea.'

'Every princess has a P,' says Theo.

'She means the fairy tale… Go on.'

'Well, you are. You're always waiting for the perfect… thing.'

'Bed,' says Theo, dead pan.

'Mattress.' Why did I have to say that? I'm turning into my mother.

Alice is going pink in the face. I might tell her that in a minute. She tells me, 'First, you don't want to play for Mum's lot because they're too rubbish. Then you don't want to do singing because it's got words in it. One minute you're too good, the next you're not good enough.'

'That's Goldilocks,' I tell her. 'Get your story straight.'

'No. Goldilocks is alright. She does a fair's-fair. She takes what's on offer. But the pea princess…'

'Yeah,' says Theo, 'the Pea Princess is just a pain in the butt.'

'If the Pea Princess found a post-punk R and B group with a finny haddy border stuck under her mattress, she'd be perfectly justified in throwing a paddy.'

'Oh, go on,' says Alice. 'Don't be the Pea Princess. Be a Goldilocks. See what's on offer. See what you can rob.'

Here I am again, outnumbered by people who only want the best for me. Alice grows serious.

'You do know, don't you, I don't always get to choose?'

'I know.'

'And you get to be so picky, you get so much practice saying ooh no, that's not quite right for me, that you end up with nothing and you're just… choosed out.'

I can feel a smile creeping across my face. She's quite an operator, my sister.

'OK. This time, you choose for me.'

Alice sends the broad smile back. 'Yes! If the band agrees. But they will.'

'Never mind the band, you've got them in your pocket and you know it. We'd have to sell it to the choir. That's going to be a lot harder.'

'Leave that to me,' she says.

'Us,' says Theo.

A little tremolo of memory plays in my ear, as I remember what happened last time I *left it with her*. Time will tell.

'OK,' I say. We have an agreement.

'Can I buy this drum, then? Love you.'

I'm still digesting all this, and wondering why neither of us sisters seems capable of getting anywhere on our own – because just then, Alice grabbed at the band to serve as a comfort blanket, just as surely as I grabbed her to serve as mine, back in November – when there's a sudden gust of air and laughter from the doorway, and two hunched figures, gripping each other in an apparent attempt to keep themselves upright, tumble in. You'd think they were escaping a tempest on the high seas, not a slight squall somewhere off Bold Street. It's Uncle Stelios and my Prof. She's leaning on his arm and giggling like a kid, and in the space of three paces has managed to catch her silver-topped cane between the legs of a table and chair.

They straighten themselves out. Stelios greets his manager, who's standing at the bar smirking, and calls for two coffees. He guides Petra to the comfiest seats in the house, a couple of armchairs by a low table quite close to us, then he realises we're there and turns to give us the full octave of his smile.

'Theo! Beth! *Yia sas!* Good to see you. And together! Petra, this is my brother's grandson, Theo. You heard him play laouto, remember? A very talented musician. And he conducts a choir. Theo, this is Professor Petra Laing. The famous.' He turns to Petra. 'And you remember Beth? Her sister's band?'

She's in a carefree mood today. 'Oh, Telis, I know Beth,' she drawls, pronouncing what I assume to be his nickname with an authentic soft *t,* which involves her top lip in a precisely placed micro-quiver. She beams. 'Beth and I work together.' Which is a nice way of putting it, because she could have said, Beth's the minion who dishes out the microphones and plugs things in.

Stelios smacks his head. 'We met before! In the faculty office. A long time ago. Before Christmas. I thought I recognised you from somewhere!'

'Did we?' I don't remember.

Petra's voice, always a rich contralto, assumes a funereal quality as she mocks him: 'Before Christmas, Telis. That was in the dark days of the dictator moustache.' Then she switches back to her normal register to tell me, 'It was impossible to see him behind that moustache.'

He likes being teased; his hands gesture surrender and he closes his eyes to nod, yes, yes, I know, it was terrible.

Petra turns gleefully to Theo, and asks, 'So, what are you two cooking up, then?'

He's excited. I look on in awe of his hutzpah as he tells her, not what we're considering, or planning, or going to do, but what we're creating. A partnership between performers and writers, which will involve me and Alice working with the Lyceum Singers and also Sky Blue Pink (yes, that's the band she heard the other night). It sounds insane.

'How simply wonderful!' she sings, open-jawed. 'What splendid *fun!*'

This surprises me, from someone whose own compositions are lucid, crystalline, refined; and who's spent years deconstructing late Beethoven. Or perhaps she thinks a tossed salad is all I'm fit to bring to table.

I can see his dream of collaboration collapsing into a muddle; and I want it to work; so I have to speak up. 'We've got to persuade the choir first. They're only really at home with the established canon. It's going to sound to them like a dog's breakfast. A mash-up.'

Theo isn't deflected. 'This is the age of the mash-up.'

'But just a minute,' says Petra. 'Aren't we hosting your sister's band? Have we got a date for that, yet?'

'I've blocked them in for a whole Saturday, after the deadline for undergrad assessments.'

Her nostrils flare, and her wild gaze skims, not the skirting board today, but all around the ceiling.

'We keep that date… but we widen out the event. Invite the choir!' she bellows. 'Invite them in. Make it a get-to-know-you. They won't turn down an invitation from the University, surely? Make it an event, a… a first meeting.   Just to encourage everyone. Let them show off a bit of *their* usual repertoire.'

'The band still gets to record, though?'

'Of course. All you have to do is devise a schedule.' She shrugs, and Theo nods confidently. I'm quite taken aback by the rate at which this half-baked idea is gathering pace. As if neither Theo nor Prof Laing can see the obvious pitfalls.

'We won't get everybody in at such short notice. In the daytime.'

'Well…' she makes a gesture as if flicking imaginary crumbs from her lap. 'All we can do is extend the invitation – my personal invitation – and see what happens,' she says. 'Energy, Beth!' I'm worried she's going to grip my wrist and assault me again, but she retrieves magisterial composure to state, 'I wish to support this initiative.'

So that's that. Decided.

She relaxes again, as the coffees appear, and thanks the barman with quiet efficiency. Then addresses me.

'Make sure you tell that young man Mr Ander what's going on. Don't look so worried, Beth, he'll be delighted!   You might get some coverage.'

She fixes me with her steel-grey eyes and gives a little sigh. 'But musically, Beth... perhaps this is just the sort of thing you need. You need to loosen up. Energy! Energy comes from outside, you can't generate it on your own. It comes from contact with other people. Encounters with aliens! No, really! That's when the sparks fly. Besides, the whole thing will be splendid. We must all do this together. We simply must.'

60 Day job

On three separate occasions this morning, a student has pitched up in the faculty office, whining – or in one case, screaming – that the system's locked them out. I say, did you update your password as requested? They swear that no such request was made. I log out of my own PC, invite them to attempt a login, and point out the little dialogue box which appears smack in the middle of the screen. *Please update your password to continue using this service.* Well, it wasn't there before. See what happens if you click on it, I say. Knock, and the door will be opened to you. Every time I perform this high-level magic trick which we in the business call *reading what it says on the screen* – and for that matter, every time I pull up the hood of my parka or step into a puddle – I remind myself, there are just two weeks to carnival. Theo's flying back to Larnaka in our mid-session break, and I'm going with him; and it's reasonable to expect the sun to shine while we are there. Bliss.

Dad rings to say they've docked. Wants to know more about our plans for this *Adopt a Composer* scheme; Mum's told him how things are moving on with the choir, and it sounds as though, between her and Alice, he already knows as much as I do. We settle comfortably back into the usual conversation: will I be coming home at the weekend, needs help with his mobile, looking forward to seeing us all, can I persuade Alice to stay over. Then, trying to sound matter-of-fact, 'I'm packing it in, you know. Time to swallow the anchor. Asked for my cards.'

It's true, then. Mum hinted as much. I'd feel better about this if I could see his face. Thirty years at sea, that's something; and he's a right softie, so there's probably a tear in his eye.

'What tipped the balance?' I ask.

'Oh, that lot! They want to send me out to the Arctic to watch the glaciers melt. Talk about a rush job! When it's gone, it's gone.'

'I thought Mum was pleased about something.'

'Fair's fair, she's been right about this all along, hasn't she? Eco-tourism, eh? Oxymoronic. With the accent on moronic.'

'Whatcha gonna do, Dad?'

'Dunno. See a bit of life with your mother before *we* both melt.' There's a pause, a mutual recognition that the odds on that plan working may be no better than even. 'Well, if ever you need a roadie, I'm your man. Just so long as you're not going to play the wildlife paradise of Costa Rica. I'm not going west of Wallasey, me.'

Some of the staff are locked out now. I consider telling them the new password is PLEASE, but nobody appreciates sarcasm. Deciding I've earned the right to be off-task for five minutes, I phone Mum, just to say hello. She's very mellow at the moment; glad to see that Allie and I are playing nicely, and super-proud of this collaboration with the choir, which Theo and Alice sold to them at her first rehearsal last week. But in a strange, mirror counterpoint to my earlier chat with Dad, this conversation too takes a sudden right-angled turn. The difference being, that Mum homes in on the big news, and saves the chit-chat for later.

'I've just had Jenny Johns on the phone. That lad Ander...'

'Jaz?'

'Did you know he's having a go at the Singers now? For the *Echo*? He's going to be there. He's coming along too, to the faculty, for our big workshop. Wants a photo. They're running a series on the Rushworth legacy, and of course, we're in the crosshairs.'

'Be fair, Mum, nobody would have been invited into the faculty if it weren't for him. He started it, by trying to promote Alice.'

'I'd feel better about that if I knew why.'

'He's trying to making amends. I believe him. There's a lot about brain injury on his socials, too. It goes back a long time. He's made a promise, to a friend, that he'd do whatever he could to fight for resources.'

'Oh? All the same, I don't want him pointing his poison pen in our direction.'

'Oh, Mum! You know the style, it'll be a double-page nostalgia-fest. Butter-knife journalism. And you can't stab anybody in the back with a butter-knife.'

She sighs. 'He's done the Welsh Choral already. I suppose they came through unscathed.'

'It's not going to be Watergate, Mum. I mean there's nothing to expose, is there?'

'You're forgetting what they wrote about us last time. *Amateur singers bring the house down.'*

'You can't pin that on Jaz. He wasn't even in Liverpool then. What did Jenny say, anyway?'

'Oh, Jenny? Our Choir Secretary, you mean? She's already done her telephone interview, hasn't she. *She's* made up, thought he was very professional. He charmed his way in there, all right. She thinks a bit of publicity is great for the choir. And so does our conductor. Well, I s'pose *he'll* be next up for an interview.' She lets out a theatrically long, loud sigh. 'Anyway, about Theo. Are you two serious?'

A few minutes ago, I was looking forward to announcing that we were going out. She seems to know already. Heaven only knows how, although she's got enough spies in that chorus. Or it could be Alice who told her.

'Yes. I'm serious.'

'Good.'

'In fact, he's invited me to Cyprus for some festival or other.'

'Bring him to lunch on Sunday, then. He can meet your father.'

So, she's not going to warn me to look before I leap? What was it she said that time? *One of these days the seventh son of a poor woodcutter is bound to strike lucky...*

I know almost nothing about Theo's family, and she can only know less. The things I don't know about him far outnumber the things I do. There are some people who just stand out, from first meeting, and the sharper the outline, the less you worry that there's a lot to fill in; in fact, you colour people in yourself, to suit your own ends at the time. Well, it's too late. I'm committed. If I've coloured him all wrong, I'll soon know.

Time to reactivate my Go Greek account. I've only got a couple of weeks to find out what you say when you step on someone's foot. Please, thank you, numbers, food. All whilst fiddling about prepping this recording session, because Alice is insisting on another band practice, and talking about mashing *Dread* and *Silence* together. I can't see how that would work. A new tune keeps nudging me in the ribs, too; it's feeling more and more like a song, but a song needs words, so that's me stuck. Still… Just the recording, and two more choir practices, for rumours of my liaison to reach the most cloth-eared of the basses in their own little time zone on the back row. Two weeks for the choir to notice, or ignore, the quality of eye contact between me and their conductor; and four weeks before, I hope, they clock my gentle tan.

61 Hotpot

'Where d'you buy those on a Sunday morning?'

We're standing together outside Mum and Dad's front door, and Theo's holding a mixed bunch of blues and yellows, flowers that won't be seen outdoors for a month or two yet. The question seems to surprise him.

'I got them yesterday. Off a barrow.'

My old key turns fluently in the lock, with none of the jangling effort it takes to get into the flat; but on stepping inside, our progress is blocked. Stacked neatly against the hall radiator are four transparent plastic crates, in which a shared childhood is held captive: a tin xylophone, jigsaw puzzles, a box of coloured wooden blocks. Two teddy bear onesies have their noses pressed up against the sides.

Mum in her pinny comes from the kitchen to greet me and Theo, with a quick kiss each.

'Hello, love. This lot's for the charity,' she beams. Dad's voice comes from the lounge: 'Unless there's anything you girls want to take and keep.'

'There's a limit to how long you should hang on to this sort of thing. Don't you agree, Theo?' Then, 'Are these for me? They're beautiful. Thank you.' And she's off to put them in water.

We go through and find my sister rummaging through another, half-emptied box. She barely looks up to deliver her hello. Dad gets up from the armchair to shake Theo's hand, and for a microsecond they mirror each other: level gaze, shoulders relaxed, sea legs steady.

'Would you look at this,' says Dad. 'We had it all tidy in here a minute ago.' He stands up to his ankles in paper. Old exercise books, lots of them, are slumped in waves on the carpet, with the shiny torso of an action man bobbing to the surface. 'This lot's for the tip,' he tells us, with relish. Then steps over it all to give me the biggest hug.

'But you can't chuck this away!' shrieks Alice, and lifts up half a recorder. 'Beth, this belongs to you!'

Dad rolls his eyes. 'The wrong end of half an instrument. Oh aye. You never know when that'll come in handy, do you?' He glances at Theo, already seeking a potential ally.

Alice turns to me. 'Beth! Remember?'

For a moment I can smell that classroom, and the red-topped desk. I can't retrieve the little person I was then, the goody two-shoes turned tough egg who pushed the kid in Alice's seat away (which I don't remember doing anyway). Imagine, how different it would have been if I'd understood that Alice really wasn't going to be back? I might have said, politely, Miss, there was the bottom half of a recorder in my sister's locker, who's got it now? That would have been a fair question on a matter of fact. But I suppose I must have been all rage, at the time.

I answer, 'Yes. I remember. But it's still no use to anyone so let's just say, hello, goodbye! And chuck it, eh?'

Alice only tightens her grip. '*I'll* keep it, then. Mental value.'

I sigh. She wasn't even there. 'Why's it got mental value for you?'

'Because when I couldn't shout, you shouted for me.' She juts her chin. Then enunciates carefully, in a mock-pompous voice: 'On my behalf.'

'She gets it from her mother,' Dad tells Theo, glancing at me. Do I? And what, exactly?

'It's a family legend,' says Alice.

Poor Theo is waiting for someone to explain.

Since Alice and I moved out, nothing much has changed at Menlove Avenue, except that – apart from the shipwreck we had to step over just now – it's a whole lot tidier. Dad hasn't had a chance to mark out any territory yet. I wonder what Theo makes of it; the dark blue carpet, the exact shade picked up by a twining leafy pattern on the otherwise beige floor-length curtains, the sensible three-piece suite from George Henry Lee's, doomed to last. Everything here is far too good to throw out.

She hates dusting, but she's done all the family photos in their various shiny frames, ready for Theo's inspection. An ancient palm cross is tucked behind one of us in our pram. Down the business end, by the piano, my certificates still embarrass the wall. That's my own fault for not taking them away with me.

Mum's gone digital since I left home – I think she was trying to prove a point – so no more back copies of *The Guardian* in the dumping place by the standard lamp, just the local freebies; and neatly arranged by order of size in the magazine rack are a couple of Union journals, Arts Alive, leaflets from the theatres, the Bluecoat, and the Phil programme 2019-20. The old hi-fi equipment is still there, and the dusty speakers on their metal stands, but on top of one of them, perched like a robin on the top of the tree, there's a neat little Bluetooth job. She streams her music now.

The bottom shelf of the bookcase is still weighted to the floor by big foreign language dictionaries, but otherwise has new tenants; she must have time for libraries; the latest Stephen Pinker catches my eye, Alain de Botton's *Status Anxiety*, next to something called *The Drunkard's Walk*; Galeano on Latin America; Caroline Steel, *Hungry City*. There are whole worlds in this low bookcase, multiple versions of all our histories, and multiple theories as to our future. Poking up cheekily from a fat tome on post-globalisation, a little red envelope from Chinese New Year is being used as a book-mark. We get one of these every year, and it usually perches on the mantlepiece looking hopeful; the contents are unintelligible to us, and, conscious that we're taking it on trust to be a message of goodwill, we come up with our own versions of what the tiny card inside might really say. It could be parking ticket. A riddle from a cracker. A secret message: *The geese are flying. Read and destroy immediately.* Or *You are doomed. Please recycle.*

Round the dinner table, the vibe is good. These days I only eat meat at home, and Mum's showing off her Lancashire hotpot. Theo gets the concept, pickled cabbage and all. For once, everyone has something to be happy about; and best of all, I can see my mum is chuffed to bits about Dad coming home for good. They keep sneaking glances at each other à propos of nothing, just because they can, like a pair of soppy teenagers.

Theo is required to give an account of his family, and when I say I'm going to meet them soon, because we're going to have a long weekend in Limassol for the festival, Mum and Dad exchange another smile across the table.

This smile, though, is like a tap on the shoulder. It's all getting real, and scary. Soon I'll be the stranger at another table like this – maybe even eating lamb and potatoes, and who knows, being offered purple food I don't like the look of; and I'll be relying on reading people's faces, because I can't expect all Theo's family to speak English all the time; and my Greek is…

'How's her Greek coming on, Theo?' asks Mum.

'Yes… good… Polì kalà…'

He has no sample on which to base his judgement. That ticks the loyalty box, and I feel a bit better.

I come clean. 'It's harder than I'd thought. I'm going to mess up and say something offensive by mistake. Misgender everyone.'

 Mum shrugs, 'I'm sure Theo's family are decent people. They'll read your intention and forgive your grammar.'

Theo grins. 'They might tease you, though.'

Alice says, 'You only tease people you like,' and sticks her tongue out at me. I screw my nose up in return.

'Did you know, Mum… In Greek, they only have one verb for *hear* and *listen*? How does that work?' I turn to Theo, who looks blank.

'It works. What's the problem?'

'Well, listening implies an effort of attention. It involves the will.'

'You mean British people hear things without paying attention?'

This goes down well with the parents.

Theo asks my dad, 'Have you ever been to Cyprus?'

'Not for years.'

'Dad probably shipped brown sauce for your Uncle Stelios. That was before the cruise liners.'

'You changed jobs?'

Dad looks at his plate. 'Well, you know. An opening came up... And there were a lot of changes, after the accident.'

Theo nods: 'You changed your job to be closer to home.'

'No. He changed jobs to be further away.' Mum smiles at Theo, but there's a catch in her voice, and it's not clear that she's joking.

'Well, he's home now,' I say, hoping we'll move on, even while I'm filing that nugget for further investigation.

But Alice can't let this pass. 'You didn't really, Dad? Did you? You didn't go to sea to get away from us?'

'I didn't ever want to be away from you, sweetheart.'

'He wanted to be away from me,' says Mum.

'Oh, Mel...' says Dad, and his head falls to one side. 'You don't need to...' His voice trails off.

This is precisely the stuff I want to know about; but I wasn't expecting it to be dished out at the dinner table, today, and in the company of a virtual stranger, at least as far as my dad's concerned. There's a silence while we all work out which knife and fork to use. The thing is, Mum doesn't look cross. She looks apologetic, and so does he.

She turns her gaze away from him to Alice, and to me. 'I don't blame your father. I was very hard to live with. For a while.'

'You were on a war footing. Fighting on all fronts,' he says, 'what with the hospital and the schools and the house and the ed psych... Getting the right treatment for Alice, the right support, fighting to get every assessment... You took control. You were brilliant. And you didn't need me under your feet.'

I'm thinking, or me...

She shakes her head, sorry. 'I was a screaming banshee, at times. You couldn't do right for doing wrong.'

They're staring into each other's eyes again, as if we're not there; yet I sense in my bones they need all three of us, as witnesses. We're like the chorus in the last act of the opera, when the Count says he's sorry and the Countess forgives him, and everything is poised on that word, *pardon*. As if it has to be public to be real. The family stage is full, and Mum needs all of us to know.

She says, 'When life's a struggle, you get used to fighting. You stop expecting doors to open. You learn to push first.'

I get it. 'You pushed the doors for me, too.'

'By the time you reached grade eight, love, kicking doors down had become a habit. I was conditioned.' Her smile is a wistful, half-regretful, what-am-I-like. Unseen by anyone, Theo reaches for my hand. I let it rest on his thigh. He doesn't squeeze or press; it's as if his hand is listening.

Alice still looks troubled. 'Why couldn't you just work in an office, Dad?'

Mum closes her eyes and shakes her head. He's powerless to explain, so I tell my sister, 'Because he had this thing he loved, that he's always loved, since before there was a you and a me. And you have to do the thing you love. Which in your case is singing, and in his case, is – was – going to sea. Makes no sense, I know. Weird but true.'

My dad has gone all pink like that time at the Caledonia. 'What's this with the third degree? When we haven't even had pudding?'

We all watch the frown on Alice's brow tighten, then slowly unravel, until she tells him, 'You can't have afters until you've finished your befores.'

'Oh, I think we're done here,' says Mum.

I'm not so sure. He's going to miss going to sea. The never-level, never-stillness. The vastness of it. The empty skies, which give you your best chance of glimpsing the green flash at a tropical sundown; and the full skies, packed with rain, or white with stars; the confusion of raggedy, mis-shaped cloud-types that you get when a storm is clearing, which, he whispered to me once, makes up for everything that went before. He's felt the crashing waves that leave your skin pecked by salt; seen the great birds that glide thousands of miles yet barely move at all, and the sun that can set in half the time it takes to boil an egg. He's known nightfall like a switch that flips from hot to cold. All these things he's told us about. Ask him about Cape Town, Singapore, Mumbai, and he'll describe the waterfront, or how you enter port.

How is he going to manage in a suburb? With no horizon? It's not without beauty; the natural world is here, in trees and shrubs; there are goldfinches on the feeder right now; but there's no sense of anything much bigger than yourself.

The price he's paid for those vast horizons has been a life cramped below decks. Dad has tolerated things that Alice, Mum and I would hate, and perhaps he's coming home because he's finally had enough of it. I can only imagine: the artificial light; the smells that can't be escaped – warm oil, diesel, cleaning fluids; no windows to be opened; and always the thrum of an engine, under your feet, inside the very walls of your cabin, running right through your body all the time. After all these years, my father must be tuned to that deep note.

Theo's been telling Dad about the choir in Clitheroe who adopted a composer, and we're heading for a discussion of our plans for the workshop at the Music Faculty, when the pudding hits the table top with a thud. It's a sherry trifle in a huge, old-fashioned cut-glass bowl. I don't like this habit, in a pudding, of exposing the viscera – all that red and brown squishy mess – through the cubist-distorted prism which is the heirloom dish; and that stripe of Bird's Custard yellow is just blatantly loud, which is why you always end up staring at a trifle. Even while we carry on our conversation, none of us can take our eyes off it.

'Starts off, Beth's prof says welcome to the Faculty of Music, enjoy the biscuits,' says Alice.

I reassure Mum: 'She won't hang around after that. It'll all be very informal.'

'Then the band plays at the choir, and the choir sings at the band. Stuff people know. To introduce ourselves. And then… Then we take a look at some of our stuff. To show them how you can bend ideas, see?'

'So, what exactly?' asks Dad.

With mirror smirks across the table, I say 'Silence' and Alice says 'Dread.'

Mum explains. 'It's a setting of a poem by Emily Dickinson. The competition – remember? There's the choral version, and the version the band played at the open mic.'

'How're you going to organise yourselves, then?' he asks, not in a cynical way, but in a voice which suggests that we're going to be able to tell him, and he's all ears.

'I'm approaching it as an experiment,' says Theo.

'Balance is going to be a problem,' says Mum. 'We're low on men.'

I say, 'We need a plan,' and we all revert to staring at the trifle. Mum lifts the serving spoon.

'Here's my idea,' says Alice. 'The choir does the dirge. Then we can sample it and get it on a loop. For backing. Or in-between bits.'

'Shit, Alice, what key though? You dropped it a third, remember.'

'Did I?'

'Well… Who's going to change?'

'They can.'

Mum's roused. 'What d'you mean, *for backing?*' The spoon is back on the table. 'You've got to let us do the proper anthem. People are taking the trouble to learn it, at very short notice, Alice!'

Alice shrugs. 'You do yours. We do ours. And then comes the… What d'you call it, Beth?'

'Mixing.' We both know this is licence to mash.

'So, there's version one, version two, and version three.' Alice narrows her eyes and one eyebrow aims for the fringe. 'Electronic magic.'

I shrug. 'Could be a recipe for chaos.'

'Theme and variations,' says Theo. 'It's a classical formula. Multiple versions…'

'Yeah, but, Alice, I don't know how that's going to work. I mean, harmonically, that could be difficult…'

Alice grimaces. 'That's my sister.   Problem-finder General.'

Mum halts the argument. 'Well, all I can say is, if you think harmony's difficult, you want to try singing in unison.'

She looks wary, but lifts the spoon and starts doling out the trifle.

'Don't give me any of those bitty bits on top,' says Alice, and swiftly ratchets up from offhand to urgent: 'That's too much cream… But I do want *some*…'

I tell her, 'Oh go on, Goldilocks, take what's on offer.'

I'm thinking, now who's the Pea Princess? Somehow, over the years, I've been cast as the awkward one, whereas Alice is allowed to be the one who knows what she wants. The two of us aren't that different. Identity is all in other people's heads.

62 Pause

Today, a strange, rhapsodic thing fell out of my ear, scored for strings. It took a matter of minutes to write it down, and I can see where to take it. It's not 'interesting,' or 'original,' or 'genre-defying,' or an 'interrogation' of anything. It's purely, pointlessly, beautiful. I'm absolutely sure of that, and don't need anybody's confirmation. Things are moving with the season, then.

The sudden brightness in my flat is shocking; I've been living under lamps through the gloom of winter for so long, it almost hurts. Blasting into the flat at this new mid-morning angle, the sun reveals that nothing is as clean as I thought: the window pane is not transparent; the keyboard and the tablet, which get the microfibre treatment several times a day, are smudged; anybody can see where I have been, and that my fingers were much greasier than I knew. So it's a good day to face the normally dingy spare room, and take a soft cloth to all my kit, ready to move forward with some serious work.

I have no idea what's been going on between my parents these last years, but I do know there's been a spring clean recently. A child doesn't ask or even wonder about their parents' private business. Then, as a teenager, you're so busy rejecting everything they might conceivably stand for, and so prone to viewing other people through the prism of your own unstable ego, that you only have a scant idea who your parents are.

Am I growing up? I think I must be, because I've started to think of my parents as people like myself. Perhaps Alice and I did them a favour, by moving out; we gave them permission to stop worrying about us. Although they still do. But it's not just that. We've stepped back, which means now we can see them better.

There's a whole lot of pigeon-porn going on over the road. Most eye-catching is that dappled white-and-brown job that keeps jumping on one of the slimy slate-grey variety. Distracting. Why that one? Seriously, what does he see in her? They skitter down the roof and into the guttering. A whole flock has descended now, fidgeting about in small pointless flights, trying their silly walk on the sloping tiles; and there's a pair shuffling sideways along the ridge, side by side, nudging each other, which must be the pigeon version of foreplay.

Today's blue sky is stark naked, apart from the scratches left by a couple of jets. I'll be up there soon, on my own morning departure from John Lennon, contributing to the carbon crisis. I feel guilty, but not so guilty I won't go. It would only be a tiny step to give up meat completely for Lent, by way of offset; but there's nothing worse than a picky guest, and I'd hate Theo's family to mistake me for someone who does any form of piety, religious or dietary. After all that effort teaching me to say moussaKAS not mousse-ARca, how can I disappoint?

It will be… what? I can't imagine how our trip will be. Just, different. Not here. Not this. Life here has soaked deep into me and it's time I dried out.

But first we have the workshop. The choir will meet Alice, and the band. I ought to be delighted. *Ice cream, pickles and jam.* Only, all on one plate? Every time I imagine this random bunch of people between the same four walls, I feel slightly claustrophobic. It's all very well Petra telling me energy comes from outside, *that's when the sparks fly* – it's anybody's guess what will happen when Mum and Jaz collide. I'll behave myself. I just can't vouch for either of them.

63 Workshop (i)

The workshop is due to start in twenty minutes. The small hall is ready for us, with corporate tea, coffee, biscuits at one end, for us to help ourselves. No sign of our conductor yet. Or the second-years who are meant to be doing the recording. Whereas the choir, irritatingly eager, have been clogging up the corridor waiting for me to let them in. I'm so used to this place I hardly see it; but as they shuffle into the empty hall, their eyes wander round, as if they're expecting some Scouse Michelangelo to have done the ceiling. It's more like a very large wood-panelled lift, achingly minimalist, and soon they're desperate for something to look at apart from each other. Hinged and folded back on itself, the open door to the store in the wall opposite the entrance attracts curiosity. My synths are propped against this wall, and a stack of music stands is half-in, half-out; we haven't set up because nobody's sure what we're setting up for. There's the rosewood Bechstein to admire, which draws my mum, although I can see she isn't going to go so far as to touch it; and a drum kit, which Jenny Johns looks worried about. So she should be, if Vilma gets her hands on it. I'm worried about it too, and consider steering it on its mini-platform into another of the concealed cupboards where it belongs, but that would be such a fag, and men would want to help; so I just grab the drumsticks and stash them in the store, deep in a corner, under the pipes. This is not where they belong, and I mustn't forget where I put them.

There's a dull swoosh and gust of air as the heavy doors open again and John steps in, all smiles, with his guitar in a well-used flight case. He's followed by Vilma. I'd forgotten how much taller than him she is. She's pale as ever, serious, with her long hair tidy in a band; all in black, apart from bright red nails.

They're greeted by Mum. They're not followed by Alice. I ask Vilma where she is, and I'm hoping Alice hasn't had a falling-out with John already...

'We didn't all fit in the lift.'

'She's coming up behind with your Prof. They were getting on like old mates,' says John.

I help with introductions, not that the singers really need me to. The noise level builds and after a while there's an ironic cheer from Patrick as Theo appears.

He's looking very bright-eyed today, and gives me a hug as well as a hello.

He checks in with Jenny for the roll call. We've enough singers to make it viable. Marsha has changed her shift to be here, and Ffi tells everyone she's thrown a sickie. I suppose that's a big sacrifice for an estate agent on a Saturday.

The second-years pitch up. I know these two. Jacob Rigby owes me a favour for pushing him over the finish line with an assessment which was technically overdue. He's brought his mate, Tarik, known as Smar. In fact, it's Jacob who's the scally; Tarik's a mild, nervous lad who shares cat pictures. He needs me to know that he's got to leave at three thirty, but if we haven't finished, he says, Ashley – *you know, that girl with the accent* – will take over. It shouldn't really need the two of them anyway.

'This it?' says Jacob.

'Nearly. This is all the singers. There's going to be one more for the band.'

Alice should be here by now. Where is she? I head out.

I find her in the faculty office, sitting at my desk, swinging round and round on my chair with a big grin on her face.

'Why would you even think of giving up this job? I mean, why?' she asks. 'Give it to me. I'd work here. Second floor! Trees!'

'It's not that glamorous, and anyway, you know I changed my mind.' Alice isn't concerned. She's on her own, excitable track.

'Tell you what, though. I got Petra Laing all wrong. In real life, she's interesting. When she thinks, she thinks all over her face.'

'That's true.'

'Me and Petra Laing get on,' says Alice. 'We're like that.' She links her two index fingers and sends one elbow into the air.

'John told me you shared a lift. You got a one-on-one with a living, breathing genius, there, Al.' I wonder what they can have covered in the space of two floors.

'She's a fan.' Alice sends her gaze up to the corner of the ceiling and bats her lashes to say, *clever me*. 'She said to wait here.'

'Result! But you need to shift yourself now. Come on. Move.'

Alice reaches for her sticks and slides carefully off the chair.

The unmistakable rhythm of Petra Laing's progress up the corridor makes me straighten. Did she overhear any of this? Not that we said anything bad.

She's upon us. Swathed in posh beige, with the dark blue vintage handbag over one arm.

'How's it going?' she asks. Looking mellow today.

'We're just about set up,' I say. 'Ready to roll.'

'I'm sure it'll all go well, if your performance at the Aphrodite was anything to go by. That was quite a night, wasn't it?'

Alice pipes up, 'D'you like Cypriot music, then?'

'Well, between you and me, I'm not so keen on the Greek vein-cutters. *Kopsoflevika.* That's what they call it, you know – the wailing and the tragedy. They did one the other night, and I didn't like it much. But I do love the traditional songs and dances. They have different norms from the music of western Europe. It always sounds fresh to my ears.'

'She's a good singer, though, isn't she?' says Alice.

'Eleni? Yes. She's very talented.'

I'm thinking, so you know Eleni then, when Alice asks straight out: 'What were *you* doing there, anyway?'

I can't believe my sister sometimes. Wades right in with her wellies. I want to soften this question, so I ask, 'Do you go there often?' This hasn't left my lips before I realise, that's not much better, is it?

But Petra answers without so much as a blink. 'The proprietor's an old friend of mine. I often go along when there's a Greek music night.' Ready for our objection, she nods. 'I know. It wasn't a Greek night, was it? Open mic. I was mistaken. Duped, in fact.' Briefly, her eyebrows knot and she clenches her teeth. 'To be honest, as soon as I saw the banjo, I knew I'd made a terrible mistake.'

She wishes us good luck, tells us she'll be with us all in a moment to start us off and give the official welcome, and she's on her way.

I'm waiting for her to be out of earshot so as to pounce on my sister and find out what the hell she was thinking, asking personal questions of a musical celebrity.

Alice gets in first.

'See? How easy was that?'

I'm so shocked that when my voice comes out, it actually sounds like steam.

'Alice! You can't… What are you even…' My head's in my hands. 'I can't believe you.'

'What?' she protests. 'What? It's what you wanted to know, isn't it?' She looks around, and shrugs. 'You know your trouble, Beth. You over-think things.'

Back in the hall, the noise is deafening; everyone's gabbing away for all they're worth and nobody's taking control. Theo appears to have deserted, but where could he have gone? Unless he's hiding in the toilets. Jacob and Tarik are standing limply at the mixer desk looking like a pair of wet socks dripping on the line. Suddenly we're all in complete darkness; seconds later, the lights come on again, and a popping noise comes from the monitors. It's as if somebody's tripped a switch to get everyone's attention. If so, it didn't work; after a brief silence, then a few oohs and groans and talk of a power cut, they're all straight back to whatever it was they were on about earlier.

Marsha is particularly animated. She's treating Sandy and Ffi to the story of how Theo's Uncle Stelios's mystery lady friend only turns out to be Professor Petra Laing, and how he's seventy if he's a day, and she's no spring chicken, and he's trying to pitch her some old-fashioned woo with this request number, and this Eleni throws a hissy fit because she wasn't warned and she hadn't practised it. I have to butt in. 'Marsha! Prof could walk in any minute!' Marsha shrugs, sorry, and drops to a stage whisper to finish her story. 'She did the whole Diva thing. Apparently.' 'Who?' whispers Ffi. 'Both of them!' she whispers back. I walk away in despair. In the meantime, my sister has disappeared again.

Her chair is parked on the far side of the hall, where John has taken his guitar out of its case and is trying to tune up. Not helped by Patrick, at his ear, in full flow. Here's another idiot whose idea of a vocal warm-up is a bit of scandal-mongering. I wander across and find him nodding in the direction of Ffion, and giving John brotherly advice: 'And you wanna watch out for that one, because she'll have the kecks off you soon as wink, nice looking lad like you.' He catches sight of me. 'Not you, Beth.' John, flushed, and unusually quiet, has fixed his attention on the neck of his guitar, and specifically, the little black tuner. Patrick reads my face. He knows Ffi and I are mates. 'Oh, go on. You know what she's like. It all starts with a little drink after choir, just friendly like, then it's ooh I love the Verdi requiem, don't you? So passionate. The next thing you know she's got you round her place with the full vocal score, and before you can say *dies irae* you've lost yer place and you're committing a carnal sin on the carpet.'

My snap assessment is that he's at that voluble stage, before the slurred speech kicks in.

'You've had lunch in the pub, haven't you?'

I can't tell whether the head-waggling is a nod or a shake. 'Never eat before a performance, me.'

And now, Theo emerges from the walk-in store cupboard. He's looking worried.

'We haven't got any drum sticks.'

'Well that's alright, because we haven't got a drummer.'

'Oh. Right…'

I wave my hand at the kit, as if to dismiss it by magic. 'It's not meant for us,' I say.

'I play drums,' says a voice. Tarik. 'I can play, if you like.'

Apparently, there's this strange-but-true thing about the psychology of listening, that a person picks up, say, their own name across a noisy room, and I have to marvel that the phrase *we haven't got a drummer* has apparently roused Tarik from catalepsy.

And it's not just Tarik. Whilst I'm saying, 'Thanks, but no thanks,' and Theo's saying, 'Wow, that's really kind,' Alice, on her sticks, appears from the store too, to announce, 'They've fallen under the pipes. He can't see them, he's too tall. I can't get them, I can't reach.' She switches on her biggest, most enthusiastic eye-pop, and turns to Tarik: 'Will you play for us, then?'

'Yeah, great.' Tarik looks delighted. Then sorry: 'But I've got to go at three thirty.' The smile returns: 'There's this girl, Ashley, she's going to replace me.' The smile vanishes: 'I don't think she plays drums, though.'

It occurs to me that somebody needs to get a grip of all this. Petra Laing will be here any minute, and it's shaping into a complete dog's breakfast. I tell Theo, 'We ought to get this lot going.'

Theo nods agreement. And just stands there.

'You're the conductor.'

'You're the creators.'

'But look at the running order! We agreed we'd start by playing and singing. Band's gonna kick it off with *I like it* and so on, the singers do their *a cappella*, then the band does *Why do you do what you do* to cheer everybody up, and they can all join in. This first section, the first twenty minutes, is the ice-breaker, the warm-up. Then we talk a bit, and that's where

Alice takes over; and then we compare *Silence* and *Dread*. So to start off with, it's performance we're talking about here, not composition. It's not our department. It's over to you, now.'

'The band won't want me to tell them what to do,' he shrugs.

At which point Alice says, 'Oh, fuff. Get over yourself, Beth,' and starts tapping the hi-hat with her walking stick so as to get everybody's attention. At the top of her voice she shouts, 'Thank you all for coming. Choir stand over there. Band here.'

Right next to the drum kit. Great.

Mum has sidled up to me, and hisses: 'Somebody needs to say something. To welcome everybody? Somebody needs to *say* something. A few words.'

'Petra Lang's doing that.'

'Well, where is she?'

'We were talking to her a minute ago, she's on her way…'

Everybody's standing around, and the chatter has died down since Alice marshalled everyone to their positions.

Ten minutes pass. People are getting bored. For the first time, I notice that John and Alice are magnetically close to each other, doing that snug fit thing that only couples do; she must have made her move, then. Good on her. She picks up a text from her flatmate Zoe, which John amplifies for the whole room: 'Wishing you a lot of flak for your event.' That fills a few minutes while we have a good a laugh at it, and discuss the merits and pitfalls of dictation. We're all chatty again. The choir wants to hear the band. Patrick asks, *why not just go for it*, belches loudly, then holds up his hands in apology.

Then the doors swoosh open and Jaz Ander buzzes in. He's travelling light today, no bouncing shoulder-bag, streamlined in dark navy, and moving at speed; he halts, scans the room, and turns abruptly this way and that, which calls to mind the fidgeting of a house-fly.

'I'm not too late for the photo, am I?' he says. 'Has Professor Laing gone already?'

His anxious gaze meets the sinisterly benign face of my mother, who knows how to pitch her voice, and speaks calmly as if to reassure and inform the whole room: 'No, she seems to have been delayed.' She looks across at me: 'Do we have any idea what might have happened, Beth?'

I'm the one who's best placed to run round the faculty trying to find her, aren't I?

'Shall I go and see, then?'

'Why not.' Mum's cruising in teacher mode. As I head for the door, though, she drops her voice and I hear her say, 'I'm glad you're here, Jaz. You and I have some unfinished business.'

This is terrible. Here I am racing around the corridors, looking into every room, desperate to find our celebrity Professor who kindly extended the invitation and without whose blessing we cannot start, when all the time I'm feeling increasingly sick at the thought of what Mum is going to say, or do, to Jaz, in that hall right now. For sure, it's going to sour the atmosphere, and this whole afternoon, which was already a challenge, will be a fiasco.

Petra's not in her office. It's locked, although I can see through the light in the door that her bag's still in there. There's nobody to ask, apart from a lonely librarian, who tells me, it's Saturday, the assessments are all in, so she hasn't seen a soul; and can I hear that faint hum, which isn't coming from the ceiling lights, she's checked. Like a buzz? Sort of fizzy? The time she's lavished on communicating the simple message 'no' suggests that this woman's desperate for a chat. I haven't got time to track down the source of her mystery noises. In the small hall, waiting for me, are not only Alice and my Mum, and Theo, all of whom I love, but a couple of dozen people whom I care about and who have given up their day to be here. To have a musical experience. A musical encounter. I find myself in a position which I have assiduously been avoiding all my life: I am *responsible*. I can't complain or moan. I'm the one who has to grip this. The show must go on.

I reason: Petra Laing is not, yet, a missing person. There will be an explanation. I can leave this in the hands of the librarian who's desperate for something to do. So I hand her the problem. She begins to discuss methodology, but I cut our discussion short with a huge in-breath, wide eyes and an encouraging reminder that she's a librarian, and if there's one thing librarians are super-brilliant at, it's finding things out; so use your professional judgement.

I need to go back into that hall and get everything going. The librarian is already on the phone as I exit and head down the carpeted corridors. I slow my pace, because I mustn't arrive in a panting sweat, and because it gives me precious seconds to work out what I'm going to say. Apologise... no, just inform them Prof Laing will be with us later, because I'm sure she will. *Welcome to the faculty, thank you for coming, we're all gathered here because...* whatever the reason is. That will have to be an improvisation. There's only time to memorise the outline: *sorry, the welcome, the thank you, the why*. I fall in step with the rhythm as I hammer it into my head: *sorry, the welcome, the thank you, the why. Sorry, the welcome, the thank you, the why.*

64 Workshop (ii)

At the heavy double doors, I pause. It's possible that Petra's there already; I hope she is; but the hum of voices from the other side suggests otherwise. I check my posture, as I've been schooled to do; I'm on next, and this time, when I deliver my message, it won't be from behind the double bass, or the piano; I'll be standing up in front of everybody; and whatever awaits, behind these fire doors, must not unnerve me. I have to stop wasting people's time, get the workshop started, and get us all pulling together.

I won't need a mic, in that acoustic. I could do with somebody to do the shushing, though, so that I can get my few words out solo, without the backbeat of people shuffling about and moaning *can't hear* or *what did she say*. Jenny, Mum, Marsha, any of them could do it. I'll grab the first one I see.

The door offers smooth, well-oiled resistance, and the straight lines of the chilly corridor are swapped for a hot mess. The singers have broken rank and spread about the room in little groups. Some sit, some stand. They've dropped bags and coats all over the place, slumped against the wall, plonked on chairs. The scene is punctuated here and there by coffee cups; the refreshment table at the back of the hall has been ransacked. Alice and Theo are relaxing on the front row of the audience, and mirror each other, with one elbow on the back of the seat, chin cupped in hand, and the other arm outstretched against the back of the adjacent chair, nodding lazily. John's strumming away in his own little world. Practising? If so, he's the only one apart from me who's appropriately nervous. Or even focused. Jacob Rigby has wheeled the drum kit on its mobile platform out into the middle of the performing space, and he's giving Vilma and Patrick a demonstration of how to operate the bass drum.

Sandy's getting technical behind the mixing desk with Tarik. Alice's hat graces the Bechstein. Jenny, who's talking to Marsha and Ffi, notices my entrance, raises her eyebrows, and points at her watch. I nod acknowledgement and hold up a hand to reassure her something's going to happen.

Standing directly opposite the entrance, and beside the open store cupboard where the serious percussion belongs, there's my mother, with a half-smile; she sees me, and starts to make her way across the room, which is great, because she's a far better shusher than Jenny – much less fazed by things going wrong, and therefore better at stopping them getting worse. Bizarrely, though, Jaz Ander emerges from said store, wearing an expression I've never seen before and can't read. He follows her in my direction.

The three of us converge, and I have to get to the point.

'Right, we've lost Petra, but we can't keep these people hanging around. We're twenty minutes behind. So, Mum, can you call this lot to order? I'll apologise for Prof and do the welcome and everything. Then we can all crack on.'

'Back to our places, then,' says Mum, loud enough for others to hear, then repeats her message at growing volume, with suitable hand gestures, and supplementary detail: *singers over here again, please ... Why don't we all sit down...*

I'd never have thought of making sure they're seated. Jaz turns his head to watch her as, wide-armed, she herds them into place.

'She's brilliant, your mum.'

'Yeah. I know.'

My mind doubles back to that conversation Jaz and I had at the traffic lights, about personality being essentially unfixed and fluid, which seeded in me the seductive idea that you might one day step out of your old character, and into another one. I've always been the quiet one, the one who never spoke in public, who resisted taking pupils, and bailed out of social media; who had nothing to say and didn't trust language anyway. But now, I'm the sister who's going to have to say a few words.

I wonder what they'll be.

Sorry, the welcome, the thank you, the why.

Silence falls on the room. I can see Alice and Theo beaming up at me from the front row, and I make a conscious effort to focus my eyes beyond all this, because if I meet anybody's gaze, I'll be lost.

'First, I'd like to apologise on behalf of Professor Laing, who has been unavoidably detained,' – (where did that expression come from? I sound like a civil servant) – 'and who I know is delighted to have you all here today. We expect to see her before the afternoon is out.'

That's a fat white lie. I haven't a clue what's happened to her. But that's the sorry over. Next, the welcome.

'In the meantime, I'd like to welcome you all to the workshop. On behalf of my sister Alice and I...'

You can't say on behalf of I, Mum'll shred me for that.

'On behalf of my sister Alice and me...I'd like to thank you for giving up your time...'

Although why would you even say, speaking *on behalf of me*? Hopeless. In the seconds it took to do the welcome and the thank you, I've managed to sound both pompous and robotic. So now, it's onto the why, and holy cow, if I don't know, nobody does, and if I don't sound like someone who gives a shit, I can't expect anybody else to.

'So, why are we all here?'

This wasn't meant to be funny, but a gentle chuckle ripples round: they're laughing at me. I can't help looking now. When I focus, though, the faces are happy. Encouraging, even. Instinctively, I smile back at them.

So far, in my maiden speech, I've said the sort of things I've heard other people say. What they call formalities. I can't be doing with that any of that crap. Time to limber up.

'Yeah, right, why are we here? Fair question. On paper... on that email and everything, that we sent round... it says, the aim of the workshop is for us all to meet each other, to hear each other's music, and... what did it say? *Explore ways...*' I look to Mum for a prompt because I can't remember the exact words.

She supplies: 'Explore ways of working together with the composers with a view to devising a piece for performance.'

'Thanks. That's the brochure-speak. I want to tell you what it means to us, to me and Alice. It feels like an audition. Whether we pass or fail, though, you're helping us both be better musicians. For as long as we can remember, music has been the thing we wanted to do. We've both studied, in our different ways. In different kinds of music, and different places.'

'Oh aye. Outside W H Smith. Like all the greats.'

That's Patrick's voice. He cheers me up enough to take a good look round the room. Alice has raised a triumphant fist.

'We've taken all sorts of routes to come here today. Not just buses, cars, feet. Whether we've trained at a conservatoire, or maybe we've had lessons from someone like Joan Pipkin when we were little, or maybe we've never had a music lesson in our life but something happened and we found a choir and we just like singing... But the best performer, the greatest composer in all the world is incomplete without an audience to come and listen. And for everybody in this room, listening's not enough; it's natural to want to make the music yourself.

'We're here by choice. The world is full of us, people who choose to turn up. There are loads of bands like Sky Blue Pink, who're just starting out, and relying on the day job; and amateurs who turn out for an open mic night or a folk club; choirs, from the Philharmonic, filling the platform, to the tiniest church choir; and they all have a special magic, because all those people spend most of their time doing other things. They raise families or they sell houses, or work in the hospital, or drive a truck, or teach, or make sandwiches for a living; the world can't function without them. Or maybe they're people who can't get out that much, because they're too busy looking after someone else, or looking after themselves. So being an amateur – joining in – is amazing. Turning up every week, at the end of the day, to do something extra just for the love of it.'

'And then getting told off because you're crap.'

Patrick's really warmed them up now; the room bubbles, as everybody moves at once, in different ways; crossing or uncrossing their legs, shifting, or leaning forward, or back, or turning to their neighbour, or sending eyes to the ceiling. He's elicited every reaction from laugh out loud to head in hands. He turns to appeal to his comrades and holds the floor: 'It's true, though, isn't it? You miss an entry, or you're under the note, or you're not on the beat... But you get better, don't you? I mean, there is hope. Only it's not easy, doing something properly, when it isn't your actual job and you've just done a twelve-hour shift.'

I'm glad of his intervention. I'd rather have a conversation than give a speech.

'You're so right. The thing is… most people give up what they can't do easily, first opportunity. When you're a kid, you think being an adult equals no more homework, and paying other people to do stuff for you, and that includes to entertain you. But you've chosen: you've chosen not to outsource your lives to a screen. We get to *make* live music together… I mean, *live*… How great is that?'

There are other things I ought to be saying, and thanks which I ought to be giving, but I'm sounding like a vicar or something; and I'm tiring of my own voice now; so I race to wrap up and move on.

'All I want to say is, what we do… what you do… is important. That's all I want to say. So let's crack on with the programme. Can we have Sky Blue Pink up please?'

65 Last Word

And now, down in the street cafe of the Everyman, we're all basking in the glorious sense of afterwards. We're like a cask ale that's settled: barm to the bottom, clear, tawny-gold, and with a faint sparkle, when you hold us to the light.

I'm leaning slightly against Theo and watching people on other tables gab away. Sandy, Ffi and Patrick, Marsha, Vilma agree: didn't they do well? Jaz Ander got his photo, in the end, and he's shared it with us already: choir, band, and Professor Petra Laing, beaming away centre screen, having recovered from her hour stuck in the lift; thank goodness there's a direct line to the emergency engineer, because there's something wrong with that alarm; it didn't exactly ring out, did it? Too weedy, nobody heard a thing. A few feet away from us, Jaz is having a serious conversation with Mum and Jenny; he's already quizzed John and Alice about Hands Free music, and Sky Blue Pink. The word *profile* came up a lot. Alice, sitting at our table now and snuggling against John, is like a dog with two tails. She's vindicated, too, because when Mum and Jaz collided back there in the hall just now, it ended in a truce, and that goes to show how wrong I can be.

Theo asks, 'Is this an English custom, to settle your scores in a cupboard?'

I say, 'That's Mum's moral code. You don't humiliate a person in public. You humiliate them in private.' I observe Jaz, a few feet away, nodding, deferential. 'Mum surprised me, though. I mean, it was inevitable sooner or later they'd come face to face. But I assumed that when they did, she'd unleash the complete Queen of the Night, you know? Skewer his brain with her blood-curdling staccato, sort of thing.'

'Perhaps, like the Queen of the Night, she reserves that treatment for her daughter.' He gives me his ironic smile. 'You should only get angry with people you care about.'

John frowns to emphasise his agreement, and sends his whole face into spasm. 'Too right!' Alice mutters, *Chicken Licken,* because I'm famous for the way I cringe around, waiting for the sky to fall.

Mum has got up. She's heading for the counter.

'Hey!' Alice calls. 'Mum! Come here!'

That diverts her to our table. 'We ordered tapas,' she says, 'but that was ages ago. Jaz's got an appointment to get to.'

Alice asks, 'What did you say to him, then? In the stockroom?'

Mum leans in, bends over our table, and lowers her voice. Which is discreet in acoustic terms, but visually quite the opposite.

'I told him he ought to have the last word. And the last word ought to be, sorry.'

'Boss,' says Alice.

'All done. Now, if you'll excuse me, I'm going after those potatoes.' She's off.

The four of us sigh, and drift along on the background music. Alice turns her attention to the lurid cocktail in front of her, rotating the stem of the glass on the table so that the whole pinky-orange tropical island revolves. Vilma's happy, having a laugh now with Ffi Johns, who's showing her something on her phone. They pass it around the singers, who take it in turns to feign shock or amusement. Jaz nods. Seen it before. I relax. I'm connected to this, and distant from it, all at once; I don't need to share my thoughts at this moment.

A mellow feeling is making me philosophical. I love the way people behave in these city bars. They mock each other, they disagree, they argue, and then they get their round in. These are the rules when you're performing as human beings, live and acoustic. When you perform as a media animal, the rules are different, and they always were. Ever since the invention of the printing press, technology has been encouraging us to shout at each other from a safe distance.

I think of the times I've sat with this bunch of aliens in the pub, after choir. Or that first night in the Aphrodite bar, watching the dancers doing stuff I'd never want to do myself. It's all so pleasurable. There's something about these gatherings. It isn't about alcohol or what you smoke or use. There's an intoxication that comes from company and words tumbling out around the circle, a sort of Bacchic dance of ideas which grips the emotions too because, seated so close to each other, we have a human longing to get on. In this heady conversation, the pedant admires the generalist, the atheist steps into the church; the ways in which we mis-perform and get things wrong, the unequal note values, the ragged entries, the ignorance of technical language and its over-use, the fumbling for the right word, the things lost in translation and sometimes frankly misunderstood – none of this matters too much because conviviality – physical proximity – breeds a high degree of tolerance. We stumble, but the dance goes on, while ever there's a way of linking hands.

'You think,' says Theo.

'Yeah. Good thoughts.'

'The end is good, everything's good,' he says, and puts his warm hand over mine.

66 Packing

My dad comes round to help me pack. When he notices the workshop photo Jaz took on my screen saver – which he's already got on his phone, because I sent it – he's drawn by some magnetic force, and stands over it making funny little noises for ages.

'Ah, look at your mother. She's mustard, she is.'

She stands straighter than anyone. She has a settled smile and looks straight into the camera.

'Yeah. She's brilliant.'

I want to say, *she's been brilliant all my life, and I never noticed*; but I'm too ashamed. Look at our dad, though… He's always known.

I lay everything I want to take out on the bed. With a grin and a shake of the head he clears a space for the suitcase, and jokingly elbows me out of the way.

'Let the dog see the rabbit,' he says, because it's what his father used to say.

He knows I hate packing. He's brisk and makes light work of it, so this is his way of thanking me for what he terms my IT support. Not that I've given him any lately.

He rolls, never folds. He gives due thought to how things will settle during the journey. He distributes the weight carefully across the suitcase from back to front, bottom to top. Most people don't give that a moment's thought, but it makes a big difference when it comes to steering the thing.

'Are you still wearing these?' he says, waving a fistful of tee shirts. 'Jeez, Beth, this is the one we had to get you for that field trip at school.' He puts them down, picks out George Harrison and shakes him out so I can see what he means. 'D'you remember when this was blue?'

I shrug: 'OK, so maybe he's looking a bit peaky…'

'Peaky?' He holds it up. 'This is Liverpool's answer to the Turin Shroud. They're not fit for dishcloths. Why don't you bin 'em?'

'What, bin a holy relic?'

He sighs, and rolls them all up together in one fat swiss roll. Then he stands up straight, feet apart, and looks me in the eye and breathes in so that his chest broadens, then nods, and lets the breath out in a little pant, the way he always does when he has something important to say to me. He's trying to be solid and reassuring, but the cottony swiss roll in one hand tells me he's just a bloke who can't talk and do at the same time.

'You need new things, love. This could be the start of a new life.'

'On the international music circuit?' Which is what my mum actually said out loud. With no irony intended. Me and Dad snort like kids.

'Oh aye, yeah!' He pulls a silly face, then falls serious again. 'But your mother's got a point. You should be thinking about what image you want to project. Not dressing like you're scared. If you're heading for the future, you don't want to be dragging a suitcase full of yesterday behind you.'

Ah. This is serious.

'Bit deep, that, Dad.'

'Hm. Yeah.'

He goes to place the roll of tee shirts in the case, but I take them from him. I extract the recent ones and gently lob the rest towards the corner of the room.

'I'll get new when I'm there.'

'Great,' he says, and turns back to stoop over the piles of clothing on the bed.

67 Faith

2020 is shaping up to be the best Valentine's ever. Mum and Dad equals true love, apparently. John and Alice are planning their own surprise, not sure how that works. And Theo and I fly tomorrow, John Lennon to Larnaca, and on to meet the family in a village somewhere with almond blossom.

My escort is merrily sober; I'm slightly drunk from all the excitement of a night at the cinema. Our voices echo round the stairwell at Faith Place; once we're in the flat, which I now know is tidy and curiously empty of belongings, Theo heads straight for the fridge. I've already taught him about cheese and jam. Lancashire and blackcurrant, on whatever bread you have. We flop on the bed and eat our sarnies.

'Do you remember the first time I came to Faith Place? Gave me the creeps, that basement. I thought for a minute you were going to kidnap me.'

'I am,' he says through a mouthful of sandwich.

'Theo… What happens next?'

'You get little white cheese crumbs everywhere, and then you panic because it feels like worms.'

'With my music. I don't know what the next step is.'

'And I,' he says.

'I used to be so driven.' The pauses in our conversation have started to lengthen.

'What did you expect?'

'A career, composing. That someone would step in and say, yes, you're good at that, here's a ton of money, carry on. I assumed this endless stream of music would all just flow from my head... driven by an inner certainty towards... perfection... That was when I was a precocious, pretentious kid. Yesterday.'

'The music's always there. It won't leave you.'

'I realise now, that this earning a living business isn't a stopgap. It's what I'm always going to have to do. Whether it's at the Uni, or somewhere else.'

We stare at the blank wall opposite, and he drawls, 'I don't see you in a blue hairnet.'

I match his lack of pace. 'You won't do that for ever, either. Does it even pay?'

'Mm, no...' His voice is grave. 'Sometimes... sometimes you have to step back, before you pounce.'

'Mm – hmm.'

This sounds as though it ought to mean something. He's either very thoughtful, or very tired.

'Look at this. See?' He holds a crumb of white cheese between finger and thumb, and in a nearly-Liverpudlian sing-song, adds, 'The state of us! I'm jiggered.' Then places the cheese crumb carefully on the paint pot which serves as a bedside table, and suggests: 'Let's just follow our *meraki*. Keep doing what we do, until we don't enjoy it.'

'*Meraki*,' I repeat, and when I close my eyes, I'm imagining what that word might look like, written down in Greek.

I'm still not quite used to this bedroom, and spend a long time dithering between sleep and wakefulness. And yet it could be home.

Perhaps these months of going backwards will help propel me forward now.

I'm warm, and tuned to someone else's sleeping breath, and not alone.

This takes me as far as memory will go; not just before the accident, or before we twins started school, but before I had a single fact in my head. Before I spoke in sentences. To the very beginnings of knowing: a time when I had scant sense of *who* I was, but certainty of *where* I was. In this memory, I'm upstairs, in the dark. Being held. Safe and warm. The three of us are too near to see each other. Maybe there's just a hint of light from the landing, sensed through half-closed eyes, eyes that close on a human smell, a human warmth; all my attention flows towards the low sweet voice that I can feel, because it resonates, and because the singer's body gently rises and falls as it supports me. We sway, ever so slightly. My sister is close by, and this is my turn.

It all started there, with the lullaby voice.

And it isn't the music lessons or the instruments or the endless hours spent listening to the rasping tones of an adolescent orchestra, or the long car journeys to festivals and competitions, or the season ticket for the Phil, or any of the many micro-wars that the tiger mother wages to protect and to promote her young that I have to be grateful for; no, the thing that started it, the thing that made all the difference to my life, is that lullaby voice. A mother sang to us, and that's what set us on this course.

***

Thanks

Hundreds of people have contributed unwittingly to the content of this novel: church choirs, school choirs, festival choruses, a cappella groups; many orchestras, many schools, folk clubs, and all their audiences.

The project acquired emotional urgency during lockdown, when singers were made to feel like criminals and, worse, professional musicians, like all performers, faced catastrophe. It seemed our world had ended. This is a record of what we nearly lost.

The composer Ian Stephens – who really can set words to music – was generous in answering my questions about classical composition.

Conversations with music therapists Rosie Monaghan and Elizabeth Clark helped build the story's foundations.

Samantha Aristotelous and Andrew Moore advised on the Cypriot dimension.

In the process of bringing *Amateurs* to a final version, however, I'm indebted to those poor souls who read the first drafts and whose honest observations were story-changing, in particular Pam Coward, Linda Bygrave, Graham Best, Maggie Nightingale, Tony Ovenell; and David Scott, who updated me on bars (non-musical) when travel to Liverpool became difficult.

Thank you to Paul Ellis, Rachel Greaves and the Sherborne Chamber Choir, for inspiring choral repertoire; to Kate and Peter Abbott for providing an alternative musical education; to my fellow-singers for their support and friendship; and to Penny Hart and the eagle-eyed Emily Williamson for practical help.

Thank you, Kate Rizzo, for invaluable, dispassionate editorial advice.

And finally, as ever, thank you to Susan Elderkin and the Somerset Friday writers for continuing to nurture my writing life.

Other Books by Gill Oliver

Joe Faber and the Optimists
Joe Faber's a funny guy, good with his hands, and great with words – until the stroke which leaves him severely disabled. But this is more than his story. His wife Fran has a job she loves. Daughter Jess, a wedding to plan. There's heartbreak and absurdity along the way - but humour is the family's greatest asset in the drive to get Joe back on his own two feet.

'A thoroughly enjoyable read whether or not you've been affected by stroke, Joe Faber and the Optimists really ought to be recommended reading in stroke clinics around the world.' – Michelle Ryles, The Book Magnet
'Engaging and uplifting.... Moving, funny and unexpected.' 'A wonderful read... It feels very real and very poignant... It's also very funny.' '... told with humour and grace.' 'A story of determination, optimism and love.' 'A book I will definitely share.'

Art My Eye (Short Stories)
Are we defined by the things that we imagine, as much as by the things we do? By turns poignant, sinister, hilarious, tragic, these short stories probe that question, dipping into very different private lives and visiting different places.

A Backward Glance
When the school Classics trip visits a volcanic region, what will rise to the surface? A re-working of the myth of Orpheus and Eurydice.

My Eye: Four Short Stories (Audio Book)
The comic stories from Art My Eye, narrated by the author.